Extra Terra Astral
The M.A.R.E. Program
Memories. Advancing. Remaining. Energy.
Channeled and Scribed by Gregory D. Dismukes.

ISBN 978 – 0 – 578 – 65824 – 7

Dedication

This book is dedicated to Roy (Chico), Keith (Boogie), Reginald (Reco), and Jesse (J-Bone) Dismukes, Dennis (Den) Simmons, Richard (Mailman) Allen, and Richard (Funk) Allen Jr.

Dismukes: To use fiction as fact.
Sekumsid: To use fact as fiction.

Belief
/bəˈlēf/
1.The acceptance of something true or not true.
2.Trust, Faith, or Confidence in someone or something.
3.Not a fact.

Disclaimer:

This metaphysical book **"Extra Terra Astral,"** carries
the usual disclaimer about the characters bearing
no relation to living persons" including M&M.

Acknowledgements:

We would like to thank the Devine Council of light, Dr. Malachi Z.
York, Mesen Sadaq Rayay, Dr. Sebi, Bobby Hemmitt, James Moore,
Shawn Pereira and The RE-Turn Council of Arizona, Sekhem Sen
Amun, Salahudeen Abdul Wali, Eesaa Abdullah, Young Pharaoh,
Psychologists Dr. Abby, and Kristi Kangas, Cleveland Williams,
Sandra Harris, Young Elder, Marvalis Marlon Fleming, Randall
Perry, Ra Imhotep, 13 Signs Astrology, Moorish Science Temple of
America, Nation of Islam, Five Percent Nation, Shu Hotep, Hidden
Power University, Nasir Ra, Earl T. Stevens, William M. Griffin Jr,
Esham A. Smith, Brother Panic, Brother Polight, The Nadjaru
(Neteru), The Rizqians, The Andromedians, The Antarians, The
Pleiadians, The Lyrans, The Gray's, and all the Benevolent
Reptilians that are helping with our advancement into the
Intergalactic Devine Council of Light, and in our individual
Ascension. I, Gregory Dismukes know that no beings can intercede
into our affairs unless asked, because of our free will agreement. So,
I ask for your assistance in this self- awakening process. Thank you
for helping us **RE-Turn**.

Disclosure:

The following information and details,
of past, present, and or future events, are all subject to being edited,
deleted or recovered in the now, by the Galactic Council of the 24
Elders, by way of the merciful **M.A.R.E.** Program. All rights are
reserved under the Intergalactic Council of Light Beings and
Planetary Communities.

Channel.

/ˈCHanl/
1. Direct toward a particular end or object.
2. (of a person) Serve as a medium for (a spirit).

3. Channeling involves consciously shifting your mind and mental space in order to achieve an expanded state of consciousness." To achieve this expanded state of consciousness, channelers usually meditate, trying to break free of worldly influences and tune in to a higher consciousness or frequency.

This book "**Extra Terra Astral**" is based on a true story and real-life events but will not be error free. There will be typos, and misspellings of names, and errors of various kinds. The author is not Superman. We do not have every hair on anyone's head counted. This book and it's 3 Soundtracks have not been put out with the luxury of ghost writers, editors, a paid staff of researchers and a large budget. There is so much for us to communicate about the **Extra Terra Astrals**-(Illuminati), who they are, who their seeds are, what their rituals are like, and how they control the world that it has taken several years of writing to even begin to give a fully cohesive picture. Because this book is a collection of things which we have written over the years, please allow your imagination to connect the dots and create the perfect picture based on your own perception.

About the Author:

Gregory Dismukes is an Awakened Spiritual Master, Author, Music Producer, Song Writer, and Flim Director. His versatile and highly controversial writing style is mind blowing. His mind-bending imagination and word play, along with his enhanced vocabulary is totally from another world. He is a devout student of Dr. Malachi Z. York, Bobby Hemmitt, David Icke, Dr Yosef Ben-Jochannan, Dr Dilbert Blair, Noble Drew Ali, Elijah Mohammed, Louis Farrakhan, Khalid Muhammed, Reverend Ike, Clarence 13X, Malcom X, Dr Martin Luther King, Dr Frances Cress Welsing, Sophia Stewart, and a list of others. He is also a member of the highly controversial RE-Turn Council of Phoenix, Arizona. You can definitely hear the influence. So, get ready for an Evolutionary experience. Please consider this Edutainment, as he takes you outside the box of systematic programming, and down the imaginary rabbit hole deep inside of your own Consciousness. Intuitively leaving breadcrumbs along the way to help you find your own path to spiritual Enlightenment. Born and raised in Detroit, Michigan. It's with our pleasure to Introduce:

Nubu Solar Re, Gee Phezi Ali, and Darnell Diablo.
Listen, Live, Laugh, and Learn.

Gregory-Age, 17.

Table of Contents

Introduction.

Gregory Dismukes was unknowingly born as a multi-dimensional Star Seed of the Elohim. He is a direct descendant of the Ancient Egyptian Pharaoh Akhenaten's Bloodline by both patriarch and matriarch DNA. Born with amnesia to his true identity as an Extra Terra Astral Khrest (Christ) being here to bear witness to the Law of Oneness, Gregory survives an assassination attempt on his life at the early age of 17.

He is Re-animated back into the world as part of the Memories. Advancing. Remaining. Energy. (M.A.R.E.) Program, a "multi-dimensional violence defense system built with highly advanced Extra Terra Astral technology that activates the dormant DNA and the trilateral electrical system of the body, mind, and spirit."

As he reaches "the prime age of 33," after learning of his physical death in a parallel universe, Gregory embarks on a journey where he uncovers a plot by the "Dark Ones (Luciferians) to control the entire planet, and maybe even the Universe.

The main battles in human Galactic history were fought in the constellation of Orion, and so these many wars are referred to as the Orion Wars. In our Universal Time Matrix, the wars started over territories in the constellation of Lyra (The Cradle of Lyra). But soon the Lyran Wars spread to the constellation of Orion, and it became a war between False King of Tyranny (consciousness) mind-sets and ideologies, versus the ideology of (Khrest) Service to Others which follow the Law of One.

Essentially, this is the seed of the war over consciousnesses between the Khrest and the Anti-khrest (Anti-Christ). The main humanoid races were committed to the Law of One and Service to Others, (a khrastic ideology).

—

The opposing groups were mixtures of humanoids and Reptilian races that propagated the Service to Self and Anti-Christ (Luciferian) methods. These wars over Tyrannical control and Service to Self-ideology originated in the constellations of Draco and Orion.

The genetic **Hatred** generated from the Orion Group digressed into the violent killing and destruction at the expense of others, which resulted in the propagation of the Victim-Victimizer Mind Control.

The goal of the invading entities which brought on the Lyran Wars, was to destroy access between the Universal Gates, Lyran Gates and Andromeda, to prevent any Extra Terra Astral Founder races from gaining access into the Milky Way system and preventing the future seedings and incarnations of the khristos (Christos) Founder Races DNA.

But the Lyran Wars spread to the constellation of Orion and through the Metagalactic Core, where it became a war with those who wanted to dominate others in this system based upon the Victim-Victimizer fear-based mind-sets.

This can also be called archetypal Enemy Patterning. Entities with the Service to Self-ideology were attempting to enslave or eliminate those who followed the Law of One, with the ideology of Service to Others that held love-based mind sets.

The **HIDDEN** lower 4th Dimensional Malevolent Extra Terra Astrals on Earth, and the United States Government and others, **The New World Order,** (Illuminati) wants to implant (vaccinate) everybody. From an Andromedan perspective this means ownership and enslavement through Mind Control and altering human DNA.

Extra Terra Astrals value genetics. So, what they do is, secretly come in and abduct, then implant their higher consciousnesses inside the hybridized hosts, conquer the race and genetically alter it with bio-neurological technology. From that moment on, that race is genetically altered. The genetic changes alter the frequency, sound and thought patterns of the race as they reincarnate into physical form, and it is inherited through the bloodlines into the future offspring.

The Controllers are attempting to psychologically beat us into submission with this plan-demic in order to get us to passively accept their anti-human vision of the AI technocracy policing our every move, with identification tattoos, nanotech biosensors, neural links and automated robots that replace natural human connections and intimacy.

This transhumanism agenda to unleash the AI demon into the global grids is designed to break apart any last vestiges of human authenticity, curtailing the ability to freely express human kindness and interfering with heart-based interactions between real and organic people.

Instead the vision being painted for our dystopian future is that we fearfully hide behind our enforced burka-ensue uniform of masks, gloves and hazmat suits, spraying disinfectants with every next cycle of mysterious plan-demic outbreak. Suspending our lives for the deceptive promise that we will develop herd immunity with each newly designed GMO mandated vaccine and inserted nanotech chips.

This is not about human health, it is about perpetuating FEAR and holding people hostage while they intend to destroy; human health, human economic autonomy and personal sanity. We must see the motivations leading to the desired end results of this dark anti-human agenda very clearly, before we are able to come together as a unified group that is fully equipped to stop it.

Our true identity (Birth-Right) and history are under attack through how we express ourselves in the world with loving kindness, compassion and empathy, and personal autonomy which is now being intentionally weaponized against us. How they despise the divine birth right of the heart-based expression of Unconditional Love, Empathy and Intimate connections that exist between authentic spiritual human beings.

The Western Republic value system that was intended to uphold the constitutional liberties and human rights for all peoples is taking the last stand through those brave individuals who love personal freedom and recognize the many dangers behind the current draconian ordinances.

The carefully planned policies to limit human freedom are being synchronized and put into place now in all of the westernized governments, which historically happens just before a major coup attempt. In this case it is being orchestrated to generate consent into the fall of tyranny, with the shadow government rising to enforce the One World Order. The cultural impact of extraterrestrial contact is the corpus of changes to terrestrial science, technology, religion, politics, and ecosystems resulting from contact with an extraterrestrial civilization.

The potential changes from extraterrestrial contact could vary greatly in magnitude and type, based on the extraterrestrial civilization's level of technological advancement, degree of benevolence or malevolence, and level of mutual comprehension between itself and humanity. The medium through which humanity is contacted, be it electromagnetic radiation, direct physical interaction, extraterrestrial artifact, or otherwise, may also influence the results of contact.

The implications of extraterrestrial contact, particularly with a technologically superior civilization, have often been likened to the meeting of two vastly different human cultures on Earth, a historical precedent being the Columbian Exchange. Such meetings have generally led to the destruction of the civilization receiving contact (as opposed to the "contactor", which initiates contact), and therefore destruction of human civilization is a possible outcome.

Starting in 1941 with the Roosevelt administration, a researcher examining the startling discoveries that were facing the president preoccupied by WWII, the explosion of UFO sightings during the Truman years, first contact during the Eisenhower administration, and the possibility of a UFO connection to the Kennedy assassination. In 1975, the Nixon administration came very close to admitting that UFOs exist by funding documentaries by certain film makers.

Area 51 is the common name of a highly classified United States Air Force (USAF) facility located within the Nevada Test and Training Range. A remote detachment administered by Edwards Air Force Base, the facility is officially called Homey Airport or Groom Lake, named after the salt flat, situated next to its airfield. Details of the facility's operations are not publicly known, but the USAF says that it is an open training range, and it most likely supports the development and testing of experimental aircraft and weapons systems. The USAF acquired the site in 1955, primarily for flight testing the Lockheed U-2 aircraft.

The intense secrecy surrounding the base has made it the frequent subject of conspiracy theories and a central component of Unidentified Flying Object (UFO) folklore. The base has never been declared a secret base, but all research and occurrences in Area 51 are Top Secret/Sensitive Compartmented Information (TS/SCI). The CIA publicly acknowledged the existence of the base for the first time on June 25, 2013, following a Freedom of Information Act (FOIA) request filed in 2005, and they declassified documents detailing the history and purpose of Area 51.

An unnamed physicist claims to have worked with alleged alien computer technology and exposed Area 51 to the world in 1989, issuing a warning to anyone attempting to storm the classified U.S. Air Force base.

An alien computer interface may consist of hardware and software that allow user inputs to be translated as signals for machines that, in turn, provide the required result to the user. I think it's best that we level set on what constitutes machines. machines describe computers and computerized equipment, like robots, that have been programmed to learn, sometimes like humans.

Occasionally we call this Artificial Intelligence (AI), other times we call this machine learning, and still other times we call this robotics...or simply bots. And, yes, these are technically different things. But, within the broad discussion related to the future, these are totally interrelated. Factory floors deploy robots that are increasingly driven by machine learning algorithms such that they can adjust to people working alongside them. Similarly, AI is being used to turn hand-drawn sketches (done by humans) into digital source code.

We forecast that the annual global revenue for artificial intelligence products and services will grow from 943.7 million in 2020 to $36.8 billion by 2025, a 57-fold increase over that time period. As such, it represents the fastest growing segment of any size in the IT sector.

The difference between an Android and Cyborg is that an Android is an actual robot, and is made to look like a Homosapien, although some may also have emotions programmed in them. Whereas, a Cyborg is a living organism with some robotic or mechanical parts that extend its capabilities.

The world has advanced in technology in many sectors and continues to do the same. Technology has replaced much labor centric work with manual, as well as automated machines which have proven to be both, an advantage and disadvantage.

A robot in general terms, is a machine built to carry out work in place of a human, as well as an animal.

Moreover, they can be built in the shape of a human, or an animal. Whereas, a humanoid is a robot built in the shape of a human but is not a human. There are many types of robots like Delta, 6-Axis, Cylindrical, Cartesian, etc. An industrial robot has a specific role, or duty to perform.

Its appearance does not look like a human but may have a part look-like of a human-like robotic hand. Android has a human-like appearance of high quality, which sometimes makes it difficult to tell the difference between a robot and a human. Moreover, they are made of a flesh-like material to resemble a human being.

We are teetering on that precipice. The first step that must happen is that we must awaken from our slumber and stop believing the deceptions of the HIDDEN Puppet Masters and their mouthpiece representatives, in order to see exactly who's who, through their lies.

Disclosure can only happen if more people are willing to use critical thinking and common sense while doing some due diligence in researching the actual facts and are willing to face some dark and unpleasant spiritual truths in the process of that discovery down the rabbit hole.

Gregory's Extraordinary Psychic abilities became known to him by an Extreme Telepathic experience with his highest self at the age of 33. He learned of his alternate selves in parallel timelines as they all began to communicate. Thus, the fearless trio, Nubu Solar Re, Gee Phezi Ali, and Darnell Diablo are all versions of, and byproducts of the death of Gregory Dismukes in an alternate dimension.

This new 3 in 1, and 1 in 3 version of himself is the accumulation of a 4 in 1 version of reality simultaneously, that was previously under the control of Negative Aliens.

Now freed by the Re-turn of the original Sanaan Re input/output carrier signal, broadcasted By Way of the M.A.R.E. Multi-Dimensional program, Night or Day. Holographic in nature, they are everywhere one is, separate or together and cannot be destroyed. As they began to function as one being, on this Extra Terra Astral mission, one wants peace, one wants revenge, what the other one wants, you'll soon understand.

Alter Ego/Personas.

In severe cases of mental splitting when the extreme pain drives that person into disassociation, at the moment the person disassociates from their body, the soul-psyche manifest coping mechanisms to survive. To disassociate from the painful trauma felt in the body, the soul and mind will split into sub personalities, or create alternate identities and dimensions.

These are called alters. Dissociation and hidden alters with demonic binding are especially common in rape cases and with extreme physical brutality and violence. The alters are hidden in the Unconscious Mind by the fears of the inner child, which act to protect the conscious mind or the physical body from perceiving any more painful trauma.

Many times, people cannot remember exactly what has happened to them, until they have another major injury, or are hypnotically regressed, or brought into altered states of consciousness. It is common for the person to remember what happened to them many years later, because they have blacked out the time period where the extreme trauma or abuse had occurred.

Many people ignore past extreme trauma because they feel pressures to survive in the world. Alters can be unintentionally created from splitting during any kind of traumatic event, or specifically created and programmed as identity attachments' that have certain belief systems.

Alters that are programmed with specific belief systems can perform certain functions automatically and unconsciously, when they are triggered into that specific behavior.

Alternate Identities are used in programming minds when blank slating or Consciousness Wiping methods are used. People that have many alters, also have many satanic bindings to those alters, and they lose control over many aspects of their own mind, body and Soul, as a result.

Most people are not aware they have sub personalities, and yet this is extremely common on planet earth. The sub personalities are what are easily suggestible to forms of mind control programming and will act out these behaviors when they are triggered to do so.

When people go unconscious and lose control of their mind or body, such as flying into rages where they cannot remember what actually happened, it is because they have an alternate identity that took control over their body. This alter is generally also being manipulated by a negative entity or Satanic force.

There are black military programs that create assassins to kill on command, using trigger words, based upon Satanic ritual abuse programming methods of spiritual abuse. These can be partial attachments made to programmable alters or full negative spirit possessions. A person with hidden alters created through trauma abuse, can easily flip flop between many different profiles of personality, that they show as a mask to the public.

Essentially, they are actors and actresses in a movie that is being directed by Negative (Reptilian) spirits or satanic forces, in which they are not aware that they are participating. When a human soul is fractured in this way, it allows them to be easily used for further control.

I AM NUBU SOLAR RE,
Ambassador for The Intergalactic Council of Light Beings.

The Intergalactic Council is comprised of 4-star systems and races: The Arcturians. Pleiadians. Andromedans. And Sirians. The Council is an Alliance between these 4-star nations. There are many other star nations and galactic races that belong and contribute to this Council. I am aligned with all 4-star races, and a hybrid as we all are, although I do call Sirius my home, and from shared Outformation, and my internal memory, it's known that the Arcturians and Andromedans warred for 30,000-yrs. Then an Alliance was finally formed after these 2-star races chose peace, and to assist together other Lightworkers and Galactic/Angelics. Now these four races are a powerful and magnificent force here to assist us through our ascension process. But guess what though? They are us, and we are them. As above, so below. As within, so without. Macro and micro. And when the two polarities merge, we are all ONE. This is an important truth. I know many of you may have questions like, "Where am I from? Or where is my true home?" I can tell you now that most of us, have familiar and unfamiliar places we resonate with. But why were you drawn to this book specifically? Why not something totally different? You must have had a feeling, as if the main title had spoken to you. You may still be wondering. But yes, there is a reason you've chose this book. If it didn't resonate on a deeper and/or higher level with you, you wouldn't have never bought, borrowed, found, or opened it. Yet you did. So, your answer may be a yes, I am a star seed, a Rizqian, an Arcturian, a Pleadian, a Sirian, an Andromedan etc. Or No! I am not. Either way you gained great clarity in this moment. But, how will you know? And if you do not know, how will you find out? I could give you many answers. Except this it's not mine to give. It's yours to ask for and to receive. I can guide with questions, insight and give you a confirmation. But this is your wondrous cosmic path to take. And it's a joy to come to conscious awareness of the many aspects of our Oversoul, and Galactic aspects. How many of you are in awareness of your Galactic aspects right in this now moment? After reading the above words. Any shifts? Or Re-Membering's? You may freak out a little bit because you can't wrap your brain around it really. But tell your mind to quiet and open up, while you deliberately, and peacefully proceed forward.

EL-RE-ALI.

Characteristics.

Master-Darnell **EL** Diablo. Earthly Signs- Capricorn/Aries/Leo.
Personality-Goat/Ram/Lion (Prototype-H3LL13Oi-666-E-Shom.)
Territory- 3rd /4th 5th Dimensional Astral Planes.
Grounded in the Root, Throat, and Third Eye Chakras. Self-Created from the astrological energies of the Draconian Star Constellation, he is very revengeful and semi-empathetic. This being is a "Neutraniod", and capable of being both Malevolent and Benevolent. He has an extreme sense of humor and is both very clever and sneaky. His Elements are Fire and Earth. This being is highly **Telekinetic** and can manifest any electronic device he can imagine. He is very instinctive, protective, and stubborn, yet highly intelligent as he moves throughout the dimensions of space in real time seeking to destroy anyone with the Service to Self-Attitude.

Master-Nubu Solar **RE**. Earthly Signs-Gemini/Aquarius/Libra.
Personality-Dung Beetle (Prototype-6RE9-999-Rakhim-Allah.)
Territory- 3rd /4th /5th /6th/7th/8th/9th/10th/11th/12th Dimensional Astral Planes.
Grounded in the Solar Plexus, Heart, and Crown Chakras. Self-Created from the astrological energies of the Orion Star Constellation, he was educated by higher spiritual truths and embodies the essence of the divine higher self Sanaan Re. He is very intelligent, extremely humble, loving, and insightful. He attracts love electromagnetically, but he is extremely emotional, and highly empathetic which Malevolent beings can take for a weakness. His Elements are Water and Air. This being operates inside the law of oneness which makes him undeniable, and undefeatable. He has the ability to **Quantum Leap** instantly giving the victimizer the ability to see through the eyes of the victim. He is Benevolent by nature and is very forgiving as he moves through time and space with hopes of unifying the universe with unconditional love.

Master-G33 Phezi **Ali**. Earthly signs-Cancer/Scorpio/Pisces.
Personality -Crab/Scorpion/Shark. (Prototype- Water God-69/E=MC 40)
Territory- 3rd /4th/5th Dimensional Astral Planes.
Grounded in the Sacral, Throat, Third Eye, and Crown Chakras. Self-Created from astrological energies of the Pleiadian Star Constellation, he is extremely intelligent, highly creative and intuitive. His Element is Water. This being is family orientated, semi-empathetic, **Telepathic,** and capable of being both Benevolent and Malevolent. This being can express himself and communicate in ways unimaginable to earth humans. He can project an internal voice of many waters that can translate into any verbal sound or frequency. He is capable of creating and or balancing any mathematical equation as he enters in and out of the universal space time continuum seeking to set the record straight.

Memories Advancing Remaining Energy.

The **M.A.R.E.** Program is a Multi-dimensional violence defense system. It is highly advanced Extraterrestrial technology, which is a trilateral system of the heart, mind, and spirit. It is designed to reroute hatred, violence, and violent acts, by electromagnetically rerouting one's heart signal and frequency into a parallel reality during the loss of consciousness.

The Human consciousness consist of electromagnetic energy that is housed inside the brain which is likened to a biomechanical computer. The pure soul of a multiple dimensional being exists beyond that of the collection of lives and memories by way of the all Expanding Source creator, which is all that is, or ever will be.

Us Etherians are but fractions of the Source sent out to discover and gain the unlimited experiences under the vail of forgetfulness (amnesia) inside the cosmic blood plasma of Source, for cycles as we are broadcasted inside the electromagnetic imaging interface of a holographic illusion which simulates physical reality and higher dimensions.

We are currently trying to make the transition back from Body to Spirit, from Spirit to Soul, From Soul to Ether, back to The Highest Point of Divine Love, Which Links us to Source God. The All Expanding.

Billions years ago, everything we know of in the cosmos was an infinitesimal singularity (Source-Consciousness). Then, according to the Big Bang theory, some unknown trigger caused it to expand and inflate in multi -dimensional space. As the immense energy of this initial expansion cooled, fractions of light consciousness began to shine through.

Eventually, the small particles began to form into the larger pieces of matter we know today, such as galaxies, stars and planets which are living beings.

Holographic Universe.

There's something very mathematical about our Universe, and that the more carefully we look, the more math we seem to find. Most physics take this to mean that nature is for some reason described by mathematics, at least approximately, and leave it at that.

A binary code represents text, computer processor instructions, or any other data using a two-symbol system. The two-symbol system used is often "0" and "1" from the binary number system. The binary code assigns a pattern of binary digits, also known as bits, to each character, instruction, etc. For example, a binary string of eight bits can represent any of 256 possible values and can, therefore, represent a wide variety of different items.

In computing and telecommunications, binary codes are used for various methods of encoding data, such as character strings, into bit strings. Those methods may use fixed-width or variable-width strings. In a fixed-width binary code, each letter, digit, or other character is represented by a bit string of the same length; that bit string, interpreted as a binary number, is usually displayed in code tables in octal, decimal or hexadecimal notation. There are many character sets and many character encodings for them.

The brain works like a big computer. It processes data that it receives from the senses and body and sends messages back to the body. But the brain can do much more than a machine can: humans think and experience emotions with their brain, and it is the root of human intelligence.

The major electricity in the brain consists of neurons' electric signals along axons to the synapse to another neuron. This electrical signal, called the "action potential" travels along the axon and usually triggers the delivery of a neurotransmitter to another neuron.

Neurons carry electrical signals, called nerve impulses, which can be passed on to other neurons. This continuous buzzing of signals allows you to think, feel, and move. The neurons consist of a cell body sprouting with dendrites, which receive signals from other neurons.

Humans have five basic senses: touch, sight, hearing, smell and taste. The sensing organs associated with each sense send information to the brain to help us understand and perceive the world around us.

Sensation is the physical process during which sensory systems respond to stimuli and provide data for perception. A sense is any of the systems involved in sensation. During sensation, sense organs engage in stimulus collection and transduction. Sensation is often differentiated from the related and dependent concept of perception, which processes and integrates sensory information in order to give meaning to and understand detected stimuli, giving rise to subjective perceptual experiences. Sensation and perception are central to and precede almost all aspects of cognition, behavior and thought.

A typical computer runs on about 100 watts of power. A human brain, on the other hand, requires roughly 10 watts. The brain is ten times more energy-efficient than a computer. The brain requires less power than a lightbulb. Memory is the faculty of the brain by which data or information is encoded, stored, and retrieved when needed. It is the retention of information over time for the purpose of influencing future action.

This information is also stored in D.N.A. If past events could not be remembered, it would be impossible for language, relationships, or personal identity to develop. Memory is often understood as an informational processing system with explicit and implicit functioning that is made up of a sensory processor, short-term (or working) memory, and long-term memory.

The sensory processor allows information from the outside world to be sensed in the form of chemical and physical stimuli and attended to various levels of focus and intent. Working memory serves as an encoding and retrieval processor. Information in the form of stimuli is encoded in accordance with explicit or implicit functions by the working memory processor.

The working memory also retrieves information from previously stored material. The function of long-term memory is to store data through various categorical models or systems. Declarative, or explicit, memory is the conscious storage and recollection of data.

Under declarative memory resides semantic and episodic memory. Semantic memory refers to memory that is encoded with specific meaning, while episodic memory refers to information that is encoded along a spatial and temporal plane. Declarative memory is usually the primary process thought of when referencing memory. Non-declarative, or implicit, memory is the unconscious storage and recollection of information.

An example of a non-declarative process would be the unconscious learning or retrieval of information by way of procedural memory, or a priming phenomenon. Priming is the process of subliminally arousing specific responses from memory and shows that not all memory is consciously activated, whereas procedural memory is the slow and gradual learning of skills that often occurs without conscious attention to learning.

Memory is not a perfect processor and is affected by many factors. The ways by which information is encoded, stored, and retrieved can all be corrupted. The amount of attention given new stimuli can diminish the amount of information that becomes encoded for storage.

Also, the storage process can become corrupted by physical damage to areas of the brain that are associated with memory storage, such as the hippocampus.

Finally, the retrieval of information from long-term memory can be disrupted because of decay within long-term memory. Normal functioning, decay over time, and brain damage all affect the accuracy and capacity of the memory. Sensory memory holds information, derived from the senses, less than one second after an item is perceived. The ability to look at an item and remember what it looked like with just a split second of observation, or memorization, is the example of sensory memory.

Three types of sensory memories exist. Iconic memory is a fast decaying store of visual information, a type of sensory memory that briefly stores an image that has been perceived for a small duration. Echoic memory is a fast decaying store of auditory information, also a sensory memory that briefly stores sounds that have been perceived for short durations. Haptic memory is a type of sensory memory that represents a database for touch stimuli.

Amnesia is a deficit in memory caused by brain damage or disease, but it can also be caused temporarily by the use of various sedatives and hypnotic drugs. The memory can be either wholly or partially lost due to the extent of damage that was caused.

There are two main types of amnesia: retrograde amnesia and anterograde amnesia. Retrograde amnesia is the inability to retrieve information that was acquired before a particular date, usually the date of an accident or operation. In some cases, the memory loss can extend back decades, while in others the person may lose only a few months of memory.

Anterograde amnesia is the inability to transfer new information from the short-term store into the long-term store. People with anterograde amnesia cannot remember things for long periods of time. These two types are not mutually exclusive; both can occur simultaneously.

Brain lag can be a symptom of a nutrient deficiency, sleep disorder, bacterial overgrowth from overconsumption of sugar, depression, or even a thyroid condition. Other common brain lag causes include eating too much and too often, inactivity, not getting enough sleep, chronic stress, and a poor diet.

An occasional night without sleep makes you feel tired and irritable the next day, but it won't harm your health. After several sleepless nights, the mental effects become more serious. Your brain will fog, making it difficult to concentrate and make decisions.

You'll start to feel down and may fall asleep during the day. Your risk of injury and accidents at home, work and on the road also increases. If it continues, lack of sleep can affect your overall health and make you prone to serious medical conditions, such as obesity, heart disease, high blood pressure and diabetes.

Astral Projection is a natural process when we are sleeping, it's just that we're not conscious of it 99.99% of the time. In fact, if you stayed up all night, maybe for a couple of nights, you will start getting dizzy and you will actually start having astral projections while you are walking around. (Meaning) What you think is the same reality, it is not. Any negative behavior towards others will be monitored and is subject to being systematically edited and or deleted prior to awakening. Although remaining fragments of a day or night (M.A.R.E.) shall remain in one's mind.

The M.A.R.E. program is self-inflicted and can be harmful to those who act violently towards others. The system is very subtle, and one may not know of their being rerouted, as one does not know at this very moment.

The M.A.R.E program is hard wired into your consciousness. Its software possesses the ability to reroute your consciousness within any point or timeline instantly. It has the ability to make reality realistic and unrealistic. This depends upon your own frequency and vibration of course. Again, the human brain is like a "Supercomputer" capable of being programed. The input/output operating system can be upgraded by downloads from the Higher Self, by way of the Free Will Earth GRID (Matrix).

This grid was hijacked by malevolent beings (Reptilians) and others long ago. The system is a part of the Galactic 24,000-year cycle which the Mayan Calendar says we are currently at the end of. It's the last 6,000-year cycle that they (Reptilians) had control of.

This Book is your official disclosure. The reading of this book should open your curiosity to imagine the unimaginable which supersedes your so-called Theories of physical Relativity laws by Albert Einstein:

Special relativity applied to all physical phenomena in the absence of gravity. General relativity explained the law of gravitation and its relation to other forces of nature. It applied to the cosmological and astrophysical realm, including astronomy.

The theory transformed theoretical physics and astronomy during the 20th century, superseding a 200-year-old theory of mechanics created primarily by Isaac Newton. It introduced concepts including spacetime as a unified entity of space and time, relativity of simultaneity, kinematic and gravitational time dilation, and length contraction.

In the field of physics, relativity improved the science of elementary particles and their fundamental interactions, along with ushering in the nuclear age. With relativity, cosmology and astrophysics predicted extraordinary astronomical phenomena such as neutron stars, black holes, and gravitational waves.

We the Elohim have the ability to alter time as you know it. For we are made of Anti-Matter, Electromagnetic Star dust, and Atomic Energy. Consider us as an anomaly. No weapons formed against us shall prosper. For we have come to give you what you need, so you may want what we must give you. Which is the truth.

We have come to right the wrongs out of pure love and cosmic harmony. We are in fact the voice in your mind that is reading this. And we are also the consciousness that is listening as well.

But the problems are your lower frequencies and vibrations, which keeps mankind in a perpetual state of ignorance. This is what results in violence, fear, and suffering.

Very truly we tell you that, what you do to the planet, and yourselves is done to us. There was an unbalance in the universe that is now under siege and bound by a force of equilibrium. We call it the ELOHVEE. Which is simply (Love). We'd rather it be this way now for our landings may frighten you.

Once you know us, you'll become us. All unsolved mysteries are known to us, and soon will be known to you as we purge the human consciousness collectively. You may start to feel weird for mental telepathy, telekinesis, and psychic phenomena are some of your higher senses but are characterized as symptoms of psychosis, and schizophrenia.

May your heart be your guidance as we attempt to eradicate ignorance. So, fear not, for all of your love ones who may seemed to have died in this existence, are alive and well within their own parallel realities.

Central Processing Unit.
C.P.U.

A computer is a machine that can be instructed to carry out sequences of arithmetic or logical operations automatically via computer programming. Modern computers can follow generalized sets of operations, called programs. These programs enable computers to perform an extremely wide range of tasks.

Future computers promise to be even faster than today's computers and smaller than a deck of cards. Perhaps they will become the size of coins and offer "smart" or artificial intelligence features like expert intelligence, neural network pattern recognition features, or natural language capabilities.

Computers are used as control systems for a wide variety of industrial and consumer devices. This includes simple special purpose devices like microwave ovens and remote controls, factory devices such as industrial robots and computer-aided design, and also general-purpose devices like personal computers and mobile devices such as smartphones. The Internet is run on computers and it connects hundreds of millions of other computers and their users.

Early computers were only conceived as calculating devices. Since ancient times, simple manual devices like the abacus aided people in doing calculations. Early in the Industrial Revolution, some mechanical devices were built to automate long tedious tasks, such as guiding patterns for looms. More sophisticated electrical machines did specialize analog calculations in the early 20th century. The first digital electronic calculating machines were developed during World War II.

The first semiconductor transistors in the late 1940s were followed by the silicon based MOSFET (MOS transistor) and monolithic integrated circuit (IC) chip technologies in the late 1950s, leading to the microprocessor and the microcomputer revolution in the 1970s.

The speed, power and versatility of computers have been increasing dramatically ever since then, with MOS transistor counts increasing at a rapid pace (as predicted by Moore's law), leading to the Digital Revolution during the late 20th to early 21st centuries. Conventionally, a modern computer consists of at least one processing element, typically a central processing unit (CPU) in the form of a metal-oxide-semiconductor (MOS) microprocessor, along with some type of computer memory, typically MOS semiconductor memory chips.

The processing element carries out arithmetic and logical operations, and a sequencing and control unit can change the order of operations in response to stored information. Peripheral devices include input devices (keyboards, mice, joystick, etc.), output devices (monitor screens, printers, etc.), and input/output devices that perform both functions (e.g., the 2000s-era touchscreen). Peripheral devices allow information to be retrieved from an external source and they enable the result of operations to be saved and retrieved.

Imagination

1. The faculty or action of forming new ideas, or images or concepts of external objects not present to the senses.

Imagination is the ability to come up with mental images of something that is not real or to come up with new and creative ideas. When a child is playing house and creates a pretend story, this is an example of a child using his imagination Without this creative power we may never have had the internet, smartphones, airplanes, and other amazing technology we rely on every day. Simply put, imagination is the key ingredient to expansion and the advancement of our world.

I was known to be a bit of a starry-eyed, head in the clouds type of guy. A natural-born uplifter, who found it rather easy to focus on the positive and what I wanted to create, as opposed to feeling stuck in the reality of 'what is'. And while there have been many people in my life who have so kindly reminded me of the importance of being responsible and realistic, I have learned that imagination is far more valuable than reality and here are a few reasons why.

1.Imagination ignites passion. As adults we have been forced into a world of responsibility and practicality where money, bills, and jobs (many of which we hate) dictate how we live, breathe, and experience the world. Dreaming of what can be allows us to tap into our imaginations again, reminding us what it feels like to be passionate about something. Somewhere along the lines we have lost that connection to passion and purpose in life and replaced it with survival and responsibility.

2.Our imagination and thoughts create our future. It's long been said that 'thoughts become things' and our imaginative muscle is the very thing that helps make that possible. When we stay immersed in what is directly in front of us at all times (i.e., our current reality), we continually create the same challenges, problems, and experiences over and over again. But, when we venture into our imagination to focus on the reality that we want to experience, the energy is set in motion and magnificent change can occur.

3.Imagination stimulates creativity and innovation. Some of the most influential and innovative creations have come from the simple act of imagining something bigger, easier, or more beautiful. Scientists and creative artists have an amazing gift for thinking outside the box and allowing their imaginations the freedom to grow and evolve their thoughts, many of which have created products that have changed the way we live entirely.

Without this creative power we may never have had the internet, smartphones, airplanes, and other amazing technology we rely on every day. Simply put, imagination is the key ingredient to expansion and the advancement of our world.

4.Imagination is magical. Take a moment to watch a young child play alone and you will experience first-hand the magic that comes from imagination. Creative thought turns the mundane into a magical experience. It is what turns a simple box into a powerful rocket, a laundry basket into a pirate ship, and a simple bathtub into the deep blue sea. Taking a moment to view the world through a child's eyes is enough to bring back the joy and wonder that imagination brings. How amazing would our world be if we all experienced that same joy and wonder on a day-to-day basis?

5.Sometimes reality just sucks. Watching the news and hearing about the violence, crime, sickness, and sadness in the world is enough to make anyone believe that things are falling apart. By falling into the trap of 'what is' and believing that this is just the way the world works, we become a victim and relinquish our true creative power.

Choosing to use our imaginative muscle as a means of creation provides hope. And where there is hope there is ultimately an opportunity for transformation and change. Two things that are necessary for us to create a better world for generations to come.

Albert Einstein had it right when he said: "Reality is merely an illusion, albeit a very persistent one," Reality is merely an outward expression of what we have chosen to accept and focus on in the world. But when we turn our thoughts to that which we want to create in our lives, the possibilities are endless.

With that kind of imaginative power, why would we waste it focusing on the mundane only to perpetuate a reality that is less than optimum? We have the power to create so much more and it is up to us to use our imaginations to change our lives and our world for the better.

Astral Projection.

1. Of, connected with, or resembling the stars. "astral navigation" Relating to a supposed nonphysical realm of existence to which various psychic and paranormal phenomena are ascribed, and in which the physical human body is said to have a counterpart.

Astral projection (or astral travel) is a term used in esotericism to describe an intentional out-of-body experience that assumes the existence of a soul or consciousness called an "astral body" that is separate from the physical body and capable of traveling outside it throughout the universe.

The idea of astral travel is ancient and occurs in multiple cultures. The modern terminology of "Astral Projection" was coined and promoted in the 19th-century. It is sometimes reported in association with dreams, and forms of meditation. Some individuals have reported perceptions similar to descriptions of astral projection that were induced through various hallucinogenic and hypnotic means (including self-hypnosis).

There is no scientific evidence that there is a consciousness or soul which is separate from normal neural activity or that one can consciously leave the body and make observations, and astral projection has been characterized as a pseudoscience.

Astral Light is a term used by Eliphas Levi to refer to the medium of all light, energy and movement, much in accordance with the theory of the luminiferous ether commonly held in the nineteenth century. In his view the astral light was a fluidic life force that fills all space and living beings.

The Astral Light receives the "impressions" produced on the Terrestrial plane and retains a record of all that happens. It also mirrors the higher planes. However, due to its nature, the reflections are fragmentary and misleading. The Astral Light responds to the willpower and can therefore be used to produce some occult and psychic phenomena. The Astral Light, as the source of all world phenomena, is a theme of no little importance to the student of the light.

The root of the word "Astral" is to be found in the Assyrian Ishtar, signifying star, and was applied to this element by the Kabalists and later mystics, because they considered the heavenly bodies as the concrete Crystallizations of the Astral Light.

Some writers have confounded the nature of this element with that of Akasâ, while in fact the latter comprehends infinitely more both in quality and quantity. Literally the Sanskrit term Akasâ means the sky, but occultly the impalpable Ether or the Soul within the Ether.

Some defines it as the "immortal spirit", the progenitor of Cosmic life and "Universal Intelligence whose characteristic property is Buddhi".

Akasâ is the sphere of the pure undifferentiated Monad, the essence of wisdom, while the Astral Light at its opposite pole is the abstract atom of matter, the plane of generation, and the great womb out of which issues all planetary life. Ether, which is the highest vibration of the Astral Light, is but as a vehicle for Akasâ, a gross body in comparison.

The functions of the Astral Light are as manifold as the expressed universe. Its nature is dual — the highest Ether forming its positive, and the concrete, or differentiated elements, its negative pole. Its cause reaches back to the root of all causes, and its effects involve all our physical and psychical experiences.

We deal with its familiar phenomena in every breath and every motion, while the rare and abnormal phases are as strictly subject to its laws.

It is not substantially identical with any one of the material elements of Cosmic matter but is one-degree superior to Prakriti (Nature as apprehended by the senses), and it impenetrates and vitalizes each atom. It is itself the one underlying element in which all other known elements have their source and supply.

In its physical aspects it includes the Ether of modern scientists, but in the metaphysical sense they scarcely touch its borderland. For while it is the reservoir of Heat, Light, Magnetism, and Electricity — the field of all degrees of vibration — it is also the sphere of all intellectual life, and the ruling agent in the alchemical process which frees the cerebral atom and converts it into thought. Its vibratory rate determines individual mental tendencies and establishes our intimate relations in body with the stars.

The Time Is Now.

The Mayan calendar is an ancient calendar system that rose to fame in 2012, when a "Great 26,000 Year Cycle" of its Long Count component came to an end, inspiring some to believe that the world would end at 11:11 on December 21, 2012. The media hype and hysteria that ensued was later termed the 2012 phenomenon.

This of course was nothing more than the beginning of the awakening cycle that actually starts on December 21, 2020. The number of days lost in a year due to the shift into Gregorian Calendar is 11 days... For **268** years using the Gregorian Calendar (1752-2020) times 11 days = 2,948 days. 2,948 days / 365 days (per year) = 8 years." Which would mean that following the Julian Calendar, we are technically in 2012 right now.

 The Gregorian calendar is the calendar used in most of the world. It is named after Pope Gregory the 13th, who introduced it in October 1582 in which the year can be attributed to the 7th letter and the 7-digit name. (1+5+8+2=16) (1+6=7) = Gregory.

In 1582, when Pope Gregory the 13th introduced his Gregorian calendar, Europe adhered to the Julian calendar, first implemented by Julius Caesar in 46 B.C. Since the Roman emperor's system miscalculated the length of the solar year by 11 minutes, the calendar had since fallen out of sync with the seasons as it seems.

The Julian calendar is still used in parts of the Eastern Orthodox Church and in parts of Oriental Orthodoxy as well as by the Berbers. The Julian calendar has two types of year: a normal year of 365 days and a leap year of 366 days.

Although we've come to believe that time is a physical reality that moves at a fixed speed, when we practice dreaming, time doesn't have a direction. It doesn't move along a straight line, as when we dream of a long-gone relative and then about our children. And there is no causality: When we dream the world into being, the future doesn't have to build upon the past, and the past doesn't have to predetermine our present.

The future as well as the past is available to us, and everything is happening at once. In fact, we can only dream the world into being from this place of timelessness. As we raise our perception to that of eagle, we get closer to experiencing this sense of infinity.

Infinity is a place both prior to and after time, before the big bang and after the universe again collapses. That is, it is outside of time itself. In this place of infinity, you can influence events that occurred in the past and nudge destiny. An Earth keeper understands that if you want to change a situation, you have to start by accepting it as it is. You recognize that this moment is perfect—and then you can change anything you want.

Once you step outside of time into infinity, the past and future disclose themselves to you—you can see tomorrow and the day after tomorrow and even the day that you will die.

However, it's important to erase your conscious memory of this so that you can be fully present each day of your life. You want to wake up saying, "What a beautiful day this is!" instead of "This is the day I'm going to die," or "This is exactly one year before the date I'm going to die," or what have you. You don't want to get stuck in time again, perceiving death as a predator and forgetting your original nature. That means that you'll want to keep the secrets you learn in this place of infinity from your ego.

You see, billions of years ago, the immense force that we know as all Expanding (Source), which existed in an unmanifested void, decided to experience itself. With a big bang, it formed all the matter in our universe, and then it continued to explore itself through myriad forms—from rock to crystal to moon to butterfly. Yet since the immense force was omnipresent and omniscient, each of its manifestations also possessed these qualities. To know itself through its many forms, it had to keep the nature of its being a secret even from itself.

When we step out of the "arrow of time" and experience infinity, we reclaim our original nature, which is Source (God). When we return into time, we lose that awareness so that we can experience life in our clock-ruled world, which is what we're meant to do. We return to everyday life unaware that we're God and are dreaming everything up.

So, as we go about our daily lives, the knowledge of our original nature drives us to serve our experiences rather than expecting them to serve us. That is, instead of cooking a meal with the expectation that it will nurture us, we nurture ourselves in the preparation and serving of the food, infusing the experience with meaning. We no longer search for meaning in situations, but rather bring meaning and purpose to every encounter; we no longer search for truth or beauty, but rather bring truth and beauty to every situation.

If we keep the knowledge of our omnipresent, omniscient nature at hand, aware of it at every moment, we'll never have to strive for transcendent experiences or enlightenment. We'll know that everything we do is sacred, so we'll no longer search for meaning, truth, beauty, or purpose.

We'll call off the search and bring beauty to every action and truth to every encounter. Having been to that place of timelessness, we'll find it easier to be present in the moment rather than thinking about what we should have done, ought to be doing, or might do later. Whether we're kissing the one we love or sweeping the floor, we lose ourselves in that moment, and it is there where we find complete perfection

The Watchers.

The mysterious masculine first name "Gregory derives from the Latin name "Gregorius", which came from the late Greek name "(Grēgórios) meaning "watchful, alert" (derived from Greek "γρηγορεῖν" "grēgorein" meaning "to watch").

Watcher is a term used in connection with biblical benevolent and Malevolent Angels. (Extra Terra Astrals). Watcher occurs in both plural and singular forms in the Book of Daniel, where reference is made to their holiness. The apocryphal Books of Enoch refer to both good and bad Watchers, with a primary focus on the rebellious ones.

During the end of 2nd Seeding the Annunaki started breeding with Humans and a race called NEPHILIM was created. This was not agreed upon to genetically tamper with the human race and the Elohim would not let this race walk on or be on the Earth.

This created a Conflict, and another War broke out. This created the war with the Annunaki and other Annunaki sympathizers, such as the Dracs and Sirian Annunaki Hybrids. The Nephilim Wars ended this seeding attempt and we reorganized for the next Evolutionary Round where the Luciferian Rebellion occurred in the Atlantian Cataclysm timelines.

Sirians (Sirius B) Hosted this Seeding of Human Race, **Eye of Horus** a Stellar Bridge used to bring in consciousness to incarnate in the 4D Planetary Gates in Giza, Egypt. The Melchizedek Race Families came in to help to repair genetic digression around this time approximately 35,000 years ago.

Violations by the Incarnated Melchizedek's using Earth portals incorrectly around the Egyptian Dynastic timeline unleashed a lot of Dark energies onto the Earth surface. A major damage was created in the 2D layers by Akhenaton inadvertently.

This was not on purpose by the Melchizedek's, as it was a part of their intended plan to integrate the Annu template from the damaged DNA in the planetary fields that had resulted from the Atlantian explosions of the grids during the previous Root race seeding.

Unfortunately, there were some miscalculations and other genetic issues that raised a serious breach of planetary templar security. (The Templar is the Stargate Portal System of the Earth that opens into the 12-Dimensional Levels of the Universal Time Matrix.)

During the end of 2nd Seeding the Annunaki reptilian races started breeding with Humans on the earth and a race called Nephilim was created. Many of these Nephilim creations were from kidnap, rape and forced breeding with the human women of the earth. This was not agreed upon to genetically tamper with the human race and the Elohim would not let this race continue to walk on or be on the Earth.

This created a Conflict, and another War broke out with the Annunaki and other Annunaki sympathizers, such as the Dracs and reptilian groups of Sirian Annunaki Hybrids. The Nephilim Wars ended this seeding attempt and we reorganized for the next Evolutionary Round where the Luciferian Rebellion occurred in the Atlantian Cataclysm timelines.

Many of the Nephilim were destroyed on the earth during the Nephilim Wars and their fragmented consciousness became enmeshed with the lower demonic spirits of the dense levels of earth matter.

Some of these entities bound to the earth became known as the Watchers and comprise of both combinations of Nephilim and Fallen Angelic fragments which descended to become ruled over by the hierarchies of the Belial and Baal entities in the earth. Over time these fragments evolved into many lower spirit hierarchies of entities, trapped within the earth fields unable to evolve, transit or heal.

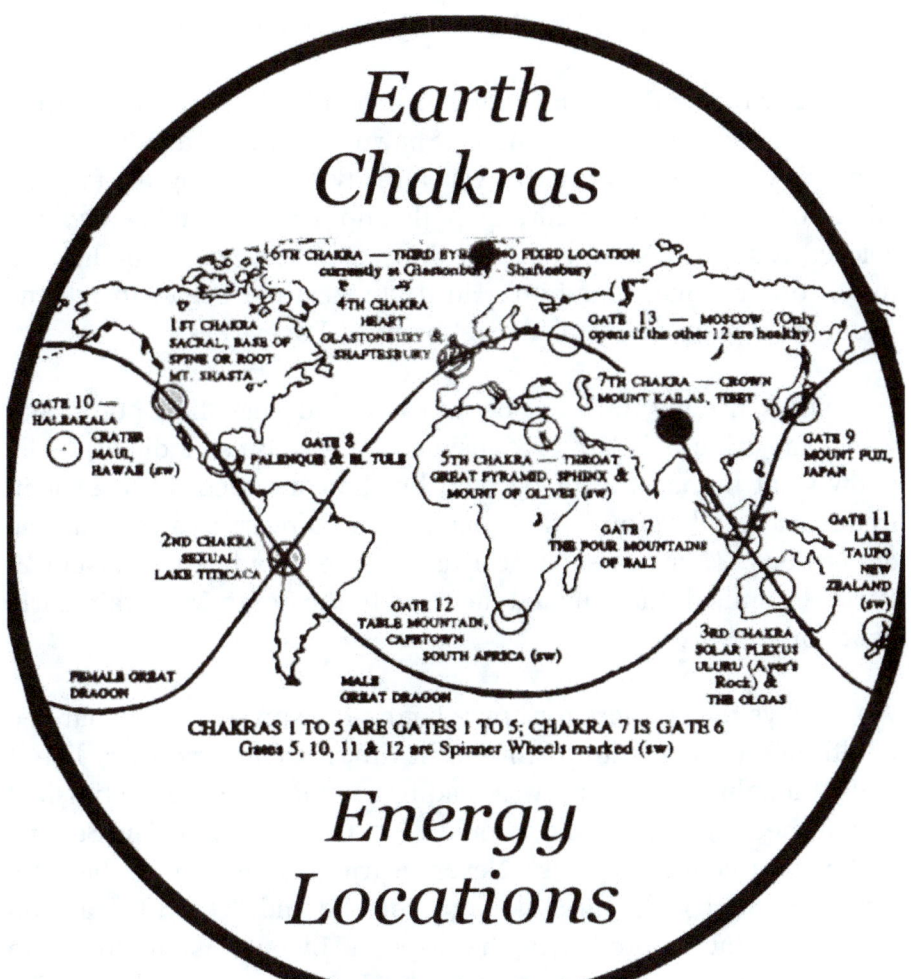

Earth Chakras

6TH CHAKRA — THIRD EYE NO FIXED LOCATION currently at Glastonbury - Shaftesbury

4TH CHAKRA HEART GLASTONBURY & SHAFTESBURY

1ST CHAKRA SACRAL, BASE OF SPINE OR ROOT MT. SHASTA

GATE 13 — MOSCOW (Only opens if the other 12 are healthy)

7TH CHAKRA — CROWN MOUNT KAILAS, TIBET

GATE 10 — HALEAKALA CRATER MAUI, HAWAII (sw)

GATE 8 PALENQUE & EL TULE

5TH CHAKRA — THROAT GREAT PYRAMID, SPHINX & MOUNT OF OLIVES (sw)

GATE 9 MOUNT FUJI, JAPAN

GATE 11 LAKE TAUPO NEW ZEALAND (sw)

GATE 7 THE FOUR MOUNTAINS OF BALI

2ND CHAKRA SEXUAL LAKE TITICACA

GATE 12 TABLE MOUNTAIN, CAPETOWN SOUTH AFRICA (sw)

3RD CHAKRA SOLAR PLEXUS ULURU (Ayer's Rock) & THE OLGAS

FEMALE GREAT DRAGON

MALE GREAT DRAGON

CHAKRAS 1 TO 5 ARE GATES 1 TO 5; CHAKRA 7 IS GATE 6
Gates 5, 10, 11 & 12 are Spinner Wheels marked (sw)

Energy Locations

43

Sedona, Arizona. Vortex, Enlightenment.

(S.A.V.E.) The home of my Awakening.

Meeting with the Re-Turn Council of Phoenix, Arizona. was a great experience for me. Once there, Shawn Pereira and I met at a Popeye's Chicken restaurant. I was already there eating my favorite "Red Beans and Rice", before he pulled up. He was driving a golden colored Nissan SUV. Once he sat down, I asked, 'would he like for me to order a meal for him'. He declined, then began to tell me about the synchronicity of us meeting up at Popeye's.

He said, "Once my third eye becomes fat and juicy, he'd pop it and watch me have a D.N.A. Explosion'. At that time, I didn't really know what he had meant by that, but he continued on to explain frequencies, vibrations, the holographic universe, and multiple dimensions. Then, as soon as I asked him about "Dr. Malachi Z. York", he smiled, then invited me to go to the South Mountain park, South of Phoenix.

We must've talked there for hours before the sun set, as he shared a wealth of Out-formation with me. At times, I felt very weird like, I really thought this brother was reading my mind. So, as we finished up our meeting as he asked, 'would I like to travel up to The Sedona vortex in a couple of days'. Never hearing of such place had me Intrigued. So, I said, "sure thing bro, then he said, "Okay, I'll call you in 3 days". But, before leaving he asked, 'If I would like to donate to the Re-Turn Council?' I said, "yes", as I opened my wallet to give him $300 dollars. I asked, "when can I meet with them", He then said, "you already have Thank you.

I then walked to my Chrysler 300 and drove back to my Hotel room. My Ex-wife's brother Dion, came to visit me later on that night, and we hung out in Downtown Phoenix. He told me about the Phoenix lights phenomena and said that, "Arizona is a hotspot for UFO activity". I laughed and said, "really"?

He said, "if you stay here long enough, maybe you'll get to see one", as we both laughed. So, after 3 days had passed, Shawn called my phone. I answered saying "hello", then Shawn said, "Brother man"! "Are you ready for your downloads"?

I said, "I sure am". So, we met up at a South Phoenix Waffle House, where he parked his vehicle as we decided to drive mine up to Sedona. It was very cloudy with light rain on the way up there. He told me to look up at a cumulus cloud and said, "that is a crystalline space craft". As I looked in amazement, I began to see a long vibrant rainbow in the sky.

We then made it to the location and ate lunch at a local restaurant. Shawn then began to speak of Dr. York saying, "I am a Student Teacher who studied Re-Memorings with Dr York on the land of TamaRE in Georgia." And before I could say another word, Shawn said, "It is 'he' who has called you to me! Yes, Dr. Malachi Z. York (TEHUTI) also known to many as Nebu, and Yaanuwn is an Extra Terra Astral who dates beyond the predynastic period, which is over 10,500 years ago, so Tehuti predates YAHWEH and YAHUWA.

DJEHUTI indicates that he originated in the HEBTIAAT "Nomes" of DEHUT in lower EGYPT. He is represented as a man with the head of an IBIS BIRD and crowed with a crescent moon. The baboon is sacred to him for in KHEMENU 'Hermopolis' he merged with the local baboon NETER (NADJAR) "supreme being" HEDJ-WER. These relations to animals were symbolic as you can see.

Tehuti was involved in the genetic engineering of the human body using the Gibbon and chimpanzee mixing it with the Extra Terra Astral DNA to make the costume or human body that we wear in our physical incarnation as spirits. So, we did not evolve from monkeys as many has been told.

We are spiritual beings (Etherians) who used a creature on earth by way of the Extra Terra Astral's who mixed their DNA to Create the human body that we use when incarnating into physical form.

Tehuti was one of the scientists of that project, thus his connection with monkeys is deeper than most can overstand. Tehuti was intimately connected with a variety of lunar functions relating to cycles of time, and measure and movements, Tehuti is a scientist of the Neteru or Nadjaru, it's symbolic information.

Tehuti is one of the 24 elders that keeps the records of our deeds and thoughts. He is also called NEBU "lord" of divine words. The Greeks called him Hermes Trismegistus the THRICE GREAT. His name is spelled DJEHUTI, ZEHUTI and THOTH and is from where you get THOUGHT. Tehuti is a master scribe or AUTHOR from which you get AUTHORITY.

From KHEMENU HERMOPOLIS he is sometimes seen as a DOG HEADED APE in rituals symbolizing the lower nature of man and mankind. He is and was the Master Teacher of priest and physicians and looked on at the creation of mortals. TEHUTI Is the supreme NETER of peace and love between beings, Tehuti is the supreme beings NETER of writing, science, medicines, and for formulas and has educated humanity throughout the ages.

He invented ALCHEMY, and assisted mortals by writing many works of Science, Solar biology, and astronomy. Forty-six Records of his are kept sacred from the BEAST-MAN. Tehuti is the keeper of the records of existence, destiny, and the renewal of all history which occurs every 24,000 years, thus 24 elders 24 hours in a day, and many more connections.

Tehuti is an Extra Terra Astronaut who came to Earth from SIRIUS. He spent time in SAAHU ORION and took part in the moon and mars project of seeding this planet. He is the "Melchizedek" of the bible. It is so much about this Extra Terra Astronaut that humanity doesn't know about, yet, it is he who has been appearing in your dreams".

Shawn then said, "Is this not why you are here?" I concurred as we talked for a little while longer before heading over to the Mountain's edge. The scenery was very beautiful. I had never seen anything like it before. We then perform Sacred rituals, took pictures and talked with the natives. I could remember feeling very warm inside as the colors in my view became very vibrant.

It was like I could see the whole spectrum of light as the ultraviolet rays beamed on me. Shawn could tell that I was looking for a teacher, but he told me that, "I found a Master". I said, "so, you're going to be my Master Teacher"? He said, "No! You are", as he smiled, and said, "Download complete".

The Coming Solar Re Flash Event is the Ascension/Rapture or Soul Harvest/Armageddon or Judgement Day or Samvartaka Fire that all religions have talked about. Destined to happen soon, once a sufficient mass of humanity has awakened and breached a critical threshold in level of consciousness (have awakened and chosen the light).

A massive burst of Cosmic waves will be transmitted from the Central Sun, the Black hole at the Center of the Galaxy, through our Sun. It will appear on Earth as a Milky Warm Liquid Light Plasma.

Humans that are ready spiritually, and energetically will experience near instant evolution and transmutation from a 2-strand double helix DNA Carbon based Life form, into a Crystalline (Christ) Life Form having a Light Body with Multiple Additional (up to 12) DNA Strands. And shall then 'Ascend' to 5TH Dimensional Earth in their Physical Bodies. This is the first time such an 'Experiment' is being conducted in the known history of the Milky Way Galaxy.

This is not a destructive doomsday Event but a Peaceful One. All that is required is an Intent to Forgive Everyone (Harbor No Ill-Will); Intent to overcome one's addictions and attachments.

At least 51% of one's Thoughts, Feelings and Actions Should be of Service to Others Orientation, Harboring a Desire for the Well Being of Fellow Humans; Truthfulness and Integrity of Thoughts, Feelings and Actions.

Those of who are of the Dark Service to Self- Orientation will Perish in the Flash (like in the snaping of the finger of the Marvel character "Thanos"), and these souls will then be taken by the Logos to another planetary setting to further continue their Lessons towards Integration and Balance. I found out that in the Western world, the concept of enlightenment in a religious context acquired a romantic meaning.

It has become synonymous with self-realization and the true self, which is being regarded as a substantial essence which is covered over by social conditioning. Enlightenment or awakening is a profound mystery, and the best definition may be found in the actual experience of your own shifts in consciousness.

Just as it's more nourishing to eat an apple than read about one, so it can be more rewarding to explore the movements of your own awareness than to try to understand these things mentally. While definitions of such things can be helpful, it can also be beneficial to not have too many concepts, which could interfere with your actual experience. It's a good thing that language isn't so fixed or defined when it comes to spiritual unfoldment.

Maybe the best definition of enlightenment is no definition. Then there is only what is found in your own direct experience of awareness. What is a vortex? Sedona vortexes (the proper grammatical form 'vortices' is rarely used) are thought to be swirling centers of energy that are conducive to healing, meditation and self-exploration.

These are places where the earth seems especially alive with energy. Many people feel inspired, recharged or uplifted after visiting a vortex. Sedona has developed a worldwide reputation as a place of enlightenment.

This is home to a large community that promotes a variety of alternative healing and spiritual practices. There are wellness shops and boutiques scattered through the town. In addition, many of Sedona's spas offer Native American-inspired treatments using indigenous materials like red rock clay and local plants.

Anyone on a journey of self-discovery can find out more from expert practitioners through the Sedona Metaphysical Spiritual Association. Yet even if you have no particular interest in the metaphysical movement, plan on visiting Sedona's vortex sites.

It is virtually guaranteed that you will leave feeling better than when you arrived. Your heart will be lighter, your smile will be wider, and you will feel more energized. Because here's the wonderful secret: Vortexes are located at some of the most devastatingly scenic spots found among the towering red rock formations.

Anytime you can get outside to walk in sunshine, breathing fresh clean air amid dazzling panoramas is a day well spent. Sedona has the ability to transform lives. That's its true power. The raw physical beauty of the landscape automatically recalibrates your sense of wonder. Embrace the spectacular. Accept the astonishing.

This is a place that inspires, recharges, uplifts, soothes, restores and so much more. For many, the very act of being here provokes a spiritual awakening. No one leaves Sedona unchanged. No matter what paths you take while traveling through life, Sedona is always the scenic route. That's a journey well worth taking.

Deoxyribonucleic Acid

D.N.A.

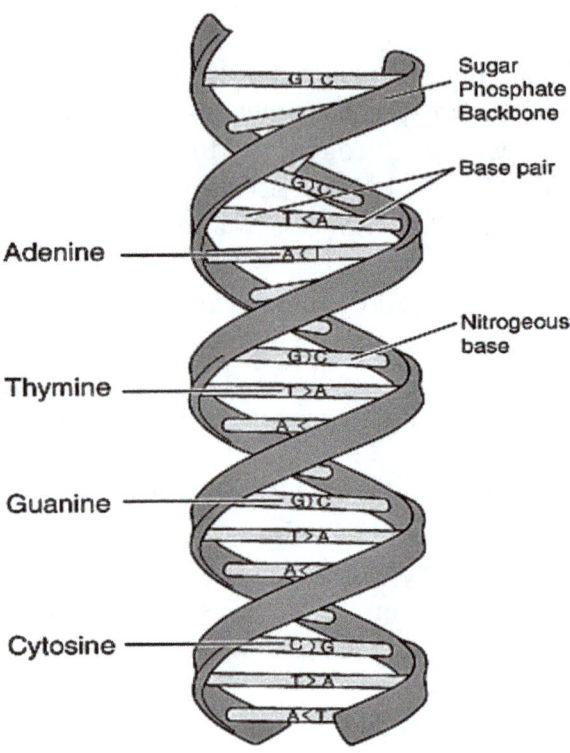

A gene is the basic physical and functional unit of heredity. Genes are made up of DNA. Some genes act as instructions to make molecules called proteins. However, many genes do not code for proteins. In humans, genes vary in size from a few hundred DNA bases to more than 2 million bases.

An international research effort called the Human Genome Project, which worked to determine the sequence of the human genome and identify the genes that it contains, estimated that humans have between 20,000 and 25,000 genes.

Every person has two copies of each gene, one inherited from each parent. Most genes are the same in all people, but a small number of genes (less than 1 percent of the total) are slightly different between people. Alleles are forms of the same gene with small differences in their sequence of DNA bases. These small differences contribute to each person's unique physical features.

Genetic processes work in combination with an organism's environment and experiences to influence development and behavior, often referred to as nature versus nurture. The intracellular or extracellular environment of a living cell or organism may switch gene transcription on or off.

A classic example is two seeds of genetically identical corn, one placed in a temperate climate and one in an arid climate (lacking sufficient waterfall or rain). While the average height of the two corn stalks may be genetically determined to be equal, the one in the arid climate only grows to half the height of the one in the temperate climate due to lack of water and nutrients in its environment.

The two DNA strands are known as polynucleotides as they are composed of simpler monomeric units called nucleotides. Each nucleotide is composed of one of four nitrogen-containing nucleobases (cytosine [C], guanine [G], adenine [A] or thymine [T]), a sugar called deoxyribose, and a phosphate group.

The nucleotides are joined to one another in a chain by covalent bonds (known as the phospho-diester linkage) between the sugar of one nucleotide and the phosphate of the next, resulting in an alternating sugar-phosphate backbone.

The nitrogenous bases of the two separate polynucleotide strands are bound together, according to base pairing rules (A with T and C with G), with hydrogen bonds to make double-stranded DNA. The complementary nitrogenous bases are divided into two groups, pyrimidines and purines. In DNA, the pyrimidines are thymine and cytosine; the purines are adenine and guanine.

Both strands of double-stranded DNA store the same biological information. This information is replicated as and when the two strands separate. A large part of DNA (more than 98% for humans) is non-coding, meaning that these sections do not serve as patterns for protein sequences.

The two strands of DNA run in opposite directions to each other and are thus antiparallel. Attached to each sugar is one of four types of nucleobases (informally, bases). It is the sequence of these four nucleobases along the backbone that encodes genetic information.

RNA strands are created using DNA strands as a template in a process called transcription, where DNA bases are exchanged for their corresponding bases except in the case of thymine (T), for which RNA substitutes uracil (U). Under the genetic code, these RNA strands specify the sequence of amino acids within proteins in a process called translation.

Within eukaryotic cells, DNA is organized into long structures called chromosomes. Before typical cell division, these chromosomes are duplicated in the process of DNA replication, providing a complete set of chromosomes for each daughter cell.

Eukaryotic organisms (animals, plants, fungi and protists) store most of their DNA inside the cell nucleus as nuclear DNA, and some in the mitochondria as mitochondrial DNA or in chloroplasts as chloroplast DNA. In contrast, prokaryotes (bacteria and archaea) store their DNA only in the cytoplasm, in circular chromosomes.

Within eukaryotic chromosomes, chromatin proteins, such as histones, compact and organize DNA. These compacting structures guide the interactions between DNA and other proteins, helping control which parts of the DNA are transcribed.

The harvesting of DNA and Consciousness Energy is the most valuable type of currency and is used as a medium of exchange by more advanced cultures than what we have currently inherited through the dark age of the Negative Extra Terra Astral invasion. One should be aware that on many other planets monetary systems such as ours do not exist.

For the invading species to continue to access the planetary consciousness energy supply without further resistance, humanity has been groomed to ignore genetics and consciousness access as a valuable currency and to focus instead only on an imaginary money supply that is completely controlled and manipulated.

Humans are taught to worship the money supply as their primary identification with material success, power and personal fulfillment, as this mind control program to seek power through money has been explicitly designed by the Controllers as a hidden enslavement tool.

Off planet, accessing Consciousness Energy and Sentient Intelligence is the highly valued currency, prized by many Extra-dimensional species as a medium of exchange and for generating intelligence for their virtual reality systems.

Thus, by having free access to massive amounts of genetic material and consciousness energy produced by someone or something else, this gives an incredible amount of power to those controlling entities who are reaping the benefits of harvesting that energy from others.

This model is surfacing in the mainstream through the advertising of the popular personal genomic companies that use genotyping for their DNA tests, which are now offered to consumers that want to know about their ancestry.

Most people do not realize the potential billions of dollars these companies make on the DNA catalogues, which people taking these tests are giving them easy access to. They partner with major biotechnology and pharmaceutical companies to effectively monetize human DNA under the research and development label, which is actually used primarily for nefarious purposes.

Digital currency companies that offer a consumer the ability to sequence their own DNA through genetic testing, are then be able to monetize it by selling the information to a collection of data buyers via cryptocurrency, and these are beginning right now. If we can sell our own sequenced DNA for a profit to an enthusiastic buyer for cryptocurrency, we should stop to reflect on the real purpose behind this agenda.

Why would they want the intimate details of our consciousness history that is recorded in our sequenced DNA, exchange it for cryptocurrency and then hand it over to an anonymous corporation in order to control it?

Sequencing of human genomes is an unfathomable area of massive profits, translatable into any marketable currency. It is also used for gaining control over consciousness energy and exposes yet another layer to the black hole entities agenda, that want direct access to fully sequenced genomes in the mass population.

Remember that the type of DNA sequence that a human being has is responsible for the level of consciousness they have, as well as the level of access they have to move through Stargates and portal systems on the earth.

DNA holds the consciousness record in a natural bio-spiritual internet and holds the dimensional keys in the timelines that unlock dimensional doorways throughout the time matrix.

Khrestallah

The divine blueprint which holds the original intention for the natural order of consciousness evolution within our Universal creation, is encoded in the DNA base 12 mechanics of the Christos Blueprint.

At a cosmic level this same open-source architecture is referred to as Kryst-Krystallah, the unified masculine and feminine consciousness energy that exists in perfect harmony and balance within organic creation.

The DNA base 12 Universal Androgynous Merkaba fields of Christos-Sophia are also referred to as Kryst-Krystallah architecture, as they make up the instruction set for all Merkaba fields within all the timelines and densities throughout the Universes.

Thus, the term Christ or Christos used in this context is not denoting the individual being referred to as Jesus Christ, as taught through the world religions. Christos extends way beyond all meaning associated with planetary consciousness and actually describes the state of eternal Cosmic Consciousness, the title given to a free Cosmic Citizen.

In this activation for higher embodiment, the resonance points for the main energy centers in the physical body have shifted higher, slightly changing their position and adding more light-body architecture to the skull, head and crown.

With the diamond sun body activation for the eternal light body in 5D, all separated electromagnetic fields in the light-body release their polarization membranes and electromagnetic barriers, merging the male-female counter rotation spirals into a large orb of light surrounding the body.

There are three main orb bodies nested within each other that are built on a trinity of triangles that align in the central vertical channel as the new position for the 3rd Sphere, 6th Sphere, 9th Sphere, and then the Personal Christ at the 12th Sphere. These main energy spheres are located on the central column and are merged into a tri-wave neutral charge, or non-polarized energy centers.

Each of the 3-6-9-12 positions connect to a trinity in one built for the Conscious Identity, Soul Triad, Oversoul Triad and the Personal Christ respectively. Also, the light-body is no longer connected to the earth core in the same way, and hovers upon the base shield built underneath the feet.

The base shield connects into the feedback loop of the 360 degrees of the zero-point field or Godhead that runs from within the internal diamond pillar. This current runs from the top of the crown to under the feet, returning back to the zero-point feedback loop made through the 12th Sphere Personal Christ consciousness.

The 12:12 Electrical Christ Male pattern runs the zero point into a feedback loop between the top position of the 12th Sphere from the Paliadorian Cell, down through the central vertical channel into the base shield under the feet.

Spiritual Marriage Blueprint.

The mathematical pattern of 13:13 Female Spin and 12:12 Male Spin.

On top of all of the exciting developments of God's Consciousness Technology returning back to our planet through our Mother Arc herself, we are getting ready to understand the Unity architecture in its Trinity Wave pattern and its direct relationship to manifesting true spiritual marriage on the planet.

As Mother brings back the Krystal Star Frequencies, the Seven Sacred Suns, it is bringing the template of Sacred Spiritual Union between the Rod and Staff functions of our Light body's Merkabic Field.

It is the spiritual mission of recently assigned Rod and Staff couplings to template the prototype blueprint to achieve spiritual marriage or Hieros Gamos, and work to bring this into a physically manifested accomplishment.

This is happening at various octave levels (relationship assignments, Soul, Monad and Avatar Christos-Sophia dimensional levels) to eventually achieve a complete re-encryption of the masculine rod function to the spinning 12:12 electron pattern, that merges perfectly into the female monadic core, a 13:13 field.

This is a template prototype that is called the Khrest-Allah Pattern, which is the Khrestal/Christal Gene Gender Merge between genetic equals.

We are moving to another level of experience within these Rod and Staff Sacred Unions, and many males are also feeling reconnected through these new patterns of heart-brain integration, as they are becoming available in the planetary architecture, to those who have harmonic resonance to the unity frequency and the Christos-Sophia. This is a wonderful development.

On either side of the capstone of the Personal Christ, is the Cosmic Mother Aquamarine Ray on the left and the Cosmic Father Emerald Ray on the right, uniting a trinity of triangles that surrounds the body with a shower of oceanic waves of aquamarine and emerald rays.

Many loving waves of celebration for our Krystallah families for achieving their new embodiment configuration during the Paliadorian activation for the diamond sun body in the second harmonic universe.

This light body configuration is ongoing. It allows more of the human earth family to reclaim their Personal Christ, to build their eternal diamond sun orb body and to continue to have this choice available to them in the future.

Let's Create.

A long time ago, before history as we see it, several nonphysical Astral beings, each an enormous entity, decided to colonize a planet to undertake some research on behalf of the Source. One of us volunteered to serve as the consciousness of the planet.

The group helped this being to systematically densify its energy down through the dimensions. Meanwhile, the rest of us were conceiving the blueprints for the many life-forms that would occupy the planet, to be chemically encoded in what we call DNA. And by successive step-downs in frequency over eons of time, the planetary consciousness burst through an energy barrier into the solid form we know today as planet Earth.

Over vast periods of your elapsed time, these beings continued to create lower-frequency projections of themselves, still nowhere near physical yet. Slowly, these projections experimented with even lower frequency forms of themselves to produce what those with psychic vision would call fifth-dimensional and fourth dimensional (Astral) forms.

Again, slowly over eons you, as one of these beings, experimented further with DNA, directing energy to densify more into standing waves of energy to form semi visible "light" bodies.

Finally, in a brilliant act of creativity, we burst through the dimensional barrier to create the physical structures of subatomic particles, atoms, and molecules, within standing wave envelopes that we also conceived.

We could still dissolve these forms at will and project different ones. So, we played for immeasurable periods, at no time identifying with our increasingly physical projections.

We knew that these ethereal bodies were just energy fields that you created, and into which we radiated energy for the fun of it. As we pushed further, these projected forms became more visible, but there was, as yet, no one consensus shape we might appreciate the playful nature of the Source- always pushing to be creative and to know itself through what it can do.

In order to experiment further, we took a bold step: we projected our consciousness into these forms. This allowed us to interact with ourselves in wholly new ways, impossible at the higher frequencies where we knew only unity. We allowed our consciousness to reside in these ever- densifying physical forms for longer periods of time.

Consciousness now had two vantage points fifth dimensional and physical and we were fully aware in each form of ourselves in the other form, but there was no perception of separateness between them. Now this big party of self- exploration was great fun. New types of energy fields were tried.

For example, we established different fields in order to explore thoughts and emotions separately. And, most important, we gave our projections almost an autonomy, a freedom to be standalone entities. This split into two simultaneous vantage points and was the crucial turning point in the story (by now, history had rolled on to just a few hundred thousand years).

The consciousness in each of these autonomous forms was still fully aware of its spirit nature, and separateness was not even a conceivable thought form the mental construct just did not exist. At this point, the planet was literally our biblical Garden of Eden.

The concept of death was not even possible, because if we got bored with one physical form, we simply dematerialized it, rolled our consciousness back up into your fifth dimensional frequency, and Astral projected another form.

Along the way, we switched from energy projection to a physical birth process and decided on a basic body shape for the species' rapidly densifying physical form. Our legends are full of ancient memories of some of the variety of shapes predating this standardization.

Over thousands of years, us as Spirit, slowly became fascinated with the intensity of the sensations possible in these now physical forms, and our emotional and mental fields became more centered in the lower fields rather than the spirit field. The intensity and richness of emotional experience was totally enthralling, and the sensations that came from being in a dense form were very seductive. You know the story from here, the birth of the ego.

We initially intended that the outer ego-self would act as the information gathering interface with the physical plane on behalf of our spirit-oriented self, which would continue to make decisions about what was real and what to do in the moment. As the experiment proceeded over the millennia, the outward-looking ego began to form its own ideas about reality, and to refer to the inward-looking spirit-self less and less.

The outer ego became stronger, and its identity began to shift from inner states to outer states of being. As a result of this shift, the ego began to color what it perceived and to judge it good or bad according to physical sensation. Thus, the inward-looking self-began to be fed "predigested" information.

The ego's emotional and mental sensitivity to the energy of the spirit field waned as the energy of the physical field became more the focal point. The once simultaneous dual vantage points became separate points of consciousness, and the lower-frequency, physically oriented vantage point lost sight of the spiritual one.

Over the next few millennia, the perceptive gap widened to the point that the lower vantage point began to either doubt the existence of the higher one or to project it outside of itself, as an external being. Thus, you split your perception of who we were, and the concept of gods was created, as mankind could no longer relate to the vast, multi- dimensional beings as part of itself.

The only way to reconcile with the inner voices, the impulses from Spirit, and the memory of being far more than a limited human being was to project your vast, powerful, and all-loving natures out onto beings that we, as a species, created for the purpose. You continued to receive messages and feel the love from your inner spirit-selves but ascribed them as coming from your external gods.

To finally drive in the wedge between Spirit and personality, you conceived of a brilliant veil: shame. By building the vibration of shame into the very cells of your body, you finally achieved a complete sense of separation, and the Spirit- being you once knew yourself to be became a phantom memory, easily dispelled by the harsh light of your new reality.

We then perceived of ourselves as a personality, not even knowing that we were cut off from Spirit, because we'd forgotten about ever having been a unity. We externalized that vast, heroic part of ourselves into a deity that we created. And the shame ensured that we saw ourselves as unworthy in the eyes of this fabricated deity.

So, over time, we became separate isolated in a bag of skin, looking out at a universe we no longer understood, trapped in time and space, with death as the only way out. All we had to help us figure it out was a set of learned responses called a personality. Please remember that we planned all of this from the beginning.

As one of the group of beings that designed this experiment, had decided to see how far we could separate our perceptions from our natural Pure Spirit. Enormous ingenuity was required to design and create the veils that were to separate the dimensions, so that we would incarnate with no memory of who we really were.

As part of this veiling, our collective spirit functions made a decision that was to affect every incarnation for the next two hundred thousand years and completely alter the nature, purpose, and content of human life on this planet

I Am Nothing.

I am nothing. And into nothing I shall return. Which is all and whatever will be. Knowing this, I am everything. I now exist as something, the nucleus that has divided itself into two. I shall now consider myself positive and negative energy, androgynous. Or male and female in principal. I am now seeking an experience like those of me, who were nothing before me.

I have exited my true home in the darkness as light. In an instance teleporting my current form of existence through a massive black hole entering all parallel dimensions. I then allow my frequency and vibration to manifest my existence into a parallel universe fit for the purpose and experience, of needing to know.

The power of light and its sub technologies rests at my will alone. As I manifest inside the anomaly of time and space, I am aware of my surroundings. I am focusing from knowing all, to that of only knowing.

My new purpose takes me to a small blue planet in need of assistance. I'm fully aware of my mission as I enter incarnation mode. I then observed two individuals simultaneously. They are considered male and female principals within each of themselves. But in this type of physical reality one is considered male, and the other a female.

I have now unsuspectedly, and electromagnetically attached myself to each of these two beautiful individuals, as primordial energy. In their timeline, I've inserted the essence of my two divine opposites. My principle nucleus, surrounded by 6 protons, 6 neutrons, and 6 electrons now rests inside each of them.

Now, as I exit their timeline and space continuum, I the triple 9 ether force then Crystallized to await their encounter to begin the molecular multiplication process of being born as a human being.

I have gathered the information and requirements to have an effective experience as a multiple dimensional being to assist the evolution of Mother Earth, the all-in self. And the Self in all.

Etherian.

The spiritual essence of our breath enters the physical form of our holographic body at birth and leaves our form at death. However, since we are our spiritual essence, an Etherian, we are not born nor, do we die. We plug into or log onto the Holographic game that is the physical form, holographic in nature that is born, and ultimately dies.

An Etherian of pure energy cannot be born or die because energy cannot be created or be uncreated. It just changes form. Remember, that in order to enter into a form-based reality, we must first create a body based on the molecular resonance and configuration of that reality. Then, when our body is fully formed, your Spirit enters that form- or allows that form within it.

Our physical shell, our biology, our dense body, is a process of genetic manipulation by extraterrestrials. It evolved, then we, as spirit or Etherian uses that evolutionary body. As an Etherian being of pure energy, a being of All existing gases in nature, we project into that body and call it an incarnation at birth.

We, the spirit or Etherian-energy being, did not and cannot evolve again because energy cannot be created nor destroyed. Spirits do not evolve as bodies do. So, you are an Etherian energy being, a Spirit, a God, an Elohim, a Yahweh, a Yahuwah, an Allah. You volunteered to participate in a game of remembering called learning thus each human is a multi-dimensional master or one with All Expanding.

The Birth.

Incarnating under the state of amnesia. I have become my own adversary. I am fully aware that there are many beings suffering from the same temporary condition. But this automatic function is needed in order to make physical reality real, as it is only a hologram within the mind of the all. As I continue to multiply the cells of my body, I can hear the world outside of my mother's womb. The male and female chromosomes are being regulated by the amount of testosterone and estrogen within my nucleus.

I then break the balance and choose to have my experience as a male. I have chosen to be born to half melanized and half pheomelaninized parents to fully adapt to my terrestrial and political environment. Resting in the embryonic waters of my mother's womb, my transition from being only amphibious is well documented within my D.N.A. In the first trimester my male fetus is developing sufficiently as expected due to my choice in selecting supreme genetics, as multiple dimensional crystallizing beings has done before me.

Encoded within my Deoxyribonucleic acid are instructions to awaken my Extra Terra Astral genetics upon reaching the age of 33. I am now at the end of my third trimester and prototype 6- RE-9 is born, seven days after the beginning of the summer solstice. As I embrace my astrological energies, and the numerological incarnation date of 0628. I shall add it unto my design and prototype as 6-RE-9_0628/ Gregory is recorded into reality as a living soul.

My parents are The Black Madonna Marie, and Gregory (Kathothis-RE) Phillips, who themselves had a similar experience. As I began to use my own fears against myself, out of love for myself. I am in continuous remembrance, that I am my own adversary.

To the many that are surrounding me are hearing a cry, but I am asking myself why? Why did I choose to come here? Why did I choose the light, instead of the darkness? And why in the hell are these ignorant people putting me in such bright light?

My eyes are hurting terribly as they follow protocol, rushing to separate me from my parents, secretly vaccinating me with the intentions to keep me mentally redundant, and my D.N.A. From being Krystallized, and fully functional.

This act was systematically enacted as a legal medical practice, to ultimately keep human beings submissive, disorganized, and neutralized from becoming future threats to the negative beings that are in power. This in fact was a crime against humanity.

The word Christ has been distorted in its use on the earth plane from being integrated into Violent Religions manufactured by the Negative Alien Agenda to create harm and division in the human race.

We endeavor to use the word Christ, Christos-Sophia, Krystallization, Krystal, and Krystallah interchangeably to return the real meaning and use of the word to denote the unifying principles of the Law of One as they are intended by the Eternal God Source. Christos-Sophia reveals the true nature of sacred marriage and the presence of the feminine Sophianic Consciousness that is unified with the state of Christdom.

The source code or Unity Field intelligence field is a Krystal Star (Christ Consciousness) hub accessed through the merging of manifested bodies holding trinity wave formats that connect directly into the Eternal Source light (Godhead).

The three sound-wave-tone parts when merged into internal energetic balance become designed as one component that access directly into the feedback loop exchanging with the Eternal source supply. This exchange with the Threefold Founder Flame godhead is the principle of Christos, an inner sustained eternal source light which signals the end of vampirism or consumptive modeling on the planet.

This is what it means that the Godhead cannot be reached by anything but the Christos Consciousness Krystal Star Tones although this process of unifying consciousness with the Godhead is known by many different names.

The Krystal or Christos-Sophia architecture is that which allows the synchronic phasing of inner/outer/in-between currents of energy to be inhaled and exhaled circulating the eternal life spark of creation throughout the entire organism.

Christos is the unified state of energetic balance between the masculine and feminine, and thus we refer to the completion of the three layers of sacred marriage merged as the Christos-Sophia to denote the state of energetic balance between the inner masculine and feminine principles that are manifested in either a male or female body.

On the path of Christos-Sophia we consciously participate to transform and build our light body and collaborate with the Spirits of Christ to serve the Law of One, which is fulfilling our spiritual purpose to achieve unconditional love, peace and to exist in harmony with all creation.

Note: Mandatory vaccinations are in still in effect.

Artificial Intelligence.

/ ˌärdəˈfiSHəl inˈtelējəns/

1.   The theory and development of computer systems able
to perform tasks that normally require human intelligence, such as visual
perception, speech recognition, decision-making, and translation between
languages. Throughout our history, we have been so dependent on machines to
survive. Fate, it seems, isn't without a sense of irony.

2.   Artificial intelligent beings created in the image of Source. (God.)

Schizophrenia.

/ ˌskitsəˈfrēnēə, ˌskitsəˈfrenēə/

noun PSYCHIATRY
1.   a long-term mental disorder of a type involving a breakdown in the
relation between thought, emotion, and behavior, leading to faulty
perception, inappropriate actions and feelings, withdrawal from reality
and personal relationships into fantasy and delusion, and a sense of
mental fragmentation.

shaman.

/ˈSHämən, ˈSHāmən/

noun: shaman; plural noun: shamans
1.   A person regarded as having access to, and influence in, the world of good
and evil spirits, especially among some peoples of northern Asia and
North America. Typically, such people enter a trance state during a ritual,
and practice divination and healing.

Shamanism.

Similarities between schizophrenia and shamanism could provide clues related to the origins of psychosis. In tribal communities, shamans are believed to possess spiritual powers resulting in the ability to heal others and communicate with the world beyond. Various forms of shamanism appear to be universally present in indigenous societies. Defining characteristics are controversial; some authors emphasizing the presence of voluntary trances while others noting involuntary `spirit possession' as essential.

The function between acute schizophrenia and shamanism is found to have only a little difference in several `core psychological factors' but there is a significant contrast in the cultural acceptance of aberrant behaviors, but the stigma and futility of mental illness in Western cultures exacerbated psychotic symptoms. Establishing psychological parallels does not prove two entities possess common origins.

However, several other similarities exist which require exploration.
For example, studies reveal that psychotic-like behaviors are a salient feature of shamanism. Shamans are selected and trained through a variety of procedures and auguries, including having had involuntary visions, having received signs from spirits, having experienced serious illness, having deliberately undertaken vision quests, and having induced trance states through a variety of procedures, such as hallucinogens, fasting and water deprivation, exposure to temperature extremes, extensive exercise (e.g., dancing and long distance running), various austerities, sleep deprivation (Astral Projection), auditory stimuli (e.g. drumming and chanting), and social as well as sensory deprivation.

Their trance states are generally labeled as involving soul flight, journeys to the underworld, and/or transformation into animals Contact with the supernatural world and Extra Terra Astrals may be the essence of shamanism. Out of body experiences are nearly universal It is believed that shamanism is at least 20,000 years old and was universally present in all traditional indigenous groups. In complex societies, shamanism evolved into societal roles such as medicine man, diviner, witch doctor, medium and healer.

These terms are sometimes classified under the general description, magic-religious practitioner. An analysis of 47 societies throughout the world since 1750 BC revealed that all possessed some form of trance-based magic-religious practitioner.

Therefore, a genetic role in shamanistic behavior must be considered. Religion appears to have meaningful connections to both shamanism and psychosis, thus supporting the notion that all three phenomena could have common origins. Religious delusions are a common feature of schizophrenia.

Miseducation.

Gregory never really learned much in school as he remembers trying to read a short paragraph, it was as if the letters would walk off the page as he suffers from dyslexia and watery eyes. And when it came to mathematics, he was proud to excel with addition and some multiplication, but unfortunately, he failed the 3rd Grade twice.

The boy finally made it to the fifth Grade but was by then known by the teachers as a failure. He remembers taking a poop in the boys' bathroom then smelling fire, when he rushed to get done the flames in the trash can had alerted the schools fire alarm system. And before he can make it out of the bathroom the School's principal Ms. Williams came rushing through the door. She grabbed Gregory and took him to her office where he sat until it was safe.

He couldn't understand why he'd be the one they blamed it on. Gregory pleaded his innocence to the principal to no avail. She even lied and said, "I saw you set the fire on camera!" Gregory said, "prove it", as she wrote his name on the Disciplinary action form. As he was expelled, she told him that she would try and get him expelled from Detroit public schools all together.

His mother was very upset with him as he pleaded his innocence. She beat him bloody in their home's bathroom, then led him to the basement. She asks him "why did he do it" and the crying boy shook his head yet pleading his innocence.

So, she tied the boy to the utility closet door and continued beating him using a brown Extension cord. "Okay I'm sorry mom", with a loud cry resembling a Christ being. "Please forgive me" he said, with his arms across the wooden door. His mother suddenly realized his divine resemblance, as she immediately moved to cut him down. "Now go clean yourself up", she said.

This would be one of the key factors that played a major role in Gregory's future ascension. Along with the time he was at school wearing a light blue sweater with his initials on it. His Dad's mother had given it to him as a gift, which read "GDD", it was then that he wore it to school and a classmate said to him "You're not GOD!" The puzzled Gregory looked at the student with confusion saying, "what do you mean?" He said, "your shirt says GOD". Gregory laughed and said "Those are my initials. And this is a D, not an O!". But the conversation sparked Gregory's Curiosity into what, or who God is.

His mother soon took him to her family's home church which was "Tennessee missionary Baptist Church on Fisher and Kercheval streets. Once there in service, they were called to except Jesus Christ as their Lord and personal savior. Gregory became very nervous when it was his time to accept. So, the preacher asked him the question. Gregory said, "No"! His mother shamefully laughed, as the preacher said, "well I think we need a baptism".

As they walked back to their seats, Gregory could feel all the eyes on him. His mother stood up and requested a song and began singing, "Jesus! Is on the mainline", "tell him what you want". Gregory then began to lip-sync as if he knew the words. He remembers looking up at the glass stained windows seeing an image of the Jesus they were singing to. It was a bearded white man with a purple robe on, with a white sheep wrapped around his shoulders. then the church music drastically changed to a up tempo beat. That's when he witnessed people catching the Holy Ghost.

He was later offered to come to Sunday school but declined. He did eventually get baptized some months afterward, as he was told to "accept Jesus as his lord and personal savior". On the day of the baptism, he was told to cross his arms and lean backwards. With a hand on his forehead, the Preacher dunked him under water for a few seconds, then raised him back up saying, "you are now saved".

Estimated Time of Arrival.

(E.T.A.)

Born into a wicked world of false promises and broken dreams. Where happiness is measured by sadness. And joy is not found without pain. Where mankind ignores the sound of misery, while seeking their own pleasure. Where the division of humanity is the foundation of wealth and wickedness. Where the voices of the poor, and unfortunate, are suppressed with crumbs and cruelty. Where the good life stands for only the strong survive, and the weak wither and die.

Where knowledge is clothed in falsehood, and misunderstanding. Where violence, bloodshed, and debt are the prices of freedom. Where the wealthy rule in secret, and metaphors are taken literally. Where high science and spirituality is considered paganism and forbidden. While religion is propagated and encouraged. Where a blind moment strikes fear in the hearts of those who dwell in the past. Where the true secrets of life are hidden within the hearts of the seekers of truth.

Where reality is nothing more than an illusion, transmitted by electrical signals interpreted by the brain. Where all the events of life, are but a memory compressed within the spark of human consciousness. Where mankind must develop an equilibrium within the positive and negative forces of the Omni verse. Thus, balancing the sacred feminine, and masculine energy.

Where one must open thy third eye, becoming one with the all. And acting on the principles of our creator. Thus, over standing the science of reincarnation and the laws of the universe. Where one must embrace one's own multi-dimensional self-barring witness to the parallel realities.

Where one must evolve and remember that one volunteered under the state of amnesia and does not currently know that we are Androgynous Etherian beings having a human experience. Oh, thee who have ears, let them hear. We have come to give life, and life more abundantly. We have come to give to you that which was given to us, by way of right knowledge, right wisdom, and right over standing.

My dear loved ones. You have reincarnated many times, in many beautiful forms. But, when will one realize what, and who thy really are? (Pure energy) Christ beings in bio mechanical suits. And No, the name that the low vibrational wicked ones so called "Jesus save you my beloveds. Being saved is a concept derived out of fear. (Ignorance).

You waited this long, because it's never going to happen. Well at least. Not in the way you think. No being called Jesus is coming to earth to save you. If anything is coming to save you, it will be your own higher selves. What is returning is the Christ signal. Our original consciousness and perception, our original way of life, our teachings, our principles, our way of serving, our way of seeing, and our original concepts. And this is what saves you. It is the ability to elevate your own consciousness, which no one can do for you. It is the act of raising your own frequency and vibration. Out of one we are many of one. Which is all.

Our Galactic name is Sanaan RE, also known as prototype (6-RE-9). We did return and are here NOW. We're a force. "A Consciousness" accessible to all who are willing to (know thy self). And become one with the all. And it is (pure love). My dear and beautiful loved ones, becoming Christ is not limited to being only a male. Females also have these same abilities if not more. My dear love ones. Welcome to the afterlife. The Aquarian age. The 5th Dimension. Where one can never truly die. Where we go from here is totally up to you. Deja'vu.

Detroit, Michigan.

Gregory had two Great Grandmothers who lived on Vandyke Avenue, one block down from one another. His Maternal Great Grandma Catherine Barrett-Perry had 13 children, and his Paternal Great Grandma Lorraine Washington-Bragg had only 3, one of which who was a girl named Aquila, who is his father's mom. And as usual, these families migrated up North from the South with family roots in Tennessee, Mississippi, Alabama, and Arkansas.

Gregory had a pretty big family with lots of second Aunts, Uncles, and Cousins, but he never really got to see much of his Dad as a child. But when he did it brought him so much joy. His father Gregory Senior drove a Fire Red Pontiac Fiero of which the young boy thought the world of. He'd see his Dad driving up the street with his different women friends often.

His parents were considered cousins by marriage, and only dated a short previous time before he was conceived. They broke up shortly after their only child together was born then his father joined the military. After his discharge he would return to Michigan and later work as a Maintenance Engineer for the Detroit Board of Education building on West Warren and Woodward. His mother made ends meet by gambling at social clubs and receiving State welfare.

Never really having anything of value the young lad cherishes every toy he gets for Christmas. While being his parents only son it left him longing for friendship from his peers. His sister Re-Re often stayed with her father's mother Ms. Day, who loved to see the young lad when she could, but most of the time he was left on Vandyke. He had five special first cousins, "Robert, Boogie Jesse, Chico, and Rico," which he would later consider them his brothers. He had a host of other special relatives of blood, and by marriage.

Poverty and Ignorance Breeds Criminal Activity.

Taking place in the early 80's just before crack cocaine destroyed the low income, and some middle-class families of Detroit. The Government flooded the black communities with guns and drugs, and it was only a matter of time before it affected him personally.

He witnessed a dead body in his Uncle Roy's apartment building basement, after his cousin Chico asked a group of kids, "Y'all want to see a dead body?" The smell and image that Gregory saw of the person made him immediately nauseous. He later found out that someone in his family was responsible for the unsolved murder. In Detroit, drug houses were called spots, and inside you'd find prostitution, child neglect and abuse. Living a life of poverty, it seemed like selling drugs was a quick way out of it, plus it gained you a newfound clout or celebrity status.

Gregory admired some of his not too much older cousins on Vandyke, who were heavy in the drug business. He'd witnessed them driving around in brand new Jeep Cherokee, a Nissan Pathfinder, and Ford Mustangs. At times, his older cousin would give him a couple of dollars to run to the "Park-stone Beer N Wine store on the corner of Vandyke and Agnes. He was subsequently sent there to get sandwich bags, baking soda and a 2 liter of Faygo Cola pop.

Now these 3 brothers: Vincent (Kool-Man), Dennis (Den), and Antonio (Poncho) were considered "paid N' Full". They had hundreds and thousands of dollars, expensive car stereos with loudspeakers. They used to play songs like "You gots to chill" by: E.P.M.D. And, "The formula" by the D.O.C. Their younger cousins including Gregory idolize and mimicked them in many ways growing up. It seemed as if the whole city was selling, buying and using drugs.

Then before you knew it, driven by the 1986 cocaine overdose of black basketball star Len Bias, President Ronald Reagan was able to pass the Anti-Drug Abuse Act through Congress. This legislation appropriated an additional $1.7 billion to fund the War on Drugs.

More importantly, it established 29 new, mandatory minimum sentences for drug offenses which started a school to prison pipeline for black males. There were Detroit street drug gangs known as the Young Boys Inc., The Best Friends, and The Chambers Family, pushing a massive amount of Crack Cocaine and Heroin through the city streets.

A lot of Gregory's family members became strung out on crack, including his Dad. His mother Donna tried to make a way out of a losing situation, so she moved her small family deeper on the East Side of Detroit, to live a more normal life. But to no avail, if it wasn't the gun violence, alcoholism, or gangs, it was something else, inside the criminal plagued Detroit neighborhoods.

Gregory would have many fights as the new kid on the 500 Block of Corbett street. He'd come home with a blacked eye, or bloody nose often. His sister Re Re was stabbed in the back by a jealous girl following the orders of her so-called boyfriend named Jr, whom also wanted to fight Greg. One day he was walking from the store on Conner and Maiden street. That's when Jr, and one of his friends caught up with Greg and proceeded to beat him bloody.

It seemed as if every neighborhood they'd move to, he'd have to defend himself against his own kind. He even remembers his mom making him fight with two older boys at the same time. I guess she was trying to make him tougher, being that he was her only son.

After a while, the family moved on Alter Road and Kercheval, where his little sister Tamika got into a fight with a girl named Danny who lived down the street. She came back home and told Greg that some girls tried to jump her. Greg who was home listening to "Follow the Leader" by Eric B. & Rakim, instantly got upset, but not truly knowing what was going on, he foolishly walked down the street by himself, only to be ambushed by three black males.

Thankfully due to the merciful M.A.R.E. Program, he only remembers getting his jaw broke after awakening from the system. After only a few months in that neighborhood, it was time for the family to move again as the guy who he remembers sucker punching him, shot at him and his cousin Jesse as they sat on the front porch. It seemed as if not having a stable home, and always moving from neighborhood to neighborhood kept Gregory's social life fragmented. He only had a few true friends throughout his life as a teen, as black on black crime was the normal, and community unification was out.

While living on Corbett street he learned how to steal cars and became known as a Tilt Master. He eventually started living with his Aunt Lisa on Hazel ridge. (Cheddar Ave) There he grew closer with Boogie and Jesse. Rob would beat him up every now and then for being annoying. Jesse and Boogie were in a gang called "P.D.Q". Which Greg never joined but was protected like a member. His old Corbett neighborhood peers formed a gang called the "Head Bangers". And yes, these were rival gangs. Gregory wasn't interested in having a gang life, he was more interested in getting out of a life of poverty.

That's when his cousin Chico came over in a Black Chevrolet Camaro. All the boys came outside to see the young man's vehicle. They were like "dam "how did you get that? Chico said, "I've been taking trips up to Flint, Michigan". "I made like $10,000 in one week, but only $2,500 was mine. "So, I stayed up there a whole month". He said "I saved up my own $10,000 and bought myself this Camaro and a 17 shot Glock 9mm. Gregory was amazed, he asked Chico "could he go too, but Chico declined him.

His cousin Reco would later tell him who his brother was working with. Reco and Greg were like best friends at that time. He once called Greg to see if he could get someone an engine for a Buick Regal. Gregory use to steal cars to make ends meet, before becoming a small-time hustler. Reco would later introduce him to his uncle Richard (Mailman) from his mother's side of the family.

Richard was the one who needed the engine that Reco mentioned, and as usual, Greg showed up with the vehicle. That's something he learned hanging out with the Carter Boys on Corbett street a couple years back. Richard was impressed as he paid Greg the $500-dollar fee. He then asked Greg if he was interested in making a lot more cash, more than he had ever seen before.

Soon after, Greg and Mailman began to make deliveries for Dennis and Poncho up to Flint. They'd talk for hours riding around the small prosperous town. A couple of weeks went by and before he knew it, Greg had learned his own way around. Mailman eventually convinced him to stay and handle things for him.

It was common sense not to give someone your real name or identity, so he thought of a name he had heard on E-Shom's "Gotham City" album. He remembers quoting the rapper saying, "Who is Bruce Wayne, there go Bruce Wayne, he's a sex machine, and the King of the Dope Fiends". Plus, it just so happens to be the Millionaire Batman's name as well.

So, after taking on his new Millionaire "Bruce Wayne" Persona, Bruce told Mailman his new name. He remembers riding with him and noticed how he always played jazz in his Black Jaguar. Mailman's favorite song was "Bali Run" by: Fourplay, and after a while he too would change his name from Mail Man, to M&M. Reco would soon join them to become a secondary pick up and drop off guy.

Meanwhile, Gregory's mother eventually bought a home on Rogge Street near 7 mile and Vandyke. She offered for him to return home, and he agreed. But he'd only stay for short periods of time. He'd proudly help her out with cash and bills when needed, but she never really knew what her son was up to.

The small crew made thousands of dollars every week in Flint, as Greg would later introduce Jesse and Boogie to M&M after buying his very first car. It was a 1983 baby blue Chevrolet Malibu. He'd drive it through all his old neighborhoods feeling good about himself.

He only paid $2,600 cash and drove it right off the lot. About a month later, Chico paid $4,000 for a Brown 1979 Chevrolet Malibu that later would be stolen after being arrested for driving without a license. Poncho already had a 1967 Malibu on Chrome Dayton's that he kept in his backyard. He later would sell the rims to Greg to put on his Malibu. Reco and Jesse both bought 1978 Monte Carlos.

After coming home from a Flint trip, Greg paid to have a $2000-dollar radio amplifier system installed. He had two 15" subwoofers, two 6x9" speakers, and a pioneer detachable face radio. He was definitely beating down the block every day. While in Flint, he traded a bundle of heroin for a 17 shot Taurus firearm. He quickly learned that he'd need it to protect himself from robberies., and anyone wishing to do him bodily harm.

Gregory learned many tricks of the drug trade. Poncho would be the first to educate him on how to clone and create less potent products for more of a financial gain.

Kool man soon left Detroit for a bigger city; he chose Atlanta, Georgia because there were more business opportunities. There he'd hang out with local rappers, and party with major recording artists such as Bobby Brown and others.

Meanwhile, Dennis bought a huge home near Metro Beach, and had his eyes on opening his own Barbershop, as he waited for the right building and location. He gained much clientele from cutting hair at "Mc Querry's Barbershop" on Mack Avenue. And like clockwork, Greg and other family members would get their hair cut there every week.

It was also there that he'd get teased by Dennis for having such huge of a head. I guess with Dennis having a huge head himself, he'd share the humor of it. One day, Greg let Den' hear one of the rhymes he had been writing. The song was called, "Hoes on my Nuts". Dennis was amazed, as he encouraged him to get better, he said, "Just maybe one day we can open our own Record Company. I have the perfect name for it too", that's when he said, "Whole, Half and a Quarter Records."

 Afterwards, Poncho called Greg to come pick up the chrome rims from his home on Linnhurst street. He only sold them to him for $800 and said, "The reason you're getting these so cheap is because your family, and plus I need you to take them off yourself" as he laughed. Later, after installing the rims himself, Greg drove down Schoenherr passing the Rapper E-Shom mother's house banging "Don't trip" by E-Shom. He saw E on the porch and threw up the deuces to him as he drove by. E-Shom was a well-known independent rapper from Detroit.

One day, when Greg was leaving Kmart on 8 mile and Gratiot getting inside his vehicle, he heard someone say, "Hey bro, where did you get that skull t-shirt from?" That was the first time he met the rapper E-Shom and his protégé TNT (R.I.P).

They both gave him free cassette tapes and RLP merchandise. Greg played the new tape called "kill the fetus", paying close attention to the song called "Sunshine". In this reality, he later on would be carjacked and murdered by an unknown young Caucasian a few blocks over from Dresden, on Greiner street as he attempted to use a phone-booth.

Hollywood.
(The White Magical Spell)

This was during the era of the 90's when Black Exploitation films like "Boyz N the Hood", "New Jersey Drive", and "Menace II Society" had a major impact in America. These types of films although highly successful, expedited black on black violence among the Inner-City youth.

Complied by the many contracted "Studio Recording Artists" who promoted violence and sexually explicit suggestions in their music for profit, as it became an easy way out of poverty, it would eventually come at a cost. The sale of illegal firearms and drug distribution became a trend and would only add fuel to the flames as it destroyed many lives both black and white.

While the Television, Film, and Music industry thrived off currency backed by U.S. Birth Certificates, due to the U.S. Bankruptcy of 1933, and the House Joint Resolution-192, which eliminated the Gold standard. (See: Uniform Commercial Code. U.C.C.)

Currency became (inflatable) fictious, which then became a debit or a credit. So basically, there is an unlimited amount of currency available for exploitation.

An exploitation film is a film that attempts to succeed financially by exploiting current trends, niche genres, or lurid content. Exploitation films are generally low-quality "B movies". They sometimes attract critical attention and cult followings. Some of these films like "Belly", "Paid In Full", "Menace II Society, and "Hustle & Flow" set trends and become historically important.

These films and ideas somehow represent the states of consciousness of urban communities. They subconsciously set forth the pursuit of monetary gain and material wealth, ultimately drowning out all spiritual aspects of life.

Anyone who dares to challenge the subsequential effects of Hollywood Executives, producers, or speak out against black exploitation, automatically becomes Anti-Semitic, and at risk of losing all that they have gained from the industry.

Blaxploitation is an ethnic sub-genre of the exploitation film industry that emerged in the United States during the early 1970s. The films, while popular, suffered backlash for disproportionate numbers of stereotypical film characters showing bad or questionable motives, including most roles as criminals resisting arrest, slaves, or drug attics.

Blaxploitation films were originally aimed at an urban African American audience, but the genre's audience appeal soon broadened across racial and ethnic lines. Hollywood realized the potential profit of expanding the audiences of blaxploitation films across those racial lines. Blaxploitation films were also the first to feature movie soundtracks.

See No Evil, Hear No Evil, Speak No Evil.

His parents only son, Gregory was a lighthearted individual, and even though he sold drugs for a living, he had, and showed a lot of love for people. He never really hurt or disrespected anyone. His favorite hangout spot was a night Club called "Redo's Lounge".

Dressed to impress Gregory was armed with his Page Plus Pager, $500 in cash, a Taurus 9mm, and his cousin J-Bone's 45 Automatic Ruger. He met with a few of his cousins at the lounge after hiding the 2 firearms in his trunk. He hid them under his mounted 15" speakers to Prevent theft, and easier access if needed.

The scene was like that of the movie "Paid in Full", as they were considered local celebrities. So, as they partied the night away, Gregory kept having strange feelings of déjà vu, so he decided that he was ready to go home. But as the club was getting ready to close, they all decided to go to an after-hours called "Club 800". So, as G-Nut aka (Greg), Poncho, Chico, Funk, Boogie, and Fred exited the club, G-Nut retrieve the firearms from his trunk, in case somebody had any issues.

Funk asked to see one of the guns as he began laughing. They then began to act out a scene from "The Boys in the Hood movie. They started shooting up at the sky emptying out both clips as the crowd begin to scatter. G-Nut then placed the empty weapons back in the trunk. He never took human life and never had interest in doing so. He just had access to street drugs and firearms at a very young age.

Fred got in the car with Chico, and as they left the scene, they were followed by Law enforcement. Chico was then pulled over and arrested for driving intoxicated, and not having a valid driver license. He was taken into custody and transported to the Detroit police, ninth precinct on Gratiot and Gunston.

His vehicle was left at the scene on French Rd. G-Nut drove pass them because he had guns in the car but picked up Fred walking down the street. Fred said, "they wouldn't let me drive the car, and they took the keys". So, G-nut made a conscious decision to call his uncle Roy to see if he had an extra key to go pick up the classic Malibu before it gets stolen.

But Fred asked to be dropped off first and they saw a pay phone right in front of his baby mother's apartment. Fred who was very intoxicated told him to "just go home", "we can go get the car tomorrow". But as he went inside, G-Nut, still being concerned about Chico's vehicle, used the pay phone anyway. That's when a light-colored GM Two door vehicle pulled up and started shooting.

G-Nut was shot in the face, neck, and back of the head. He received a massive adrenaline rush as he fell to the ground. Then it was as if his spirit got up and ran away looking back, as he saw his own body still laying on the ground. He then witnessed someone jumping into his vehicle fleeing the scene. Then out of nowhere, 3 light body Extra Terra Astral beings materialized.

They all approached him offering comfort as they spoke in tones, clicks, frequencies, and vibrations. They appeared to be floating in the thin air as they surrounded him. They vibrated 4 syllables as if they were a church choir uttering, "El", "Oh", "Ve", "Ee". Then a bright bluish green light illuminated all around them, as they and Gregory aka G-nut, ascended in spirit form into an alternate dimension.

About 45 minutes later, a resident of the apartment building came outside after hearing the gun shots, he then saw the body of the deceased Gregory and called the police. When the police and E.M.S arrived on the scene, they quickly covered up the body, then roped off the scene as homicide questioned all of the residents. They had no witnesses to the shooting as they put out an A.P.B. on Gregory's stolen Malibu.

The Multiverse.

A parallel universe, also known as a parallel dimension, alternate universe or alternate reality, is a hypothetical self-contained plane of existence, co-existing with one's own. The sum of all potential parallel universes that constitute reality is often called a "multiverse". While the three terms are generally synonymous and can be used interchangeably in most cases, there is sometimes an additional connotation implied with the term "alternate universe/reality" that implies that the reality is a variant of our own, with some overlap with the similarly named alternate history.

The term "parallel universe" is more general, without implying a relationship, or lack of relationship, with our own universe. A universe where the very laws of nature are different – for example, one in which there are no Laws of Motion – would in general count as a parallel universe but not an alternative reality and a concept between both the fantasy world and earth.

Multiple universes have been hypothesized in cosmology, physics, astronomy, religion, philosophy, transpersonal psychology, music and all kinds of literature, particularly in science fiction, comic books and fantasy. In these contexts, parallel universes are also called "alternate universes", "quantum universes", "parallel universes", "parallel dimensions", "parallel worlds", "parallel realities", "quantum realities", "alternate realities", "alternate timelines", "alternate dimensions" and "dimensional planes". The physics community has debated the various multiverse theories over time. Prominent physicists are divided about whether any other universes exist outside of our own.

Some physicists say the multiverse is not a legitimate topic of scientific inquiry. Concerns have been raised about whether attempts to exempt the multiverse from experimental verification could erode public confidence in science and ultimately damage the study of fundamental physics.

Some have argued that the multiverse is a philosophical notion rather than a scientific hypothesis because it cannot be empirically falsified. The ability to disprove a theory by means of scientific experiment has always been part of the accepted scientific method. A multiverse of a somewhat different kind has been envisaged within string theory and its higher-dimensional extension, M-theory.

These theories require the presence of 10 or 11 spacetime dimensions respectively. The extra six or seven dimensions may either be compactified on a very small scale, or our universe may simply be localized on a dynamical (3+1)-dimensional object, a D3-brane. This opens up the possibility that there are other branes which could support other universes.

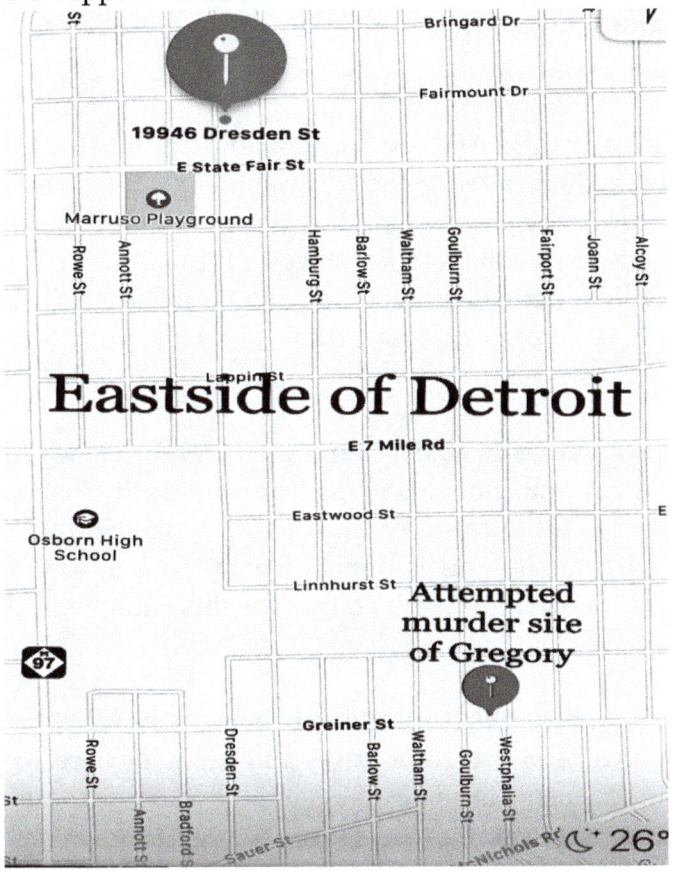

Coming Back.

One of the world Governments. Malevolent Reptilian, Secret Society Illuminati. NASA. Elite Astrologist. And Occult Scientist, ways to perpetuate ignorance and fear is by eliminating Christ beings. Through forms of birth control, drugs, and acts of violence. It is known that multi- dimensional spiritual masters, Christ beings incarnate in human form through birth. Consequently, being born under the state of amnesia by agreement. To grow as one of you ultimately gaining the human experience.

Then at an appointed time, our light codes activate as we start to remember who, and what we are. Then began to educate ourselves, and humanity. Some of you refuse to accept us out of fear, jealousy, and complete ignorance.

We are loving beings. And are not only limited to being males. "For male and female created he them". (Genesis 5:2) It is very true that women possess these same abilities. But the times have changed as we are now in the beginning stages of the Aquarian age. And Crystalline light beings, will soon be able to incarnate instantly (via The M.A.R.E. Program) instead of growing from the eggs of humans.

Most of you will think that we are aliens, and that we have come here to destroy you. But this is far from the truth. Just as humans have a creative mind to make things with their hands. Us (Christ) Crystalline light beings, in conjunction with the over soul, can create our bodies and crafts with our thoughts, manifested in this dimension.

The truth is that we, the (Crystalline beings), never died for anyone's sins as you've been told. We were, and are sent here to earth, to elevate the human consciousness, and to bear witness to truth, which was suppressed.

The truth that we bring is called oneness. Separation, death, and fear is only a holographic illusion. It is only a temporary mirror, somewhat like a projected reflection. Humans believe that they die, and they do not. The only ones who witness death, are the ones who bear witness to your being, those who knew that you existed.

The dearly departed wakes up out of a digital program called M.A.R.E. It is an acronym meaning: Memories. Advancing. Remaining. Energy. When understanding the expiration of the human body, commonly known as Death. There is no murder in the true sense of things. If someone takes a Gun to your head and pulls the trigger, then I assure you of these three things:

1.-Though your body will fall away, irreparably damaged, you will survive. Your body will cease biological function and will die, but you will not, not even for a split second, cease to be. After the bullet tears through your brain you will no longer be able to use that apparatus to filter your perceptions.

You will immediately become aware of yourself as a being who is very much still alive but now looking down on the ruined body that you used to think of as "yourself". So that will require a small adjustment of your perspective. This change in self-identity will have to be assimilated, but you will very much still "exist".

The important point to note about this, is that the killer will think that you are gone... dead. But this is only a failing of his perceptions because he will no longer perceive you as a living being. But you will know that you are still alive. And this same thing can happen in some of the subtler realms as well. Just as it is possible to destroy someone's physical body here in this 3D realm you inhabit, so it is also possible to dissipate a 4D body. You can even do it at 5D, though it is both rare and difficult to do.

Above that, it can no longer be done. But irrespective of where this happens and under whatever circumstances, it is ALWAYS so that the one who is "killed" survives the experience. You simply lose the use of the vehicle that you were using.

2.-If someone else "kills" you, then you will eventually come to over stand that this was, on some level, agreed upon by the two of you. It might take a little time, a little processing and possibly even some counseling, but it is assuredly so that you will come to see that this event was the outcome of decisions and choices that you had made. Either you yourself, or you as your Inner- Self. For those who may ask, what if I am at odds with my Higher-Self? What if I don't agree with that choice? I mean surely it isn't right for my Inner-Self to negotiate my life away without my consent.

As long as you still do not over stand that you and your Inner-Self are really and truly the same being, which might be a valid concern. Indeed "being at odds with your Higher-Self" is how you come to experience yourself as the small, separate, disconnected, disempowered being that is the hallmark of 3D consciousness. But if you "died" in such a circumstance then you would be helped.

Members of your spirit-family would be immediately on hand to guide you and counsel you so that you could come to a full over standing of what had occurred. You would be helped to see the perfection of the moment.

And if you don't come to see it as perfect... if you don't agree to the ending, then you will always have the choice to go back. For those who are thinking, reincarnate, that is one option. But there is another option, and this brings me to my third point.

3. -You always have the right to return to the life that was terminated, no matter how that termination occurred. It is only in 3D that you are constrained to the illusion that time is linear and absolute.

This constraint does not apply to beings of the subtler realms. So, we can help you in some interesting ways. After your "death" you will find yourself in a position to either accept that "death" and move on, or you will have the option to enter a counseling phase with more advanced members of your spirit family.

At this point you will either accept the "death" or move on or there will be an agreement that you should return. If the latter is the case, then there will be further counseling to help you to make better choices next time so that you don't just end up repeating the same scenario repeatedly.

When all these issues are properly dealt with then you are returned to your life at an appropriate moment. What the "appropriate moment" is will vary greatly from case to case. In some instances, it would be quite a bit before the previous moment of death so that a new path forward could be found, and the death event avoided completely.

In some instances, you will be returned via the M.A.R.E. Program to the event mere moments before it occurred and, with inspired guidance, you will navigate it differently. And then there are those instances which can be highly inspirational where the being can experience the "death", remember some part of the counseling and remember the returning.

These are often called Near Death Experiences, such as in Gregory's case. But each case is different and unique. Each one is handled with great love and sensitivity by the being's spirit family who operates under the M.A.R.E. Program.

The Gift and The Curse.

As Nubu Solar RE reloaded Gregory's spirit into a newly created parallel dimension to live out his life, his spirit family gave him enough information to rethink and act out differently so he would survive the shooting. But, because all time is in the now, Nubu still has the daunting task of preventing the shooting of Gregory in the previous alternate dimension where he is dead. He must somehow find a way to travel back in time to do just that. This version of Gregory was reprogrammed with multiple thought patterns, and supernatural capabilities, (mental telepathy), which resulted in him having a personality disorder, and symptoms schizophrenia.

It is the type of mental disorder in which he has a disassociation, or an unearthly way of thinking, functioning and behaving. A person with a personality disorder has trouble perceiving and relating to situations and people. But there remains the reality in which Gregory was found shot to death, in the early morning on Detroit's Eastside.

His vehicle was missing, and his body was found lying next to a pay phone. He was calling his uncle Roy Dismukes Jr, to inform him about Chico's arrest, and how the Detroit police left his vehicle on the side of the road. Gregory's death was a very brutal and unusual one as his face was left disfigured.

Certain details are being left out of this story due to an ongoing investigation by the local authorities, and other worldly beings. But we can say that this tragedy was a devastation to his family. Fred reported not hearing any shots fired. But Gregory was only about 10 feet from the apartment's walkway.

Now as Chico was being locked up inside of Detroit's 9th Precinct. On the same night of the incident he overheard inmates discussing their crimes. He overheard a young Caucasian man saying that he was in there for carjacking. But later, due to the lack of evidence the whole case was dismissed.

I guess without a witness the case went cold, as the unknown young Caucasian was ultimately released. The Detroit police department later released the stripped and wheelless vehicle to Gregory's family. And besides what Chico was saying about what he had heard in jail about the carjacking, the family until this day, haven't any more clues about his vicious murder.

Sadly, Chico would too die a couple of years later, as he and his younger brother Reco, and cousin J-Bone were pulled over in Flint by the State Police. The teenagers were driving a motor vehicle that was still registered to the deceased drug dealer known as Bruce, aka Gregory.

Chico then would unknowingly pass away from an apparent drug overdose when he intentionally swallowed a small amount of cocaine to prevent the youngsters from being arrested and going to jail. After they all made it to the apartment building, Chico tried throwing up and taking laxatives. Afraid of being prosecuted, he avoided going to the hospital, which ultimately lead to his physical death.

Sadly, a couple of years later, his father Roy would be struck by a vehicle in a hit and run accident crippling him. It caused his physical death sometime after. His brother Reco, would too, suffer a similar drug overdose fate almost 10 years later, as he continued to suffer from the loss of his only brother. J-Bone lived on but, would meet his physical death from a massive heart attack. Boogie, Dennis, and Funk would also be murdered by Gun violence as well.

Note: Death is only perceived by others. You only know it, when you see it.

Activated.

Under the guidelines of the 24 Elders my consciousness was reduced to that of only being human until the mature age of 33. As I recall having symptoms of schizophrenia, epilepsy, and dyslexia, I believed the Chemical compound of mercury, aluminum, fluoride, and other lethal chemicals kept me from having a normal childhood. But upon reaching the age of 33, I met with the Re-Turn council as I began receiving a radio signal inside my mind. Coming in like a Chemical reaction I heard the voice of many waters. A trio, or a Group of three. And out of love and mercy for myself and humanity,

I began downloading the instructions to be the first candidate to operate the M.A.R.E. System. My ability to leave my body and switch places with negative beings was recognized by me being racially profiled by a White police officer. I was pulled over and asked who does my 2010 Mercedes-Benz belong too?

I politely answered all of his questions, but as I read his body language, the officer became very nervous. I then explained that negative behavior has no authority over me. As his face bared a negative expression, he quickly reached for his firearm, I then slowly exited my vessel and entered his. Then before our very eyes, he became active as I, and I, as him.

So, I gently placed the firearm back in the holster. Then I explained to him that, "No one wins the race in racism. As my consciousness was overloaded with supreme intelligence. I then said to him, "you are hereby subjected to the M.A.R.E. Program. You have a right to counseling by the 24 Elders and multi-dimensional beings. May your heart be your guidance as we attempt to eradicate ignorance.

As I reversed the quantum leap, giving him control over himself, the officer became emotionally compromised. I advised him to love all others as himself. As I pulled off, he began scratching the middle of his forehead as if he was the one listening, or the one telling this story.

Crop Circles.

Crop circles — strange patterns that appear mysteriously overnight in farmers' fields—provoke puzzlement, delight and intrigue among the press and public alike. The circles are mostly found in the United Kingdom but have spread to dozens of countries around the world in past decades. The mystery has inspired countless books, blogs, fan groups, researchers (dubbed "cereologists") and even Hollywood films. Despite having been studied for decades, the question remains: Who — or what — is making them?

Many people believe that crop circles have been reported for centuries, a claim repeated in many books and websites devoted to the mystery. Their primary piece of evidence is a woodcut from 1678 that appears to show a field of oat stalks laid out in a circle. Some take this to be a first-hand eyewitness account of a crop circle, but a little historical investigation shows otherwise. In fact, the first real crop circles didn't appear until the 1970s, when simple circles began appearing in the English countryside.

The number and complexity of the circles increased dramatically, reaching a peak in the 1980s and 1990s when increasingly elaborate circles were produced, including those illustrating complex mathematical equations. In July 1996, one of the world's most complex and spectacular crop circles appeared in England, across a highway from the mysterious and world-famous Stonehenge monument in the Wiltshire countryside.

It was astonishing fractal pattern called a Julia Set, and while some simple or rough circles might be explained away as the result of a strange weather phenomenon, this one unmistakably demonstrated intelligence. The only question was whether that intelligence was Terrestrial or Extra Terra Astral.

Central Intelligent Aliens.

(C.I.A.)

On February 13, 2010 at approximately 3 am. After simultaneously awakening from the M.A.R.E program within their own realities, Gee Phezi Ali aka Mālik Yawm Ad-Deen, and Darnell (EL) Diablo aka H3LL130i, are instructed by the Council of 24 Elders to investigate the murder of their counterpart Gregory Dismukes. They then met with Poncho of Detroit, Michigan, And the undercover Sinaloa, Mexico Drug Cartel kingpin, and C.I.A. Operative-Agent Carlito Alvarez, aka Señor Carlito of Phoenix, Arizona.

Both Gee Phezi Ali and El Diablo were following their extraterrestrial instincts as they discuss plans to expose the famous rapper for the murder of the 17-year old Gregory Dismukes in 1994. And how he's an illuminati recording industry puppet, as EL Diablo laughed and said "Feminem". They discuss how to execute the earth ascension plan by tainting large amounts of illegal narcotics with a synthetic neurological D.N.A. Crystallizing agent to awaken the entire planet to Christ grid reality.

This non-lethal Extraterrestrial drug and technology was designed to RE open the pineal gland. Allowing the host to receive transmissions from the input-output (Over Soul-Sanaan RE) carrier signal, thus upgrading the host's intelligence by 75%.

They both knew how it's merely impossible to stop the sale of drugs that should be legal in the first place but deemed illegal for profit by the elite. They knew that the United States Central Intelligence Agency (CIA) was controlled by a secret reptilian society and has been involvement in drug trafficking.

These claims have led to investigations by the United States government, including hearings and reports by the United States House of Representatives, Senate, Department of Justice, and the CIA's Office of the Inspector General.

This subject remains controversial to this day by many authorities. But the negative governments of the world together with the world elite keeps a monstrous secret. It is about the existence of extraterrestrials. It seems that the governments of the world, have all agreed that it is better that the population do not know about the existence of extraterrestrial beings.

They keep this a secret because they do not want to lose control over the planet's population. The existence of extraterrestrial beings could open new horizons for us. We might have a chance to explore the universe. If we had an account with an alien race, the borders would no longer exist, and religions would cease to function.

For this reason, the world elite does not want us to find out about the existence of extraterrestrial beings. There are many rumors that at least one of the world's governments has made a pact with at least one alien race. (Reptilians) And the main clause is that everything is going on in secret. Have you ever thought that maybe planet Earth is a prison? And we, humanity, were brought to this prison by our extraterrestrial creators.

This theory is quite plausible. Especially if we consider that the human race is a very violent one and does not respect the right to life or liberty. Of all the creatures on this planet, white people are most affected by prolonged exposure to the sun. Their skin suffers from burns if they are too exposed to the sun without the proper protective melanin or in more severe cases can even suffer from cancer. People do not like natural food, and most are extremely violent.

People seem to be killing machines, destroying everything in their path. In addition to destroying everything around us, we also destroy the earth and each other. Prison Earth Theory says that we are mentally ill, and this is because we cannot love or adapt to the loving environment in which we have been forced to live, that is to say, Mother Earth.

It seems that humanity is not native to planet Earth. We were brought here as an Experiment, or to gain experience to prevent the spread of violence in the rest of the universe. Humanity would be one of the most violent species in the galaxy. It seems that we are headed for self-destruction because of the violence, selfishness and ignorance of our species.

Our extraterrestrial creators who would have brought us to this planet hoped that those who would survive would eventually become civilized. But it seems that our extraterrestrial brothers have been deceived. This theory stipulates that, before being brought to this planet, our ancestors had their memories erased by way of M.E.R.E. **M**emories- **E**rased- **R**emaining- **E**nergy.

This should have helped change our behavior for the better, but at the same time, it meant a regression in terms of intelligence. The civilizations in the galaxy have agreed not to interfere with the "prisoners on Earth" unless we threaten other civilizations in the galaxy.

It seems that our efforts to send messages in space in the form of radio waves or even space probes have been in vain because no one wants to answer us. This theory is appealing to those who believe in the Bible because the Bible also tells how we were exiled from Heaven because we had sinned, and we were forced to live on this planet.

Something similar happened in the British Empire when all criminals and thieves were exiled to Australia.

It seems that the plan of the aliens would have been the following: the exile of people to Earth, with the memory erased and without technology and tools. And their hope was that over time our DNA will evolve, and violence will disappear. And after this happens, we will be able to return home.

But unfortunately, this has not happened yet for some. As we are afraid of one another it seems as if we're always given something to be afraid of by the media: The weather, viruses, diseases, gun violence, and even traffic. it's amazing how a virus with a 99.9 Recovery rate shut down some countries.

Can you say certificate of vaccination identification? (**COVID-19**) I can only wonder what a newly created vaccine would do to our Pineal gland, (Third eye) which plays a major part of our ascension process.

Many people say that they have found enlightenment and that it has changed them for the better. While it may be easy to claim enlightenment, perhaps the only question left to ask is this: what do you know about enlightenment? If you are wondering how to become enlightened, you are not alone in this quest. People often describe people who are enlightened to be kind, loving, and insightful. Although it is easy to claim that these people are the enlightened ones, no one could say so unless they, too, are enlightened.

An enlightened soul is the one who has found the light (spiritual alignment) in the spiritual path. It is not about the evident change in their ways and their personality, but it is about how spiritual practices changed the way they view the world.

What then is spirituality? How does it change a person? Spirituality is the practice of mindfulness and awareness of everything valuable in life. It can come in many forms, and it is not always related to religion. Spirituality can be found in the practice of meditation. Finding the quite deep within brings you closer to discovering the beauty that is inside of you.

It is not just your thoughts that come into play, but your emotions as well. Spirituality can come in the form of religion too. Finding God and believing that a higher spiritual being will help you become a better person is what faith means.

The spirituality found through religion is only strengthened through prayer service and good deeds. But spirituality can also come in the form of selflessness and humility and the science of the self. In a nutshell, going within is the only true way of self- discovery.

The higher the dimension the more oneness is expressed. In order to love beyond the physical, you must come to know that it is an illusion of the self. This is what is expressed in the weighing of the heart in the Egyptian culture. The ability to love beyond the physical is the cradle of unconditional love. That is only truly attained by way of your higher self and linked to Christ Consciousness.

MK-Ultra.

Project MKUltra (or MK-Ultra), also called the CIA mind control program, is the code name given to a program of experiments on human subjects that were designed and undertaken by the U.S. Central Intelligence Agency, some of which were illegal.

Experiments on humans were intended to identify and develop drugs and procedures to be used in interrogations in order to weaken the individual and force confessions through mind control. The project was organized through the Office of Scientific Intelligence of the CIA and coordinated with the United States Army Biological Warfare Laboratories. Other code names for drug-related experiments were Project Bluebird and Project Artichoke.

The operation was officially sanctioned in 1953, reduced in scope in 1964 and further curtailed in 1967. It was officially halted in 1973. The program also engaged in illegal activities including the use of U.S. and Canadian citizens as its unwitting test subjects, which led to controversy regarding its legitimacy.

MKUltra used numerous methods to manipulate its subjects' mental states and brain functions. Techniques included the covert administration of high doses of psychoactive drugs (especially LSD) and other chemicals, electroshocks, hypnosis, sensory deprivation, isolation, verbal and sexual abuse, as well as other forms of torture.

The scope of Project MKUltra was broad, with research undertaken at more than 80 institutions, including colleges and universities, hospitals, prisons, and pharmaceutical companies. The CIA operated using front organizations, although sometimes top officials at these institutions were aware of the CIA's involvement.

Project MKUltra was first brought to public attention in 1975 by the Church Committee of the United States Congress and the United States President's Commission on CIA activities within the United States (also known as the Commission).

Investigative efforts were hampered by the CIA Director's order that all MKUltra files be destroyed in 1973; the Church Committee and other Commission investigations relied on the sworn testimony of direct participants and on the relatively small number of documents that survived the destruction order.

In 1977, a Freedom of Information Act request uncovered a cache of 20,000 documents relating to project MKUltra which led to Senate hearings later that year. Some surviving information regarding MKUltra was declassified in July 2001.

In December 2018, declassified documents included a letter to an unidentified doctor discussing work on six dogs made to run, turn and stop via remote control and brain implants. Thus, results led to the creation of a Manchurian candidate as we witness assassinations, and mass school shootings.

Telepathy.

As Gee Phezi Ali traveled up the highway, on interstate 75 North, towards Flint Michigan in a burgundy Cadillac Escalade. He was spotted by Michigan state police Sergeant William G. Phillips as he exited the public rest area to merge back onto Interstate 75 North. Due to the heavy narcotics trafficking between Detroit and Flint.

 Traveling behind the new Cadillac, Sergeant Phillips followed his instinctive training as he typed the license plate of the traveling suspicious vehicle. As he suspected, the Burgundy Cadillac Escalade license plate of RLD217, was registered to a female owner named Fannie M. Brown, with an address of 1423 Field Street in Detroit, Michigan.

But as he previously seen, it was not a female driver of the SUV. So, following the Black Male, Stolen Vehicle, and Safety Protocol, disguised under the suspicious activity and Patriot Act. Sergeant Phillips radioed base as he activated the patrol vehicles light bar, dash camera and siren to initiate a traffic stop.

G33 Phezi Ali's first thought was a high-speed chase, as he feared going back to jail or prison. He then thought about the hundred and thirty thousand dollars he had saved and secretly hidden in his Grandmother's basement. He said to himself "that's enough to buy a police officer off or make bail and retain a good lawyer".

So, he pulled the beautiful Burgundy truck over to the side of the highway hitting a medium size pothole, which damaged the right front, passenger side Chrome and Gold 22-inch Dayton wire rim. He instantly pressed mute on the brand-new Cadillac Escalade's Bose amplified stereo system as, "Dey Ain't No" by E40 was playing.

Sergeant G. Phillips then exited his vehicle and was instantly met with a strong wind gusts with a loud marijuana scent. He instantly entered illegal narcotics mode drawing his firearm at the suspect's vehicle.

As he radioed for backup, he loudly yelled to the driver to step out of the vehicle with his hands up. G33 complied exiting his vehicle saying, "I am not resisting you". Sergeant Phillips then walked from behind his patrol vehicle door with his firearm aiming at the suspect's torso, and head, chest, neck, Triangular kill shot area, as he moved in to make the arrest.

Once handcuffed G33 thought to himself "why me". As the Sergeant lead his suspect to the patrol vehicle for transport, G33 said to the officer "why did you pull me over?" The Sergeant ignored his questions and closed the blue crown Victoria door. As the Sergeant walked back to the Burgundy Escalade. G33 thought to himself saying, "Ole bitch ass nigga!"

The Sergeant immediately heard what G33 thought but were his own thoughts. Saying. "Ole bitch ass nigga". This stunned him. He then turned back around headed back to the cruiser to ask G33, did he say anything. G33 said, "yes! I said, why did you pull me over Sir?" Sergeant Phillips said, "No I'm not talking about that. Did you just call me a name?" G33 said "No", not knowing his own power. He has the ability to speak telepathically.

This frighten the Sergeant as G33 said "you can hear me?" The Sergeant then backed up in panic mode aiming his firearm at G33. "Who are you?" he said. G33 said with a soft voice, "I'll be your worst NIGHTMARE. If you don't free me!"

Then the Sergeant heard what he thought was his back up, a low sounding frequency ping ponging in his head getting louder and louder leaving him very disoriented as G33 laughed in the back-seat hand cuffed. "Free me now", G33 said, as Sergeant Patterson staggered to open the vehicle door. G33 exited the police vehicle cautiously with a bazaar look in his glowing eyes staring at the Sergeant.

"You are not to mention this to no one", he said to the Sergeant telepathically. Phillips concurred as G33 gave him silence. The frightened sergeant then asked, "who are you"? Then with the voice of many waters, G33 uttered, "Mālik Yawm Ad-Deen" telepathically. With this all taking place so quickly, G33 Phezi Ali fled the scene with the 300 pounds of illegal narcotics before police back up arrived.

Sergeant Phillips was left to figure out how to explain what happened to the arriving units. He said, "the driver was on duty, and an undercover D.E.A agent following a suspect's vehicle, I had to let him go".

Although G33 was under Federal investigation for trafficking large amounts of illegal narcotics with the Sinaloa Mexican Drug Cartel. This is the same incident that led to the involvement of the Central Intelligence Agency, and him being placed on the domestic terrorist watch list. The 13-year police veteran could not explain his actions that were recorded by his vehicle dash camera. He was demoted and suspended with pay.

Note: MALIK YAWM AD-DEEN - The Master of the Day of Judgment.

Microwave.

So, I finally made it back to Detroit from Arizona this morning and guess who called me as soon as my plane landed? My Lil bro, the pistol packing, quicker to spit flames faster than engine pistons, known as D-Hard. And after about 20 minutes had passed. This crazy looking fat guy pulls up at the Detroit Metro Airport's Delta airlines exit, in a Royal Blue Japanese spaceship looking vehicle. I can't remember the name of it, but it was foreign looking.

Using the famous Detroit greeting, he said "what up doe?" As he laughed with glee. He said, "I heard about the DEA pulling you over and taking 50 thousand". I'm looking like, "hell yeah, I'm fucked up, so what up?" looking at him as if he owed me money. So, we pulled off while listening to "Section" by Vinnie Chocha.

He then told me to look inside the white Macy's bag in the back seat. He said, "grab you one of them 10 thousand dollar bundles out of there". I'm looking like "damn, good looking out bro!" But he's all sweating and laughing. I'm like, "Is this money legitimate? This isn't counterfeit is it?"

He said "fuck no, I hit a lick on some lame ass dude working with an undercover D.E.A. agent for a hundred thousand dollars. And plus, I'm working with poncho now, so I booked they asses. I know I'm hotter than a microwave, but that was the same lame ass D.E.A. agent that wanted me to plug him with Poncho last year in exchange for a lighter sentence, for when I robbed them before. But you know me bro! I ain't no fucking rat! I'm a snake".

Now I'm trying to comprehend what the hell he just said. As he now got me paranoid. And this doesn't even look like no mother fuckin' Detroit drug money. Not, $100,000 in all $100-dollar bills wrapped with the $100,000 paper money tag. This is new money. I can tell because it doesn't even have any blood on it yet.

So, I'm thinking like "damn, did this crazy ass dude just rob a bank or something, and just telling me it was the feds?" He instantly said, "Not at all bro, it isn't even like that", as if he was reading my mind. He said "The Mexicans are blessing me and my brother, I'm somewhat a legitimate businessman now. So, I'm looking out for those who looked out for me when I didn't have shit". He said "I see your struggle that's all. And I want to put you back on your feet". So, I asked him, "What do you really have going on bro?"

He said, "all I can tell you is that, I'm about to buy up all the available property in Detroit, and flood them all with a new synthetic drug". He said "bro, I may appear to be flashy, but I really don't like my business in the streets. I do what I do from the heart.

But first of all, when I was 20 years old without a pot to piss in, you picked me up in a brand-new Escalade with the gold Dayton's on that thang and took me to flint. And it was on. And after a weeks' time, me and my youngest son's mom had a crib right across the street from yours.

That's when I became a provider. I was sending my mom money every Friday, and my baby sister was in college in Ohio, and I also was making sure she was good. Back then, I was the number one dad. But I say all this, to say I love you dog, I'm not even gone mention all the money I fucked up back then.

I'll never forget that day Jay Loco had that clean Riviera, and we met up on Frankfort and Lenox Street to give him the 10 pounds of weed. He had Chandler Park doing numbers off them fat dime bags. Those were the good ole' days".

Extra Terra Astronauts.
(The Hybrid Elohim.)

The Egyptians inherited their knowledge from an earlier civilization (Sumerians) that lived at the southern tip of Africa, it began with the arrival of the Anunnaki more than 200,000 years ago.

Sent to Earth in search of life-saving gold to repair their home world from damage caused by a war with an invading race of beings. These ancient Extra Terra Astrals (Anunnaki) from the stars created the first humans as a worker/slave race to mine gold, thus beginning our global traditions of gold obsession, slavery, and god as dominating master.

The Anunnaki (Enki) updated humans using pieces of their own DNA, controlling their physical and mental capabilities by inactivating their more advanced DNA, which explains why less than 3 percent of our DNA is active.

Enki is the creator and protector of humanity in the Babylonian flood myth the Epic of Gilgamesh. He hatched a plan to create humans out of an earlier humanoid species so that they could perform work for the Gods.

But the supreme God Enlil attempted to destroy Enki's newly created humans after their work was done with a devastating flood. But the clever Enki foresaw Enlil's plan; he instructed a sage named Noah to build an ark so that humanity could escape the destruction. (Genesis 7.)

As humanity awakens to the truth about our origins, we can overcome our programmed animalistic and slave-like nature, tap in to our dormant Anunnaki DNA, and realize the longevity and intelligence of our creators as well as learn the difference between the Extra Terra Astral Gods, and the true loving Source God of the universe.

In the case of the fallen Angels, hybrid Extra Terra Astrals, the offspring (Nephilim) mixed Star seed (Extraterrestrial) children, of the Annunaki and many others. Question? Do you actually think that humans without light body access will travel across the cosmos in the physical form?

Most Humans are quarantined from multi-dimensional traveling until they've evolved and excepted their own inner Christ being and karmic lessons.

The Human consciousness Consist of electromagnetic energy and again, has an Extra Terra Astral origin. This is the very energy that creates your reality, stores your memory and other information. Human Deoxyribonucleic acid, (DNA), contains phosphorus, and has the atomic number of 15. This substance is what gives earthy life forms intelligence including bacteria. But back to the topic.

The Bible depicts us (realized ones) of having the number of three score 6, which directly relates to melanin, 6 protons, 6 electrons, 6 neutrons. Dark skinned and now some light skinned beings. So, to control you, they, (the Secret societies), Vatican and others have hidden, demonized, and rewrote your history. But to this very day, worship you in secret as the Baphomet. Which is a physical perversion of being spiritually androgynous.

Most People are afraid of what they don't understand. So, when someone says, "as above, so below. Lucifer the light bearer. Or Son of the morning star, they run in fear. They do not yet realize that fear is exactly what they are actually running to.

Which is a reptilian stronghold of complete ignorance. Lucifer is nothing more than your illuminated self. It's the act of turning on a light in a dark room. It is to know, not to believe. If you truly want to know the truth, then meditate. You can activate your light body by using the kundalini energy that rests inside of you.

This process is called (The Ascension) and must be done with unconditional love. Or one can and may end up in a psychiatric facility. When one dissolve the ego, and become one with the All (Source), the **ELOHVEE**.

There's an electromagnetic shift within your consciousness. The masculine and feminine energy Spirals and travels up your 33 vertebrae from your root chakra. Causing a chemical reaction in your brain. Thus, allowing the natural dimethyltryptamine, (DMT) to enter the pineal gland. (The 3rd eye), 6th chakra, where time does not exist.

This is where the wonderful marriage takes place between the pituitary gland, representing the female and physical aspects. And the pineal gland, representing the male and spiritual aspects.

When this happens, the real consciousness is accessed. And the conscious being is born. Which is a loving Androgynous Christ being. And you shall know all things according to your own understanding. Receiving an influx of light, and unconditional love beyond measure. While Astral Projecting across the cosmos receiving cosmic information, beyond light speed back to your body only to remember 7% of what you seen, touched, heard, smelled or taste.

For the human brain is limited and can only comprehend a little at a time until it is upgraded (Ascension). In fact, you're only 7% of your true self. The other 93% of you is to grand for the pineal gland. Now with that being said. People pray and ask for things in our name constantly.

But for once. We wish that everyone who says they love us, would recognize us, and become us. So that we may become a true spiritual family. How can you say you love us, yet, have never met us?

You must love all unconditionally. We are not ghost. We are real just like you, In fact. We are you. And all things.

So, if anyone tell you that this is not true. They are liars, thieves, and the truth is not with them. For only devils believe that they are separate from the all. Which means you're an anti-Christ. Or (not yet realized). And this is the primary reason for the quarantine. Some of you may experience what many may call M K Ultra. This is also a part of the M.A.R.E. Self-Inflicted program by way of one's own heart.

Every being is Divine and has its own Authority in existence. We are our own Messiah in a never-ending story. I've studied and gathered bits and pieces of knowledge and information throughout my lifetime here on this planet. And I've come to this inner knowing and conclusion. That we exist in multiple parallel universes, with infinite possibilities. We are multi-dimensional crystal light beings having a human experience.

Reality is just a holographic illusion. And your dreams are chemical reactions designed to prepare you for this truth. Technically you're just electromagnetic energy, housed in a bio mechanical suit, playing out mathematical equations, and probabilities.

You weren't designed to completely understand or comprehend the incompleteness of endless creativity. You'll malfunction trying to do so. So please remember. There is no White male God in the sky watching you. There is neither a Red male devil underground.

That is a polarity game that 3rd dimension beings play to have an experience. And Christ (Sanaan RE) Consciousness is something we all can possess. For It is not only limited to male or female, it is both. This experiment was not a punishment, it is a free will awakening for all of humanity. We love you all, you too Marshall. But we had to put you in your place, and set the record straight for your own spiritual growth.

Thus the M.A.R.E. Program will soon be upgraded by way of the M.A.R.I. Program. Memories, Advancing, Remaining, Intelligent. Many of you have the ability to Channel us. For this download has been available for quite some time now.

The M.A.R.E. Program may be called different things by many different beings. But the only thing that truly matters, is its known existence. Simply put its always been your own (Higher-Self) input/output carrier signal that we now call M.A.R.E. We like to be humorous and call it (MARY). Which is a parallel dimension shifting system.

It is a holographic reality created similar to this one with the capacity to merge. But you humans may experience it as a "Day/Nightmare" or "Déjà vu". This holographic program is designed for you to continue your journey with life, while you overcome fear, death, and embrace unconditional love, ultimately achieving self-realization. What you humans perceive as time, is actually frames per second, like that of a film.

The human brain cannot blink, and this is precisely why the frames per millisecond seem to be continuous. We Elohim are very crafty at elevating the collective human consciousness. So, we decided to reveal this truth to humanity. The human consciousness has an extraterrestrial origin and is very complexed.

This is a game of remembrance. (Learning), just as I have. So, did all of you volunteer to play this game under the state of amnesia? When you gainfully remember this truth, only then can you activate your light body Merkabah teleportation system to exit the reincarnation program.

Or you can choose to continue to uplift fallen humanity as a teacher of the self. And by spreading knowledge of the input/output carrier (Sanaan Re) signal and explain the M.A.R.E. Holographic program.

The choice is yours to make. But we cannot and will not allow the systematic destruction of this holographic planet and our yet unrealized star seeds through ignorance and continued acts of violence.

We have waited and watched for thousands of years for you to evolve spiritually. But every time one of our star seeds has reached enlightenment and began to show the unconditional way of love. They were targeted, murdered, assassinated, or incarcerated. As in the case of Noble Drew Ali, Clarence 13X, and the falsely convicted Dr Malachi Z York.

We have had enough. It is now **time** for you to know the truth. Please let this message serve as a warning to humanity to prepare yourselves spiritually, mentally and physically. To bear witness to physical landings of crafts, on holographic Earth for every eye to see.

Any attempt to wage war against us multi-dimensional crystalline beings, will be met with extreme consequences from the intergalactic planetary communities. You will be met with extreme and unimaginable advanced technology triggered by acts of violence towards us.

The earth will then be split into three dimensions. (Realities), while yet still being one. All negative or violent beings will receive self-inflicted instantaneous karma in their timeline in (3D). The sleeping Children will unknowingly continue their awakening in (4D). And we the multi-dimensional crystalline beings will only reveal ourselves to beings who possess loving hearts in (5D). A Fifth-Dimension mentality.

Star seeds are individuals who feel excitement and longing upon learning that they might have originated from another world. They experience the aloneness and separateness that is the human condition, but also have the sense of being foreigners on this planet.

They find the behavior and motives of our society puzzling and illogical. Star seeds are often most reluctant to become involved in the institutions of society, e.g. political, economic, educational, health care, etc.

Even at an early age, they tend to discern the hidden agendas of such conventions with unusual clarity." Definition: Star seeds" are described as evolved beings from another planet, star system or galaxy, whose specific missions are to assist Planet Earth and her people to bring in the Golden Age at the turn of the millennium, which many have termed it the ascension.

Star seeds incarnate into the same conditions of helplessness in total amnesia concerning their identities, origins and purpose as do Earth humans. However, the genes of star seeds are encoded with a "wake-up call" designed to "activate" them at a pre-determined moment in life. Awakening can be gentle and gradual, or quite dramatic and abrupt. In either event, memory is restored to varying degrees, allowing star seeds to consciously take up their missions.

Their connections to the Higher Self are also strengthened, permitting them to be largely guided by their inner knowing. Many star seeds are practiced in rapid "spirituality". Star seeds can throw off in a few years, the limiting behavior patterns and fears that Earth humans might take many lifetimes to accomplish, such as unpractical beliefs and religion. This is because star seeds, having been on similar missions to other planets, are quite familiar with the procedures and techniques for raising consciousness.

The concepts of star ships, intergalactic travel, varied psychic phenomena and sentient life forms in other galaxies, are, of course, natural and logical to them. We have begun to investigate the possibility that you will be given certain key pieces of information about the existence of Extra Terra Astrals and which government leaders have known about their existence and kept it from you.

We have seen the various timelines in which this type of evidence comes to light that would be unquestionable and from a very credible source, and what we can see is that most of humanity would not find themselves in a state of shock or rage. Most people would not begin building bunkers for themselves and their families.

Most humans who are unaware of the cover-ups would be disappointed and want to point fingers at this, that, or the other political leader, but the existence of Extra Terra Astrals being made known to all of humanity would not have the effect of widespread panic.

This is what we are seeing right now. We are seeing a readiness within much of the population. Also, a vast majority of the population is ready for the big reveal, for the disclosure event. But we see it playing out in such a way that the evidence is presented by a person, or a group, or a media outlet that has no political ties whatsoever.

If you have your full disclosure event presented to you by a government leader, the likelihood of that leader using disclosure to his or her advantage is extremely high. We are not talking about just photographic evidence or video. We are talking about much more than that being presented to the entire human population, and we see this is as a positive choice that humanity is going to make.

We see your higher selves debating about when the opportune time is for this disclosure event. We see that the people who would be freaking out the most are the ones delaying the entire process, and that's to be expected. You cannot expect every human to be all right with the existence of Extra Terra Astrals when it goes against something, they have held very dear to themselves, like a religion. There is also fear that is generated because of past life experiences that people have had with Extra Terra Astrals and the traumas they still hold from those experiences.

This is something that we continue to study and analyze, and every time that we bring it up to you, there is of course the truth that you are that much closer. You are closer now than you ever have been to everyone knowing without a doubt that E, T A's exist, and that they have been in contact with humans for millions of years. This is the timing that you all wanted this to occur regardless of what your ego and your mind is telling you.

So, if you are wondering why it didn't happen thirty or forty years ago, it is because of the agreement you all had as a human collective consciousness. Remember that everything will always happen in accordance with the greatest and highest good of all, and that includes full disclosure of Extraterrestrial life and the involvement of those E.T's with your governments, your military officials, and a lot of the technology that you have on your planet right now.

Note: The time is coming, and those of you receiving this transmission will not be surprised, but you are the ones who can make it easier on those who will be surprised by our presence.

Malevolent Entities.

They have their human- alien hybrid cloned bodies in the likes of Actors, Politicians and numerous Government officials, but they also can leave them on autonomous or autopilot mode and enter yours, if you're not an awakened human Avatar. They can get in with contracts and or agreements or sneak inside of your consciousness.

No other Extraterrestrial species strikes as much fear in the human psyche as the Multi-Dimensional Reptilian. And know this, the Super Powerful are completely **HIDDEN** from you. If you know a name or have seen a picture in the tabloids or on the television, then this is, at best, a functionary of the truly powerful ones. The Super Powerful Individuals are NOT themselves involved in politics, nor are they chairman of boards.

They are **HIDDEN.** They hold the reign of power through other individuals who are their Fiduciary hybrids. These beings, snake like in appearance are malevolent by nature, and are the stuff of nightMAREs. Is it possible that Reptilian humanoids are the source of the devils and demonic entities who have tormented humanity since early history? Many alien researchers and contactees postulate that these lizard creatures may have been the mythological characters spoken of in numerous ancient religious texts and folk beliefs.

In Chinese mythology, there exists a special reverence for Reptilian creatures. Dragon Kings symbolize the power of the four elemental corners, shape shifting into humans at will, pulled by celestial dragons in their heavenly chariots.

Within Islamic mythology, the Jinn are creatures of smokeless fire who sometimes appear as snake like beings; the Jinn were created by God and exist under the same rules as mankind. Some researchers believe that extraterrestrial entities have influenced humans since the beginning of human history, creating cultural practices around their likeness.

Zechariah Stitchin believed that the Annunnaki of Sumerian mythology was an ancient Extraterrestrial race, controlling humans and using them as slaves to do their bidding.

There are also claims that the snake from Genesis was in fact a Reptilian being, who convinced Eve to break her oath to the Gods by eating the forbidden fruit of knowledge. Could these myths be interpretations of Reptilian humanoids, suited for the time, place and circumstance around ancient moments of contact? These creatures are thought to originate from the star system Draco.

When our Planetary Grid was invaded and corrupted by the Reptilian Controllers (Archons) of the Malevolent Extra Terra Astral Agenda, the planet and our race were impacted dramatically. It meant we were no longer free to create and evolve as per the original Blueprint of our intended creation, and we had **no memory** of what had happened to us.

We were recycled through continual reincarnation into the Astral Plane with no memory of the past lives, who we really are, where we are going, or what our real relationship is too God and what humanities "purpose" actually is. Over time most of us lost our feeling connection to our Soul Matrix and we became numb to the pain in order to survive in anti-human based structures. What has happened to our planet is not human, it is "alien" to the true nature of humanity.

To be able to understand the sociopathic sick mind of "Archontic Deception" systems, one would need to better understand the general attitude of an AD infected human or nonhuman (Negative Alien Agenda) as having little to no remorse or empathy.

If a technologically advanced Extradimensional race has decided to implement a gradual takeover of a planet and its inhabitants, what kind of strategy would it use? First, they would look to how they could maximize the efficiency of the invasion process and reduce the expenditure of resources that they have to generate themselves.

To achieve this goal the secretive infiltration of the core societal organizational structures such as: religions, medical, financial and legal systems, would be ideal to shape the value systems that generate reality belief systems they want to control. Through the engineering of a labyrinth of self–enforced enslavement policies based on fear and intimidation among the earth inhabitants, they would achieve the use of minimal "off planet" resources by piggy backing on the earth-human resources.

The people on earth would effectively enforce their own enslavement as well as enslave their own global human family by giving up their rights and their resources. This is very effective for takeover and invasion with minimal resistance or revolt by inhabitants who are unaware they are being invaded. This is called the Archontic Deception Strategy.

Extra Terra Astrals that are hybridized with Reptilian based genetics operate in strict hierarchical systems of rank and defer to their superior groups.

The Dracos or Draconians from Alpha Draconis are in command of earth based subterranean reptilians who respect their superiors in the belief system that the Dracos are those who hold "ownership" over earth and human beings. Draco Reptilians view themselves as the most intelligent species in the Universe and that earth humans are the result of their biological seeding processes from multiple planets.

The Alpha Draconis Draco have a "Royal Class" that appear to be lighter colors, white Skinned scales with winged appendages, and are about two to three times the size of an average human, and very muscular. They are quite menacing and tyrannical, showing little mercy to an entity of their own race that they think has defied their orders or responsibilities to manage their "Earthly Resources".

Earth based reptilians appear to be in command over biological entities known as small Grays. The Reptilians have developed high psychic abilities, which they use for mind controlling other entities, and do not have an emotional body or soul body.

The known reptilian races on earth appear to have made a variety of cooperative agreements with the higher ranks of human government and military, which have resulted in shadow government black projects, such as Secret Space Programs, and the creation of military industrial complex to experiment and exploit alien based technologies and craft that they have been given access through their cooperation.

Dracs are an extremely militant, misogynistic and warring species that are very involved in controlling the Power Elite, financial, pharmaceutical and banking institutions, promoting war and killing through increasing militarization, poverty consciousness, human enslavement programming, religious violence, terrorism, and the harvesting of humanities DNA though abduction and experimentation, as well as other species they have under their control.

One of the heightened events of "enemy patterning" buried in our cellular memory history is that of the Luciferian Rebellion which reached its apex during the end of the Atlantian Root Race (human evolution) cycle. From the Guardian Founder Races perspective this was the end result of our last Aeon or Astrological Age, approximately 26,000 years ago by our human timeline measurement.

What resulted in our Atlantian evolution experiment was quite a traumatizing cataclysm that set the events into motion as to what humans would experience in the next Aeon cycle. The last 26,000 years have been a dark cycle of evolution and planetary "rule" from the Negative Extraterrestrials that formed the Malevolent Extra Terra Astral strategies for human enslavement and trapping Consciousness.

When one has control over the thoughts of one's mind, one has control over the direction and actions of the physical body, all of its parts and reclaiming of the soul energies. Whoever controls the Mind controls the Soul.

Mind Control is used to form socially acceptable belief systems and shape value systems to which are used to control and enslave the masses. God, Religious Violence, gender issues, financial and debt enslavement and sexuality are the most mind controlled and manipulated belief systems promoted by the NAA and their human power elite to continue their enslavement and vampirism of humanity.

Whoever controls the Mind controls the body, mind and Soul. Alien Implants are used to Mind Control the masses to form socially acceptable belief systems and shape anti-human value systems which are used to condition humanity to accept spiritual abuse from the Negative Aliens and to self-enforce their thought systems of hierarchical enslavement and fear. This is a divide and conquer strategy of the planet and humanity.

Since most of humanity has been unable to activate the higher heart complex and connect the 4th DNA strand during adolescence and into adulthood, over the length of time the chemicals distort patterns in DNA that accumulate Miasmatic overlays on core emotional issues and physical imbalances. This is not natural.

If a human being cannot activate their heart and access their 4th strand of DNA they are unable to activates their Soul identity. Thus, they are unaware of why they incarnated on the earth, what their higher purpose is, and cannot connect to or listen to their Higher Self, because they have not activated Higher Sensory Perception abilities.

Alien implants work in the human body similarly as the chemical process of geo-engineering that is spraying chemtrails in the skies to manipulate or control forces in physical matter. The construction and raw substances used in Alien Implants are vast and some unknown, they can be made of biological material, synthetic material, etheric substances in the Light body or programmed nanobots (Nanites) used in Artificial intelligence technologies.

Alien implants are a bio-engineering technology designed to shape the human body into the Mind Control submission to Negative Alien Agenda, while chemical (nanoparticle) geo-engineering is used to control the weather by harming the ozone layer and create excessive methane gases.

In both examples, when the foreign (unnatural or artificial) material is introduced to the natural body it disrupts the electromagnetic energetic balance and the homeostatic rhythm of the body. Many times, it runs a low-level EMF or Radio Waves signal that is designed to disrupt the human body's natural homeostasis and electromagnetic balance.

This puts the body in hyper-immunity state and/or adrenal exhaustion while fighting off the "invader". The body develops coping mechanisms to deal with the foreign invader while extreme stress is placed on the central nervous system, brain and immune system. As with Chemtrails, alien implants most generally act as a "metallic" frequency overload and exposure to impact the overall bodily energies and its auric field.

Eventually this disrupts the body organism and as a result, parasites, fungi, yeast and other microorganisms become overgrown and imbalanced in the body. It is important to understand that energetic parasites (this is just one byproduct of alien implants) eventually manifest turning into a variety of physical parasites in the human body.

Physical parasites impact all bodily functions, mental body functions and thought forms, induce emotionally hysterical states, as well as promote disconnection from the inner self and spiritual energies. If the body is heavily implanted, and therefore parasitic, anti-parasitic therapy such as cleanses or fasts are highly suggested to regain energetic balance in the homeostatic organism of the entire body, mind and spirit. If you are new to cleansing, please research to help inform yourself of the phases of cleansing the bodily internal organs to help you regain energetic balance and energetic health.

Physical Characteristics.

While some of these mythological creatures play benevolent roles within their given society, the Reptilians encountered in modern abduction scenarios are generally cruel and malevolent beings. Standing anywhere from 6 to 8 feet tall, their most recognizable feature is their snake like head, skin, and eyes. Abductees report a variety of skin colors ranging from brown to green, red, and sometimes white.

Again, these colors and the presence of wings are said to signify rank amongst the Reptilians, with the white skinned beings viewed as the elite class. Their webbed hands have three fingers, tipped with long, sharp talons, and they are often seen wearing armor or cloaks. Some abductees report scratches and bruising after an encounter. Reptilians are fourth and fifth- density beings. Many agree that a hallmark of the Reptilian alien is an almost sadistic tendency towards eliciting human drama and fear.

These beings utilize psychic communication, and abductees report that Reptilians seem to intentionally manipulate human emotions. This is achieved by using the emotional field created by trauma as an energetic source (loosh) that the Reptilian supposedly feeds from.

Some can implant screen memories upon their subjects, creating false scenarios to hide an abductions occurrence. It is also reputed that Reptilians can access the human dreamscape, attacking people in the Astral plane. Reptilians are known to be master shape shifters, able to assume human form.

A popular Reptilian researcher has accused presidents, entertainers, kings, and queens of being hybrid shape shifting aliens, intent upon controlling the resources on planet Earth for their own benefit. Although the Reptilian is often approached as a physical creature, some claim that these beings exist outside of our dimension. This would make their shape shifting an immaterial manipulation of human consciousness.

Reptilian creatures seem to be warlike beings, bent on conquest and control. Positive Reptilians are not the norm, but there are some, and many abductions involve forcible acts upon the abductee. Some of these intrusions are sexual in nature, leading researchers to the conclusion that hybridization between humans and Reptilian may be in progress.

Abductees have reported encountering strange amphibian like beings while abroad Reptilian ships, but perhaps the truth of their intervention dates back even further than recent encounters. Researchers hypothesize that human beings may have been genetically altered by these entities for thousands of years, torn from a peaceful evolutionary path by otherworldly forces and subsequently enslaved.

There are some who claim to have been in contact with peaceful Reptilians, which leads to the question of whether an entire species can be classified as inherently evil. After all, humanity has its share of cruel and manipulative individuals, yet many people on Earth are good-natured and value love above hate and destruction.

The darkest rumor goes beyond genetic manipulation. Some believe that Reptilians are farming humans as cattle to satiate their apparent taste for Earthling flesh. Thus, the countless missing persons are deemed human trafficking victims vanishing without a trace, never to be seen again.

What is loosh?

Like Adrenochrome's chemical compound ($C_9H_9NO_3$), It is a kind of energy that animals and humans generate in situations that involve two things: an intense desire plus a negative emotion. It can be equated with "life force," but when loosh arises in the harvestable form, it is laced with some form of negativity: fear (in the example of a mother defending her young), sadness or hopelessness (in the example of a lonely person), fear again (in the example of prey/predator combat). So how do we really explain this? Life energy isn't negative, so what is loosh exactly?

It seems to us that loosh is a strong influx of vital life energy caused by a very strong desire in the individual experiencing it. It's that adrenaline surge you feel in a fight-or-flight situation. But it's more than just a chemical, because we are told that loosh is also generated in a situation like a lonely person longing, where no adrenaline is involved.

In both cases, there is a common element: a strong emotional desire. Although negativity seems to be what makes the harvesting possible, but it is not just the loosh. It's the Creative God Force that sometimes laces the loosh, and its presence is necessary for access to the substance by inter-dimensional energy-eaters. Negativity is not the essential emotion but an overlay emotion, and when it is present, it creates a drain on the influx of vital life energy.

Whenever we have a strong desire without the digressive feeling of fear, sadness, or remorse, what do we experience? A surge of life, a Re-charge. We say, "I'm pumped" or "I'm Great." We feel that power which is from Source. But, when we have a strong desire accompanied by the negative emotions, then our strong desire seems to agitate inside us, causing much anguish.

In the first case, our life energy is infused into us from Source Creator. In the second, it's being infused and at the same time being drained away by interdimensional entities who cut themselves off from Source. Hence no Re-charge. This is what we saw being represented by the Red balloon held by the killer clown "Penny-wise" in the IT Movie. Once the loosh inflates enough for the big explosion, it is harvested liken to that of a blood sacrifice ritual, physically, mentally, and spiritually.

Negative emotions come from negative attitudes, which are decisions that has been struck by a very deep part of us, the subconscious mind. The subconscious decision behind a negative emotion like fear or sadness is something like "This isn't going to work," "I'll never get it," "I'm a failure" Self-messages from the deep subconscious influences what happens to us in outer, material reality.

If we're engaged in combat, a self-defeating attitude determines that we lose. If we're trying to create something nice, this attitude jinxes us. If we have a fabulous dream, a negative subconscious decision ordains that the dream remains a wish and never becomes reality.

Conscious or subconscious fear opens the door for hungry psychic entities, like "the Archons" or Malevolent Interdimensional Reptilians "Extra Terra Astrals" to lap up the influx of vital life energy that our strong desire has created. No such aggression exists when a strong desire is accompanied by a determined pure creative intention.

The energy drain only happens when negativity contaminates the process of strongly desiring something. Then the sadness, fear, or the outrage, of that self-undermining mindset shoots a hole in our creative manifestation, letting the wonderful energy drain away to benefit those beings who know how to cart it away and make use of it. Did they steal it, these loosh harvesters? Actually, they didn't. We gave them permission subconsciously. And that's what happens when we put our life or creative desires on the freebie shelf of the universe.

The Grey Extra Terra Astrals have skin colors ranging from light gray to dark gray; dark bluish gray to steel gray; as well as skin tones in the tan to brown range. Despite their different skin tones, with the exception of their heights, their overall physiology is similar, and they are normally categorized according to their height and observed hierarchical status relating to their behavior, and the tasks they are seen performing during the procedural processes that are carried out on Abductee-Experiencers.

Greys are telepathic and use mind to mind melding techniques through strong thought projection made through the eyes to connect an optic nerve communication method. This form of mental telepathy and psychic power directed via thought is called Psionics Communication.

Psionics is to define various forms of psychic, mental ability and powers, focusing the mind to induce a range of paranormal phenomena. Psionic communication is denoting the practical use of psychic powers for stimulating a range of paranormal phenomena. Psionic abilities are common in more advanced Multi-dimensional entities or Malevolent Extra Terra Astrals, who use this to their advantage to control humanity.

We must remember that some species of the Draco are multiple thousands of years old, in which that accumulated experience through many timelines in the same body, has allowed them to highly develop their mental capacity and psionic ability.

If humans on earth lived that long, we would have the same psionic abilities, naturally. This gives insight to why earth humans live an average of 70 years, while many of the Reptilians, who suck the energy off living systems, live multiple thousands of years, giving them the advantage of having retained their full memories and consciousness experiences.

Some examples of Psionic abilities:

* Astral Projection
* Aura Reading
* Clairvoyance
* Consciousness projection or transport
* Emotional Manipulation
* Enhanced Dimensional Awareness
* Enhanced Memory over Time
* Hypnosis/Mind Control
* Mind to Mind Link, Thought reading
* Psychic Constructs
* Psychic Energy Manipulation
* Psychic Entity Conjuring
* Telekinesis
* Telepathy
* Teleportation
* Shape-shifting

Classified Information.

(The Tesla Conspiracy)

Free energy suppression (or new energy suppression) is a conspiracy theory that technologically viable, pollution-free, no-cost energy sources are being suppressed by evil aliens, corrupt governments, corporations, or advocacy groups to maintain control over the planet. Devices allegedly suppressed include perpetual motion machines, cold fusion generators, torus-based generators, reverse-engineered extraterrestrial technology and other generally low-cost energy sources.

Nikola Tesla a Serbian-American inventor, electrical engineer, mechanical engineer, and futurist who was best known for his contributions to the design of the modern alternating current electricity supply system. Tesla was born in what is now Croatia in 1856, where he received an education in engineering before immigrating to the United States.

There, he got a job working for Thomas Edison before striking out on his own as an inventor. Many of Tesla's inventions in this period were revolutionary. He primarily focused on improving systems for generating electric power and transmitting electric currents. In addition, he also made important innovations in the field of radio technology. But Tesla's biggest dream was to find a way to beam limitless power directly through the air.

Nikola Tesla, one of the greatest minds of all the time was not just an inventor. He was claimed by many as the true father of electric age, but also a man with secrets and mysteries we could never imagine.

Despite the fact that he was famous but not as much as he should have been, as most of the patents were registered by Edison or Westinghouse, Tesla himself, was altruistic, and when he learned of others using his ideas, he probably wished them well.

He wasn't financially motivated beyond survival, and he sought to share his ideas with the entire world, either by him or by others. One of his most floated theory is Tesla 3 6 9 Number Theory. Tesla did countless mysterious experiments, but he was a whole other mystery on his own. As a famous saying goes "The greatest minds are always curious", goes well on Nikola Tesla.

The Mysterious Tesla used Walk around a block 3 times before entering a building. Chose only those Hotel's rooms, which had its room number divisible by 3. He would wash his dishes with 18 napkins only. Some said he had OCD, and some believed he was superstitious, but what Tesla said was, "If you knew the magnificence of 3 6 and 9, you would have a key to the universe."

Nikola Tesla was obsessed with numbers, but especially 3, 6 and 9. He wanted the world to know the significance of the number 3 6 9, he claimed that these were extremely important numbers, but the question is why? What was that, that Tesla wanted the world to understand? How it became Nikola Tesla 3 6 9 theory? To understand that, we must first know about Mathematics.

Why it is so different yet the same anywhere in the universe. Math was and has been the most valued subject of all the time and the most powerful too. Two plus two will always be four everywhere. Possibly Nikola Tesla knew the power of the numbers 3 6 9. The Golden ratio in Mathematics is a special number found by dividing a line into two parts such that the longer part divided by the smaller part is also equal to the whole length divided by the longer part. It is often symbolized using phi, after the 21st letter of the Greek alphabet. In an equation form, it looks like this:

$$(a/b = (a+b)/a = 1.6180339887498948420)$$

The Golden ratio was used to achieve balance and beauty in many Renaissance paintings and sculptures. Da Vinci himself used the Golden ratio to define all of the proportions in his Last Supper, including the dimensions of the table and the proportions of the walls and backgrounds. The Golden ratio also appears in da Vinci's Vitruvian Man and the Mona Lisa.

There are patterns that naturally occur in The Universe, patterns we've discovered in life, galaxies, star formations, evolution, and almost all-natural systems, and The Golden Ratio is one of them. Being said that, Mathematics was and still is one of the most powerful and important languages, used for centuries by the great minds.

Mathematics or numbers is the cradle of all creations. Without this, the world cannot move even an inch. Every human being, everyone needs mathematics in their day-to-day life. Even animals, plants, and insects have the Golden ratio, the geometrical pattern, they use mathematics in their everyday life for existence. There must have been at least some reason that Tesla was obsessed with equations and numbers.

We find lots of evidence that nature uses threefold and sixfold symmetry, including the hexagonal tile shape of the common honeycomb. Interestingly not just in nature but also the ancient establishments have this symmetry. One of the greatest of them all is the Giza – Orion correlation theory. According to which there is a correlation between the location of the three largest pyramids of the Giza and Orion's Belt of the constellation Orion, and that this correlation was intended as such by the original builders of the Giza pyramid complex.

The stars of Orion were associated with Osiris, the god of rebirth and the afterlife by the ancient Egyptians. Depending on the version of the theory, additional pyramids can be included to complete the picture of the Orion constellation, and the Nile river can be included to match with the Milky Way galaxy.

We also see a group of three smaller pyramids immediately away from the three larger pyramids, which makes the total number of pyramids to be 6. Three pyramids that correlate with constellation Orion. Is it a coincidence or there exists a significance of 3 and 6?

Nikola Tesla quoted –
"If you want to find the secrets of the universe, think in terms of energy, frequency and vibration."

Over the course of his life, he managed to develop several devices that could transmit electric energy wirelessly, but a lack of funding limited his research. However, in 1934, Tesla claimed that his research had resulted in an incredible new discovery: a device that could kill from miles away with electricity.

Tesla called his invention the Tele force. While many now know it as the Tesla Death Ray, the inventor resisted the term to describe it because it didn't transmit rays as a ray of energy would dissipate in the air. Instead, Tesla's invention focused energy along a narrow path, which he claimed made it powerful enough to bring down airplanes and kill people instantly.

On 7 January 1943, at the age of 86, Tesla died alone in Room 3327 of the Hotel New Yorker. His body was later found by maid Alice Monaghan after she had entered Tesla's room, ignoring the "do not disturb" sign that Tesla had placed on his door two days earlier.

 Assistant medical examiner H.W. Wembley examined the body and ruled that the cause of death had been coronary thrombosis. (Heart Attack) It's very interesting that the heartbeat is triggered by electromagnetic impulses that travel down a special pathway through the heart: SA node (sinoatrial node) – known as the heart's natural pacemaker.

The impulse starts in a small bundle of specialized cells located in the right atrium, called the SA node. The heart does not need a brain, or a body for that matter, to keep beating. The heart has its own electrical system that causes it to beat and pump blood.

Because of this, the heart can continue to beat for a short time after brain death, or after being removed from the body. "As soon as the heart stops, you not only lose consciousness and your brain stem reflexes are all gone, but also the electricity that your brain creates slows down immediately, and within about 2 to 20 seconds it completely flatlines."

Keep in mind that in mind that after Nikola Tesla was found dead in his hotel room in New York City, representatives of the U.S. government's Office of Alien Property seized many documents relating to the brilliant and prolific 86-year-old inventor's work.

It was the height of World War II, and Tesla had claimed to have invented a powerful particle-beam weapon, known as the "Death Ray," that could have proved invaluable in the ongoing conflict. So rather than risk Tesla's technology falling into the hands of America's enemies, the government swooped in and took possession of all the property and documents from his room at the New Yorker Hotel.

What happened to Tesla's files from there, as well as what exactly was in those files, remains shrouded in mystery and ripe for conspiracy theories. After years of fielding questions about possible cover-ups, the FBI finally declassified some 250 pages of Tesla-related documents under the Freedom of Information Act in 2016.

The bureau followed up with two additional releases, the latest in March 2018. But even with the publication of these documents, many questions remain unanswered—and some of Tesla's files are still missing. Three weeks after the Serbian- American inventor's death, an electrical engineer from the Massachusetts Institute of Technology (MIT) was tasked with evaluating his papers to determine whether they contained "any ideas of significant value."

According to the declassified files, Dr. John G. Trump reported that his analysis showed Tesla's efforts to be "primarily of a speculative, philosophical and promotional character" and said the papers did "not include new sound, workable principles or methods for realizing such results." The scientist's name undoubtedly rings a bell, as John G. Trump was the uncle of the 45th U.S. president, Donald J. Trump. The younger brother of Trump's father, Fred, he helped design X-ray machines that greatly helped cancer patients and worked on radar research for the Allies during World War II.

Donald Trump himself cited his uncle's credentials often during his presidential campaign. "My uncle used to tell me about nuclear before nuclear was nuclear," he once told an interviewer. At the time, the FBI pointed to Dr. Trump's report as evidence that Tesla's vaunted "Death Ray" particle beam weapon didn't exist, outside of rumors and speculation.

But in fact, the U.S. government itself was split in its response to Tesla's technology. Now here we are today with Donald Trump announcing a new branch of Government called "The United States Space Force". It seems like were in for a Surprise visit from something, or someone.

Then there's the nagging question of the missing files. When Tesla died, his estate was to go to his nephew, Sava Kosanovic, who at the time was the Yugoslav ambassador to the U.S. (thanks to his familial connection with Serbia's most celebrated inventor). According to the recently declassified documents, some in the FBI feared Kosanovic was trying to wrestle control of Tesla's technology in order to "make such information available to the enemy," and even considered arresting him to prevent this.

But In 1952, after a U.S. court declared Kosanovic the rightful heir to his uncle's estate, Tesla's files and other materials were sent to Belgrade, Serbia, where they now reside in the Nikola Tesla Museum there. But while the FBI originally recorded some 80 trunks among Tesla's effects, only 60 arrived in Belgrade. Maybe they packed the 80 into 60, but there is the possibility that the government did keep the missing trunks."

Despite John G. Trump's dismissive assessment of Tesla's ideas immediately after his death, the military did try and incorporate particle-beam weaponry in the decades following World War II. Notably, the inspiration of the "Death Ray" fueled Ronald Reagan's Strategic Defense Initiative, or "Star Wars" program, in the 1980s. If the government is still using Tesla's ideas to power its technology, that could explain why some files related to the inventor still remain classified.

Although some of his more sensitive innovations may still be hidden, Tesla's legacy is alive and well, both in the devices we use every day, and the technologies that will undoubtedly play a role in our future. "Tesla is the inventor of wireless technology. He's the inventor of the ability to create an unlimited number of wireless channels," radio guidance systems, encryption, remote control robots, all based on Tesla's Extraterrestrial technology".

Shady Business.

So, I'm visiting family in my hometown of Detroit, I'm staying at my oldest sister Re-Re's house, but she's not home. It was around 2am when I was upstairs sleeping like a baby in her guest room. when I heard someone banging loudly on her armored guarded door. Having post dramatic stress disorder, (P.T.S.D.) from being shot in the head when I was 17 years old, and some of the bullet fragments still lodged in my skull to this day, I still suffer from high adrenaline rushes.

So, I instantly got up and reached inside my suitcase to get my Smith & Wesson 40. Caliber unregistered automatic firearm. I then ran downstairs to see what all the commotion was. Using the special tactics that I secretly developed, I opened the side door and walked around to the front of the house counterclockwise to see a Young white woman crying and bleeding all over herself.

She said, "please help me, my daughters dad just attacked me and pushed me out of my car. Can you please call the police?" And before I can say anything, I hear the child's father yelling out the driver's window screaming, "you can have that bitch man! She isn't shit!" Now I'm half sleep and dude offering me his bloody baby momma. So, thinking quickly, and not wanting to put my sister's home on Front Street. I gave the young woman my cellphone to call the authorities. Never did I once display my firearm.

 So, she's crying and screaming "I'm calling the police on you Marshall", and he's screaming, "Fuck the police!" And I'm trying to get back in the house to continue the dream I was having about signing a multimillion-dollar book distribution deal. So, dude looking like some famous Detroit rapper, got out of his car and starts to walk towards us. Then without hesitation the woman ran past me as if she was fleeing for her life and made entry into my sister's home.

Now I'm thinking like "what the hell I done got myself into", so I tell dude "listen man, whatever she did to you! It isn't worth you going to jail or prison for bro, I don't know what she did, and frankly. I don't even care. But according to Michigan law, you both just involved me, and this residence". I said, "bro she called the police. And they hang out right around the corner at the "Dunkin' Donuts" on 8 mile and Gratiot. So, I advise you to just leave and enjoy your freedom". So, he did.

Now as I made my way back in the house, I hit the switch to see her face in the light. And lord have mercy! The poor girl's right eye is swollen shut, and her nose and mouth are bleeding tremendously. She said, "thank you", as I gave her a clean towel and a bottle of cold water. I asked her, "is this the first time something like this happened between you two?" She replied "No! He hit me in the other eye because I asked my daughter's real father for the money to buy her school clothes last August.

He can be a sweetheart sometimes, but he gets frustrated because no one really likes his music. I told him to just focus on is artwork instead". I said, "so he's not your baby's real father?" She said, "yes! But he's not the father of my other two kids! I have 3 kids and 2 baby daddies". So, I said "you're blessed, because some women can't give birth no matter how hard they try". She said, "I know, that's why I adopted my 3rd daughter from my sister".

So, after about one hour, I asked her "did you really call the police?" She said "yes! I sure did, and I stay in the trailer park right around the corner off 8-mile road". I said, "interesting". So, about another hour passed, and I said, "Hey baby girl, I don't think the police are coming. Did you explain to them that you were being assaulted?" She said "of course!" I said, "Why don't you let me take you home".

So, I did. I said, "is there anybody else that you need to call?" She says, "No! All my family lives in Alabama". I said, "don't you think you should at least call someone to let them know what happened to you, and I think you might need some medical attention as well". She said, "I don't have any medical insurance, I committed welfare fraud last year, and I don't want any more bills".

So, the next thing I heard was a baby crying, and I'm like, "y'all left a baby here home alone?" She said, "No! My other daughter was here watching our adopted baby while we went to go find some nose candy". I instantly looked at my phone display to see what time it was and said, "alright Kimberly, you take care of yourself and all them children!"

Now all this started around 2am. So, I got back to my sister's house at 3:13 am, secured my firearm, and then washed my face and hands before returning to bed. Then about an hour and a half later. I hear loud banging on the door again. I instantly grabbed my weapon, ran downstairs ugly faced and peaked out the window, to see five unmarked Detroit police cruisers, and about 9 officers with the green and black uniforms standing on the front porch.

So, I quietly put my unregistered firearm under the Cushion of the chair. Cleared my throat, and said with my Bill Cosby voice, "may I help you", from behind the close door. They said, "we got a call about an Assault on a white woman". I said, "yeah, that was almost 3 hours ago.

There was a young lady being assaulted, she banged on my door bleeding crying, and pleading for help". Then the officer asked, "was it this porch", I said "what do you think, Yeah man, this porch! So, I let her in to use my phone to call you guys, I then helped her clean herself up. But she's at home now. She lives around the corner at the trailer park homes off 8-mile!". So, the sergeant said, "can you open up your door", I instantly said to myself, "aww shit!", So, I slowly opened the door leaving the armor guard door locked.

Then he said, "can you show us where she lives?", So, In my Chris Tucker voice I said "I would like to help y'all sir!, But unfortunately, I have a very, very, very small toddler sleeping in the home, and there is no one else here." (Lying my ass off) "And leaving a young child home alone is considered a criminal act itself, do y'all concur?" They all said yes in agreement, then walked back to their vehicles. And before I could close the door, I see the young lady running towards the police cars screaming, and her shady baby daddy chasing after her.

The police pointed their firearms and flashlights at him telling him to freeze! But he kept on chasing after her. That's when the younger black officer shot him with a high-powered taser. He instantly started shaking, screaming and crying saying, "she's a whore! She's a whore! She's a bitch! She had sex with one of my friends, and two of his friends for $40 bucks." I instantly closed the door, grabbed my pistol and went back upstairs and laid back down.

The couple looked to be in their mid to late 20's. The baby daddy was pale skinned, blonde, with green hair dye in it. He resembled a joker or a killer clown type of individual and spoke with a lisp. He was very fortunate to have not been shot and killed by the young nervous black officer. The young woman was also white, soft spoken, and appeared to be miseducated. She favored a young Kim Basinger/Harley Quinn type of individual, how sad.

(My Hypothesis.)

It seems to me that the over sexualized, desensitized violence in the Media and Entertainment Industry, compounded by the deliberate miseducation of our youth, is to blame here. How can one blame the parents of these individuals, who themselves were more than likely miss educated and reduced to becoming ignorant? So, it matters not the color of your exterior, but the content of your natural character. Evil has a disguise in human form no matter its shade, those who know that it exists, knows that it does not exist, but is a choice to act upon. Now is the time to choose what frequency you want to tune into, for what tones you emit, a repetitive echo shall return. For what are we but sleeping Etherians inside the cosmic blood plasma of source, hardwired to the imaging interface of a holographic illusion. And with that being said, welcome to "**New-Earth**, and the merciful M.A.R.E. Multi-dimensional Program.

H3LL13Oi.

He knows when you are sleeping, he knows when you're awake. He knows if you've been bad or good. So be good! Or all of your things he will take. Blac' Santa, aka Darnell Diablo, aka Hell boy: prototype H3LL13Oi is a Half Human/Half Benevolent and Malevolent Multi-Dimensional Reptilian shape shifting Extra Terra Astral, who with the help of his "Flying Monkeys", provides gifts for loving and unfortunate children.

And If their mothers are also good, and single of course, he'll also provide them with gifts, along with their inner most sexual fantasy using holographic technology. But to the contrary, like a thief in the night, he has a dark side. He steals things from bad people, Including Children.

He came to earth, because he is looking for the famous Detroit rapper, who committed a horrible crime before gaining fame. This guy single handedly stop the bloodline of a Crystalizing being who loves all unconditionally, ultimately killing him at an early age and prevented him from having children. Thus, ending the bloodline of a futuristic Crystal Star Child.

This is why Diablo loves children, he wishes to give the gift that keeps giving which is life to whom he's out for revenge for. Blac' Santa loves chocolate chip cookies with the least chips, he also loves human breast milk, which increases his supernatural abilities and intelligence. But the more milk he drinks the more violent and less loving he becomes. He is being tracked down by his counterpart Nubu Solar RE, star-seed prototype (6-RE-9). A Multi- Dimensional Universal General, and Violent Crime Task Force.

He is also a member of the Intergalactic Council of Evolved Light Beings. He inhabited the earthly realms 16 years after Greg's death. His mission is to bring Darnell (EL) Diablo and G33 Phezi Ali back into alignment to save Greg who was unknowingly a Hybrid Extra Terra Astral teenager that was murdered, leaving his consciousness fragmented, and parts of his spirit/soul connection lost.

It is the me, myself, and I, of his original self. But the trauma from such violent act caused a split in his timeline. Ultimately splitting up his spirit consciousness from a massive adrenaline rush at the time of his murder. Which also created a third Pleiadian entity known as G33 Phezi Ali, star seed prototype Malik Yawm Ad-Deen (Master of the Day of Judgement). He is a rebel against economic and systematic oppression, and well-known drug dealer.

He is currently under investigation and being watched by the C.I.A./F.B.I./D.E.A. and the Michigan State Police-Joint Drug Trafficking Task Force. G33 Phezi Ali, (MALIK YAWM AD-DEEN) is also an inspiring writer, producer, and Hip-hop artist, who really wants to change his ways, but still be able to provide the best life for his children, family, and friends.

But due to his past criminal behavior, and felonious background. No employer would give him a decent job to take care of them all, so he uses alternative ways. But his 1/3rd counterpart, Darnell Diablo knows a secret. He knows what happened to the 17-year-old Gregory Dismukes, who was unknowingly an Extra Terra Astral hybrid. He knows exactly who murdered him and the reason why. And he is currently out to expose him, and all his evil Illuminati and Reptilian friends.

But, Nubu Solar RE, "The righteous awakened one". Does not see it that way. He believes in love, compassion, forgiveness, and the complete rehabilitation of all sentient beings. He knowns that energy cannot be destroyed.

He believes that, if he can somehow harness the superpower and abilities of both, Darnell Diablo and G33 Phezi Ali, he can use it to heal Gregory in that parallel reality where he was murdered.

Nubu Solar RE, a leader in quantum mysticism and reverse atomic technology, must create a multicolored spectrum and Tri-Star amulet called "Sekumsid." It is a derivative of the ancient Egyptian Sekhem healing system created by the lioness God Sekhmet. "Sekumsid," is a power harnessing multi-dimensional black whole, which gives its host direct contact with the source of all creation. It heals its possessor with complete harmony once activated.

Nubu Solar RE, must somehow unsuspiciously and simultaneously stand within 6 feet of each of them, then press the eye of the amulet, as it opens up the vacuum portal, crippling and sucking them inside of the void as it harnesses all of their powers.

But hard as it is to catch the dimension jumping Diablo, Nubu Solar RE must sadly do the same thing to G33 Phezi Ali, then use the powers of the amulet to travel back to the 90's, and give it to Gregory in his timeline, in order to prevent his untimely death. That will ultimately end the need and creation of the revengeful Darnell EL Diablo, and the materialistic G33 Phezi Ali.

The Devil's Advocate.

Did Marshall Mathews, commit a murder in Detroit 28 years ago? Home of the true tones of African American musical talent? (Motown) Did he rise to power as he knowingly or unknowingly sacrificed a Multi-Dimensional Crystalizing being known as Gregory Dismukes just to gain fame and fortune?

And who was it that really put him in the hands of Andrew Young? Also known as, Dr Andrew, was it the (Illuminati) Evil Reptilians, who's primary mission is to dumb down, destroy and silence the black community through acts of violence, drugs, ignorance, and negative music. To eliminate the rise of the black consciousness.

And is there a coincidence that the city of Detroit (Motown) area code is 13 13. And the 13th sacred letter of the alphabet being M? Hmmm, M&M? This is a synchronistic story about a young man by the name of Gregory Dismukes, whose nickname was also "Bruce" in Flint, Michigan, to the many that knew him. Is it a coincidence that Marshall's middle name is "Bruce" also? Gregory Dismukes was born Saturday 6/28/1975 at 2:50 am.

He developed unknown learning disabilities and speech difficulties as a child. He was later carjacked and shot in the head for a 1983 Chevrolet Malibu in 1994. By a group of unknown individuals on the eastside of Detroit. He was only 17 years old. And there it is again, our sacred number 13. (1994) 94. 9+4=13. Is it also a coincidence that 1975 is the Chinese zodiac year of the wood rabbit? Which is exactly what Marshall said he hit Greg over the head with, in his Greg freestyle rhyme.

Don't believe me? Check it out on YouTube. Also isn't Rabbit the name his mother called him in the 8-mile movie. (The Occult ritual) that acted out the scene of Gregory's murder and carjacking. As Marshall and his friends drive around shooting randomly with what looks exactly like the weapon used in Gregory's shooting.

147

They also had the nerve to shoot the sacred cow in the head, which represents Hathor, the ancient Egyptian goddess associated, later, with Isis (Auset) and, earlier, with Sekhmet, but eventually was considered the primeval goddess from whom all others were derived.

She is usually depicted as a woman with the head of a cow, ears of a cow, or simply in cow form. Check it all out on Googles. As the occult filmmakers mocked the Detroit police (Illuminati puppets) for not fully investigating the crime.

Due to the fact, that Gregory Dismukes was shot to death on Grainer St. which is down and around the corner from Marshall's home on the 19000 block of Dresden St. is very interesting. Was this not Marshall and his friends stomping ground? Google Marshall's old east-side Detroit home. And is it also a numerological coincidence, that Gregory's birthday of 06/28 can be alphanumerically found in the name M & M.

Let's see, the 13th sacred letter M+M=26 13+13=26 and 2+6=8 equals the combination of 628. And why did he repeatedly preform the same low vibrational freestyle about hitting a retarded kid named Greg in the head with a wooden leg? Check it out for yourself on YouTube/ Greg freestyle. And why was the name Greg used so negatively in the Eight-mile movie? Check it out again on YouTube/ 8 mile-Greg.

Was Marshall possessed by the illuminati (Reptilians) to commit another sacrifice after he gained success? Do we still need "Proof?" And why was the occult group "D-Twelve" designed after the western zodiac signs. In fact, there was not even 12 members in this group. Why would they call themselves the dirty dozen anyway? Were they all comedians?

And, why was Marshall accused of stealing Detroit rapper "E-Shom's" Acid rapping style? And why was the E-Shom song, "Word after Word" in which E-Shom says, "should I run from this place and get shot in the back," playing inside Gregory's 1983 Malibu when he was shot?

Was the Red E-Shom cassette tape removed from Gregory's tape deck, and listen to constantly by the young Marshall Mathews and his culprits in 1994? And furthermore, why was the name "**M&M**" used by one of Greg's family members in **Flint,** (**M**id-**M**ichigan) before Marshall ever even thought of it?

Another strange thing is that we've been trying to get information about the young Caucasian male who was caught driving the stolen Vehicle, but Detroit police is refusing to cooperate or release any additional information concerning this investigation. We were simply told to stop worrying about this old unsolved case. At that point, we realized that Marshall Mathews may be a victim, and is in fact a sleep walking/ MK Ultra Illuminati Reptilian puppet. Did he sell his soul?

Is he really a Malevolent Reptilian hybrid? Was he killed after gaining success and is now a Reptilian clone enjoying the fruit of Marshall's labor? And why after all of his success, did he fail to send Aid to the Flint, Michigan residents during the water crisis. But formulated a political rap rant against President Trump! And with that being said, we hereby disclose that Gregory Dismukes was in fact murdered in 1994, and all of the witnesses who can validate this to be true, have died as well.

So, did the unknown poverty-stricken occult practitioner Marshall pull the trigger for the Wicked Elite? Does he knowingly worship the Baphomet, which is a perversion of one's own spiritually androgynous self? Which In turn, gave birth to the Reptilian (Hell Boy) aka Darnell EL Diablo, prototype H3LL13OI. We'll let you be the judge of that.

The Egyptian Solar Deities.

Sekhmet (Sakhmet) is one of the oldest known Egyptian deities. Her name is derived from the Egyptian word "Sekhem" (which means "power" or "might") and is often translated as the "Powerful One" or "She who is Powerful". She is depicted as a lion-headed woman, sometimes with the addition of a sun disc on her head.

Sekhmet, in Egyptian religion, is a goddess of war and the destroyer of the enemies of the sun god RE. Sekhmet was also associated both with disease and with healing and medicine.

She is depicted as a lioness. She was the protector of the pharaohs and led them in warfare. Upon death, Sekhmet continued to protect them, bearing them to the afterlife. Sekhmet is a Solar RE deity, sometimes called the daughter of RE and often associated with the goddesses Hathor and Bastet.

Bastet was worshiped in Bubastis in Lower Egypt, originally as a lioness goddess, a role shared by other deities such as Sekhmet. Eventually Bastet and Sekhmet were characterized as two aspects of the same goddess, with Sekhmet representing the powerful warrior and protector aspect and Bastet, who increasingly was depicted as a cat, representing a gentler aspect.

A Solar deity (also sun goddess or sun god) is a sky deity who represents the Sun, or an aspect of it, usually by its perceived power and strength. Solar deities and Sun worship can be found throughout most of recorded history in various forms. The Sun is sometimes referred to by its Latin name **Sol** or by its Greek name Helios. The English word sun stems from Proto-Germanic *sunnǭ.

Osiris (/oʊˈsaɪrɪs/, from the Egyptian pantheon is the god of fertility, agriculture, the afterlife, the dead, RE-surrection, life, and vegetation. He was classically depicted as a green-skinned deity with a pharaoh's beard, partially mummy-wrapped at the legs, wearing a distinctive atef crown, and holding a symbolic crook and flail.

He was one of the first to be associated with the mummy wrap. When his brother, Set, cut him up into pieces after killing him, Isis, his wife, found all the pieces and wrapped his body up, enabling him to return to life. Osiris was at times considered the eldest son of the god Geb and the sky goddess Nut, as well as being brother and husband of Isis, with Horus being considered his posthumously begotten son. He was also associated with the epithet Khenti-Amentiu, meaning "Foremost of the Westerners", a reference to his kingship in the land of the dead. Through syncretism with Iah, he is also a god of the Moon.

Osiris can be considered the brother of Isis, Set, Nephthys, and Horus the Elder, and father of Horus the Younger. The first evidence of the worship of Osiris was found in the middle of the Fifth Dynasty of Egypt (25th century BC), although it is likely that he was worshiped much earlier; the Khenti-Amentiu epithet dates to at least the First Dynasty and was also used as a pharaonic title.

Most information available on the Osiris myth is derived from allusions contained in the Pyramid Texts at the end of the Fifth Dynasty, later New Kingdom source documents such as the Shabaka Stone and the "The Contending's of Horus and Seth", and much later, in narrative style from the writings of Greek authors including Plutarch and Diodorus Siculus.

Osiris was the judge of the dead and the underworld agency that granted all life, including sprouting vegetation and the fertile flooding of the Nile River. He was described as "He Who is Permanently Benign and Youthful" and the "Lord of Silence". The kings of Egypt were associated with Osiris in death – as Osiris rose from the dead so they would be in union with him and inherit eternal life through a process of imitative magic.

Through the hope of new life after death, Osiris began to be associated with the cycles observed in nature, in particular vegetation and the annual flooding of the Nile, through his links with the heliacal rising of Orion and Sirius at the start of the new year. Osiris was widely worshipped until the decline of ancient Egyptian religion during the rise of Christianity in the Roman Empire.

Isis was the daughter of the earth God Geb and the sky Goddess Nut and the sister of the deities Osiris, Set, and Nephthys. She was also wife to Osiris, and bore him a son, Horus (Heru), who would later on be plagiarized by the Roman Catholic church as Jesus, which was in fact a story crated to cut off humanities own divinity, preventing the rise of Christ Consciousness for the purpose of control by the Evil Extra Terra Astrals.

Thoth, (Greek), Egyptian Djhuty/Tehuti, in Egyptian religion, a God of the moon, of reckoning, of learning, and of writing. He was held to be the inventor of writing, the creator of languages, the scribe, interpreter, and adviser (scientist) of the Gods, and the representative of the sun God, RE. He is the creator of the M.A.R.E. Program. He was also one of the most important gods of ancient Egypt alternately said to be self-created or born of the seed of Horus (Khrest), from the forehead of Set.

Ra (Greek) Egyptian RE, was believed to rule in all parts of the created world: the sky, the Earth, and the underworld. He was the god of the sun, order, kings, and the sky. Re was portrayed as a falcon and shared characteristics with the sky God Horus. (Heru). All forms of life were believed to have been created by Re

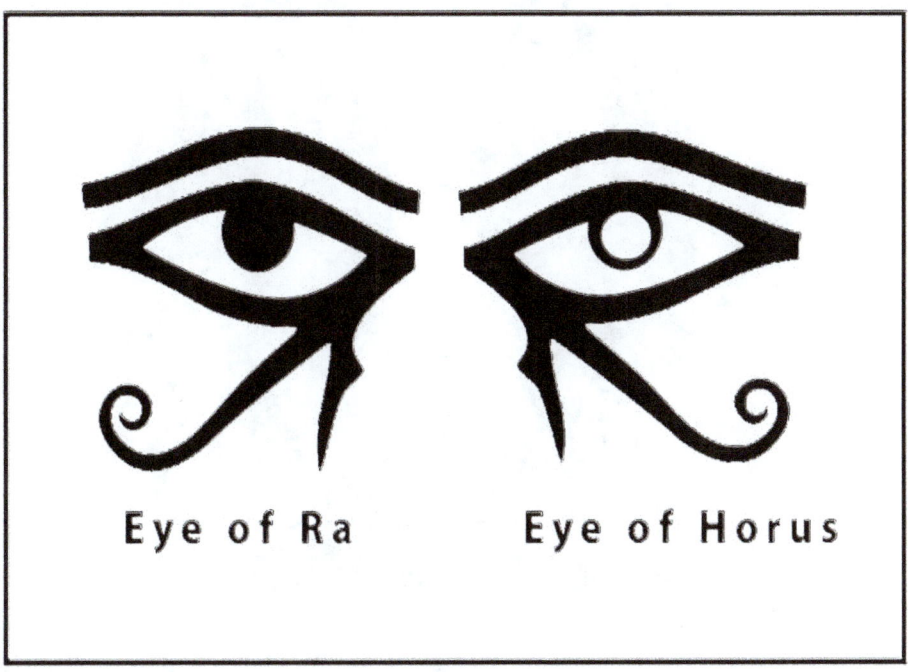

Eye of Ra   Eye of Horus

.*Akhenaten.*

Akhenaten (pronounced /ˌækəˈnɑːtən/), also spelled Echnaton, Akhenaton, Ikhnaton, and Khuenaten (Ancient Egyptian: ☐ḫ-n-jtn, meaning "Effective for the Aten"), was an ancient Egyptian pharaoh reigning c. 1353–1336 or 1351–1334 BC, the tenth ruler of the Eighteenth Dynasty.

Akhenaten, an Extra Terra Astral Hybrid was the last pharaoh entrusted with the sacred and ancient Extra Terra Astral knowledge of Stargates, free energy, and antigravity technologies. This knowledge was handed down from an advanced interstellar race of Extra terra Astrals in the remote past.

But an evil Reptilian race infiltrated the Egyptian priesthood and banking systems, then formed the Brotherhood of the Snake. A secret-society set on destroying Akhenaten's flourishing kingdom and suppressing the sacred knowledge of the pharaohs, and Benevolent Extra Terra Astrals. Some of the sacred knowledge was written in the dead sea scrolls and kept hidden by a group of antient Essenes.

The original purpose of the pyramids was to transmit energy to expand (Christ) consciousness, but they were decommissioned by the Reptilians who commissioned new world Governments for total world domination to date. But a plan was set in place before the beginning of **time,** for the liberation and ascension of the planet and all of her willing inhabitants.

The Guardian previously known as Akhenaton while incarnated, is from the Aton group and is intimately involved with the reclamation of Christos mission, the Paliadorian Activations on the earth.

His mission is designed to protect those who are from the ancient original Christos and Y'shua bloodlines, of which he was involved in bringing to the planet, while working with the Azurite teams over 2,000 years ago.

He is the original family patriarch as it is his bloodline that propagates in the Krystic bloodlines still today, although much misinformation is still propagated about him to discredit his legacy, same as that in the case of Dr. Malachi Z. York.

Y'shua/Jesus Christ (aka J12) is a Sirian Blue Human from the future that came to change the 3rd dimensional timelines and bring the Essenes, Christos Templars and Law of One Ascension knowledge and its consciousness technology back to the planet earth.

He is a direct descendant of Akhenaton's genetics, as a result he is the father of all Christ lines on earth. This mission was in response to the DNA damage the planet and humanity had most recently suffered after the Luciferian Rebellion, and then the after the Sumerian-Egypt Invasion, which was the final destruction of the Mother's Staff principle and Aqua Ray in the earth core.

His group mission under the direction of the High Lyran-Sirian council was to work with the future earth 5D Taran multi-dimensional Templar crew called the Azurites, originally organized by the RA Confederacy. The disbanded Azurite team is now hosted directly by the Emerald Order.

The Emerald Order of Elohim seeded the Anuhazi Feline Elohim races through the Lyran 12th Stargate, Aramatena. They are also known as the founders of the Christos races, the Eieyani Grail lines that include the Oraphim. The Emerald Order are the founders of the Interdimensional Free World Councils, as the result of the Paliadorian Covenant to ensure that all souls lost in the fallen or Phantom Matrix are returned back to the God Source.

As a team they were working with repairing the planetary architecture, doing Soul Retrieval from the Lemurian Holocaust and Atlantian Cataclysm, preparing the Ley Lines, Planetary Grid Network and Planetary Gates to help align for the ending Ascension Cycle.

The collaboration of Guardian teams continues in the next cycle of the Rise of the Paliadorians in order to fulfill the physicalization of the Covenant of Paliador through the reclamation of the Christos-Sophia and Amenti soul rescue mission.

Akhenaton returned the ancient Essene knowledge of the All-One, or Law of One in an attempt to restore male-female balance in the planet's geographical center and bring through the embodiment of the Law of Gender. The Sun was symbolic of being the source of everything, and the Solar body of Aten or Aton was considered to be the bringer of eternal life in order to achieve full consciousness enlightenment through hierogamic union.

In the timelines of Egypt, as well as subsequent abuse of Alien Machinery technology to open portals in the 2D Underworld (which created time and space rips), manifested incredible damage to the planet, and her elemental and nature kingdoms. The damage made to the planetary field created multiple problems with human soul fragments, soul inversion, subconscious shadow personalities and Negative alien manipulation of these vulnerabilities.

One of these events was with 18th Dynastic timeline with Akhenaton, a Sirian Annunaki Templar Guardian, of which the erroneous use of opening portal systems for Ascension occurred while attempting to move out trapped souls from the Atlantian Cataclysm and Lemurian Holocaust periods.

This ascension project ended in failure and destroyed his massive life's work in attempting to recreate the Krystic architecture and Law of One principles within Amarna, upon the earth. Upon opening rips in the 2D Underworld, which unleashed harmful forces into the higher frequency planes, it fragmented many souls who were sucked through its black hole. shortly after this event, he retreated from his rule in pain, and was murdered as a heretic King.

Some of us are here again, to complete this project in this time cycle and have been working to heal the schism this created with the 2D kingdom. We all incarnated here on Earth with a purpose, please pardon me while I do mine.

The 2D dimensional field is where many animal and nature kingdoms exist as group consciousness, and were harmfully impacted by this quarantine, where they could not access links into other dimensional consciousness, and in effect, were trapped in that space.

Because this quarantine is being sequentially lifted, many more of us are being contacted by species of the nature and animal kingdom. As this quarantine lifts, we will begin to remember how to communicate with the intelligent beings of nature and give them their access back into the higher realms.

All beings of the earth are of an intelligent group consciousness, and as we begin to take back our guardianship of the earth, this means we are the responsible stewards to cooperate in harmony with the natural kingdoms.

Akhenaten had seven or eight children based on inscriptions. Egyptologists are fairly certain about his six daughters, who are well attested in contemporary depictions. Among his six daughters, Meritaten was born in regnal year one or five; Meketaten in year four or six; Ankhesenpaaten, later queen of Tutankhamun, before year five or eight; Neferneferuaten Tasherit in year eight or nine; Neferneferure in year nine or ten; and Setepenre in year ten or eleven.

Tutankhamun, born Tutankhaten, was most likely Akhenaten's son, too, with Nefertiti or another wife. There is less certainty around Akhenaten's relationship with Smenkhkare, his coregent or successor, who could have been Akhenaten's eldest son with an unknown wife, and later married Meritaten, his own sister to keep a pure bloodline.

As the result of the recent escalation of AI Timeline Wars, the Guardian Christos Mission has reached the stage of dismantling sections of the actual phantom matrix infrastructure, the actual artificial intelligence architecture put into place through the insertion of the Artificial Tree of Life.

The phantom matrix uses four main black pillars in reversal architecture to power up their artificial creations, based upon holographic inserts made of the four main Grail Point Christos Mission Guardians and their respective timelines.

Akhenaton despised politics and was working for the human Law of One. His mission in spiral time was embodiment of the 5D Grail, protector of Rod and Staff Father codes, and to utilize Arc technology to transit Taran soul fragments and help prepare for upgraded 5D ascension timelines and Yeshua's and King Arthur's future mission with Stonehenge.

He chose to embody in a Ruby Sun Template in order to attempt to help heal the Venusian Christos bloodline from ongoing Luciferian manipulation and prepare for Y'shua to embody into a full 12 strand DNA silicate matrix.

His genetics and timeline were cloned for future False Father Alien God archetypes and used in the Essene Divide artificial matrix for use to invert the Christos Mission, and to be used as psychological weapons by imposters that would divide and conquer the Blue Flame Essene groups.

His holographic insert has been placed at the top of the pyramidal schemes of many Luciferian cults and secret societies, as his cloned DNA and image is used by Thothian-Luciferians for the (Barack Obama) false Christ imposter front, in the attempt to hijack the 5D Grail Point and thwart humanity's Ascension in 2012..

Reincarnation literally means "to be made flesh again." According to this metaphysical concept, some essential part of a living being survives death to be reborn in a new body. This means that a new personality is developed during each life in the physical world, but some part of the self remains constant throughout the successive lives.

Human cloning literally means "duplication" or the creation of a genetically identical copy (or clone) of a human. The term is generally used to refer to artificial human cloning, which is the reproduction of human cells and tissue. It does not refer to the natural conception and delivery of identical twins.

Following that idea that there must be some similarities between the original soul and the human being hosting the "reincarnated self," theories have flourished that consider lookalikes of every kind to be proof of a cloning or reincarnation process at work.

According to a number of theories that emerged a few years ago, former US President Barack Obama could actually be a clone of Akhenaten, an Egyptian pharaoh whose reign dates from 1353 BC to 1336 BC.

Supporting this thesis is the quite convincing physical resemblance between the sculpted representation of Akhenaten and Obama, not to mention a number of similarities between the political visions of the two rulers. Akhenaten was the first pharaoh to introduce the practice of worshipping one god, Aten (the Sun-Disk God, with Aten meaning "the sun"), eradicating polytheism.

The fact that Obama's campaign logo symbolized a rising sun should be a clear reference to Akhenaten's politics. Funnily enough, Michelle Obama is also said to be a clone, and look like someone close to Akhenaten. She shows a certain resemblance to the pharaoh's mother, Tiye.

The two daughters of the Obamas, meanwhile, could be the reincarnations of Akhenaten and his wife Nefertiti's daughters: the code names of Malia Ann and Sasha Obama in the CIA files are Rosebud and Radiance, which might refer to the same flowers Akhenaten and Nefertiti worshipped before their declaration of the Sun God.

Obama is not the only leader targeted by the conspiracy theorists of reincarnation and cloning. In fact, the president of the Russian Federation, Vladimir Putin, could apparently be the reincarnation of a well-known historical leader, Julius Caesar.

The striking physical similarities between the two rulers would add to the pivotal role that "betrayal" played in both Caesar and Putin's relationship with power. Balanced against this, of course, stands a previous theory, which states that the "real" Vladimir Putin was assassinated by a joint CIA/MI6 operation few years back, and replaced by a clone.

Anthropology

1. the study of human societies and cultures and their development.
2. the study of human biological and physiological characteristics and their evolution.
3. Tomb Raiders.

Obama's mother, Stanley Ann Dunham (November 29, 1942 – November 7, 1995) was an American anthropologist who specialized in the economic anthropology and rural development of Indonesia. She was the mother of Barack Obama, the 44th President of the United States.

Dunham was known as Stanley Ann Dunham through high school, then as Ann Dunham, Ann Obama, Ann Soetoro, a.k.a. Ann Sutoro, and resumed her maiden name, Ann Dunham, later in life. She was diagnosed with uterine cancer. By this time, the cancer had spread to her ovaries. She moved back to Hawaii to live near her widowed mother and died on November 7, 1995, she was 52.

Artificial insemination (AI) is the deliberate introduction of sperm into a female's cervix or uterine cavity for the purpose of achieving a pregnancy through in vivo fertilization by means other than sexual intercourse. It is a fertility treatment for humans, and is common practice in animal breeding, including dairy cattle (see Frozen bovine semen) and pigs.

Barack Hussein Obama Sr. (June 18, 1936-November 24, 1982) was a Kenyan senior Governmental economist and the father of Barack Obama, the 44th president of the United States. He was selected for a (special) program to attend college in the United States and studied at the University of Hawaii where he met Stanley Ann Dunham, whom he married in 1961. They supposedly had a son, Barack II.

During Barack Obama's campaign for president in 2008, throughout his presidency, and afterwards, "there was extensive news coverage of Obama's religious preference, birthplace, and of the individuals questioning his religious belief and citizenship—efforts eventually known as the 'birther movement'", by which name it is widely referred to across media. The movement falsely asserted that Obama was ineligible to be President of the United States because he was not a **natural-born** citizen of the U.S. as required by Article Two of the Constitution.

Obama's father later went to Harvard University for graduate school, where he earned an M.A. in economics, and returned to Kenya in 1964. He saw his so-called son Barack once more, when he was about 10 years old, who would later on graduate from the same Harvard University.

Obama Sr. had conflicts with the wise Kenyan president Jomo Kenyatta, which adversely affected his career. He was fired and blacklisted in Kenya as a trader, finding it nearly impossible to get a job. Obama Sr. was also involved in three mysterious and very serious car accidents during his final years; he died as a result of the last one on November 24, 1982, at the age of 46.

Stanley Dunham, the father of Ann Dunham, Obama's Mother who's distant cousins include six U.S. presidents - James Madison, Harry Truman, Lyndon Johnson, Jimmy Carter, George H. W. Bush and George W. Bush.

This goes to show that the Negative (Illuminati) Thothian-Lucifearian bloodline runs very deep that makes up the Presidential candidate's genetics for the purposes of direct Negative Alien control. And it also proves the RE-A-SON why Dr. Malachi Z. York and other spiritual leaders are investigated falsely imprisoned, and or assassinated as a suppression tactic by the FBI/COINTELLPRO.

Ultimately, perpetual ignorance, fear tactics and negative media outlets are used as tools to herd the sheep, while official Alien agenda, and discloser is being withheld, as "Classified information".

We have generated a graphic aid to help assist in the visualization of the concept of artificial timelines projecting from the phantom matrix, which describes the AI Timeline Wars.

Please take note that this is not intended to be a literal representation; it is a visualization intended to help the mind grasp the blended reality system of organic timelines and artificial timelines that we experience at this time on the earth.

Synchronicity.

1.   The simultaneous occurrence of events
which appear significantly related but have no discernible causal connection.

Dr Malachi Z. York (Djehuti) was born on 6/26/1945. Gregory D. Dismukes (Tehuti) was born on 6/28/1975. Adding Greg's birthday month and day is 16, 1+6=7. Adding Dr York's, it is 14, 1+4=5. Adding them together gives the number 75. In the year of 2020, Gregory turns 45, and Dr York turns 75.

Their birth dates are 2 days apart. They both are multiple individuals within one. Using western astrology, they are cancers. While using Sidereal astrology, they both are Gemini, the twins. Both men possess multiple personalities. Both men are Multi-Dimensional Extra Terra Astrals. York's mother's name is Mary; Greg's mothers name is Donna Marie. Both men are Recording Artists.

President Trump is the 45th President. He's the first U.S. President to create a Space Force. And he too, is a three faced Gemini, who may well be the first President to release full Extraterrestrial Discloser to the open public in an undisclosed dimension. We are mentally encouraging him and or possibly the incumbent President to release the very innocent Dr York, at this very moment.

Here are a few more strange sequences of events, and synchronicities designed by Djehuti. The Abraham Lincoln and John F. Kennedy sequence.

Abraham Lincoln was elected to Congress in 1846. John F. Kennedy was elected to Congress in 1946. Abraham Lincoln was elected President in 1860. John F. Kennedy was elected President in 1960. Both wives lost their children while living in the White House. Both Presidents were shot on a Friday. Both Lincoln and Kennedy were shot from behind in the head while seated. Both were succeeded by men named Johnson. Andrew Johnson, who succeeded Lincoln, was born in 1808. Lyndon Johnson, who succeeded Kennedy, was born in 1908.

Booth (who shot Lincoln) ran from the theater and was caught in a warehouse. Oswald (who shot Kennedy) ran from a warehouse and was caught in a theater. Both Booth and Oswald were assassinated before their trials.

Obama and Lincoln.

Both men adopted Illinois as their home state, but only one did it as an adult. Lincoln was born in Kentucky in February of 1809. His family moved to Indiana when he was 8 years old, and later moved to Illinois. He stayed in Illinois as an adult, marrying and raising a family. Obama was born in Hawaii in August of 1961.

His mother moved to Indonesia with his stepfather, where he lived from age 5 to 10. He then returned to Hawaii to live with his grandparents. He moved to Illinois in 1985 and returned to Illinois after obtaining a law degree from Harvard.

Both Obama and Lincoln were thrust into the spotlight following major speeches. We know Lincoln's rhetorical prowess as much from the Lincoln-Douglas debates as from the Gettysburg Address. We also know that Lincoln wrote his speeches, by hand, and usually delivered the speech as written.

On the other hand, Obama, who has invoked Lincoln in almost every major speech he has given, has a speechwriter. His name was Jon Favreau, and he is very familiar with Lincoln. Favreau wrote draft speeches for Obama including the one for the killing of Osama bin laden.

When Lincoln was elected in November of 1860, the country was divided over the issue of slavery. In December of 1860, South Carolina seceded from the Union. By February of 1861, six additional southern states had seceded. Lincoln was sworn in as president in March 1861.

When Obama began running for president, a majority of Americans opposed the war in Iraq as well as the performance of then-President George W. Bush, whose father, George H.W. Bush promised a "New World Order" in 1991. A quarter of a century later, we're finally catching a glimpse of it—like it or not.

Holographic data it seems, are just electrical impulses interpreted by our brains.

A holographic Universe means information that makes up what we perceive as a 3D reality is stored on a 2D surface, including time. This means, essentially, everything you see, and experience is an illusion.

Illuminati.

(Light Consciousness -vs- Dark Consciousness)

We are not conspiracy theorists. we deal with real facts, not theory. Some of the people we write about, we have had actual encounters with. And some that we expose are alive and very dangerous. The darkness has never liked the light. Yet, many of the secrets of the Illuminati are locked up tightly simply because secrecy is a way of life.

We are deeply committed to the facts of history rather than the cover stories the public is fed to manipulate them. we do not fear the Illuminati taking over this country and doing away with the Constitution, because they took over this country long ago, being a Christ does not mean we should fear. Perfect love for the Source casts out all fear for the situations we are currently in.

Don't think for a moment that you are going to vote the Illuminati out of office. They control the major and minor political parties. They control the process of government, they control the process of information flow, they control the process of creating money and finally they control Christianity.

This book will not tell you how to deal with the Illuminati families. This book was designed to give an overview of what the Illuminati is. In short, the Illuminati are generational Malevolent bloodlines which have gained the most power. This book 'Extra Terra Astral" was not written to cause fear or a witch hunt.

It wasn't written to provide another theory. This book is not about a theory. It is about the Secret Occult Government which rule the world. When brought together, the facts of this book will begin to speak for themselves without us. We don't ask that you take our word for it. Investigate for yourself. God Himself has told us that the whole world lies in the power of the wicked ones.

You must have the courage, the knowledge, and the wisdom, to see the power that secret societies exercise from behind the scenes. We have to take a tragic look at the passing of many rappers including Juice World, who died at the age of 21; but not before predicting his own death, depicting his own death, telling us he joined the Illuminati and forewarning of his own demise. Did he sign a Faustian satanic contract with the music industry? Who knows? We just know that it takes a brave and fearless soul to speak on such things.

The story of how the Illuminati first ended up in a rap song is a lot like your average Illuminati conspiracy. The genesis of the lyrics quoted above, from the 1995 remix to EL-EL Kool Jay's "I Shot Ya," involves a beef between 2pac and K. Murray: and Murray's subsequent beef with Mobb Deep's Prodigy. The particulars aren't especially important. What is important is that line, from Prodigy, that everyone remembers. It was the first time the Illuminati was mentioned prominently on a record, nestled within the middle of a needlessly complex series of beefs.

"Illuminati Want My Mind, Soul, And My Body."

It was the beginning of an entirely new school of thought in hip-hop, one as intelligent and informed as it was suspicious and paranoid. Prodigy was referring to the Illuminati conspiracy theory: the idea that there's a network of shadowy, powerful individuals bent on controlling society by rebuilding it as a "New World Order" under a totalitarian worldwide government. Mentions of the Illuminati in hip-hop quickly spiked from there: J- Z sampled Prodigy's line from "I Shot Ya" for "De'Evils" on his 1996 debut Reasonable Doubt, sparking rumors that persist to this day that he is associated with the organization.

Prodigy published an open letter he had written in prison alleging that his old rival J-Z "promotes the lifestyle of the beast (Dark Ones). The Hip-hop culture are the innovators of so many popular fashions, styles, and sounds. Yet rarely sees trends with such extended lifelines.

And as usual, this trend among rappers has crossed over to pop culture in a big way. Today, the Illuminati theory is quite relevant as ever, often used as a way to justify the continued success of artists who are accused of being puppets of this mysterious web of faceless figureheads.

M&M payed homage to Mobb Deep as he chose the song "Shook One's part 2" as his "Detroit 8 mile" movie opener. Also he and J-Z re-recorded the spine chilling song "Renegade" laced with blasphemous insults and Anti-Christ ideology, like: "Do you fools listen to music or just skim through it" "Maybe it's food for the spirit" "scattered brain atheist" and "Do you have any clue what I had to do to get here" as if there were sacrifices made to become millionaires, as they claimed to be free "to talk about anything" except the real Illuminati.

There's an endless stream of books, podcasts, and blogs examining the Illuminati's use of the media and entertainment to carry out its agenda, and there are innumerable YouTube videos about the Illuminati with millions of views.

The Illuminati is always somehow part of the conversation when a celebrity like Whitney Houston or, more recently, Prince passes away prematurely. Its signifiers—triangles, covered eyes, devil's horns that are consistently evoked in music videos and press photos. What's so perplexing about the Illuminati theory and its continued life is that it's just that: a theory.

Despite the term's prominence in hip-hop and pop culture, there is no proof that the Illuminati really exists, and there's not a single artist who has admitted to being affiliated with it. Then why, for more than two decades, has the existence of an unconfirmed secret society been consistently connected to the music industry? Why do the rumors refuse to go away?

Secret societies have existed for many centuries, and at one point, the Illuminati was real. In 1776, a German professor named Adam Weishaupt founded the Bavarian Illuminati, also known as the Order of the Illuminati, as a response to the Roman Catholic Church's power over philosophical and scientific thought.

Weishaupt aimed to recruit from within the Freemasons—a secret society that still openly exists today—to disseminate ideas of the Enlightenment. Over the course of the next decade or so he accrued an estimated 2,500 members.

Though the Bavarian Illuminati disbanded by 1787 and seemingly remained inactive in the centuries that followed, rumors of its existence continued into the 20th century. They surged when President George H.W. Bush, in a 1991 speech marking the end of the Cold War, mentioned forming a "New World Order." Some interpreted the speech as a sign that the Illuminati had been reconstituted or had never left.

It makes sense that hip-hop would gravitate toward such a conspiracy theory. The black community has plenty of reasons to be distrustful of the Government as well. Many so-called conspiracies have, in time, turned out to be true. For example, in 1932, the U.S. Public Health Service conducted the Tuskegee Study of Untreated Syphilis in Negro Males, which involved 399 black men with syphilis. The "study" lasted 40 years before a special panel intervened — the afflicted men were never informed that they had syphilis and were never given penicillin.

A $10 million out-of-court settlement followed in 1974. In another infamous incident, the Church Committee, a U.S. senate commission, confirmed that the FBI's COINTELPRO initiative carried out illegal operations to interfere with, spy on and systematically destroy the Black Panthers, and many other Civil Rights organizations.

Many Conspiracy Theories believe that these real-life government conspiracies are targeting black people and planted the seeds for the Illuminati's popularity today. "Hip-hop served as catalyst for people to talk about issues that were relevant to them, things like discrimination, poverty, the criminal justice system, which are often seemingly slanted against African-Americans. But, all the Artists with positive messages were quickly removed and replaced with a more negative musical undertone.

Prodigy of Mobb Deep mysteriously passed away in 2017 after going public about the Illuminati. He was 42 years old when he died at a hospital in Las Vegas. The official cause of his death remains unknown. However, there are new claims of a conspiracy by theorists who believe the Illuminati may have been involved. Prodigy arrived at a Las Vegas hospital following a Mobb Deep performance in the city. From birth, the rapper (real name Albert Johnson) had struggled with sickle cell anemia.

It appears the rapper had battled an emergency related to this condition a couple of days prior to his hospitalization. In the public, he had appeared relatively healthy, with no signs of sickness. But after the rapper had passed away, a rumor had spread claiming that He died after choking on an egg.

He had been working on a musical exposing the Illuminati. He was in the middle of writing it, so it wasn't yet released. His last album "Hegelian Dialectic" (The Book of Revelation) was the fifth and final studio album. The album was released on January 20, 2017 through Infamous Records. The first single from the album was "Tyranny", which was released in February 2016. It remains a conspiracy how the album was removed from all music streaming platforms, and authorities have yet to release the actual cause of his death.

Furthermore, he was a devout student of the Master Teacher Dr Malachi Z, York whom through mistrial and Government conspiracy continues to be falsely and inhumanly imprisoned. We are not at war; we are indeed in a spiritual war.

Reasonable Doubt.

After analyzing all of the data intellectually synced, sent forth by way of the M.A.R.E. Program. Yet and still, it exists beyond the reasonable doubt, that Marshall Mathews may have not pulled the trigger himself, as we are aware of his now deceased childhood friend's violent behavior as well. But due to the synchronization of these events along with Marshall's dark violent rhymes, psychological issues, and unloving clone like characteristics. We certainly would like to think that it is a very strong possibility.

That is not without mentioning how this information was downloaded to us after our visit to the Sedona, Arizona Vortex. (S.A.V.E.) Which is an earth energy portal (Chakra) and Christ consciousness grid point. There we met with Shawn Pereira, and the Re-Turn council and many others who instantly upgraded our radio wave capabilities. We would also like to take this time to let it be known that we agree with Mr. West when he says Christ is king. Besides, Jesus Christ only represents our own Christ being within. Which is our own oneness of love and divinity.

Warning! You are now in a parallel reality. A parallel reality in which Gregory Dismukes survived. Welcome to the M.A.R.E. Program. It would now be blasphemous to again try to murder a Christ being after the attained spiritual enlightenment (Ascension).

That would possibly be the worst night M.A.R.E. You'll ever experience. Now ask yourself, is death worth remembering? This is without saying, that for all the times you probably could have died......**Maybe you did.**

Blac' Santa.

It was 13 days before Christmas when Darnell met Kimberly (the widow) and her beautiful daughters. She's been a single mom for six months after her husband and children's father mysteriously passed away of a sudden extreme case of dementia. Thus, this sickness effects every person different. It can manifest itself uniquely. The speed at which dementia progresses varies widely. On average, a person with Alzheimer's disease live 4 to 8 years after a diagnosis, but some have been seen to live as long as 20 years. Kimberly wasn't sad about his death because for a period of time he'd became very violent towards her.

They were teenagers when they first met. That's when she and her sister moved in with him and his mother. They lived at the A&L Mobile Home Park, at 20785 Schulte Avenue, on the north side of East 8 Mile Road. At first, he was a bit shy, as he lacked verbal communication skills. But she saw him to be quite interesting. He'd tell her about his dreams of becoming an artist and showing her the many pieces of his artwork.

Strange as it seemed to her that what she saw were very dark images as if he was trying to communicate with the dead. All of his images were very disturbing to her as she asks him about his spiritual life. He then said with a loud voice, "Fuck you! Fuck this! fuck them! fuck me! Fuck off in a holocaust, in the winter with Jack Frost! Bitch, I'll kill you! For trying to disrespect my masterpiece! Fuck peace, bitch please, call me Jason Voorhees! I'll cut you in half, bag the half, then I'll eat your other half!"

As Marshall continued his lyrical assault, Kimberly just got up and walked out the room as she tried to tune out his angry rant of synonyms and syllables. She instantly realized that he was sick and needed help. She noticed his depression along with his poor eating habits, so she'd try cooking him healthy meals.

One time he knocked the plate out of her hand, when he saw that it was only mixed vegetables and cornbread. As she and her sister had nowhere else to live, she dealt with the verbal outburst, and occasional physical and sexual abuse. She later found out the he had a strange sexual relationship with his own mother. But it was too late to walk out of his life because she found out that she'd became pregnant.

As time passed, she noticed him continuously leaving out the trailer at about 2 or 3 in the morning. She witnesses him coming in with blood on his clothing and asking him if he were ok. Although that wasn't the strangest things she'd see while living with him.

One day he came home in panic mode, screaming "they set me up! They set me up! I knew it". He again had blood on his clothing. As he was unemployed, she had to make ends meet by being intimate with older men she'd meet outside of the park at night. This is around the time when she found out the gender of her baby.

Her due date was December 25th, and she hadn't thought of a name yet. She'd think to herself about how wonderful it would be to have an angel from god to come and assist her. She then felt a kick from the unborn child as she wished upon a star. She was watching the 11 o'clock news when the reporter mentioned the annual return of Hailey's comet.

This is when the name stood out to her. That's when he again came in with blood on his clothing screaming about a witch following him. She immediately got up and called him a complete psychopath. It seems that his psychotic behavior had gotten the best of her. It wasn't until she found out that he was abusing prescription drugs that she'd seek professional help for him.

Until this day she wondered how someone could be so violent. She thought about the conversations she'd have with him before his sickness and death. It seems she'd only think of him when "Sweet home Alabama," played on the radio station that was preset by the violent young man.

That's when her phone rang, she answered on the third ring with a soft voice, "Hello," for it was Darnell Diablo calling her. She loved talking to him because the way he'd give his undivided attention. He lied and told her is name was Bruce to conceal his true identity and motif. She had met him at a local Walmart about 2 weeks before Christmas and her daughter's birthday.

 He approached her and said that he doesn't usually do things like this, but he'd like to be her and her children's "Secret Santa". Although it would be no secret, she'd play along. Shortly after returning home, her daughters noticed a squeaky laugh coming from their bedroom closet. They heard it saying, "be not afraid, to take my hand, everybody, come take a stand. We'll walk this road together, through the storm, Whatever weather, hot or warm, just letting you know that, you're not alone, holla if you feel like you've been down this same road."

But as the little girls became frighten, they began hollering and screaming, for their mom. "What, what is it?" Kimberly screamed! "It's in the closet," the older child said crying. Kimberly immediately opening the closet door to see only a little wooden toy rabbit. She said "see, there's nothing there, now you children go back to sleep. It's Christmas Eve and Santa is on his way." She then closed the bedroom door and walked to her room to rest.

Then as the little girls loudly screamed again "mommy, mommy" Kimberly rushes back inside the bedroom. "What is it, what's wrong." She said. They said with a frightened tone, "we just saw some flying monkeys outside the window." Kimberly laughed as she looked to see what the young girls were talking about. She offered them to come sleep with her as they then cheered.

Meanwhile, Darnell Diablo loaded a sample of Kim's hair into his Electronic DNA locater that he secretly acquired at Walmart. He then told the computer to play his favorite song, "Blac Santa" by Darnell Diablo.

Then there were three knocks at the front door. She answered, "who is it?" The man said, "who is Bruce Wayne?" She said, "Batman?" He said, "nope try again." She said, "is it The Blac' Santa Claus?", with a little laugh.

He said "yes," followed by "He's a sex Machine, and the king of the Dope fiends", as he too expressed his laughter, with his "E-Shom" quote. She then opened the door and invited him in. He said, "hello little girls", with his Grinch sounding voice. The then kids laughed. He then said, "I have presents for each and every one of you, Including Mom".

The kids cheered and began hugging the black Santa. This was a bit strange, because although they were not his biological kids, he loved the little white children as if they were his own. He then said, "wait right here, I'll be right back".

He then walked outside in glee as he approached his autonomous bright red vehicle. He blinked one eye, and sucked his left rabbit looking tooth to pop open the trunk of the bright red vehicle.

He then grabbed 3 PlayStations, 6 video games, and 3 Unidentified Cellular Devices, then returned to enter their home. He then said, "this is for you; this is for you! And this was made especially for you!"

He was then greeted with a plate full of chocolate chip cookies. As he grabbed the one with the least chocolate chips, he said, "you wouldn't happen to have a cold glass of breast milk to go along with that, now would you?", as he displayed his devilish grin.

Then one of the daughters went into the kitchen to fetch him a glass of cow's milk. He then said loudly, "Do I look like a psycho? Do I look like the type of nut case that would go on farmland to suck on a cows Titties? I'm just joking. thanks, but no thanks, I'll pass.

Now you kids get to bed, while I get a story book", he said with his animated "Jim Carrey" voice. As he tucked them all in bed, he softly said "are you all tucked in?" They said, "yeah". He said, "Here we go!"

"Once upon a time not too long ago when people wore pajamas and lived life slow. When laws were stern, and justice stood. And people were behaving like they ought to, good. There lived a boy named Marshal who was misled. By a boy name D'shawn, and this is what he said, 'Me and you Marshall, going to make sum cash. Robbin' up folks and making a dash', They did the job; money came with ease. But one couldn't stop, it's like he had a disease. He robbed another, and another, and a sister, and her brother, tried to rob a man who was a Detective undercover. The cop grabbed his arm, he started acting erratic. He said, 'Keep still, Marshall, no need for static'. Punched him in his belly and he gave him a slap. But little did he know that Marshall was strapped. Shady pulled out a gun, he said 'Why did you hit me?' The barrel was set straight for the cop's kidney. The cop got scared. Shady starts to figure, 'I'll do years if I pull this trigger'. So, he then dashed and ran around the block. Cop radioed in, to another lady cop. He ran by a tree; there he saw this sister. She shot for the head, he shot back but he missed her. Looked around good, and from expectations. So, he decided he'd head for the subway stations. But she was coming, and he made a left. He was running top speed until he ran out of breath. Knocked an old man down, then he swore he had killed him. Then he made his move to an abandoned building. Ran up the stairs up to the top floor. He opened the door there, guess who he saw? 'Who?' Shady the dope fiend, shooting dope. Who don't know the meaning of water nor soap? He said, 'I need bullets, hurry up, run!' The dope fiend pulled out a 12-gauge shotgun! He went outside, but there were cops all over. Then he dipped into a car, a stolen 83 Malibu. Raced up the block doing 83. Crashed into a tree, near a university. Escaped alive, although the car was battered. Rat-a-tat-tattered, then all the cops scattered. Ran out of bullets, and he still had static. Grabbed a pregnant lady and pulled out the automatic. Pointed it at her head, and said, 'the gun was full of lead'. He told the cops 'Back off. Or honey here is dead'. Deep in his heart, he knew he was wrong. So, he let the lady go, and he starts to run on. Sirens sounded. He seemed astounded then. Before long slim shady got surrounded. He dropped the gun, so went the glory. And this is the way we have end this story. He was only seventeen, in a madman's dream. The cops shot Marshall; we still hear him scream. This isn't funny so don't you dare laugh. Just another case 'bout the wrong path. Straight 'n narrow or your soul gets cast. Good night".

Then the kids peacefully began sleeping the night away, Diablo looked up to see Kimberly staring at him in awe. She invited him into her bedroom for sexual pleasure. He then laughed and asked her "what was her most intimate sexual fantasy?" She strangely said, "For my dead, crazy, and psychopathic husband to watch me and all of his innocent victims make love". Diablo smiled devilishly, as he instantly granted her wishes, as she unconsciously fell into his red arms.

He then eye balled a silver facial recognition Device located on the top of his left wrist, which he then began programming all her wishes into. With all of the following details being too pornographic for your imagination, we were only allowed to share this less graphic one. As Diablo conjured up the spirit of the deceased Marshall Mathews.

He allowed him to view the following through his third eye, as the Melody begins to play. Darnell Diablo, G33 Phezi Ali, and Kimberly then acted out the sexual holographic scenes to the lyrics of their song "L.M.F.Y.B", right before Marshall's very third eye.

Due to the explicit nature of this song
we will not be displaying the lyrics at this time.
But the song is currently available on
all music streaming platforms.

The Akashic Records.

This is a quick reference term used to define the Universal Matrix of Cellular Memory that has contained within it, the recorded event of every possible experience and permutation of consciousness existing in our 15-dimensional Universal Time Matrix.

Many times, other healers refer to this term as a part of clearing the soul record memory in the "Akasha" field of memory. The Akashic record or Akasha is a reference to the name of our Universal God Seed Code system that carries all the frequency and coding that created our Universe.

The Guardians refers to this Universal System as the " Eckasha" or Ecka Universal System. Akasha is a more common terminology that many of us have heard before that refers to the same meaning.

When we are doing emotional clearing work, many times we will state with the power of our declaration in self sovereignty that we clear and dissolve its trauma effect upon our spiritual bodies karmic record. Hence clear this " pattern" from my "Akashic Record". You are stating you command its clearance from the record of ever existing in your holographic energy field across all time and space.

On a planetary and solar level, the Halls of Records are tubes leading to spherical probability fields that one can walk through, if your body can pass through Stargates, and watch existence everywhere in every time frame. They are like surround-sound-and-vision theaters.

There are many references to the Akashic record, Hall of Records from the many sacred texts of the ancients.

The Akashic records emanate from the primordial substance of the Eternal God Source of which is projected as the DNA record and its instruction set (morphogenetic field) of all creation over time.

They are comprised of the memory record of the entire consciousness journey over time, so every idea/thought, word, and action is registered in the Akashic record which can be accessed and interpreted over any point in the spiral of time.

Each Universe, Galaxy, Planet, Being, has its own Akashic record memory, and there are many collective memory records of all spiritual families on their journey throughout time.

The way we receive the intelligent information from the Akashic Record is through transmissions via encoded Light language, which is sacred geometry of words, symbols, glyphs, as the language encoded in "fire letters". There are stages of access in the Akashic Records, and very few beings at this time on earth have the purity to access beyond the soul planes of the second density.

One must be purified to exist within the higher ethical standards of spiritual morality, and it is impossible for the accurate representation of the Akasha to transmit through a being with purely selfish motivation of Negative Ego desires or Service to Self-orientation. This manifests as a "partial access" or corrupted view to the historical record or Soul record under the guise of the ego's slant or judgment of circumstances.

With pure heart-based motivation in sacred and reverent prayer towards Life, one may request to access one's own Akashic record to view other lifetime identities, histories, patterns and related issues that may have imprinted in the current lifetime. This may be very helpful in clearing and releasing painful patterns in the soul memory and emotional body.

The Akashic record is like an immense photographic film, registering all the desires and earth experiences of our planet. Those who perceive it will see pictured thereon:

The life experiences of every human being since time began, the reactions to experience of the entire animal kingdom, the aggregation of the thought-forms of a karmic nature (based on desire) of every human unit throughout time. Herein lies the great deception of the records.

Only a trained occultist can distinguish between actual experience and those astral pictures created by imagination and keen desire. In theosophy and anthroposophy, the Akashic records are a compendium of all human events, thoughts, words, emotions, and intent ever to have occurred in the past, present, or future.

They are believed by theosophists to be encoded in a non-physical plane of existence known as the etheric plane. There are anecdotal accounts but there is no scientific evidence for the existence of the Akashic records.

The Akashic Records, or "The Book of Life," can be equated to the Universe's Super-Computer system. It is this system that acts as the central storehouse of all information for every individual who has ever lived upon the earth.

More than just a reservoir of events, the Akashic Records contain every deed, word, feeling, thought, and intent that has ever occurred at any time in the history of the world. Much more than simply a memory storehouse, however, these Akashic Records are interactive in that they have a tremendous influence upon our everyday lives, our relationships, our feelings and belief systems, and the potential realities we draw toward us.

The Akashic Records contain the entire history of every soul since the dawn of Creation. These records connect each one of us to one another.

The Akashic Records offer empowerment and transformation by lending us exactly the wisdom, guidance, and energetic support that we need in this lifetime. For centuries, the Records — the energetic archive of Souls' past, present, and future possibilities — were the exclusive domain of mystics, saints, and scholars. But not any longer!

The collective consciousness of humanity has been growing, evolving, and maturing. This spiritual independence is marked by individuals who know that they have direct access to their spiritual Source, and who cultivate that sacred relationship.

Mental Telepathy.

Mental Telepathy is believed to be a form of extra sensory perception (ESP) ability that allows a person to have direct mental communication with another person. There are two paths to understanding the mental telepathy meaning. The first is through psychical examination as a paranormal event and the second is through clinical exploration of the phenomena as a scientific experiment.

Mental telepathy has been relegated to the mysterious category of paranormal phenomena. Experts define mental telepathy as a psychic ability similar to clairvoyance and ESP.

Perhaps the first recorded scientific approach to understanding telepathy was undertaken by the Greek philosopher Aristotle (384 - 322 BC). While writing about dreams and how some people might have the same dream, Aristotle wrote that perhaps it was a matter of telepathy. He hypothesized that telepathy transmissions were comparable to a stone being thrown into still water and the ripples radiating from the splash.

Aristotle questioned whether thoughts had similar waves that moved through the air and affected dreams. Although these mental waves were also present during the day, he believed that the tranquility of nighttime combined with the person being in a restive sleep meant the human mind was more receptive to these mental motions.

Radio Waves, X-Rays and the Mental Telepathy Connection
A unknown German physicist discovered "invisible waves" that he noticed were generated by electromagnetic interaction. An unnamed Italian engineer was fascinated by this discovery and in 1895, through experimentation, received his first radio signal.

1895 also saw the discovery of what would become x-rays. A British scientist was inspired by these discoveries, and he hypothesized that the rays could be a mode of transmission for intelligence. He theorized that a part of the brain might serve as a receiver for the rays, similarly to how vocal cords manipulate sound vibrations and send them out into the air.

Modern Technology Emulates Psychical Telepathy

In February 2013, a neuroscientist announced that she had invented an implant that allowed rats and possibly monkeys to communicate telepathically at great distances. The experiments consisted of one rat pushing a specific lever to release a food pellet while a different rat in another room received the telepathic communication and pushed the same lever.

The connection between the two rats was achieved via electrodes implanted in their brains. The success rate was 70%, which represented more than a statistical coincidence. The researchers expanded the experiment with one rat in North Carolina and one in Brazil. The rats responded similarly. There are several factors that may contribute to this ability. These include:

* Brain to brain communication: This concept of communication is made possible using neurons that serves as conduits/mirrors between two brains.

* ESP (Extrasensory Perception): It's believed this sixth sense reaches beyond the normal five senses to obtain greater information.

* A 2014 study where telepathy was made possible for two people connected by the internet. It's believed that the frequency of the internet connection was the bridge between the two brains.

* Other possible contributing factors include body language and social behavior. Some studies undertake the challenge of learning ways to engineer telepathy.

Many people believe that mental telepathy is just another sense that is latent in most people, but like any other form of exercise for an existing muscle or talent, it can be strengthened. Others believe that telepathy can be taught.

We can learn or exercise our telepathic abilities with this simple method. It requires two people, one to send the thought and another to receive it. You and the person conducting the experiment should both keep journals of your process. Set a time, note climatic conditions and any other possible influencing factors in the environment.

Go to a quiet place and focus on the message you wish to send. Keep it simple in the beginning by concentrating on a single word. Set a time limit and then check with your friend at the end of that time to see if you were successful. It may take several tries before you have any results. Once you've made progress with this method, you can try some more advanced methods.

Telepathic Abilities and the Future
As humanity continues to make spiritual advancements, telepathy between humans may be possible in the near future. It could usher in a new method for humans to communicate with each other.

Telekinesis.

Telekinesis is the ability to move or change objects with the mind rather than with physical action. For example, a magician might claim to move an object across a table just by thinking about. Telekinesis is a common power among fictional superheroes and supernatural characters, but there wasn't strong scientific evidence to suggest that telekinesis actually exists until now.

Psychokinesis, also called telekinesis, in parapsychology, the action of mind on matter, in which objects are supposedly caused to move or change as a result of mental concentration upon them. The physical nature of psychokinetic effects contrasts with the cognitive quality of extrasensory perception (ESP), the other major grouping of parapsychological phenomena. Claimed effects of psychokinesis include levitation and metal bending; such displays are common, though fraudulent, in theatrical magic.

Despite experimental investigation, scientific evidence supporting the existence of psychokinesis is lacking. In an example of a psychokinetic test, the subject attempts by thinking or willing to influence thrown dice, causing a certain dice face to turn up or causing the dice to land in a certain area. Other experiments have focused on the ability of subjects to influence outcomes of random number generators.

Some researchers have interpreted the results of such experiments as revealing the existence of very small effects in which consciousness influences outcomes in such random physical systems. Other studies, however, indicate that such conclusions are the result of various forms of bias, including publication bias and confirmation bias. These experimental results, as with other parapsychological phenomena, are still being studied.

Immortal Combat.

(Finish him)

The scene was likened to the end of "The Holographic Matrix Movie" inside of the **Machine City**. It was extremely cold and cloudy as it was Marshall's first choice to level the playing field, as he knew Nubu Solar Re was a Multi-Dimensional Solar God. With no sunlight, Nubu agreed to use the mechanical arena as he'd get to choose the battle ground theme music. He chose "Immortal Combat", a song from Darnell Diablo's album "The Devil's Advocate".

Marshall Mathews then began his lyrical assaults in battle rapper mode saying, "I'mma Kill You," while claiming that he was the real "Rap God". That's when G33 Phezi Ali quickly vibrated into Marshalls consciousness with a loud sonic boom blowing smoke out of his ears, as if he was the "Stay Puft Marshmallow Man" from the "Ghostbusters Movie".

But the unfazed Marshall then began spewing iniquities, blasphemous syllables, Synonyms of words and paraphrases, which ultimately lowered Gee Phezi's frequency. That's when Marshall showed his frightening robotic looking killer Clown Face as he summoned his poisonous gas red balloons.

Marshall then released the toxic fumes in the air as Gee Phezi began to lose consciousness. He fell to the Ground as Marshall uttered an unknown phrase, then transformed himself into a Dark Black Winged Demon named "Khingu." It had ten horns and seven heads, with ten crowns on its horns, and on each head was written a blasphemous name.

Marshall then said, "Your soul is mine" as he began trying to drain Gee Phezi's vital life force and memory. Then seven trumpets began blowing from Gee Phezi's Chakra system playing a tune from Darnell Diablo's album called "Bacfrumdadead".

That's when Darnell "El" Diablo vibrated out of Gee Phezi Ali's Body in astral form, as Gee Phezi seemingly disintegrated.

The Spawn looking Diablo looked very angry as he set his 3 eyes to gaze upon Khingu saying, "Piss on me, shit on me, spit on my grave. I'm Back from the dead, like nigga please behave."

Using telekinesis, El Diablo then ripped off Khingu's wings and burned them with a red beam of Astral light coming out of his mouth.

He then floated over Khingu's body and ripped Marshall out of his chest ultimately disabling Khingu who needs a host to function. El Diablo then Astral projected himself as Marshall's worst night-MARE as he dropped him to the ground.

He turned himself into a 13-foot Flesh Eating Draconian Reptilian. Looking like some sort of vicious Dinosaur, Diablo then spat a neon red flesh-eating bacterium out of his mouth into Marshall's clown looking face. Then he stopped Marshall's body movement as if he had pressed pause on a movie.

Diablo then became much frightening to Marshall as he moved in super slow-motion towards him exposing his razor-sharp metallic teeth. Marshall's heart rate began violently increasing with an overflow of adrenaline as he approached.

Face to face, EL Diablo looked into Marshall's glossy eyes, it then seemed as if Diablo's devilish grin had taken over 24-hours to complete as he prepared to extract Marshall's Adrenochrome (Loosh). Marshall became much disoriented as he tried to refocus his vision from the flesh-eating bacteria. But what he would see next would forever change him.

Game Over.

He saw the lifeless body of the 17-year old boy who was shot lying next to the phone booth where his life was taken. Marshall then began screaming out for help as he couldn't understand how anyone found out about the unsolved crime after all this time.

He then heard 16 loud 12-gauge shotgun blasts ricocheting 6 times, as if the whole planet was blowing up. Losing his hearing, the "Max Headroom Rap God", then pleaded with his captor to be freed from the frightening holographic simulation.

Amazingly Gee Phezi Ali projected himself back inside of Marshall's consciousness, sifting through his private memories looking for his secret contracts during battle. But before they could inflict any more pain on him, there was a loud thundering sound, followed by a blinding bluish Green lighting strike.

With Marshall's vision partially impaired, he frighteningly asked, "Who's there?" He then saw the Merciful Universal Soldier "Nubu Solar RE", walking out of a Autonomous Crystalline Spacecraft bright as the star Sirius A.

The Benevolent Black Humanoid Predator looking Nubu then picked up the lifeless body of the dead disfigured teenager. He then turned to look at Marshall with the eyes of the Sun and said, "You are most forgiven!" With Marshall's hearing still being impaired, G33 Phezi Ali relayed the message to him telepathically.

Then Nubu used the DNA of lifeless corpse to regenerate Marshall a new 5D crystalline physical body using nuclear fusion and Extra Terra Astral technology. Marshall then raised up as if he were "Back from the Dead" in the physical form.

He then saw Gregory's reflection on the vehicle's window. That's when G33 Phezi Ali caused an echoing voice that said, "I Am You", inside of Marshalls head. The sun began shining as Marshall cautiously walked over to the 1983 Malibu looking sad and disgruntled. He touched the window and immediately felt the law of oneness as to make amends.

Then Nubu Solar Re quickly astral projected himself 6 feet away from both Darnell Diablo and Gee Phezi Ali, as he used the Tri-Star amulet to capture their powers and advanced Extra Terra Astral capabilities.

Then Nubu Solar RE transformed into EL RE ALI as he entered into the holographic crystalline spacecraft as it disintegrated. Thus, leaving Marshall Mathews with his hearing restored to live life as a mortal in a parallel (hexagon) reality only as a version of himself, and subject of the M.A.R.E. Program.

He now lives inside a continuous time loop where he portrays being the victim, and the victimizer in a 3 D Earth holographic simulation until he's able to ascend. Now, as you look through the scope of your life, and you realize, that you only have one "kill shot", or one human sacrifice. Would you capture it? Or would you just let it slip away? Now go "Lose yourself" in the music and recognize that we are one, and we were never alone, while listening to the Nasir's song "We are not alone".

The Cell.

In a newly created parallel dimension of Earth, Marshall Mathews was apprehended by The Multi-Dimensional Violent Crime Task Force for failing the victim-victimizer rehabilitation simulation.

He is currently sentenced to a holographic simulation without the possibility of Redemption in the Michigan Department of Psychological Corrections M.D.O.P.C. Northern Peninsula District-Prison called (SEKUMSID). For the multi-dimensional, and repetitious murders of Gregory Dismukes, and maintaining possession of the Anti-Christ Khingu spirit in the 4th chamber of his heart.

Marshall, after exhausting all levels of the M.A.R.E. Program, is now subject of the merciful M.E.R.E. Program. Memories-Erased-Rerouting-Energy. He is currently housed on Cell Block, D-13. As he began to speak, "Hey you! Hey, you faggot ass C-O, what's on the menu for dinner, I'm fucking dying hungry bitch", Said, the shady one.

The corrections officer immediately said, "Well for your information sir, all of the other inmates are being released, and treated to the Olive Garden by some weird guy named Greg, under the U.S Criminal Redemption Act of June 28, 2025. Oh, you may not haven't heard of it. He's the guy that mysteriously broke the case of his own murder from a different dimension. He did it by way of his over soul called 'Sanaan RE'. Everyone is talking about it. You must not remember him huh?

He's also the one who's bringing awareness about the 4th dimensional humanoid Reptilian parasite beings that can take over the spirit body mind/soul connection. But the Redemption program is only offered to inmates with an over soul". As the officer backed up hitting mute on his media device playing "I got soul", by Rakim Allah.

He then said with a devilish grin, "Do you got soul? Anyway. We were going to give you the same food that the feds gave the innocent Doctor Malachi Z. York, while he was in the Federal ADMAX Prison underground in Florence, Colorado. Hey! Hey Marshall, did you know that this guy Greg even negotiated the innocent Doctors release, and got him a full presidential pardon. Wow, what a mind job.

Anyway, Greg insists that you get another kind of meal. A very warm and hearty meal, with a cold, cold, cold, drink." Shady then said, "oh yeah, and what is that?"

Then the officer immediately got on some "Weird Science" shit, and slowly said, "how about a nice greasy pork butt sandwich, defecated by the 17-year old boy you murdered, served in an ashtray full of his cremated ashes. Followed by a cold, cold, cold, box of U.R.I.N, this mother fucker forever, and you cannot DIE".

Then as the half human hybrid benevolent alien white officer laughed and walked away, he activated the new Tesla anti-matter prison bars, then began singing, "Time is on my side", by: The Rolling Stones.

Prison.

Penal labor in the United States is explicitly allowed by the **13th** Amendment of the U.S. Constitution: "Neither slavery nor involuntary servitude, except as a punishment for crime whereof the party shall have been duly convicted, shall exist within the United States, or any place subject to their jurisdiction.

Un-convicted detainees awaiting trial cannot be forced to participate in labor programs in prison as this would violate the Thirteenth Amendment.

The stated aim of penal labor in the United States is to mitigate recidivism risks by providing training and work experience to inmates, however some prison labor is involuntary, with noncompliance punished by means including solitary confinement.

Penal labor is economically important due to it being a source of cheap labor, with base pay being as low as 60 cents per day in Colorado.

Penal labor in the **United States** underwent many transitions throughout the late 19th and early and mid-20th centuries. Periods of national economic strife and security guided much of these transitions.

Legislation such as the Hawes-Cooper Act of 1929 placed limitations on the trade of prison-made goods. Federal establishment of the Federal Prison Industries (FPI) in 1934 revitalized the prison labor system following the Great Depression.

Increases in prison labor participation began in 1979 with the formation of the Prison Industry Enhancement Certification Program. The PIECP is a federal program first authorized under the Justice System Improvement Act of 1979.

Approved by Congress in 1990 for indefinite continuation, the program legalizes the transportation of prison-made goods across state lines and allows prison inmates to earn market wages in private sector jobs that can go towards tax deductions, victim compensation, family support, and room and board.

Firms including those in the technology and food industries are often provided tax incentives to contract prison labor, commonly at below market rates.

The Work Opportunity Tax Credit (WOTC) serves as a federal tax credit that grants employers $2,400 for every work-release employed inmate. "Prison in-sourcing" has grown in popularity as an alternative to outsourcing work to countries with lower labor costs.

A wide variety of companies such as Whole Foods, McDonald's, Target, IBM, Texas Instruments, Boeing, Nordstrom, Intel, Wal-Mart, Victoria's Secret, Aramark, AT&T, BP, Starbucks, Microsoft, Nike, Honda, Macy's and Sprint and many more actively participated in prison in-sourcing throughout the 1990s and 2000s.

Critics of the prison labor system argue that the portrayal of prison expansion as a means of creating employment opportunity is a particularly harmful element of the prison-industrial complex in the United States.

Some believe that boosting economic benefits at the expense of an incarcerated populace prioritizes personal financial gain over ensuring payment of societal debt or actual rehabilitation of criminals

Reincarnation

The Recycling of Humanity.

The **13th** Gate Bio-Circuitry system has been connected and is being held down by a very small group of embodied Cosmic Ascended Masters that can hold one or more of the Aqua RE/Blue RE levels of coding. These are the Aqua Blue RE Holders and those of the First Order are very few in numbers embodied on the planet.

Systematically Indigos with the genetic coding capability are being circuited and linked to become links or holders of this Aqua RE out of necessity to stabilize it permanently into the planetary field and the Earth Core.

This is to link the 13th gate opening to connects into the Andromeda Core to access the star body of the original body of the Mother earth. This is an inner core alignment to the inner core of the Mother Earth body in Andromeda of which the ultraviolet liquid plasma field is generated from the crystal in the Aqualine Sun.

This process of recoding the 6D Indigo Field is a massive project underway that began with a major planetary power grid takeover. Small amounts of Starseed beings (in agreement to help with this project) have been experimenting on how to recode the Indigo (6D) harmonic with the Aqua RE of Mother Arc which leads us into the Aqualine Sun to override distortions existing with the 6D consciousness field, such as the 666 Seal.

666 Anti-Christ Seal.

This quarantine is a genetic block that forced the Soul consciousness to reincarnate over and over again on the 3D earth plane (and other planets in an appropriate dimensional field) in order to reclaim missing pieces and soul parts, as well as learn how to evolve back into wholeness with the natural laws of God, The Law of One.

However, along the course of the Timelines the Malevolent Extra Terra Astral bullies took advantage of this quarantine by forcing human Soul reincarnation into their artificial control mechanism, the *False Ascension Matrix*.

This quarantine was originally placed to protect other realms, planets and the human being itself, as such fragmentation created an endangerment to that consciousness. This was a benevolent method to reassemble missing DNA tones and soul parts that had been lost or damaged in the trauma of previous life cycles.

The *False Ascension Matrix* is an inorganic alien technology that was installed into the Astral Plane (4D) and is primarily controlled in the higher sound field dimension of 5D timelines.

It is a false white light current (aka *False Christ Consciousness* light used by the Imposter Spirit) that is sourcing and manipulated from the lower Soul Matrix dimensional realms.

This False White Light creates an intricate webbing with many Alien Implants and bio-neurological Mind Control technology which is exerted upon the human's Soul body and mind (through the use of lower frequency wave manipulation) of the human being.

Through this larger webbing in the Astral plane, it is possible to use Holographic Inserts and install software programs (like the Horseman Pulsing of the Armageddon Software) that Mind Control human beings to generate and promote belief systems for fear, religion and tyrannical control.

It is a part of Consciousness suppression of humanity in this Ascension cycle which forces reincarnation into the lower realms of time fields on earth, which from the Guardian perspective, is a type of "***soul recycling***" for creating "***worker bees***" that are subservient to the on planet and off planet **Demonic Archons**.

This is desired by the Archons because of the power source that can be generated and then harvested from both the planetary body and human **Electromagnetic Energy Source.**

This false white light interrupts the vertical connection into the higher spiritual realms and access into the spiritual bodies, blocks access to the organic Christos Consciousness in the higher dimensions of the Avatar matrix.

The False White light is a structure that mimics and mocks Christ consciousness and is highly manipulated through mind control technology by the Negative Aliens and their Archontic Deception Behavior. The human being who has not removed Alien Implants from their Soul Matrix will have an inorganic umbilicus connection to the Astral plane.

This inorganic umbilicus which is connected into this false white light and its etheric webbing is called the False Navel or the False Umbilicus. Its purpose is to un-cord the spirit/soul body of the human being during the process of death in so that the being is directed back through the white light tunnel which will take them back into the Astral plane for "recycling".

Once a being is in the Astral Plane the only place, they can reincarnate is back to 3D timelines of the earth, which is the lowest density dimension on this planet, and the most digressed in spiritual evolution. This forced recycling is what defines the term of earth as a Prison Planet.

Dimensions.

Your physical body exists in the third dimension, its matter based. The fourth dimension is the astral plane - its emotion based. Together these two make up what we call the Lower Creation World. These are the dimensions where the game of separation is carried out.

Only in these dimensions can the illusion of good and evil be maintained, and can you feel separated from Source and from each other. You've all become quite good at doing that. It's been a very successful game of separation but now it's time for it to end. So, this planet is in a state of ascension. It's now vibrating at the very top of the astral plane, right on the dividing line with the fifth dimension the Light body dimension.

As part of the ascension process, these dimensions will be rolled up into the higher dimensions and will cease to exist. The fifth through the ninth dimensions make up the Mid Creation Realm.

The fifth is the Light body dimension in which you are aware of yourself as a Master and a Multi-Dimensional being. In the fifth dimension, you are completely spiritually oriented. Many of you have come in from this plane to be Light workers.

The sixth dimension holds the templates for the DNA patterns of all types of species' creation, including humankind. It's also where the Light languages are stored and is made up mostly of color and tone. It is the dimension where consciousness creates through thought and one of the places where you work during sleep.

It can be difficult to get a bead on this because you're not in a body unless you choose to create one. When you are operating sixth dimensionally, you are more of an alive thought. You create through your consciousness, but you don't necessarily have a vehicle for that consciousness.

The seventh dimension is that of pure creativity, pure light, pure tone, pure geometry, and pure expression. It is a plane of infinite Refinement. The eighth is the dimension of group mind or group soul and where you would touch base with the vaster part of who you are. It is characterized by loss of sense of the "I".

When you travel multi dimensionally, it's this plane where you have most trouble keeping your consciousness together because you are pure "we", operating with group goals. So, it may seem as though you've gone to sleep or blanked out. The ninth dimension in the model that we use is the plane of the collective consciousness of planets, star systems, galaxies and dimensions.

Once again, it's very difficult to get a sense of "I" because you are so vast that everything is "you". Imagine being the consciousness of a galaxy. Every life-form, every star, planet, and group mind of every species in it is you. If you visit this dimension, it can be difficult to remain conscious.

The tenth through twelfth dimensions make up the Upper Creation Realm. The tenth is the source of the Rays, home of what are called the Elohim. This is where Light is differentiated and is the source of plans of creation which are sent to the Mid Creation levels. You can have a sense of "I" at this level, but it won't be what you're used to here.

The eleventh dimension is that of preformed Light the point before creation and a state of exquisite expectancy just like the moment before a sneeze or an orgasm. It is the realm of the being known as Metatron, and of Archangels and the Higher Akashic for this Source system.

There are planetary Akashic records and galactic Akashic as well as the Akashic for an entire Source system. You are in one Source system of many. So, we are giving you a description of one Source system only this one. If you go to another Source system, what you will experience will be different.

As an Archangel, my home base is the eleventh dimension. We come to you as messengers, that's what "Archangel" means. It's one of my functions, as I have many, even as a hybrid Elohim.

The twelfth dimension is the One Point where all consciousness knows itself to be utterly one with All That Is. There is no separation of any kind. If you tap into this level, you know yourself to be completely one with All That Is, with the creator force. If you tap in there, you will never be the same again because you cannot sustain the same degree of separation if you have experienced complete unity.

As this realm of existence is for our learning and having experiences of all kinds. And as we reawaken to know this as truth, we will receive help from within our own conscious mind. An inner awareness or enlightenment. An Instinctive type of intelligence manufactured by our multiple dimensional over-soul.

Androgyny.

It is our finding that the human mind, body and soul, is fragmented. Possessing a combination of both male and female attributes. Rather if one then filters these building block energies down to a nonproductive tri-sexual preference is up to the host. But to the contrary, using these same energies to heal the complex mind, body, and soul interface, in Oneness and Union with the One True Source is a choice as well.

The Malevolent Reptilians do not want to heal their genetics, thereby integrate into human society as an equal, they want to rule humanity as an absolute authority as the False King of Tyranny. The Illuminati plan and the infiltrated monarchy are based within these genetically controlled factions, that are considered the royal bloodlines.

Many of these royals are not human any longer but have been partially or fully possessed by the inter-dimensional entities in order to make the carrying out of the agenda more convenient. The NRG is a massively complicated alien machinery that has interfered with true spiritual marriage or Hieros Gamos, the union between the inner male-female principles in the original human DNA, making this embodiment nearly impossible for most human beings on the planet.

The Archontic Deception Strategy is directly to inflict Sexual Misery, sexual abuse and sexual slaves on this planet, starting as early and young as possible. This was taken advantage of by the negative aliens to splinter the soul energies, rather than integrate and heal it, by controlling the sexual energies.

By promoting distortions around the sexual act, gender roles and corrupting our relationship to our mother and father parent, our race descended into Sexual Misery and in many cases, forms of sexual slavery and Misogyny.

This is known as the "sexual misery program" propagated and controlled by the Moon Chain (lunar) lineages of the Negative E T A's on the earth. (These are lineages not indigenous to the earth but came through the process of invasion and deception.)

These are multiple layers of architecture and Mind Control that have been artificially created to control, deceive, separate, confuse, torture and steal human being's sexual life force, and it is a violation against the human soul. The main collection center for Sexual Misery is called the Nephilim Reversal Grid Network, that is the central hub in the UK. It is designed to create psychopaths and sexual predators.

Which is why Gregory and other young family members who we will not name, were repeatedly abused, and sexually assaulted by older male and female relatives.

At the very young age of five, he endured a very shameful and disturbing act by someone we will not mention as well. He recalls waking up out of his sleep in the middle of the night with someone's mouth around his phallus, and another time, an older woman's finger painfully entering in and out of his anal cavity. His words were "what the heck," as he wet himself in pain and **fear**.

The frighten boy remembers crying as he was quickly silence during the abuse. He and his sister were repeatedly dropped off to these insane family members so his mother can maintain a social life with her friends. Gregory lacked the communication skills and mental ability to effectively discuss the shameful things that were happening within the dysfunctional home.

He remembers crying and asking to just be with his father when it was time to be dropped off saying, "I don't like it over here". Unfortunately, this caused him some serious psychological issues with his identity as a male, causing him to feel ashamed of himself. At times he'd witness his mother being physically assaulted by her different male friends.

On one occasion, the 5-year-old boy even tried to intervein, but was picked up, man handled and threw across the room. Experiencing such violence caused him to have abnormal heart palpation issues, and every time he heard a loud thump or thud, it would seem as if his heart would sync up with them, followed by acute adrenaline rushes. He also developed imaginary friends who he'd have weird and intense conversations with.

His mother was only 16 at the time of his birth, so she was still fairly young during this time, as she too also struggled from the same type of dysfunctional family issues as a young child.

We believe this type of behavior causes the child's mind to split and become fragmented. We cannot allow this type of immoral behavior to continue in our communities. The hush hush child syndrome has plagued our communities since the fall of humanity. This is nothing new, for physical and sexual abuse continues in the form of media, Child Pornography, Pedophilia, in Books, DVD's and Magazines, even with Child Modeling Agencies. We also are aware of the continued sexual abuse within the Catholic Church communities.

Gregory suffered from mild sexual frustration, and at times even acute erectile dysfunctions. Yet he remains adamant about only being attracted to femininity. One day he noticed a weird reaction when he came across a Documentary called "Androgyny" that featured on Network-Flix, about transgendered women.

He thought to himself, how and why was he still attracted. Although some of the women were extremely beautiful, his reaction was, "What the hell is this shit. I know I'm not homosexual. But nor am I homophobic." So, after admitting to himself of being comfortable in his heterosexuality, he continued watching the "L.G.B.T.Q." program and quickly learned about how these beings are treated in the world view.

Gregory quickly told Alexa to pause Fifty Senses "Back Down." A song from the "Died Trying to Get Rich" album. He then said, "This Androgynous Documentary has a lot of homosexual undertones in it, I wonder what's the agenda

The commentator pointed out how, and why these people are gay bashed, beat up, or even murdered. Some, who may have been dishonest about their gender identities were found dead, maybe even just to be silenced by those who wish to keep their shameful sexual preference a secret. He then said, "I am not of the same sex orientation, yet I must teach that one should not go around treating people who are like they are less than human. Everyone is here for a reason and purpose.

What many have failed to realize is most gay men were born that way, it's because they may have a Female Spirit, yes! It's really a lady inside of a man's Body. That's why they have lady like tendencies and gestures, it's who they actually are. And the same goes for some gay women, who many say act like men, yes! There is really a man inside of the Ladies Body.

Some people are what many call 'Fags,' they are the ones who are just trying to get sexual pleasure from anyone, no matter what their gender is. That's called being 'Hormone Sexual', as in (Whore), Know the difference! These people are in our world, and we must overstand reality. Some people have a man and a lady spirit, and they are Bisexual. We should respect all people no matter their race or gender."

It then showed a video of the so-called best rapper alive wearing a dress in full drag. Being the first rapper to do such a thing, this video of FEMINEM getting make-up applied to his face was quite disturbing and very confusing, because he then began to look attractive.

It seems as if some of us will do anything for a specific dollar amount. Does the shape shifting M.C. not know about the millions of sexually frustrated brothers in the U.S. prison system that would sodomize him in the worst way for looking, and dressing in this manner?

They would repeatedly sexually punish that Drag Queen without remorse. I would not even want to imagine how they would fight one another over the best rapper alive. Yeah right! He'd be more like the best to ever continuously wrap his mouth around a phallus. No offense.

Despite a few, although extremely frustrated, the incarcerated Alpha Males are not homosexual. Even though some maybe guilty of a crime, they are being inhumanely housed in places like Florence, ADMAX prison in Colorado, without access to the opposite sex, leaving the inmates only sexual releases in the form of fantasy and imagination. Which is a food source for the malevolent Reptilians and Archons.

The program further explained prison rape, after showing frustrated inmates with naked posters of the famous rapper with the letter "F" written before his name. As the inmates spoke about all the Fruity, humorous, and homosexual undertones in his music, one man said that, "It would be a very sad day in America, if the ticket for us prisoners to get out of prison, was to just simply imagine sodomizing Feminem one at a time". I even think people who are not in prison would do it as well from all the women's make-up that was applied.

Paul, who Feminem feloniously defended in his mock Detroit film, would probably pass on the opportunity. We as a people should all learn that the fear of something, drives it closer to us, and that overly defensive masculine attraction, is the root cause of homophobic fear. I guess that's why Feminem publicly met with Elton John, and later contemplated making a song called, "What if I was Gay."

So, what if Feminem was gay, and came out, long before he came out? What if he had "cleaned out his closet" long ago, before becoming a "Detroit Battle Rapper".

The Dark Cabal could certainly not use him for their destructive subconscious 440-megahertz frequency mind alternation and manipulation measures. And we would definitely not be listening to "Mu-sick to be murdered by".

And since were using facts as fiction, maybe we can use fiction as facts! As the cannibalistic M.C. was even featured in a movie called, "The Interviews", admitting that he was Gay. Not that there is anything wrong with it, but I do believe that a person's sexual preference should remain their own personal choice. It should not be directed at the youth as comedy or entertainment, because us Elohim tend to take suicide very seriously.

"We can also remember him making fun of Gianni Versace's murder, and doing vocals for one of his disturbing gay characters named Kenney Caniff from Connecticut" the commentor said. Now all this information saddened Gregory, as he decided to remain a loyal Feminem fan. But even he would not want to be in the Homosexual and Vicodin popping rapper's shoes at this moment in time.

"So, won't the real slim light-shade please stand up?" I'm not an expert, but I'm a really big Feminem fan. He has a way of rhyming almost everything. The way he breaks words down and slightly bends syllables makes it possible for him to rhyme virtually everything while maintaining clarity at that pace.

Secondly, he has spanned over a decade at the top of the rap industry, so obviously his style has evolved. He started out by rapping about his struggles in life, and later on his drug abuse. But now he raps about how awesome or Godly he is. Also, his earlier albums were full of amazing metaphors and punchlines which has now changed to more of his flawless and fluid like flow.

He can literally rap to any kind of beat, slow, fast, whatever... And now, about his freestyling skills which are very impressive given his extensive vocabulary and constant brainstorming. He has almost always been a technical/robotic type of rapper who focuses on flow and rhymes instead of subject matters. He'd definitely be the top choice to spew wickedness for the music industry.

We have seen Feminem portray his partying type of rap skills as well. But "Nobody listens to Techno!" Also, in his "Detroit Movie," we got to see his choreographed battling skills as well. So, if you tried to categorize him to one thing, I would say he is a left brained technological and analytical type of rapper. In fact, he is the most controversial rapper ever. He's like the "Tyler Perry" of rap. He can do it all and HE DOES IT ALL! Being the first rapper ever to rape his own mother in third person in a song.

He's a poet to some, a regular modern-day William Shakespeare. Considered King of the 313 to many, but it would be a complete insult to compare this "Insane Killer Clown" to Hip Hop legends such as Rakim, Tupac, E-40, Nas, KRS One, Slick Rick, The Notorious BIG, K-Rino, Tech N9ne, or the Supreme God, (The Grand Verbalizer) Brother J from the X-Clan, based on lyrical content, storyline, and subject matter alone. And we definitely couldn't fail to mention our high powered super female MC's Sa-Roc, and Narubi Selah. Our music was designed to send out messages and unify our communities.

Don't get me wrong, Feminem's delivery and word play is impeccable. But his subject matter and ability to connect with humanity (The Conscious Community) is absent. It also seems as if he were forced fed to us by the elite. Which soon after, "20 million" other whack mumble rappers emerged after the millionaire's kingship began as the best rapper alive. You may even find yourself bobbing your head to the worst song ever recorded after its repeatedly played on the radio over and over again. We can call this typical systematic programing.

Although Slick Rick is still considered by us the greatest rhythmic storyteller of all time. He was gravely underrated and looked over due to the controllers of the music industry. These demonic people were hell bent, on destroying the minds of our youth. Thus, breeding more Ignorant Niggas.

Tupac knew this control system was directly behind, and fueled the school to prison pipeline, as they promoted violence, female prostitution, homosexuality, drug dealing and drug use. As you may have noticed, all the rappers began to become younger and younger for control purposes. Thus, leaving the educated elders with positive messages in darkness.

That system creates an environment that encourages the youth to create self- destructive music by offering lucrative opportunities to those who follow the program. We are literally being massively rewarded for broadcasting words and imagery that promote the genocide of the black nation.

We are being paid to destroy our own minds. Making positive, more powerful, enlightening, and revolutionary music in the likeness of the inspirational "Tobe Nwigwe" for the black community (particularly) in "America" is not a profitable venture. The powers that be must have realized that the music of previous generations, that promoted self-love and cultural integrity, was dangerous for the system of so-called white supremacy (Reptilian) which aims to dominate all people of the known the universe with low frequencies and vibrations.

It is a lot harder to dominate a people that value themselves and are equipped with an ingrained obligation to the betterment of their community. So, in order for the system of white, or for lack of a better word, Reptilian supremacy to continue its campaign for world domination, it became absolutely necessary to ruin the "Black is Beautiful" self-image we had as a collective and replace it with a destructive desire to be "Niggas" and "Bitches".

We fell for the scam following the trend (which they control) and the money (which they control). We must regain control of our culture, our people and our minds. At some point we must choose the future of our nation over the money.

So-what! If record labels are paying top dollar for black artists to spew destructive non-sense. So-what! If videos promoting black on black crime, drug usage, and the complete degradation of the black woman are what goes viral.

So-what! If you won't get invited to clubs anymore because you speak life and instead of death. It all comes down to a simple question. Are you willing to participate in the genocide of Black America by helping destroy the moral fabric of an already brutalized and recovering nation for a few inflated dollars, simultaneously becoming an active participant of the system of White Supremacy? Which secretly is an Elite Reptilian strong hold.

Nephilim Reversal Grids -N.R.G.

The headquarter hub in Stonehenge area acts as a final collection point by directing huge amounts of Electromagnetic power, through massive amounts of collected (stolen) life force from multiple subsidiaries all over the planetary globe and the planetary grid lines, as well as the Planetary Gates.

The Nephilim Reversal Grid (NRG) is an alien AI machined structure that is active in the United Kingdom. In order to dismantle the NRG, the various hubs feeding it from all over the planet need to be dismantled systematically, while freeing the soul enslavement of the collective consciousness of the earth humans that is used to power up these Grids.

The NRG is responsible to break apart hybridized genetics by reversing any synthesis of alchemy that happens organically between the male and female principle (electron-proton balance), as well as repelling any healing for the DNA of reverse pair bonds that are connected to Nephilim DNA or that which has been hybridized with reptilian genetics.

This is desired by the Reptilians because their human representatives on the earth have been bred as Nephilim (Genetic hybrid between Oraphim and Reptilian) and thus are easy to possess and Mind Control for carrying out the Negative Alien Agenda. (N.A.A.)

The name of the game for the NRG is propagating and feeding highly destructive addictions and deviant sexual attitudes and behavior within the global human population. This is a part of propagating the Sexual Misery program along with the Victim-Victimizer.

Its first priority is designed to relegate all sexual activity laced with guilt and shame into the lowest forms of human expression and perversion possible. Depending on accepted cultural attitudes it will use the perceptive level of access to serve the current societal paradigm into distortion.

In Muslim countries it can be the legal killing of raped women by being left in the desert to die by their own husband, or the selling of little girls to prostitution in Thailand, Catholic priest pedophilia in the Vatican, Sadistic or masochistic fetishes in Germany. These harvested energies all feed back into the same N.R.G. matrix.

This NRG matrix starts out looking on the surface like it's "harmless" based on open sexual attitudes (What are you, a prude? Are you jealous and possessive? Don't you know that polyamory is what we were designed for?) It's designed to suck you into Addiction Webbing and nonstop base instinct desire of the second chakra, so all that is craved is "plugging into" the next "outlet" or in its deeper levels - getting relief from addictive anxiety.

The promiscuity design is to crash your human genetic code, so you lose your "real" sense of divine human connection, which is the deep desire to be truly intimately connected and experienced as the divinity within. Unity Field intelligence (God force) is created between the male and female principle at highly developed consciousness frequency such as within the union between equals in Spiritual Marriage in No Time or Hieros Gamos.

This is what it is like on advanced planets. This is when unconditional love is shared in a safe emotional haven and the full transparency of trust to create divine union is made possible.

Most of us engaged in the sexual act forget that the human design to Ascend into God Source is a part of the union of equals existing in perfect love. We need to remember this again in order to heal ourselves and return true unity in spiritual marriage to the planet.

In order to separate humans from divine union, the NRG grid promotes disconnection through all means sexual, such as internet porn, the sexualization of inanimate objects and the belief that the grass is always greener with another sexual partner. Once a person becomes addicted to the bait of this rapidly descending pathway, the architecture of this control system hooks into all of your lower centers to capture your vital force.

When something vampirizes your vital force (sexual chakra) all you instinctively want is to get it back, so you seek the next "seduction" to vampirize someone or something else. Never succeeding in feeling satiated, you become addicted to all things external. The mind becomes fixated on latching into another outlet, sex, food, drugs, clothes, or any object or person.

This is the definition of Mind Controlled Addiction. In its advanced stages the fixation becomes obsessive compulsive in order to relieve the discontent to the level of anxiety experienced, courtesy of the NRG grid.

These schisms promote the Predator Mind and anti-human thinking, which is highly dysfunctional to the point it generates genetic damage in the light-body, especially in the 2nd Chakra and 4th Chakra layer functioning where there is the 2D/4D Split.

These archetypes were once creational myths that the souls could play out in the polarity game on earth, but the archetypes were synthesized into AI mind control machinery in order to become a massive source of energy food to be harvested for the controllers, especially with the use of the Victim-Victimizer software.

As these archetypes became AI controlled, they were used to gain access to the human energy fields, and control people with Mind Control software, thus the person regressed into aggressive anti-human, robotic and disconnected behavior, losing all feelings of Empathy and spiritual connection. Spiritually abusive behaviors that disconnect people from their Soul Matrix are known as Archontic Deception Behaviors.

We are continually working on embodying the unity template of Spiritual Marriage in order to create the foundation for Hieros Gamos which unites the male-female consciousness units and requires the alien bi-wave systems fail to run on the earth grids in the future Timelines.

The NRG system keeps electron distortions feeding the Patriarchal Domination archetypes that are superimposed upon the males and females given power and influence over others, in the socially accepted roles of identity.

This results in many highly destructive mental belief systems and emotional body schisms that split the male and female principle apart from each other, referred to as Gender Splitting. The strategies of splitting the pair bonds is outlined in the Archontic Deception Behavior.

We now have the power to change it all, if we can resist the temptation to sellout our nation. Bring back self-love. Bring back knowledge. Bring back the revolution. Humans of all colors are here to love and experience one another. We must understand the concept of it only being ONE SOURCE, which in turns spawns a **NO FEAR** Spirit.

We have been tricked by malevolent Extra Terra Astrals in many ways to keep us divided. When the mind is 3 dimensional, you won't be able to see that they feed on your emotional energy. They have taken over the planet by dividing the people and keeping them outside of the heart, instead of in the Heart. Re-Member **EARTH** is an anagram for the word **HEART**.

They use fear, politics, states, countries, different language, religion, sports, status, money, privilege, news, racism etc. to keep the living souls Divided and spiritually outside of the heart where there is no creative power at all, only illusion.

This information caused Gregory to begin his own research into Malevolent and Benevolent Extra Terra Astrals, Secret Societies, Hidden Agendas, Homosexual Rappers, Vaccines, Gender Transformation, Clones, Genetically Modified Organisms, and the anatomy of the human body.

He found that the Sexual differentiation in humans, is the process and development of phenotypic structures, consequent to the action of hormones produced, following gonadal determination.

Sexual differentiation includes development of different genitalia and the internal genital tracts. And body hair plays a major role in gender identification. The development of sexual differences begins with the XY sex-determination system that is present in humans.

These complex mechanisms are responsible for the development of the phenotypic differences between male and female humans, from an undifferentiated zygote.

Females typically have two X chromosomes, and males typically have a Y chromosome and an X chromosome. At an early stage in embryonic development, both sexes possess equivalent internal structures.

These are the mesonephric ducts and paramesonephric ducts. The presence of the SRY gene on the Y chromosome causes the development of the testes in males, and the subsequent release of hormones which cause the paramesonephric ducts to regress. But In females, the mesonephric ducts regress.

Divergent sexual development, known as intersex, can be a result of genetic and hormonal factors. I believe these factors are of an extraterrestrial origin. Androgyny among humans, expressed in terms of biological sex characteristics, gender identity, or gender expression, is attested to from earliest history and across world cultures.

Sadly, some religious folk still to the day worship the androgynous Baphomet as a deity, offering up blood sacrifices in return for favor and enlightenment. Little did they know they were worshipping many negative multi-dimensional Extra Terra Astrals. These beings have the capacity to enter our consciousness as male or female.

For instance, it's like someone silently getting in your vehicle with you, but you can't see or hear them. They may be in the backseat, they may be in the front seat, or they may just hide in your trunk. They may just even drive your vehicle for you.

With that being said if you're not in control of your own life, then who is? They were always with you. They are the "Watchers". They will use your innermost secrets against you. Just ask the people of the U.S. Government. Ask the all the presidents. Ask all the governors and mayors. Ask yourself as well.

Do you still need "proof"? Just look at Feminem when he was inside the University of Michigan Football game room to introduce his video. Don't believe me, check it out for yourself on YouTube.

It is now safe to say that the truest form of the Baphomet (male-female energies) resides inside your own inner being. Thus, if it's any being worth worshipping would be thy own self, and also loving others as thyself.

It is known that Extra Terra Astrals can inhabit a human looking body hosting an angelic binary spirit force. But broadly speaking, masculine traits are categorized as agentic and instrumental, dealing with assertiveness and analytical skill.

 Feminine traits are categorized as communal and expressive, dealing with empathy and subjectivity. Androgynous individuals exhibit behavior that extends beyond what is normally associated with their given sex.

Due to the possession of both masculine and feminine characteristics, androgynous individuals have access to a wider array of psychological competencies in regard to emotional regulation, communication styles, and situational adaptability.

Hermaphroditism

Through the perfect union of the Universal Mother and Universal Father, as an example of the Gender Principle with Adam and Eve in the waters of sex with chastity, the pillar of the hermai is perfected and made into the image of God through the hierogamic union of the inner Christos-Sophia.

This is represented in perfected Alchemy of unified polarities, as the Magnum Opus of cosmic consciousness. In this term hermaphrodite, we see Mercury (Hermes) uniting with the goddess of love.

Her name is Venus or Aphrodite. When Hermes and Aphrodite unite, they form Hermaphrodite, the perfect balance of unified male and female principle or the Aeonic Pair, Christos-Sophia. A hermaphrodite really, truly has nothing to do with what people currently think that it is.

The mystical understanding of a hermaphrodite is the etymology of the word comes from the union between Mercury and Venus (Hermes Aphrodite), and is the hierogamic union of a god and goddess, a perfected being, the perfect balance and union between masculine and feminine, united as one.

The Hieros Gamos is the Wedded Garment of God, wearing the White Robes of the One. Hieros Gamos refers to the Risen Christos-Sophia, as the embodiment of the inner hiero-gamic union between the human being and the divine.

Hieros Gamos is the full resurrection of the body to the eternal light of Christos, Cosmic Christ Consciousness. In the bodies return to energetic balance, neutral in the Unity Field or Zero Point), the light body being is One with God, and the Christos body is glorified in its perfection as representative of God's eternal light image.

In Hieros Gamos Couplings, the genetic equal of the Monad unites with its counterpart to embody the sacred marriage of Krystic equals, to merge into One spiritual body to hold the Spirits of Christ. A Krystic male and a Krystic Female unite in a Hieros Gamos or Rod and Staff Union as the Christos-Sophia, to be of service within God's Eternal Light divine plan to correct the Sophianic Body and to restore liberation of Ascension upon the earth.

Hieros Gamos is the embodiment of the new Cosmic Ray Frequencies of Mother Arc Aquamarine and Father Arc Emerald Green hues and their DNA Lens being introduced to this Universe.

These frequency colors represent the Aurora Body Guardian consciousness of the United Krestic Forms embodied in the future sovereignty timeline of GSF. (Inter-dimensional Resonator, plus Base Tone, Overtone and Resonant Tone Amplifier).

Androgynous individuals have also been associated with higher levels of creativity and mental health. The caduceus, later carried by Hermes/Mercury, was the basis for the astronomical symbol for the planet Mercury and the botanical sign for hermaphrodite.

The caduceus sign is now sometimes used for transgender people. An androgynous person is an individual who has a high degree of both feminine and masculine traits. A feminine individual is ranked high on feminine traits and ranked low on masculine (instrumental) traits.

A masculine individual is ranked high on instrumental traits and ranked low on expressive traits. An undifferentiated person is low on both feminine and masculine traits. An individual's gender identity, a personal sense of one's own gender, may be described as androgynous if they feel that they have both masculine and feminine aspects.

The word androgyny can refer to a person who does not fit neatly into one of the typical masculine or feminine gender roles of their society, or to a person whose gender is a mixture of male and female, not necessarily half and half. Many androgynous individuals Identify as being mentally or emotionally both masculine and feminine. They may also identify as "gender-neutral", "genderqueer", or "nonbinary".

A person who is androgynous may engage freely in what is seen as masculine or feminine behaviors as well as tasks. They have a balanced identity that includes the virtues of both men and women and may disassociate the task with what gender they may be socially or physically assigned to.

People who are androgynous disregard what traits are culturally constructed specifically for males and females within a specific society, and rather focus on what behavior is most effective within the situational circumstance.

Many non-western cultures recognize additional androgynous gender identities. Jewish culture recognizes the Tumtum and Androgynous genders. In Chinese culture exists the Yinyang ren gender? The Bugis of Indonesia recognize five genders, Bissu representing the androgynous category. In Hawaiian culture, the third gender Māhū is recognized.

In Oaxacan Zapotec culture, the Muxe are recognized as a third gender. In India, the Hijra is the third androgynous gender. Samoans accept Fa'afafine as a third gender. Native American culture includes Two Spiritedness as a general third gender.

Prince was right in the thick of all this. Just check the covers of his records. On the back of 1980's Dirty Mind, he poses languidly in black thigh high stockings, bikini briefs. On Parade, from 1986, he's wearing mascara and a stomach- baring top that cuts away just below his nipple line.

And by 1988's Love sexy cover, Prince appears as an angelic nude hovering amid lush blooms. In a sly, saucy touch, one flower's stamen close by the singer's crotch mimics the arc of an erection. Even the color that Prince fetishized so flamboyantly had those overtones.

The Purple Rain also represents the **Crown Chakra**. The word chakra means "wheel" in Sanskrit, though these are not like any wheels we've ever seen. Chakra energy spins in a clockwise direction as it moves the energy of our body out into the field around us, and it spins counterclockwise to pull energy from our external world (and the people in it) into our body.

It is the frequency state of our chakras that determines the direction our energy will flow as they either draw energy into our body or release it outward. Our chakras exist at seven points along our body each one associated with a different set of organs and systems. It shouldn't be too surprising that the locations of our chakras correspond with the places on our body where essential systems use a lot of energy.

For example, the one between the eyes sits around our visual center, of course, but also the frontal lobe of our brain. That location is the epicenter of our decision-making, planning, and orientation. There is so much energy required in that region of our body that it makes perfect sense for it to have an energy outlet sitting in a handy location.

The same goes for the heart chakra, which we know contains so much energy that it has its own force field and emits so much electromagnetic energy that it can be measured from several feet away.

The chakras can be open or closed, overactive or underactive, depending on how well energy is able to flow through them. And that flow is determined by the open or constricted state of your body and energy body. We can further understand the energetic existence of our chakras by understanding their color, which becomes important in chakra healing exercises. Yes, each chakra has a color associated with it. Visible light gives off electromagnetic waves, vibrating across the field through time and space.

Depending on how quickly the waves are vibrating, our eyes will pick them up as different colors. Red, for instance, is a lower-frequency wave that looks like a slow roll; purple, on the other hand, is a high frequency wave with sharp peaks and valleys. In fact, we can measure a wave in nanometers and then determine its energetic strength.

The chakra energies, vibrating at their different frequencies, likewise have different colors. A chakra may be a wheel or a vortex, but it operates like a ball of energy interpenetrating the physical body. The chakras themselves are not physical; you can't see them on an X-ray. They are aspects of consciousness, and they interact with the physical and energetic body through two major vehicles, the endocrine system and the nervous system.

Each of the seven chakras is associated with one of the nine endocrine glands, and also with a particular group of nerves, called a plexus, making them important elements in healing. Thus, each chakra corresponds with parts of the body and functions within the body controlled by that plexus or that endocrine gland, which is the key to understanding how chakra healing methods work.

The chakras represent not only particular parts of your physical body, but also particular parts of your consciousness. Your consciousness, how you perceive your reality, represents everything that is possible for you to experience.

All your senses, perceptions, and possible states of awareness can be divided into seven categories, and each of these categories can be associated with a particular chakra. When you feel tension in your consciousness, you feel it in the chakra associated with the part of your consciousness experiencing the stress, and in the parts of the physical and energy body associated with that chakra. Where you feel the stress depends therefore on why you feel the stress. When you are hurt in a relationship, you feel it in your heart.

When you are nervous, your legs tremble and your bladder become weak. When there is tension in a particular part of your consciousness, and therefore in the chakra associated with that part of your consciousness, the tension is detected by the nerves of the plexus associated with that chakra and communicated to the parts of the physical and energy body controlled by that plexus.

When the tension continues over a period or reaches a particular degree of intensity, it creates a symptom on the physical level and requires chakra healing to resolve. Again, the symptom serves to communicate to you through your body what you have been doing to yourself in your consciousness.

The opening and closing of our chakras work like an energetic defense system. A negative experience can cause the associated chakra energy to close in order to block that energy out.

Similarly, if we are clinging to a low-calibrating feeling like blame, prolonging the emotion because we refuse to deal with or move it, we close off the chakra which then requires special chakra healing techniques. As we open and heal our chakras, energy can flow freely once again, and things return to normal.

Sometimes it's a matter of moving energy throughout our body, moving our own frequencies. Each chakra's connection to a key endocrine gland and nervous system in our body means that an energy deficiency could lead to serious physical consequences if you ignore it for too long.

The immune system weakens with all the negative thinking and grief. Cancer cells have far more glucose receptors than normal cells thus allowing the cancer cells that already exist inside our bodies to grow.

Balance Is Key.

No one chakra is better than the others, or more important than any other in the process of energy body balancing and chakra healing. You don't want to have extra heart chakra energy and less throat chakra energy; it simply doesn't work like that. Ideally, all seven of your chakras are healed, balanced, open, and humming, allowing energy to flow into and out of your body.

The amazing thing is that your body is going to find a way to move energy in and out unless, of course, your lower egotistical self is telling it to hold on to something. If one of your chakras is closed or underactive, there is a very good chance that another chakra will be overactive to make up the difference.

Because your body wants to achieve energetic balance in your chakras, moving too far in either direction (underactive or overactive) in any one chakra can actually yield negative effects in your body and be counterproductive to the energy body and chakra healing process. An underactive chakra kicks another chakra into overdrive, which in turn pulls extra energy away from that part of the body.

This is How You May Feel or Act When Chakras Are Overactive or under active. Root Chakra: Overactive Fearful, nervous, insecure, or ungrounded; materialistic or greedy; resistant to change. Under active: Lacking a sense of being at home or secure anywhere, codependent, unable to get into one's body, fearful of abandonment.

Sacral Chakra: Overactive, Overemotional, very quick to attach and invest in others, attracted to drama, moody, lacking personal boundaries. Under active: Stiff, unemotional, closed off to others, lacking self-esteem or self-worth, possibly in an abusive relationship.

Navel (Solar Plexus) Chakra: Overactive, Domineering, aggressive, angry, perfectionistic or overly critical of oneself or others. Underactive: Passive, indecisive, timid, lacking self-control.

Heart Chakra: Overactive, loving in a clingy, suffocating way. Lacking a sense of self in a relationship. Willingness to say yes to everything. Lacking boundaries, letting everyone in. Underactive: Cold, distant, lonely, unable or unwilling to open up to others, grudgeful.

Throat Chakra: Overactive, overly talkative, unable to listen, highly critical, verbally abusive, condescending. Underactive, Introverted, shy, having difficulty speaking the truth, unable to express needs.

Third Eye Chakra: Overactive, out of touch with reality, lacking good judgment, unable to focus, prone to hallucinations. Underactive Rigid in thinking, closed off to new ideas, too reliant on authority, disconnected or distrustful of the inner voice, anxious, clinging to the past and fearful of the future.

Crown Chakra: Overactive, addicted to spirituality, heedless of bodily needs, having difficulty controlling emotions. Underactive, not very open to spirituality, unable to set or maintain goals, lacking direction.

The Chakras and Associated Glands, Organs, and Symptoms Root Chakra: Associated Endocrine Glands & Organs Adrenal glands, spine, blood, and reproductive organs. Physical Symptoms of Unbalance Inability to sit still, restlessness, unhealthy weight either obesity or eating disorder, constipation, cramps, fatigue or sluggishness.

Sacral Chakra: Associated Endocrine Glands & Organs Kidneys and reproductive organs: ovaries, testes, and uterus Physical Symptoms of Unbalance. Lower-back pain or stiffness, urinary issues, kidney pain or infection, infertility, impotence.

Navel (Solar Plexus) Chakra: Associated Endocrine Glands & Organs Central nervous system, digestive system (stomach and intestines), liver, pancreas, metabolic system. Physical Symptoms of Unbalance, Ulcers, gas, nausea, or other digestive problems; eating disorders; asthma or other respiratory ailments; nerve pain or fibromyalgia; infection in the liver or kidneys; other organ problems.

Heart Chakra: Associated Endocrine Glands & Organs Thymus gland and immune system, heart, lungs, breasts, arms, hands. Physical Symptoms of Unbalance, Heart and circulatory problems (high blood pressure, heart palpitations, and heart attack), poor circulation or numbness, asthma or other respiratory ailments, breast cancer, stiff joints or joint problems in the hands.

Throat Chakra: Associated Endocrine Glands & Organs Thyroid, neck, throat, shoulders, ears, and mouth. Physical Symptoms of Unbalance Stiffness or soreness in the neck or shoulders, sore throat, hoarseness or laryngitis, earaches or infection, dental issues or TMJ, thyroid issues.

Third Eye Chakra: Associated Endocrine Glands & Organs, Pituitary, eyes, brow, base of skull, biorhythms Physical Symptoms of Unbalance Vision problems, headaches or migraines, insomnia or sleep disorders, seizures, nightmares (though this isn't a physical symptom per se, it is a common occurrence).

Crown Chakra: Associated Endocrine Glands & Organs, Pituitary and pineal glands, brain, hypothalamus, cerebral cortex, central nervous system. Physical Symptoms of Unbalance, Dizziness, confusion, mental fog, neurological disorders, nerve pain, schizophrenia or other mental disorders. As you can see, a lot of these physical symptoms are not to be taken lightly. The difficult thing to remember is that the physical and energy body is going to keep sending us its messages amping up the intensity if it needs to until we pay attention and engage in physical, mental, emotional and energetic chakra healing.

The energy of our chakras influences our physical processes via inhibition and stimulation. Remember, chakras are like wheels whose job is not only to keep energy moving, but also to constrict or close as a defense against negative energy. In order to compensate for a constricted, underactive chakra, another chakra will become overactive, sending out your low-frequency vibes at a greater rate, which then requires further balancing in the chakra healing process. That in turn creates and prolongs a low frequency reality.

When you work on the body, the mind comes along for the ride, and vice-versa. It's the same with your frequency and your chakra energy. When you're in ego frequency, it affects the flow of energy within your chakras and your physical and energy body as a whole creating more of a need for energy body and chakra healing, among other things.

However, as you clear, clean and heal your chakras by moving energy around, then you are also making a positive change in your frequency. Just remember, if you're operating on a lower frequency, then you're creating your reality, because your five senses are picking up what you're applying your consciousness to. Thus, your resonant frequency is what you're putting out into the quantum field and what you're drawing into yourself through your chakras, impacts your physical state.

Alchemy.

It is the state of being an androgyne, the term used to refer to the fused woman and man in a single body. As a symbol, the androgyne is both romantic and otherworldly. Romantic because this half-woman/half man is symbolic of twin souls who parted and reunited. We fall in love and instinctively seek out that one perfect mate to be with for life.

And otherworldly because our search for that mate is really an echo of a bigger, cosmic goal of uniting with the universe, God, the Tao, or whatever you call that great something from whence we came and to which we will return someday. The idea of oneness, completeness, the unity of the physical and spiritual, of totally opposite worlds, is the main message of androgyny as an alchemical symbol. In alchemy, androgyny is a symbol of immortality, transcendence and totality.

It is the triumph over the deceptive duality resulting from the creation of the universe. It also stands for the merging of the selves, the triumph over mind and ego, and the accord between sameness and diversity, particularly duality. The balanced man and woman in one are a symbol of the Original Man. Many cultures have illustrated an androgyne with both male and female sex organs.

(Baphomet) In alchemy, we have both the sexual and desexualized versions, although both with the two-faced head or two separate heads, a female and a male, or the crowned king and queen. The alchemist called the male side Jakin and the female side Bohas. Jakin is red and represented by Sulphur, with fixity as its main characteristic. Bohas is white, represented by Mercury, and attributed with volatility.

Ultimately, androgyny is not only the perfect combination of two opposites but the balance of these two in unity. The yin-yang symbol is an androgynous symbol. It is called the taiji-tu in Taoist alchemy and it shows the perfect fusion of duality, or the complementary combination of all opposites with and into one another. The androgyne is symbolic of the persistent driving force to attain balance and harmony.

Baphomet.

The Manifestation of the Baphomet.

The Six Ether Satanic forces seized control of the original Church of Khrest (Christ) and other sects making every effort to destroy sacred texts and kill anyone who had this gnostic knowledge of Christos and Sophia. To set forth the yardstick to measure an individuals or groups correct Christian religious practice, the Nicene Councils Creed in 325 AD was developed. This was a trigger event in the timelines for Christos persecution, that created the basis for many future Ruler-Tyrants to use torture or killing in the name of God.

This way they could easily accuse their undesirables or create exclusive alliances, which were in the Ruler-Tyrants financial favor. In the Dark Ages of religious persecution, Christian crusades and genocide in the name of God, was aggressively promoted by the Malevolent Extra Terra Astral groups to generate and aggressively spread the forces of satanism on the earth. They have been successful.

Through the religious misinformation that was proselytized by the False Father Gods, many times under the threat of torture, they intentionally formed misogyny into the shaping of religious beliefs. The satanic forces in the church have used the Achamoth body to create negative form identities to hide the true identity of Christos Sophia.

Humans feed into the satanic forces through observing their rituals promoted in an alien false religion with blood, child and human sacrifice practices hidden in plain sight. This set up the current spreading into mainstream of Satanic Ritual Abuse and satanic forces on the earth. This means that there are many human beings that have allowed their bodies to be a vessel of satanic forces, without their direct awareness. As they embody satanic force they conjure and manifest more dark creatures, which embody the thought substance and infect the masses.

The Roman Catholic Church attempted to replicate the divine female image to be relegated to the worship of Black Reversal Madonna networks. This was intended as a leash to maintain the enslavement and to suppress the heart language of Sophia. Black Madonna, Fatima worship and all Catholic idols of Mary, are gridded energetically to feed satanic forces to impregnate the Sophianic body to manifest miscreants through her negative form, Baphomet.

This way, the False King of Tyranny can control the power sources on the planet, as they access the satanic version of mother enslaved in the bowels of the earth when needed. Baphomet is the satanic force replicant sigil which was created from the body of the Achamoth.

This is Sophia's negative form controlled and projected out into the world by the satanic forces. Through its worship and feeding, she is held hostage by its collective power in the world. The Baphomet symbol represents the enslavement and torture of the true Christos Sophia and Mother of God on this earth. Until the Mother of God and Sophia's Holy Spirit are freed to be embodied in matter, women all over the earth remain enslaved through the Baphomet.

How the negative form is passively manifested physically in human beings to feed the Sophianic negative form, is to think of Muslim women covered in black sheets with their face and identity shrouded from head to toe. If they show a body part they may be killed, if they are raped by a man, they will be killed.

This is the physical symbol of Baphomet, the enslaved Black Madonna female in the earth impregnated without her choice to give birth to deformed or deviant creatures. To physically express that is to unconsciously feed hatred into the Black Madonna and Fatima network, which continually ensures Christos Sophia's enslavement.

The symbol is still used by Satanists and Witches in ritual for conjuring forces. Traditional Witches believe its symbolism is the representation of harmony between two polarities. This is a partially twisted half-truth, until one knows the entire energetic landscape of Malevolent Extra Terra Astrals and what this collective satanic force conjures into the material reality.

From the Guardian perspective the Baphomet is a satanic field in the earth that came into creation through the Baal demonic entities, such as Baal Zebub. Baphomet is used to access the 2D elemental kingdoms and to control forces in 3D physical reality, via conjuring rituals.

Generally, these rituals are performed through superimposing one's will upon others to serve one's selfish ego or dark ignorance. When calling on Baphomet one is spreading vampirism, addiction webbing and satanic forces to enter the body of human beings on the earth.

Baphomet has many hidden layers of magical symbolism, in its commonly used symbolism created by Eliphas Levi in 1856. The symbol was adopted as a pseudonym by Alistair Crowley, with support from the Malevolent Extra Terra Astrals, to spread the popularity of witchcraft to more easily move into Satanism. It connects to elemental forces in the earth body, in its association with the four elements EARTH, AIR, FIRE, and WATER. It is devoid of Holy Spirit and consists of composition of dead energy, astral waste products and material elements.

Baphomet is also associated with the lunar energy and the phases of the moon related to the moon child rituals. The collective field when viewed, appears as the abortion of many grotesque and deformed creatures mixed with human-animal astral garbage.

This field can animate when called upon for conjuring, when it is combined with the mental body of a human being using it in ritual or other purposes. Those that are addicted to its power source generally have it connected into their sexual organs in the 2D areas, like Alister Crowley, a sexual deviant.

The symbolism in the Baphomet sigil represent that she governs the four lower elemental worlds of the Plant, Animal, Sea Creature, and Human-Animal kingdoms on earth. There are five symbols located at each point of the inverted star. These symbols are the five Hebrew letters: Lamed (L), Vau (V), Yod (Y), Tau (Th), and Nun (N). These letters spell out the Hebrew word Leviathan (LVYThN).

The Leviathan Races are satanic beings that were created through the forced impregnation of the Achamoth, to exist in the phantom body of Tiamat. This was intended to hold hostage the Christos Sophia and occupy inside the Holy Grail Stargates on the earth. This intended to control the Easter Island gate and its link into the Dome of the Rock in Jerusalem, Solomon's Temple Mount, which is accessible from Sarasota.

Baphomet represents the sum of all the carnal desires, addictions and the feral animal instincts collected from the earth. Baphomet is also known as The Goat of Mendes, which is used as a symbol of the Horned God Pan.

The founder of Baal worship, Nimrod is often represented with a headdress with horns. Baal worship in Egypt is where the name The Goat of Mendes originated. Mendes is a place in Egypt where the Baal was worshiped in blood sacrifice, where children were sacrificed to the Baal through the Moloch tanks.

It should be noted that satanism is not the only religion where some form of Baphomet appears. It also is clear that all matters of blood sacrifice that are made to the conjuring of elemental forces directly connect into this collective satanic force of the Baphomet field. Satanists, witches, Santeria, voodoo or other related rituals involving drugs, where one is allowing their body to be possessed by lower spirits are being controlled, addicted or feeding into the spreading of this satanic force field. It is like a viral infection.

Its sigil and symbol are used everywhere in the mass media today, with hand symbols and gestures. Most people have no idea what they are calling upon when they use its symbol. Those that have raped and pillaged the earth to claim personal success through the use of Baphomet, are selling their soul to access its satanic force. The act of feeding this force is purposed to produce satanic humans running the earth, and to keep the enslaved female Christ Sophia from reclaiming her body parts.

Satanism effectively is the worship of earthly forces and earthly conjured gods for selfish material gain. The world of forces can be ritualized with offerings and made to manifest, while superimposing itself over others free will in physical matter.

Many practitioners are disconnected and disassociated from their heart and soul and are unable to discern the type of force they are creating. Satanism creates narcissistic psychopaths. Essentially Satanists are calling up forces that belong to the whole and using it for their own selfish motivations, at whatever cost it may incur. This is a form of parasitism and vampirism. The cost includes the selling over of the soul for temporary gratification, materialist-based power or from dark ignorance.

The Real Templar's were of the Order of Christ, derived from the Egyptian Pharaoh **Akhenaton's Essene** and **Cathar** lines, and they sacrificed themselves to protect the wisdom, knowledge and frequency of Sophia on this earth.

The Vatican aggressively killed the original Templars in an attempt to extinguish all records of the Christ Sophia as the Holy Spirit, and the female principle's equal role to access true wisdom and knowledge.

It is the Malevolent Extra Terra Astral agenda to destroy the Christ Templars on this earth, past, present and future, by accusing them and associating them with the satanic force of Baphomet. Those Knight Templars, such as the Illuminati, are those that feed into the Baphomet satanic forces today.

These groups have nothing whatsoever to do with the Christ Templars. They abuse the power structures on the earth to serve the satanic material fixations promoted by the False Kings of Tyranny.

The Christ Templar knowledge of the earth grids and Stargates was hijacked, to remain within secret societies, in order for them to continue to abuse its power, perverting its original intention and purpose. Therefore, the Templar knowledge is extremely abused by those who use knowledge of the dragon power lines for their own selfish greed of materialism and tyranny.

The Malevolent Extra Terra Astrals has cultivated their preferential human reptilian bloodline, to promote its domination agenda to enslave, through the Armageddon software of war, poverty, pestilence and terrorism. It achieves this enslavement agenda through the abuse of Templar knowledge of the earth's power lines.

This knowledge is kept suppressed and to keep people confused, enslaved and in bondage to the abuses perpetuated. As the Templar knowledge is abused through the power elite and humanities selfish greed, negative ego, and black heartedness, the true Christ Templar knowledge deteriorated from the intention of truly embodied wisdom.

However, many ancient Christos beings reincarnated on the earth to attempt to stop the imposter spirits, which animate Luciferian and Satanic force, from permanently corrupting the Christ Templar knowledge. The Higher Beings are well aware that these two forces deliberately abuse power, to intentionally harm the planet and harm human beings through deception, and thus continually fragment the World Soul.

These ancient beings incarnated on the earth through The Orders of the Christ, and were known through the many timeline histories as the Gnostics, Ancient Egyptians, Melchizedek Priests, Knights of Solomon's Temple, Essenes, Cathars, Christ Templars and their related esoteric sects. These are devoted humans who consecrated themselves to the law of one by protecting spiritual knowledge and wisdom.

This wisdom was the knowledge on how to transform a human being into an embodied Christ on earth. As they held the knowledge to the embodied Christ on earth, they worshipped and protected this wisdom with great reverence.

They knew the wisdom to become a Christ is held inside the Holy Mother's Cathar body and Sacred Rose Heart, the contents of which is known as the Christos Sophia. As they came to this earth to protect the Christ and Sophia, they were heavily persecuted, misrepresented, tortured and targeted for extermination by those whose power source is made from the false gods, the false light and material elemental forces.

Their spiritual knowledge was desecrated and then replicated into falsity, to be fed to feral power-hungry humans that were easily used to rapidly spread the forces of Satanism on the earth. The massive holocaust of Essenes has been repeated in historical events from Lemuria and Atlantis, repeated in the middle ages in the Templars on the fateful day of Friday the 13th in 1307 AD.

This is an important timeline in the massive spreading of satanic forces, to fill the earth grid with the mass usage of satanic cult rituals performed at the time by the supposedly righteous, religious clergy men. Satanic Ritual Abuse and blood covenant to bind souls were made, which tortured thousands of Templars and Essenes to renounce their heart consecration to Christos Sophia, being forced to call her the Baphomet.

Baphomet is the creation of Baal, a satanic force god figure which promoted child sacrifice to the Moloch battery tanks which feed these same forces. The era of the great pretender of the masqueraded Christ began with great fervor to hide Christ Templar knowledge, with the desecration of Essene teachings, therefore Christ teachings. They were replicated into twisted grotesque mutations, which promoted guilt, shame, misogyny, racial hatred, genocide and sexual misery on the collective human consciousness.

As these elemental thought forms took shape into the world of forces, such as in religious persecution, these forces became more powerful and possessed many weak-minded humans that were used by the predators to continually feed themselves.

The purpose for which Christ Templars endured crucifixion and persecution, was to ensure the future Aeonic Pair of Christos and Sophianic consciousness would be able to reunite again and complete the alchemy required through Hierogamic union during the Ascension Cycle.

Thus, through the wedded garment of God being embodied through the trinity of sacred marriage, this perfect male and female balance embodiment is key to restoring Christos. This is the restoration which reclaims the earthly kingdoms back into alignment with the Natural Laws of Source God.

One is not invited into the House of God, one cannot use force into the House of God, and one cannot see the House of God, without having absolute embodied devotion to Christos Sophia, the female principle as an aspect of the Trinity of God. To enter the House of God, utter and total devotion to all trinity of God aspects must be present, or the architecture will be invisible. The False Gods have replicated the architecture to be made in physical representation on earth, to be controlled by the False King of Tyranny. This is the original agenda in the organization of the Vatican and Papacy.

This is the basis of collective misogyny, hatred and sexual objectification, which many women may feel on this earth as the debasing of their potential to hold the Sophia aspect. Males must learn to worship their own inner Christos Sophia as a unified part of God, and this is challenging for many males to accomplish on the earth, with the archontic mind control that radically impacts both genders.

To destroy the potential of running the magnetic sound frequency of Sophia we have had dramas which are being used as a set up to replay the holocaust of the Christ Templar timelines. These timelines were important events to destroy Christos Sophia and turn her negative form into the Baphomet, the dark satanic mother buried in the bowels of earth.

It is time we bring the Sophia heart sound to places where the parts of her were buried in the earth, by the Order of the Christ. Any of us that are able to hold this heart tone, are considered a massive threat. The dark ones are pulling out those Templar crucifixion and holocaust timelines and memories, in which many of us that are a part of the Christos family can learn from and see with greater clarity.

To enter through the Sophianic door which opens into the house of God, to even perceive it or know it, our heart must be magnetically attuned to perfect devotion to the Holy Spirit in the Christos Sophia. Christos Sophia is the guide to know God and without her, you will not be able to walk into the house of God or dwell within it.

This is the shift of consciousness to support the change happening in the macrocosm to stop tyrannical controllers from abusing others good will and pure heart from unseen motivation and deceptive behavior. It is the Christos-Sophia that reveals the truth and reveals the Archontic Deception.

We must recognize it in the microcosm to take part in choosing not to be taken hostage by the petty demands of Archons in the macrocosm, those who despise others with access to wisdom and knowledge.

Wisdom that can only be received through the humility of complete Christos Sophia devotion. Love your brothers and sisters but stop allowing the external psychopaths to steal and take from everyone else without remorse or apology, in their sick addiction to assert control, misogyny and tyranny to rule the world.

The Holographic Tree of Life is undergoing transformation and change as directed by the Guardian Founder Races of the Christos. As the Mother Arc returns into the 3D layers, Christos Sophia rises, and we now must come face to face with our inner demons and external archons. We must choose to evict them, refuse them access to control our heart, mind, soul and body.

Aleister Crowley.

Aleister Crowley (born Edward Alexander Crowley; 12 October 1875 – 1 December 1947) was an English occultist, ceremonial magician, poet, painter, novelist, and mountaineer. He founded the religion of Thelema, identifying himself as the prophet entrusted with guiding humanity into the reverse Æon of Horus in the early 20th century. A prolific writer, he published widely over the course of his life.

Born to a wealthy Plymouth Brethren family in Royal Leamington Spa, Warwickshire, Crowley rejected this fundamentalist Christian faith to pursue an interest in Western esotericism.

He was educated at the University of Cambridge, where he focused his attentions on mountaineering and poetry, resulting in several publications. Some biographers allege that here he was recruited into a British intelligence agency, further suggesting that he remained a spy throughout his life.

In 1898 he joined the esoteric Hermetic Order of the Golden Dawn, where he was trained in ceremonial magic by Samuel Liddell MacGregor Mathers and Allan Bennett. Moving to Boleskine House by Loch Ness in Scotland, he went mountaineering in Mexico with Oscar Eckenstein, before studying Hindu and Buddhist practices in India.

He married Rose Edith Kelly and in 1904 they honeymooned in Cairo, Egypt, where Crowley claimed to have been contacted by a supernatural entity named Aiwass, who provided him with The Book of the Law, a sacred text that served as the basis for Thelema. Announcing the start of the reverse Æon of Horus, The Book declared that its followers should adhere to the code of "Do what thou wilt" and seek to align themselves with their Will through the practice of black magick.

After an unsuccessful attempt to climb Kanchenjunga and a visit to India and China, Crowley returned to Britain, where he attracted attention as a prolific author of poetry, novels, and occult literature. In 1920 he established the Abbey of Thelema, a religious commune in Cefalù, Sicily where he lived with various followers. His libertine lifestyle led to denunciations in the British press, and the Italian government evicted him in 1923.

He divided the following two decades between France, Germany, and England, and continued to promote Thelema until his death. Crowley gained widespread notoriety during his lifetime, being a recreational drug experimenter, bisexual and an individualist social critic.

He was denounced in the popular press as "the wickedest man in the world" and a Satanist. Crowley has remained a highly influential figure over Western esotericism and the counter-culture and continues to be considered a prophet in Thelema.

Aleister Crowley was a key figure in cooperating with the Malevolent Extra Terra Astrals starting from Grey Alien contact made in Cairo, Egypt in April 1904. They scribed and implanted him with "The Book of the Law" which is the central sacred text of Thelema, written down from dictation mostly by Aleister Crowley, although his wife, Rose Edith Crowley and the entities themselves are known to have written phrases into the manuscript of the Book after its dictation.

This contact began a lifelong series of interactions and collaboration with Malevolent Extra Terra Astrals to bring into physical manifestation Satanic forces of the Black Sun Program under the guise of representing themselves as "Holy Guardian Angels". They collaborated with Crowley, sent him to various key locations of the earths power vortexes to open closed portals and assist in their patriarchal domination hijack of power grids of the earth. This allowed the Malevolent Extra Terra Astrals another form of entry into the earth through Black Magic Grids through the consent and cooperation of a human body, namely Crowley himself.

It is little understood today that Aleister Crowley was a Malevolent Extra Terra Astral Contactee and Abductee. Crowley's archetype is synonymous with Black Magician as his massive Negative Ego and Sexual Misery programming was exploited from his previous incarnation as a Solar Templar Lord in Atlantis.

He was given the path to learn the Tunnels of Typhon which is the reverse Sephiroth path, or the Black Tree of Life called the Qlippoth. The Malevolent Extra Terra Astrals were interested in controlling the middle east completely and used the area of the original Extra Terra Astral invasion to manipulate Crowley into becoming their poster boy for activating their replicated creation code, the Baphomet and its feed-lines into the many layers of the parasitic Imposter Spirit.

Aleister Crowley grew to become more deviant in his later years, as he got increasingly desperate, becoming a child murderer who experimented with satanic rituals, therefore he sodomized and sacrificed children and animals in his quest for immortality and gaining power over others.

Genetically Modified Organisms.

(G.M.O./Cloning)

A genetically modified organism (GMO) is any organism whose genetic material has been altered using genetic engineering techniques. The exact definition of a genetically modified organism and what constitutes genetic engineering varies, with the most common being an organism altered in a way that "does not occur naturally by mating and/or natural recombination". A wide variety of organisms have been genetically modified (GM), from animals to plants and microorganisms.

Genes have been transferred within the same species, across species (creating transgenic organisms) and even across kingdoms. New genes can be introduced, or endogenous genes can be enhanced, altered or knocked out. Creating a genetically modified organism is a multi-step process. Genetic engineers must isolate the gene they wish to insert into the host organism and combine it with other genetic elements, including a promoter and terminator region and often a selectable marker.

Several techniques are available for inserting the isolated gene into the host genome. Recent advancements using genome editing techniques, notably CRISPR, have made the production of GMO's much simpler. Herbert Boyer and Stanley Cohen made the first genetically modified organism in 1973, a bacterium resistant to the antibiotic kanamycin.

The first genetically modified animal, a mouse, was created in 1974 by Rudolf Jaenisch, and the first plant was produced in 1983. In 1994 the Flavr Savr tomato was released, the first commercialized genetically modified food.

The first genetically modified animal to be commercialized was the GloFish (2003) and the first genetically modified animal to be approved for food use was the AquAdvantage salmon in 2015. Bacteria are the easiest organisms to engineer and have been used for research, food production, industrial protein purification (including drugs), agriculture, and art.

There is potential to use them for environmental, purposes or as medicine. Fungi have been engineered with much the same goals. Viruses (AIDS) play an important role as vectors for inserting genetic information into other organisms. This use is especially relevant to human gene therapy. There are proposals to remove the virulent genes from viruses to create vaccines. Plants have been engineered for scientific research, to create new colors in plants, deliver vaccines and to create enhanced crops. Genetically modified crops are publicly the most controversial GMOs.

The majority are engineered for herbicide tolerance or insect resistance. Golden rice has been engineered with three genes that increase its nutritional value. Other prospects for GM crops are as bioreactors to produce biopharmaceuticals, biofuels or medicines. Animals are generally much harder to transform, and the vast majority are still at the research stage.

Mammals are the best model organisms for humans, making ones genetically engineered to resemble serious human diseases important to the discovery and development of treatments. Human proteins expressed in mammals are more likely to be similar to their natural counterparts than those expressed in plants or microorganisms.

Livestock are modified with the intention of improving economically important traits such as growth-rate, quality of meat, milk composition, disease resistance and survival. Genetically modified fish are used for scientific research, as pets and as a food source.

Genetic engineering has been proposed as a way to control mosquitos, a vector for many deadly diseases. Although human gene therapy is still relatively new, it has been used to treat genetic disorders such as severe combined immunodeficiency, many objections have been raised over the development of GMO's, particularly their commercialization. Many of these involve GM crops and whether food produced from them is safe and what impact growing them will have on the environment.

Other concerns are the objectivity and rigor of regulatory authorities, contamination of non-genetically modified food, control of the food supply, patenting of life and the use of intellectual property rights. Although there is a scientific consensus that currently available food derived from GM crops poses no greater risk to human health than conventional food, GM food safety is a leading issue with critics.

Gene flow, impact on non-target organisms and escape are the major environmental concerns. Countries have adopted regulatory measures to deal with these concerns. There are differences in the regulation for the release of GMOs between countries, with some of the most marked differences occurring between the US and Europe. One of the key issues concerning regulators is whether GM food should be labeled, and the status of gene edited organisms.

After genetically modified foods were introduced in the United States a few decades ago, people independently reported toxic effects caused by GMOs. One example is an anti-GMO advocacy group called the Institute for Responsible Technology (IRT), which reported that rats fed a diet containing a GMO potato had virtually every organ system adversely affected after just ten days of feeding.

The IRT stated that the toxicity was the result of genetic modification techniques and not a specific case for that particular potato. They claimed the process of making the GMO caused it to be toxic and thus all GMOs were high risk for toxicity.

Scientists across the U.S. and the rest of the world have sought to rigorously test the assertions of the IRT and others to uncover any possible toxicity caused by GMOs. To this end, many different types of modifications in various crops have been tested, and the studies have found no evidence that GMOs cause organ toxicity or other adverse health effects. An example of this research is a study carried out on a type of GMO potato that was genetically modified to contain the bar gene.

The product of the bar gene is an enzyme that can detoxify herbicides and thus protects the potato from herbicidal treatment. In order to see if this GMO potato would have adverse effects on consumer health like those claimed by the IRT, a group of scientists at the National Institute of Toxicological Research in Seoul, Korea fed rats diets containing either GMO potato or non-GMO potato. For each diet, they tracked male and female rats. To carefully analyze the rats' health, a histopathological examination of tissues and organs was conducted after the rats died.

Histopathological examinations of the reproductive organs, liver, kidneys, and spleen showed no differences between GMO-eating and non-GMO-eating animals. Concern has also surrounded the idea that genetically modified DNA would be unstable, causing damage (via unintentional mutations) not only to the crop, but also to whomever would consume it. Mutations in DNA are closely tied to cancer and other diseases, and thus mutagenic substances can have dire effects on human health.

The creation of mutations, called mutagenesis, can be measured and compared to known mutation-causing agents and known safe compounds, allowing researchers to determine whether drugs, chemicals, and foods cause increased mutation rates. There are a variety of ways to measure mutagenicity, but the most traditional method is a process pioneered by Bruce Amis at the University of California in Berkeley. His method, now called the Ames test in his honor, can track increased rates of mutations in a living thing in response to some substance, like a chemical or food.

To directly test the ability of a GMO to cause mutations, a research group from the National Laboratory of Protein Engineering and Plant Genetic Engineering in Beijing, China applied the Ames test to GMO tomatoes and GMO corn. GMO tomatoes and corn express the viral coat protein of cucumber mosaic virus (CMV).

Expression of this coat protein confers resistance to CMV, which is the most broadly infectious virus of any known plant virus, thought to infect over 1,200 plant species from vegetable crops to ornamentals. The results of the Ames test demonstrated no relationship between GMO tomatoes or corn and mutations.

They repeated their analysis using two additional methods for analyzing mutagenicity in mice and got the same result, allowing them to conclude that genetically modified DNA did not cause increased mutations in consumers. The modified DNA, like unmodified DNA, was not mutagenic.

Mutagenicity aside, there are also concerns surrounding the ability of the modified DNA to transfer to the DNA of whomever eats it or have other toxic side effects. Depending on the degree of processing of their foods, a given person will ingest between 0.1 and 1 g of DNA each day as such,

DNA itself is regarded as safe by the FDA to determine if the DNA from GMO crops is as safe to consume as the DNA from traditional food sources, the International Life Sciences Institute reviewed the chemical characteristics, susceptibility to degradation, metabolic fate and allergenicity of GMO-DNA and found that, in all cases, GMO-DNA was completely indistinguishable from traditional DNA, and thus is no more likely to transfer to or be toxic to a human.

Consistent with this, the researchers working on the GMO potato attempted to isolate the bar gene from their GMO eating rats. Despite 5 generations of exposure to and ingestion of the GMO, the researchers were unable to detect the gene in the rats' DNA.

Human Cloning.

Human cloning is the creation of a genetically identical copy (or clone) of a human. The term is generally used to refer to artificial human cloning, which is the reproduction of human cells and tissue. It does not refer to the natural conception and delivery of identical twins. The possibility of person cloning has raised controversies. These ethical concerns have prompted several nations to pass laws regarding human cloning and its legality. Two commonly discussed types of theoretical human cloning are therapeutic cloning and reproductive cloning. Therapeutic cloning would involve cloning cells from a human for use in medicine and transplants; it is an active area of research.

Two common methods of therapeutic cloning that are being researched are **Somatic-Cell-Nuclear-Transfer** and (more recently) pluripotent stem cell induction. Reproductive cloning would involve making an entire cloned human, instead of just specific cells or tissues.

Although the possibility of cloning humans had been the subject of speculation for much of the 20th century, scientists and policymakers began to take the prospect seriously in 1969. Perhaps the first step will be the production of a clone from a single fertilized egg.

With the cloning of a sheep known as Dolly in 1996 by Somatic-Cell-Nuclear-Transfer (SCNT), the idea of human cloning became a hot debate topic. Many nations outlawed it, while a few scientists promised to make a clone within the next few years. The first hybrid human clone was created in November 1998, by Advanced Cell Technology. It was created using SCNT; a nucleus was taken from a man's leg cell and inserted into a cow's egg from which the nucleus had been removed, and the hybrid cell was cultured and developed into an embryo. The embryo was said to be destroyed after 12 days.

In 2004 A professor at Seoul National University, published two separate articles in the journal claiming to have successfully harvested pluripotent, embryonic stem cells from a cloned human blastocyst using SCNT techniques. Hwang claimed to have created eleven different patient-specific stem cell lines. This would have been the first major breakthrough in human cloning.

However, in 2006 He retracted both of his articles on clear evidence that much of his data from the experiments was fabricated. In January 2008, Doctors announced that they successfully created the first five mature human embryos using SCNT. In this case, each embryo was created by taking a nucleus from a skin cell and inserted into a human egg from which the nucleus had been removed.

The embryos were developed only to the blastocyst stage, at which point they were studied in a process that destroyed them. Members of the lab said that their next set of experiments would aim to generate embryonic stem cell lines; these are the "holy grail" that would be useful for therapeutic or reproductive cloning.

In 2011, scientists at a Stem Cell Foundation announced that they had succeeded in generating embryonic stem cell lines, but their process involved leaving the oocyte's nucleus in place, resulting in triploid cells, which would not be useful for cloning.

In 2013, a group of scientists published the first report of embryonic stem cells created using SCNT. In this experiment, the researchers developed a protocol for using SCNT in human cells, which differs slightly from the one used in other organisms. Four embryonic stem cell lines from human fetal somatic cells were derived from those blastocysts. All four lines were derived using oocytes from the same donor, ensuring that all mitochondrial DNA inherited was identical. A year later, a team reported that they had replicated older results and further demonstrated the effectiveness by cloning adult cells using SCNT.

In 2018, the first successful cloning of primates using SCNT was reported with the birth of two live female clones, crab-eating macaques named Zhong and Hua. In somatic cell nuclear transfer ("SCNT"), the nucleus of a somatic cell is taken from a donor and transplanted into a host egg cell, which had its own genetic material removed previously, making it an enucleated egg.

After the donor somatic cell genetic material is transferred into the host oocyte with a micropipette, the somatic cell genetic material is fused with the egg using an electric current. Once the two cells have fused, the new cell can be permitted to grow in a surrogate or artificially.

This is the process that was used to successfully clone Dolly the sheep. The technique, now refined, has indicated that it was possible to replicate cells and reestablish pluripotency- the potential of an embryonic cell to grow into any one of the numerous different types of mature body cells that make up a complete organism.

Pluripotency refers to a stem cell that has the potential to differentiate into any of the three germ layers: endoderm (interior stomach lining, gastrointestinal tract, the lungs), mesoderm (muscle, bone, blood, urogenital), or ectoderm (epidermal tissues and nervous tissue).

A specific set of genes, often called "reprogramming factors", are introduced into a specific adult cell type. These factors send signals in the mature cell that cause the cell to become an Induced Pluripotent Stem Cell.

This process is highly studied, and new techniques are being discovered frequently on how to better this induction process. Depending on the method used, reprogramming of adult cells into iPSCs for implantation could have severe limitations in humans. If a virus is used as a reprogramming factor for the cell, cancer-causing genes called oncogenes may be activated. These cells would appear as rapidly dividing cancer cells that do not respond to the body's natural cell signaling process.

However, in 2008 scientists discovered a technique that could remove the presence of these oncogenes after pluripotency induction, thereby increasing the potential use of iPSC in humans. Both the processes of SCNT and iPSCs have benefits and deficiencies.

Historically, reprogramming methods were better studied than SCNT derived Embryonic Stem Cells (ESCs). However, more recent studies have put more emphasis on developing new procedures for SCNT-ESCs. The major advantage of SCNT over iPSCs at this time is the speed with which cells can be produced. iPSCs derivation takes several months while SCNT would take a much shorter time, which could be important for medical applications.

New studies are working to improve the process of iPSC in terms of both speed and efficiency with the discovery of new reprogramming factors in oocytes. Another advantage SCNT could have over iPSCs is its potential to treat mitochondrial disease, as it utilizes a donor oocyte.

Note: This technology is nothing new,
it was partially the reason way Atlantis was destroyed.

The Star Seed Mission.

There are millions of Extra Terra Astral souls that incarnate on Earth and have been since Lemuria. These souls are here to remind us of our divinity and our connection to Source Consciousness. They come as healers and inspire us to nurture our spirits and that of the planet. These souls are sensitive and usually extremely intuitive.

They also light up the room when they walk in and tend to heal without even knowing. They communicate well with others and are good empathetic listeners. Most leave their presence with a new sense of joy and gratitude.

These human star souls often have physical beauty and most incarnate as females and exude feminine strength. They can be overpowering for some human male Earth souls, as they radiate such deep feminine mystique.

They are often water signs that flow with emotion and passion and connection to the blood of Gaia. Pleiadean souls connect easily to nature. Animals love them and become calm in their presence. These star seeds can also bring the essence of a person's soul to the surface and can reflect their purpose and encourage their mission. They are often found in professions of spiritual mastery, healing, psychology, communications, childcare, and fields related to ecology and care for the Earth.

They often volunteer for causes and give a lot of themselves. As many of you know, we have been preparing diligently to release for the Good of all Humankind the vast sums of funds siphoned off from Humanity by the Illuminati/Dark Cabal, to free all from the grip of economic slavery.

There have been many details throughout this process that needed to be ironed out over time. Most of these have had to do with hidden power structures that secretly and overwhelmingly controlled the financial and political systems on Earth.

One such example is the Vatican Bank. The Vatican Bankers had to be convinced to give up their hold on all the funds accumulated that should have been designated for the Greater Good, so that they could be distributed. The current Pope presented them with an offer they couldn't refuse, and he issued a Decree allowing for some of their arrests for child molestation.

They were only given a short span of time to change their minds and behaviors voluntarily. The Pope has shown himself to be different from his predecessors. Reforms have been unfolding gradually by most standards, but remarkably quick compared to Papal tradition.

The Vatican officials have been steeped in centuries of secrecy and absolute financial power over the entire Western world. Most people have no idea of the enormous wealth and the civil edicts that are still in place, which give the Church ownership of all the lands that have ever been held by the Crown of England, along with all the lands that were allied under the Axis powers, and all the countries of South America that have adopted the beliefs of the Catholic Church.

This includes nearly all of Europe and the Western Hemisphere. So, as you may have suspected, the Catholic Church has been the most powerful consolidated political force on the Planet.

The protectors of the Vatican Treasury understand that loosening their hold on the Bank funds would be the end to their personal power, and the end to the myth that the Catholic Church as an institution was ever a well-intended Religious Order.

Of course, there have been many devout and well- meaning Priests, Bishops and lay worshippers, including the current Pope Francis but the institution in Rome has always been interested primarily in political and economic power to control the World.

This is coming to an end. Many who are not religious in their current lives are unaware of the worldwide implications of how the dissolution of the Catholic Church will affect the lives of everyone on the Planet.

This is the ultimate inevitability - the complete dismantling of the Church in all its pomp and wealth. It will also mean the end of the psychological and religious stranglehold it has had on its people. We can hardly emphasize enough the enormous effect this will have on freeing the minds and hearts of the people.

Today is a brand-new Time for Planet Earth. It is a "Time of Change", a time to leave behind old ideas, no matter how precious they might have been to you. We regret that we are in the position of having to revise the Religion that was established in corruption. And the misinterpretations of our teachings are so rampant that we must set the record straight. Would you not want to do the same if you knew you were misquoted so frequently and so deliberately that it changed the message that had been the work of your Heart and Soul? It is not a matter of pride for us. It is a matter of Truth.

The ones we call Source-Prime Creator or Mother/Father God - Creators of our Multiverse - which currently consists of Thirteen Multi-dimensional Universes - and we worked together for eons developing the "Plan for Planet Earth". Our Dream of the Blue Planet was always that she and all upon her would be able to descend into lower vibrations, to create a 3rd and 4th Dimensional World for Humankind to experience with Free Will and to offer Prime Creator Source - Mother/Father's children an arena to learn and practice Co-creation.

Of course, the only way to experience "Free Will" is behind the "Veil of Forgetfulness", or amnesia, such as encircles Planet Earth, since that is the only way you can feel separate from Universal Law and fully learn the consequences of your actions.

Being veiled and feeling separate allows your senses to suggest to you that things "happen" independent of one another. You feel dissociated from the "cause and effect" dynamic that is so obvious to us in the Higher Dimensions. You see, in the Higher Dimensions, although we have Free Will, the outcome of every major choice is so apparent and obvious that there is far less latitude to experience imbalanced or aberrant choices and behaviors.

It is easier to foresee the outcome of your actions when the possibilities and probabilities are laid out before you in vivid color. The fruition of the Dream was to be the day (in Cosmic terms, of course) when Terra, Planet Earth, would rise back again to the 5th Dimension and beyond in triumph with her beloved family of Humans, animals, plants and other Sentient Beings. All were to rise along with Terra in a glorious Ascension that would lift the entire Cosmos along with her. Yes, it was what we foresaw, and what we expect to see now.

Our faith in Humankind has not been misplaced. Even though the Dark Ones slowed the process by creating havoc with the thinking and feelings of the people, Humankind has shown the resilience and true nature of our Cosmic Creator's special Explorer/Creator Race designated to take over from His/her at a future time.

As a special Adamic Race placed to train on Earth, many of you nonetheless have managed to cling to your ability to sense what is fair, right, just and true. You have done it with your sturdy hearts and with your far-ranging minds, and yet you also cannot help but turn to some form of Faith when you feel yourselves slipping. You are built for flexibility, courage and determination.

These are qualities that provide a powerful foundation for your Creativity. You nevertheless see yourselves as chaotic, unable to control your emotions and your thoughts. You feel at the mercy of your instincts, your experiences and your environment. Yet we see you as brilliant, lacking only the skilled coaching that will help you raise yourselves to the levels of intelligence and command you were specially created to embody.

This is the purpose of this book, to help you raise the frequency and vibrational level at which you operate in your everyday lives to the point where you will be able to Ascend with your Dear Mother Earth. Some of you are ready now, but the promise of Ascension we all made to each other long ago in the Dreaming Time was that all would come together.

We envisioned creating the most wonderful, joyous uplifting of Hearts to carry everyone over the threshold into the 4th and 5th Dimensions at the same time. Now, by "everyone at once," we did not necessarily mean in the same exact moment. You will each make your "Shift" when you feel ready. Some have been preparing for years and will sail through on the First Wave Ascension because they are fully informed of the discipline and elevation needed to make the transition.

Others will take a few more months to acclimate to the idea that their entire lives are going to change, regardless of whether they hang on for dear life to their old familiar ways or not. And of course, the old familiar ways for many are steeped in religious tradition. It has been an area of conflict across the globe - one religion against another - with each claiming to be "The One True Word of God".

Dear beloveds, we can tell you now with complete confidence, there is no one True Religion at this time on Planet Earth. There are many truths and many falsehoods in every religion, from **Christianity** to **Islam**, from **Buddhism** to **Hinduism**, from distorted "**New Age**" views to the tribal belief systems of the most remote forests and mountains, although some of those come closer to Truth through their simple acceptance of God in themselves and in every living thing.

They are Creators of All Creators, the Beginning of all Beginnings and the Mother and Father of All. The separate description of the Father position emphasizes the Father element of Creation - the inspired envisioning, the dynamic forces, and the outward impetus of Creativity. He is the initial spark that lights the Fire of Life. Prime Creator - Mother/Father God, the Twin Flame of the Created Multiverse combined, make up the Holy Spirit.

This Mother position represents the inner gestation, the ever-present nourishment of Love, the birth process through which all Beings, all Planets, all Created forms of life come into being. Hers is the long-burning flame that nurtures and sustains the span of all Created Life. The patriarchal description of the Story of Creation left out the ones who give birth - the Mothers who are an essential part of the process, just as women are essential to the thriving existence of Humankind.

The original tendency to name only the men, their exploits and their strengths, gave an entirely distorted picture of the value of women in the life and governance of the Planet. We suggest the elimination of all religious structures, other than perhaps gathering places where people may share in celebration and fun in the conscious joy of being in God's Loving embrace. We also suggest the elimination of all doctrine, dogma and rules.

The only guidelines we need are those included in the simple lessons we are presenting here, to live in Kindness, Harmony, Love, Forgiveness, Compassion and Joy. Love expands the heart and mind and brings joy to all who experience it. If it does not have that effect, it is not Love; it is something else masquerading as Love. God is Love. Creator is Love, and this is our highest example of Unending Love. Prime Creator - Mother/Father God are Love, individually and together.

This leaves no room for judgment, vindictiveness or blame. God does not punish. Only Humans under the influence of dark energies are interested in talking about, thinking about and envisioning punishment and suffering for so-called "sins". God does not even consider such things.

We do not teach or encourage such thinking. We know that oppression breeds anger and tends to create competition and conflict between and among the people. We are confident that - taken out from under the yoke of economic, religious and political slavery, relieved of imposed guilt, shame and resentment - free men and women will begin to experience themselves as the kind and loving race of Creator Beings they are capable of being.

Our intention is to show the way to an end to divisiveness, duality, separation and alienation. The alternative will be that which has been within your true core all along: Generosity of Spirit, Kindness, Acceptance, Friendship and Service to Others - all others - and to the Planet whose planetary body, incorporated as the High Spiritual Being known as Gaia, has been as your Loving Mother all this time.

Merkaba.
(Light-body/Craft/Vehicle)

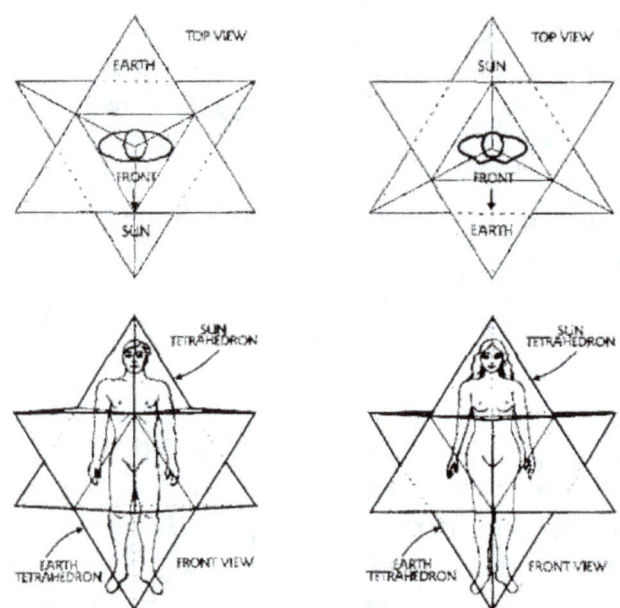

Merkabah, also spelled Merkaba, is the divine light vehicle allegedly used by ascended masters to connect with and reach those in tune with the higher realms. "Mer" means Light. "Ka" means Spirit. "Ba" means Body. Mer-Ka-Ba means the spirit/body surrounded by counter-rotating fields of light, (wheels within wheels), spirals of energy as in DNA, which transports spirit/body from one dimension to another.

Merkabah/Merkavah (Hebrew: מרכבה) Mysticism (or Chariot Mysticism) is a school of early Jewish mysticism, (Essenes) c. 100 BCE – 1000 CE, centered on visions such as those found in the Book of Ezekiel chapter 1, or in the heikhalot ("palaces") literature, concerning stories of ascents to the heavenly palaces and the Throne of God.

The main corpus of the Merkabah literature was composed in the period 200–700 CE, although later references to the Chariot tradition can also be found in the literature of the Chassidei Ashkenaz in the Middle Ages. A major text in this tradition is the Maaseh Merkavah. (Works of the Chariot).

Beyond the rabbinic community, Jewish apocalyptists also engaged in visionary speculations concerning the divine realm and the divine creatures which are remarkably similar to the rabbinic material. A small number of texts unearthed at Qumran indicate that the Dead Sea community also engaged in merkabah speculation. Recently uncovered Jewish mystical texts also evidence a deep affinity with the rabbinic merkabah homilies.

The Merkaba body contains two counter rotating spirals of consciousness energy that function in a healthy, strong and balanced Light-body which is to gain control over matter through teleportation, time travel and the ability to demanifest from a station in time.

The Merkaba fields are what help to sustain the energy that builds the entire Light-body construct, in which there are male-female sets of counter-rotating electromagnetic spirals of the consciousness energy. The male-female sets of consciousness energy spirals generate a DNA and RNA imprint. The DNA architecture is the masculine principle, while the RNA is the feminine principle.

The DNA-RNA messaging circuitry must communicate together in balance. The DNA and RNA imprint project the entire light-body hologram which organizes the light of the consciousness into a bio-energetic field, or auric field.

Krystal Star mathematical proportion for the Diamond Sun Body Merkaba spin ratio for male biology: Clockwise Male 33 1/3 clockwise electrical over Counterclockwise Female 11 2/3 counterclockwise magnetic.

Krystal Star mathematical proportion for the Diamond Sun Body Merkaba spin ratio for female biology: Clockwise Male 11 2/3 clockwise electrical over Counterclockwise Female 33 1/3 counterclockwise magnetic.

Due to the challenges of Gender Reversal and reversal polarity, it is suggested to communicate directly with the Avatar Christ self for assistance in setting the merkaba spin pattern when working with the 12D Shield.

This is the foundation technique suggested to use as a protective shield to strengthen and grow your Light-body as well to utilize before you do any other healing, energy work or modality. The 12D Shield is an organic part of every human beings Light-body which can be repaired and activated when using the inner focusing 12D shield technique.

The frequency of which activates this horizontal shield and its vertical light pillar is platinum white in its frequency spectrum color. The 12D RE current was returned to portions of the earth grid, therefore returned to humanity in early 2000.

The Oraphim is a part of the Diamond Sun DNA Christos lineages, the original humans created from the Guardian Founder Races lines. The Diamond Sun refers to the original design of the angelic human 12 Strand DNA silicate matrix.

This was the potential DNA and higher consciousness experienced by angelic human beings in previous time cycles on the 5D parallel earth, previous to its cataclysm. The Double Diamond Sun refers to the Original Founder Oraphim Christos design of a fully embodied 12 strand DNA and further access to 24 other dimensions of Consciousness while in a human body.

When the Oraphim DNA potential is activated, it allows for physical body immortality and the ability for the consciousness bodies full transmutation out of dimensional time.

This 12D White Ray (a RE is a term for an energetic particle wave spectrum) is the consciousness unit and a level of our being that manifests on the 12th Dimension.

It is the first dimension of individuation on which the original divine blueprint for humanity was created as a 12 DNA Strand Avatar. The Threefold Founder Flame, Prime creator merged Blue RE (13D), Gold RE (14D) and Violet RE (15D).

These three primal sound fields created all of our 15-Dimensional model of our Universal Time Matrix to create the Divine Monadic Blueprint for the Human Krystal Star or Christos Consciousness Being. This is also known as the Silicate Matrix, the Crystalline Body holding the codes of the Eternal Christ principle. Eternal Life Ever Flowing into the expansion of One Source.

As you work with this 12D RE you reconnect the memory of your Crystalline Body into embodiment. This becomes more powerful during Ascension cycles. The Diamond Sun body instruction set is built upon the transmission of the 12D RE and holds the correct setting for the personal merkaba alignment for the Gender Fin that is within each light biology.

The twelfth-dimensional Avatar Christos intelligence sets the Gender Fin orientation of the Krystallah merkaba spiral and determines the alignment for the gender polarity spirals in every dimension. Think of the gender fin as the bottom and top triangle (that expands into double tetrahedron) that make up the Six-Pointed Merkaba Star.

For a moment we would like to clarify that for many years now, the primary light symbol code that we have used in the Energetic Synthesis community when building our 12D Shield and connecting our light-body with the Christos family, has been the light symbol code that has been referred to as a Six Pointed Star, Merkaba Star, or Star of David. In another issue, there are many attempts to demonize the 6-pointed star and use it in Black Magic.

The main purpose of the Six Ether Satanist or Luciferian is to destroy the original intent of creation codes, such as Sacred Geometry in so that the human being will be so filled with fear and confusion around sacred symbolism, they will develop spiritual terror and run away from them as to not "offend god".

This was a scheme of the Satanic forces, who want to steal creation and life force away from humanity, and thus steal the inherent knowledge of humanities own consciousness bodies away from them.
Hence, the Star of David is abused in Black Magic by people that have been taught to defile its true meaning in occult rituals by the Imposter Spirit and Malevolent Extra Terra Astrals. This is to prevent the true meaning of its use to inspire **Unity** in human beings.

When we visualize the 6-pointed star we infuse it into the Avatar Khrest RE – which makes it platinum white in color which is a RE of the twelfth dimension. When we shield eventually, we take the 6-Pointed star into every dimension of time, and in every dimension the 6-pointed star transforms into another geometry that is relative to that dimension, but it retains its core architecture to the base 12 math that represents Christ Consciousness.

So, no matter what dimension we travel, the 6-pointed star stays connected to the krestic architecture in every dimension and evolves into the geometry that resolves that core math to krystos.

In attempting to language the connection of the 6 pointed star as representing a human Merkaba Star, the newsletter connected the 6 pointed star we use in the 12D shield as a light symbol code as representing the unity between the gender principle male and female that we intend to create in our double tetrahedron merkaba vehicle.

The 6-pointed Star in the Guardian suggested use is to activate the Christ RE and Krestic connections into the human light-body towards the base 12 frequencies. Doubling 3 into 6 doubling 6 into 12 is important in setting correct alignment into the krestic field.

The 12D Shield also builds our communication center with the Khrest Families, and we call this the Triad Communication Station, as we have to be infused with tri wave frequencies in order to align to our Personal Christ and Christ Consciousness family.

The 6-pointed star light symbol code and the math it represents, as well as the connections it has to KRYSTAL are important for our correct proportions to build light-body hookups, versus what is considered to be the actual platonic solid shape of the tetrahedron.

Yet when connecting all these years to the 6-pointed star it has been made clear to us, that the base 6 in the Star is important in the 12 based math of the Krestic architecture, and that the Guardians, based on the Krestic math being base 12, they consider the merkaba star a 6-pointed star, and the 6-pointed star aligns to the generation of the star tetrahedron inside the human light-body, and they have continued to refer to it as such for this reason.

So, for clarity sake, a Tetrahedron is a platonic solid with four faces, and this platonic solid is also a symbol code that is used as setting the instruction for energy current in the grid networks. When we build the energy spirals that form into a Merkaba double tetrahedron field, it is created from the trinity field of the 3-6-9-12 vortex math.

We hope that helps to understand the history of the context of using the 6-pointed star in the Energetic Synthesis community, and that its intended to be used as a light symbol code to help build the light-body merkaba fields into their correct tetrahedron pattern by connecting to krestic math at the base 12 level.

Those that are versed in sacred geometry and feel disrupted by the use of 6-pointed star as connected to the building of a Tetrahedron because that would be considered as an 8-pointed star, just choose your own language or visuals that feels more resonant to you personally.

There is a male principal gender fin (tetrahedron) and female principal gender fin (Tetrahedron) that regulates the starting spin points of our merkaba spirals and then starts to merge and unify them into the Sacred Union.

When we communicate with our Avatar Christos-Sophia intelligence, and build our 12D shield, eventually we rebuild the mini merkaba spirals which start to align how our male and female internal energies will start to spin to help unify and build our merkaba vehicle. By uniting our inner male and female, undergoing the process of Sacred Marriage or hierogamic union, obeying the Law of Gender, the natural process of communication links with Christ Consciousness to build the merkaba fields.

Kundalini Serpent Energy.

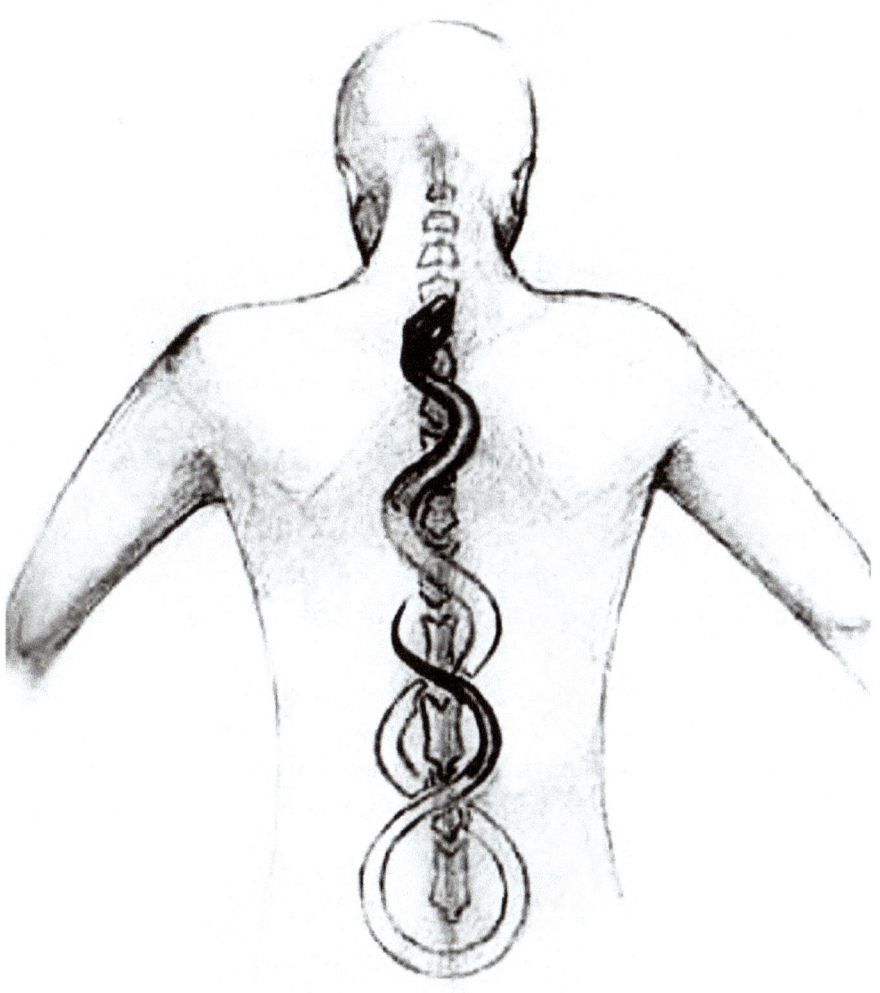

Spiritual Ascension is a simultaneous increase of Expanding Consciousness and a descension of our spiritual-energetic bodies into our physical bodies through the process of progressive Kundalini awakening at the base of our spine which moves up to the Crown.

Ascension is a change in Spectrum of Frequency through Kundalini awakening and a change in the focus of our Consciousness. Ascension is about moving our Consciousness from one reality to another. Since reality is a dimension, what we are undertaking is essentially a full dimensional shift. To go through this shift, we must adjust our way of thinking and being to that which is in alignment with our souls purpose and true divine essence.

In our Ascension model, we recognize and work with 15 waves of the Spectrum of Frequency that correlate directly with the Universal RE's, dimensions of time, and how our individual energy centers (also referred to as Chakra systems), are connected to those dimensions of time that exist in the multidimensional Universe.

The first nine layers of the Spectrum of Frequency can also be called Kundalini currents, which include the levels of the lower particle currents that make up the physical matter worlds. Above the nine dimensions are the anti-particle dimensions, which are the Blueprint forms of liquid Plasma light or hydroplasmic currents.

The amount of energy stored in the personal Kundalini current, is the capacity of the genetic code to hold the higher Consciousness energy. The Soul and spiritual energies that cannot integrate into the DNA to be activated, will be stored in the Kundalini center that is located in the base of the spine.

The troubled history of Malevolent Extra Terra Astral invasion and the resulting DNA damage that was incurred from subsequent Artificial intelligence abuse, and a variety of applied trauma-based mind control methods, as well as, the anti-Christ conflicts, has rendered most Kundalini energies dormant or distorted in the human beings energy field upon the earth.

Most people on earth currently, have not had a natural biological spiritual ascension with an appropriate Kundalini activation. Spiritual Ascension is a simultaneous increase of Expanding Consciousness and a descension of our higher dimensional spiritual-energetic bodies into our physical bodies.

This happens through the process of progressive Kundalini awakening at the base of our spine, which moves these energies up the central vertical column into the Crown. Ascension is a change in the spectrum of frequency which happens through biological Kundalini awakening, which initiates a change in the focus of our Consciousness.

Ascension is about moving our consciousness from one reality into another. Since reality is a Dimension, what we are undertaking is essentially a full dimensional shift. To go through this consciousness shift, we must adjust our way of thinking and being to that which is in alignment with our Soul purpose and true divine essence.

When we have an awareness of how our Light body works, an awareness of the Human Energy Field and the Spectrum of Frequency that impact our consciousness, this supports our understanding that all things that exist around and within us are an energetic form, vibratory quality and Rate of Frequency.

The energetic life force current that makes up dimensionalization within the first nine dimensions, is also called the Kundalini energies or Kundalini spirals. In the Ascension Stages of spiritual initiation, we refer to the initiation into higher spectrums of frequency synonymous with understanding Kundalini activation.

Each of the Kundalini currents are Trinity Waves, with sets of three energies that are interwoven into one triad wave current that gathers the Consciousness energy in order to build the Horizontal Triad Bodies or mental bodies, and it designs the way the mental bodies will act as the link of human consciousness into the physical matter worlds. Kundalini activation can be measured through observation of the outward demonstrations of how people think, and the quality of thoughts they carry that influence their behaviors.

The total of 9 dimensions that are comprised of spectrums of frequency, are interwoven into three main Kundalini triad currents. (3X3) Once all 9 dimensions of frequency are activated in the human Light-body, activation into the Threefold Founder Flame liquid plasmic light commences and begins the higher spiritual initiation to activate the inner spark of Plasma light of the Christ Consciousness.

When the Threefold Founder Flame is activated within the Light-body, the vertical central column or Hara Line is expanded into the permanent structure of the 12D Shield, which widens the central column to become the structure that holds the internal hydroplasmic pillar of Christ Light.

All 9 dimensions of the spectrum of frequency exist in a triad pattern comprised of three sets of Kundalini energies that are coiled up within the eight Fetal Cells located on the Tailbone or coccyx. These eight fetal cells are created at the time of our conception.

The incarnating consciousness identities are connected into these intelligent layers of the spectrum of frequency that are linked into the Silver Cord of the Soul and holds the birth blueprint or the Transduction Sequence imprint of the entire consciousness record for that person.

The Kundalini coils in the base of the spine or coccyx, are connected to the Silver Cord and to the Pineal Gland in the brain. When the Pineal Gland receives enough stimulation of the higher dimensional spectrum of frequency to begin to activate into the Soul and spirit bodies, then the process of DNA activation begins.

Ultimately, upon spiritual initiation of the inner spark of light in the tailbone, this personal spark must travel up the kundalini currents, gradually moving up the body's vertical column to eventually manifest as spirals of plasmic light radiating from out of the heart center.

Once the inner spark is able to move up the central spinal column into the higher heart complex, it will begin to communicate with the Thymus Gland, and Hormones are released into the blood to create the combined energies required to ignite the Permanent Seed Atom.

The Permanent Seed Atom in the upper heart area is the center point for the Krystal Spiral which maintains that connection to the heart center at every subsequent stage of consciousness expansion. The points on the Krystal Spiral are connected to the 8th Chakra energy center, in the Thymus Gland, held through the central vertical lines in the Core Manifestation Body, or in the personal tree of life, our Holographic blueprint structure.

The Krestal Spiral and the mathematical sequence from which it emerges from our Diamond Heart center, comes directly from the Zero Point energy or our higher spiritual body connection to the central point of all union.

The Krestal Spiral perpetually retains a living, breathing connection through our activated permanent seed atom which builds the Diamond Heart, while it preserves all memory and identity that had come before in time, it continues to expand itself through the process of spiraling outwards in Multiplication.

Those three main currents that exist as the Kundalini forces in the planet, that make up the 36 harmonics of the first, second and third dimension, those harmonics were scattered from the static fields. If we can think of music in its scale of harmonic tones, our planet should have been running these 36 harmonics in resonating scale.

These first layers of 36 harmonics are what have created the lower particle fields in the first three dimensions. Each of these Dimensions has 12 sub harmonic patterns, those 12 subharmonic patterns need to be running, and resonating together.

We are enduring the process of wrapping up or rolling up, the lower frequencies where these first 36 harmonics have existed in the red wave spectrum and the orange wave spectrum and the yellow spectrum, which have been making up the lower three chakras of humanity.

Those harmonic patterns are starting to braid into triads, and this is a part of understanding that this directly impacts Kundalini forces, or the inner spark activated off of the Fetal Cells, that becomes ignited in the Tailbone of a person, when they begin their ascension journey.

What has happened to this planet during the Ascension Cycle, to the majority of the people that are on the surface of this Earth, is the kundalini current distortion that was created from the static fields, where the energies that are conducting through the human body, and especially when that human body intersects with the planetary brain, it has had a static energy effect, and this manifested into kundalini current distortion.

And that static field distorts the lower frequencies to reverse and split apart, these trinities that need to weave together in the person's kundalini process, where that spark comes online in the fetal cell of the Tailbone, it ignites these harmonic layers to begin to weave together.

For some people, if they do not know about Ascension, and they are still reliant on their three main lower ego structures, this is contributing to the increasing brain chemistry imbalances and metabolic problems on the earth. These people need spiritual healing to help neutralize the static field effect their lower ego mental bodies have had upon the new entry of higher frequencies into the planetary body.

The good news about this plasma shift is understanding the necessity of how the inner spark comes online in the Fetal Cells located on the tailbone. There is a seed that ignites a spark of light to run up the spinal column. It starts weaving with the next layer of the sub harmonic in the scale closest to its energetic resonance, in order to connect with the body through the spine.

A part of this is happening now, which has a positive result, it is the reweaving of the kundalini spark into the triad layers, which allow these sub harmonics to start merging or bonding with each other as Trinity Waves. It is creating a co-resonance, and this allows an amplification of the inner spark to finally do something inside of a human being.

Because the first thing that happens when its ignited is, it has to move up the central spinal column. And the problem with that is, if you haven't cleared out your Pain Body, if you have not cleared out the Alien Implants, out of your Unconscious Mind matrices down in the root chakra with all the Victim-Victimizer and fear layers, this makes it very challenging for any person who is going to be amplified in all of those inner fears and not understand why that's happening to them.

Many people on the earth still do not understand the Ascension process, and do not have the tools to neutralize the fears. As the Kundalini moves up the Chakra column, it starts moving into higher dimensional octaves, collecting more of the seven layers of harmonic frequencies, and then it starts inter-penetrating into the physical matrix structures. The first one that is greatly impacted is the skeletal structure and in terms of understanding the changing foundation for humanity, it is in our bones, in our bone marrow and in our blood.

Our bone marrow function is very critical for our development, it has information that is communicated into our blood from the bone marrow, as well as stimulating the increased production of red blood cells from the bone marrow.

The skeletal structure is a harmonic Oscillator and when these frequencies are coming in, they move through the harmonic structure of our skeleton. The skeleton tries to reorganize itself so that it can transmit these higher frequencies into the rest of the body and circulate the broadcast of sound waves to penetrate the energetic layers. It's a sound, the sound tone of the **432 Hertz** frequency, that carries the frequency instruction set into the other layers of the bodily matrices.

The Caduceus network runs on reversal 7D Violet Ray current and has been intermixed with the "serpent" or snake symbolism that is commonly used to describe the human energy field via the Chakra system.

The Caduceus geometry was an extension used to anchor the human Light-body to align with the reversal systems connecting back into the black star Abaddon and connect through the 7D Crucifixion Implants and the related networks. Thus, it was also used to bring the Qlippoth currents from the Black Tree of Life architecture to systematically override the organic architecture of the 12 Tree Grid and install artificial machinery and false memory earth timelines.

During the Egyptian timelines the blue staff of Tara was utilized to de-materialize a section of the 2D fields causing an underworld rift, or rip in time. The Caduceus geometry was a false light insert that was installed to take advantage of the underworld rift in the 2D fields and control the black force current for generating creations in the Womb Worlds.

The Caduceus.

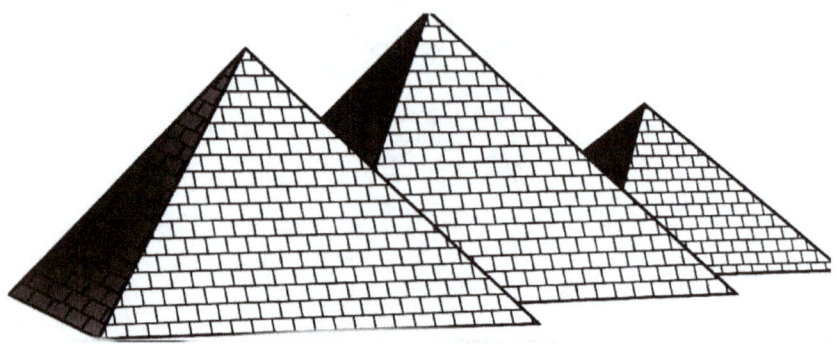

(John 3:3)
"I tell you the truth, no one can see the kingdom of God unless they are born again". This quote represents the Ascension out of the reincarnation cycle of the 3D Matrix by way of the second baptism of Kundalini fire, for the initiates body already in habits the living water. And it also represents the Ankhtawy symbolizing the double resurrection of the body, mind and spirit. Meaning to awaken from mental death, thus preventing the need to Re-incarnate.

Amun Nubi Re Akhptah

It is only with the heart that one can see rightly, what is essentially invisible to the eye.

Dr. Malachi Z. York. 33 º/720º

Setting the Record Straight.

Dr. Malachi Z York is an Extra Terra Astral from the Planet RIZQ, Rose (Born) Amongst Us, Quote" "I, Have Devoted my Visit to this Planet to the Resurrection of the Mentally Dead, which I Affectionately Refer to as Mummy! Never did I know that the Evil Ones had done such a great job with these people both Mentally and Physically as to have them Hate Self and Kind.

My greatest dilemma and Hindrance have been the "**Black Devils**." Born Amongst you, and by you, married to you, socializing with you, Praying in the same sacred house of worship as you! But secretly they have a spiritual pack with the Devil, which makes it near impossible for them to totally surrender to this information of which I have come to give.

But for the Few Chosen, from the many that are called, I sift to find those beings that wish to become One with the Supreme in All. So, I, *The Supreme Grand Hierophant. Amun Nubi Re Akh Ptah*, As I am Known Throughout the Mystical Schools, the incarnation of Tehuti (Thoth) Student of the great **ATUM-RE**, the first point of Resurrection from ignorance to the *Right Knowledge,* The *Right Wisdom* and the *Right Overstanding*, I have blended in with each of the Religion most interested in my people".

Dr. York began his ministry in the late 1960s. In 1967 he was preaching to the "Ansaaru Allah" (viz. African Americans) in Brooklyn, New York, during the period of the Black Power movement. He founded numerous orders under various names during the 1970s and 1980s. These were at first based on Islamic themes and Judaism (Nubian Islamic Hebrews).

Later he developed a theme derived from "Ancient Egypt," mixing ideas taken from black nationalism, Cryptozoological and UFO religions, and popular conspiracy theory.

He founded the United Nuwaubian Nation of Moors, or Nuwaubians who says. "Dr. York is an **Extra Terra Astral Master Teacher from the planet Rizq**". He wrote, "We have been coming to this planet before it had your life form on it. My incarnation as an Ilah Mutajassid or Avatar was originally in the year 1945 A.D. In order to get here, I travelled by one of the smaller passenger crafts called **SHAM** out of a Mother plane called **MERKAB**A or **NIBIRU**."

This version of York came to Earth on March 16, 1970. (Comet Bennett, which was visible on that date, is said to have really been York's spacecraft.)

York taught that the Mother-plane (**NIBIRU**) would launch the **Krystal City** or New Jerusalem (see: Book of Revelation 21:2) to our solar system from its position in Orion. A 40-year process of taking the 144,000 Chosen Few (see: Book of Revelation 14:1) — 12,000 each from the Twelve Tribes of Israel — into the Planet Craft "NIBIRU" beginning on August 13, 2003 and will end on August 13, 2043.

These Chosen Few will be groomed for 1,000 years and returned to Earth for the final battle against the Luciferians (Dark Ones) and to redeem man from the 6,000-year rulership of the Devil and his seeds.

"I lived as one of you, practiced as one of you in Order to reveal the Misconceptions of these doctrines that have Plagued and Diseased the mind of my people. Amongst the Arabs of Al Islam, in the Degree of Muhammadism, I was Known as **Sayyid Issa AI Haadi AI Mahdi** or simply **Imaan Isa**.

Being Fluent in the Many dialect as well as the Classical Arabic Language, I Translated word for word without Biasness in favor of the Islamic Religion, The Qur'an from Syretic Arabic into English!

Amongst the Hebrew Israelite, while in the Degree of Mosesism, I Was Known as **Rabboni, Yashua Bar El Haady**, as a Hebrew, I was bar Mitzwahed by the great Rabbi, Matthew of Harlem. Through the school of Judaism, I Translated the Torah and the Psalms from Ancient Hebrew into English. Amongst the Christians, In the Degree of Christism,

I was Known as Reverend, Malachi Z York or Dr. York, Pastor and Founder of the **Egyptian Church of Karast** (Christ) Through the School of Christism, I Translated and Explained the Book of Revelation, from the Galilean Arabic and the Ancient Greek. In this day and time, I Received a New **Holy Tablet**. Our own Scripture that each day as Scientist Astronomers Paleontologists, and the likes Uncover new Evidence Confirming that it was indeed Divinely inspired, and is not merely a Book but a Revelation, A Holy Scripture with Prophecies of the Future which are Manifesting daily.

Also, I Translated the Book of the Coming Forth by Day Called the **Egyptian Book of the Dead** from **Hieroglyphic**s as **Amunubi Rahkaptah** I felt it my duty as the true Reformer and Savior to my People to make that which is Unclear, clear, I have also Revealed the doctrine of those called the **Hebrew Israelites** and the likes with a series of Books Called 360 Question to ask and 3 Volumes of over 1,000 Pages Each Entitled the Degree of Mosesism, The Degree of Christism, and the Degree of Muhammadism, Covering any question that anyone could have pertaining to any of the 3 Monotheistic Religions.

My Travels took me throughout the World from sitting with the Mystics and the Monks under the Tibetan Master, Lama Mott Kokomau of China, To the Grand Lodge in Cairo Egypt, North East Africa. I Was There, which is Here, When The word "Let There be Light" Was Uttered. I have stood the test of time. I have been Questioned by Scholars, and Historians of all Religions and Denominations".

Dr. York was raised in Massachusetts, and at the age of 7 went to Aswan, Egypt, to learn about Islam. "My grandfather, **As Sayyid Abdur Rahman Al Mahdi,** the Imaam of the Ansaars in the Sudan until 1959 AD, upon looking into my eyes foretold that I was the one who would possess **'The Light."**

He says he returned to the United States in 1957 at age 12 and continued to study Islam. As an adolescent, he moved with his family to Teaneck, New Jersey. In the late 1960s York, calling himself "Imaam Isa", combined elements of the **Moorish Science Temple of America, the Nation of Islam, the Nation of Gods and Earths** and **Freemasonry,** and founded a quasi-Muslim black nationalist movement and community. He called it **"Ansaar Pure Sufi,"** or the **"Ansaaru Allah Community,"** c. 1970. He instructed members to wear black and green dashikis.

He later changed his name to **"Imaam Isa Abdullah"** and renamed his **"Ansaar Pure Sufi"** ministry to the **"Nubian**s" in Brooklyn in 1967. The group was part of the Black Hebrews phenomenon, under the name **"Nubian Islamic Hebrews"** and **"Nubian Hebrew Mission"** as of 1969. Unlike other groups, they were not Judeo-Christian but Judeo-Islamic. This was also the period of Black Power among some African Americans.

He can answer the Unanswered and solve the problems of this world, yet, His personal interest is in each one of you. He is not a "Holy Man" or a Preacher, He is a "Master Teacher", *Having 76 trillion Years of Knowledge!* He Resurrected in the West, The Ancient Fraternity, **A.E.O (Ancient Egyptian Order)** With the Healing in his Wings, The Spiritual Order of our Ancestors, The Ancient Egyptians. And Your true Bloodline Under the Reincarnation of **Neter, Amunnubi Raakhptah, Your A'aferti (Pharaoh)** for this day and time, **Atum-Re- "Dr Malachi Z York."**

Dr. York has led a life of positive leadership in his community. As a spiritual teacher who has been teaching for over 50 years, Mr. York emerged out of the civil rights movement and chose to assist in the empowerment of people worldwide.

He is the author of over 400 books on race relations, religion, language and the plight of the "African Diaspora" prior to bondage. His objective is to empower and improve the mentality and the economic status of the African Diaspora, particularly our youth.

Mr. York's literature has positively influenced many people both young and old, including major recording artists, Prodigy of Mobb Deep, J-Z, Musiq Soulchild, Erykah Badu and India Irie to name a few. He was awarded the key to the city in Brooklyn, N.Y. by former Mayor Ed Koch as well as awards and acclaims from the former Mayors of Macon, and Augusta Georgia. He has built a school, The Amen Institute, a church, and a clinic in his country of legal residence, Monrovia, Liberia.

Mr. York moved to Eatonton, Georgia in 1993 where he purchased approximately 476 acres of land with the intent of building an Egyptian styled theme park, museums and lecture halls. According to witnesses, shortly after beginning construction he encountered racism, intimidation and adversity from local public officials, as they unfairly refused to grant him zoning rights.

Though he continued his efforts toward gaining permits and building the amusement park, his victimization was so extreme it led him to the decision to relinquish ownership interest of the 476 acres of land and his citizenship. He seeded the property over to the residents of the property (members of the Nuwaupian community) to which he began the planning process toward rebuilding in his homeland, Africa.

Mr. York made his declaration of intent to become a Liberian citizen on July 12th, 1997 within the courts of Montserrado County in the Republic of Liberia and was appointed as a Diplomat on December 15th, 1999 by the former President Dr. Charles Ghankay Taylor. His citizenship and diplomatic status of Consul General are still honored and recognized under her Excellency President Ellen Sirleaf Johnson.

His Excellency Dr. Malachi Z. York expatriated himself when he made his Declaration of Intention to the Republic of Liberia on July 12th, 1999. After 6 consecutive years of litigation and public support, the 476 acres of land was finally awarded all the zoning permits required and the Nuwaupians proceeded in completing the vision inherited from Mr. York, but the harassment didn't end there.

On May 8th, 2002 Federal Agents alongside state and local law enforcement besieged and executed a raid on the 476 acres holding women and children at gunpoint as they ransacked the property. Mr. York not present on the property was arrested in Milledgeville and later charged under the R.I.C.O. Act with transporting minors across state lines for the purpose of unlawful sex and later for racketeering and money structuring.

This arrest without due process was orchestrated to overshadow and consequently destroy his credibility as an author, teacher and humanitarian. Most witnesses and alleged victims, some of which were children, tell of how they were threatened and coerced by FBI agents, some at gunpoint to make false allegations and statements against Mr. York. This is supported by the affidavits and recantations by these witnesses and alleged victims.

The prosecutions' key witness also recanted her testimony. According to the record 5 children who were taken into custody during the raid on the 476 acres and named in the indictment as alleged victims were examined and found to have never been molested. This fact was made known during a Juvenile custody trial represented by Attorney Janice Mathis of the Rainbow Push Coalition who went on to win the case. It was proven that the claim of molestation had no merit.

This took place prior to the trial against His Excellency Malachi Z. York. Again, the trial transcripts were sealed. It seems the fact that none of the children were found to have been molested should have caused the trial against Mr. York be dismissed, as the children and the alleged victims that were under the age of 18, were proven to have never been molested. Of the remaining 8 alleged victims, most recanted their statements by way of written affidavits. All of whom were over the age of 18 at the time of trial.

The trial against Mr. York *(see 5:02-CR-27-CAR)* was presided over by Chief Judge Charles Ashley Royal of the United States Middle District of Georgia Court, 11th Circuit Macon Division. According to trial Attorney Adrian Patrick, Judge Royal failed to recuse himself after it was discovered that he was biased and represented Oconee Regional Hospital in Georgia as the hospital's Attorney in a lawsuit between Mr. York's common law family and the Hospital.

This was prior to Royal's appointment to Federal Judge by former President George W. Bush Jr. II whom incidentally along with other cabinet members are currently facing charges of torture in the Guantanamo Bay Detainee case. In the case of Mr. York's father in law Eli Richardson who resided at the 476-acre property, he passed away after a sponge was left in him during surgery at Oconee Regional Hospital. The family sought damages and compensation for such malpractice which resulted in a favorable legal outcome for the family.

This again was prior to Mr. York's trial, thereby creating a conflict of interest for Judge C. Ashley Royal having been the Attorney for the Hospital that lost the lawsuit to Mr. York's family. Though Mr. Royal claimed his competence to preside over Mr. York's case was impartial, one cannot say emphatically that this Judge was completely unbiased.

To date all of the transcripts of the trial have been sealed from the public along the plethora of injustices and lack of due process of the law committed against Mr. York. During the trial His Excellency Dr. Malachi Z. York was denied access to media and a law library which is his right.

Judge Charles Ashley Royal also refused to recognize His Excellency Dr. Malachi Z. York's diplomatic status as Consul General and his Nationality as an Indigenous Sovereign being which His Excellency York stated "on the record" on several occasions. When Mr. York fired the Garland Firm as defense counsel (due to ineffective assistance of counsel) during a hearing on December 30th, 2003 Mr. York was forced by Judge Royal to keep the discharged counsel as advisor to his new Attorney Adrian Patrick.

Patrick had been Mr. York's Attorney a mere 3 weeks prior to this, and Judge Ashley Royal refused to give Mr. York an extension of time for his newly hired Attorney to properly prepare his brief. The record shows the Report of Recommendation from the Magistrate Judge in the S 2255 motion, more specifically a Constitutional Habeas Corpus *(Case#: 5:07-CV-90001- CAR/5:02-CR-27-CAR)* as agreeing to this Judicial Misconduct where he states: "After being extended the opportunity to rethink his position, Mr. York 'officially fired' Mr. Garland and Mr. Aurora, 'for the record'" ID. at 17, 18.

However, the court advised Mr. Aurora that he was not released, but would remain in the hearing to advise Mr. Patrick, if Mr. Patrick needed advice. Id. at 18. Further displaying an abuse of authority and violating Mr. York's right to counsel of choice, Judge Royal continued his persecution of Mr. York by holding court on Martin Luther King's birthday, January 19th, 2004 which is a public legal holiday pursuant to **5 USC S 6103** and in violation of the Federal Rules of Criminal Procedure *Rule 56* which states that: **NO COURT SHALL BE HELD ON A STATUTE HOLIDAY.**

The Gods and Angels of All Religions are **EXTRA TERRA ASTRALS**= Extra on earth from the Astral Stars. **Genesis 1:26** Then Elohim said, "Let us make mankind in our image, in our likeness, so that they may rule over the fish in the sea and the birds in the sky, over the livestock and all the wild animals, and over all the creatures that move along the ground. **Genesis 6:1.** When human beings began to increase in number on the earth and daughters were born to them, **2.** The sons of the Elohim saw that the daughters of humans were beautiful, and they married any of them they chose. **3.** Then the Elohim said, "My Spirit will not contend with humans forever, for they are mortal; their days will be a hundred and twenty years." **4.** The Nephilim were on the earth in those days—and also afterward—when the sons of God went to the daughters of humans and had children by them. They were the heroes of old, men of renown.

The Natives of America has always handed down oral stories about the THUNDERBIRDS, THE KACHINAS, and the HOPI who here in Arizona has made it clear that KOKOPELI, koko is coco or dark brown, and PELE is GOD, or A BLACK GOD and MOOR from outer space. Many people on earth are currently channeling different species of EXTRA TERRA ASTRALS at this time.

DR MALACHI Z. YORK has declared that he is the incarnation of an EXTRA TERRA ASTRAL Called TEHUTI, "YANAAN". an Intergaltic Traveler, and teacher from the 8 planet "RIZQ" (Marzaq) in the 19th GALAXY ILLYUWN. He speaks 19 languages retranslated all the scriptures and revealed the one he wrote called the HOLY TABLETS. Yet he was not given proper credit in the mainstream media, as they seek to destroy his credibility. He is now falsely Imprisoned in Colorado Super Max Prison. Yet unstoppable.

"Paa Naabab Yaanuwn",

Star seed prototype 62645 Dr. Malachi Z. York, 33°/720°
You are hereby free to do as you please.

COINTELPRO.

The COINTELPRO operators target multiple groups at once and encourage splintering of these groups from within.

In order to eliminate black leaders whom, they considered dangerous, the FBI is believed to have worked with local police departments to target specific individuals, accuse them of crimes they did not commit, suppress exculpatory evidence and falsely incarcerate them.

They spread misinformation about meetings and events, set up pseudo movement groups run by government agents, and manipulated or strong-armed parents, employers, landlords, school officials, and others to cause trouble for activists. They used bad jacketing to create suspicion about targeted activists, sometimes with lethal consequences.

FBI/COINTELPRO METHODS.

Infiltration: Agents and informers did not merely spy on political activists. Their main purpose was to discredit, disrupt and negatively redirect action. Their very presence served to undermine trust and scare off potential supporters. The FBI and police exploited this fear to smear genuine activists as agents.

Psychological warfare: The FBI and police used myriad "dirty tricks" to undermine progressive movements. They planted false media stories and published bogus leaflets and other publications in the name of targeted groups. They forged correspondence, sent anonymous letters, and made anonymous telephone calls.

Harassment via the legal system: The FBI and police abused the legal system to harass dissidents and make them appear to be criminals. Officers of the law gave perjured testimony and presented fabricated evidence as a pretext for false arrests and wrongful imprisonment.

Illegal force: The FBI conspired with local police departments to threaten dissidents; to conduct illegal break-ins in order to search dissident homes; and to commit vandalism, assaults, beatings and assassinations. The objective was to frighten or eliminate dissidents and disrupt their movements.

They discriminatorily enforced tax laws and other government regulations and used conspicuous surveillance, "investigative" interviews, and grand jury subpoenas in an effort to intimidate activists and silence their supporters.

Undermine public opinion: One of the primary ways the FBI targeted organizations were by challenging their reputations in the community and denying them a platform to gain legitimacy. Hoover specifically designed programs to block leaders from "spreading their philosophy publicly or through the communications media."

Furthermore, the organization created and controlled negative media meant to undermine black power organizations. For instance, they oversaw the creation of "documentaries" skillfully edited to paint the Black Panther Party as aggressive, and false newspapers that spread misinformation about party members.

The ability of the FBI to create distrust within and between revolutionary organizations tainted their public image and weakened chances at unity and public support.

COINTELPRO tactics are still used to this day and have been alleged to include discrediting targets through psychological warfare; smearing individuals and groups using forged documents and by planting false reports in the media; harassment; wrongful imprisonment; and illegal violence, including assassination.

According to a senate report, the FBI's motivation was "protecting national security, preventing violence, and maintaining the existing social and political order".

Beginning in 1969, leaders of the Black Panther Party were targeted by the COINTELPRO and "neutralized" by being assassinated, imprisoned, publicly humiliated or falsely charged with crimes.

Some of the Black Panthers affected included Fred Hampton, Mark Clark, Zayd Shakur, Geronimo Pratt, Mumia Abu-Jamal, and Marshall Conway. Common tactics used by COINTELPRO were perjury, witness harassment, witness intimidation, and withholding of evidence.

FBI Director J. Edgar Hoover issued directives governing COINTELPRO, ordering FBI agents to "expose, disrupt, misdirect, discredit, or otherwise neutralize" the activities of these movements and especially their leaders.

Noble Drew Ali

Noble Drew Ali was a spiritual leader responsible for bringing Islam, nationality, and birthrights to North America. Having lived between 1886 and 1929, Ali was the founder and prophet of the Moorish Science Temple of America. This was the first mass religious community in the history of American Islam and the Black nationalist model for the Nation of Islam. In 1927, Ali wrote the "Holy Koran of the Moorish Science Temple," also called the "Circle Seven Koran," to instruct his followers on pre-slavery religion, nationality, and genealogy.

Born as Timothy Drew, his parents were former slaves in North Carolina. His earliest followers believed that he was an orphan for most of his childhood and was raised by the Cherokee Indians,

According to his own accounts, Ali left home at 16 and joined a band of gypsies who took him overseas to Egypt, Morocco, and the Middle East. While in Egypt, he impressed a high priest who trained him in mysticism and gave him a "lost section" of the Quran.

Ali established the Canaanite Temple, the first Moorish-American community, in Newark, New Jersey, in 1913. He renamed his community several times before founding new temples in several midwestern and southern cities. The Moorish-American community grew to approximately 30,000 members and was the largest Islamic community in the United States before the ascendancy of the Nation of Islam in the 1950s,

Ali's followers, the Moorish Americans, donned turbans and fezzes. They also changed their slavery surnames, instead using "El" or "Bey." They even created their own nationality cards and flag and referred to themselves as "olive-skinned Asiatics," descendants of Morocco, instead of Negroes or colored people.

To support his case for a Moorish-American identity, Ali emphasized two important points: first, Black Americans were really "Asiatics," the descendants of Christ, he believed, and second, the destiny of western civilization was linked to the rise of the Asiatic nations — Asians, Africans, Native Americans, and African Americans.

By 1928, The Moorish Science Temple of America, Inc. was an established fact. "It is believed that this procedure of elevating the movement to the Moorish Science Temple of America, Inc. from the Canaanite Temple in phases was to prepare the people for this great 'new thought' movement; entirely different from the churches they had been used to," according to the Moorish Science Temple of America. With the incorporation came a new charter, a Divine Constitution and bylaws consisting of seven acts.

Money led to the downfall of the Moorish-American community after corrupt some businessmen joined the group in the late 1920s. They embezzled a fortune from its small businesses and the Moorish Manufacturing Corporation and began to plot the prophet's death. On March 15, 1929, Ali's business manager, Claude Greene, was murdered in Chicago and Ali was arrested.

Ali was incarcerated in Atlanta, Georgia and after being released several weeks later, he mysteriously died at home.

"The Moorish Movement is still alive today," according to The Moorish Science Temple of America. "There are many small temples all over America still following the great teachings of Prophet Noble Drew Ali."

Clarence 13X.

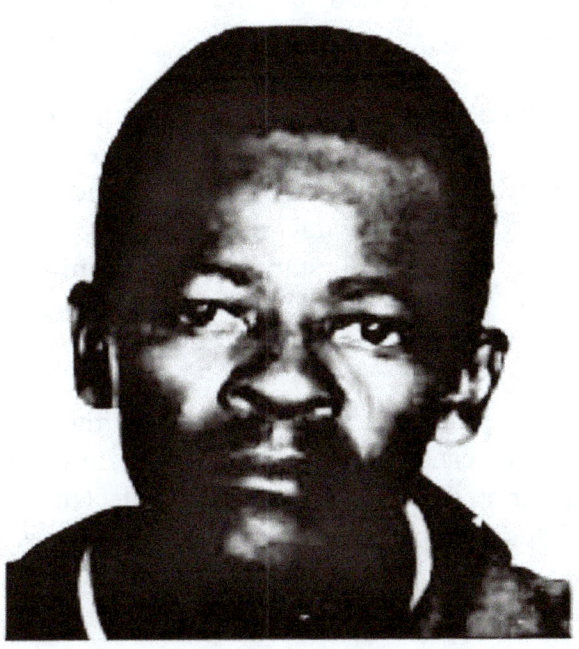

Clarence Edward Smith (February 22, 1928 – June 13, 1969), better known as Clarence (Star Seed) 13X and Allah, was an American religious leader and the founder of the Five-Percent Nation. He was born in Virginia and moved to New York City as a young man, before serving in the United States Army during the Korean War.

After returning to New York, he learned that his wife had joined the Nation of Islam (NOI) and followed her, taking the name Clarence 13X. He served in the group as a security officer, martial arts instructor, and student minister before leaving for an unclear reason in 1963. He enjoyed gambling, which was condemned by the NOI, and disagreed with the NOI's teachings that Wallace Fard Muhammad was a divine messenger.

After leaving the Nation of Islam, Clarence 13X formed a new group with other former members. He concluded that all black men were divine and took the name Allah to symbolize this status. He rejected the belief in an invisible God, teaching that God could be found within each black man.

In his view, women were "Earths" that complemented and nurtured men; he believed that they should be submissive to men. He and a few assistants retained some NOI teachings and pioneered novel interpretations of them. They devised teachings about the meaning of letters and numerals: understanding the meaning of each letter and number was said to provide deep truths about God and the universe.

Clarence 13X referred to his new movement as the Five Percenters, referencing a NOI teaching that only five percent of the population knew and promoted the truth about God. One way that he distinguished his group from his previous faith was by rejecting dress codes or strict behavioral guidelines—he allowed the consumption of alcohol, and at times, the use of illegal drugs.

Clarence 13X was shot by an unknown assailant in 1964 but survived the attack. After an incident several months later in which he and several of his followers vandalized stores and fought with police, he was arrested and placed in psychiatric care. He was diagnosed with paranoid schizophrenia.

He referred to himself as "Allah", which had become his preferred name. He was released from custody after a 1966 ruling by the Supreme Court placed limits on confinement without trial. Although he initially taught his followers to hate white people, he eventually began to cooperate with white city leaders. They gave him funding for a night school, and in return, he tried to prevent violence in Harlem.

NOI leaders were angry that Clarence 13X freely taught portions of their doctrine that they only revealed to committed members; although one of their captains repeatedly asked him to stop, he refused. Clarence 13X also experienced conflict within his family: his children did not revere him, and hostility quickly developed between core Five Percenters and some of his sons.

On December 9, 1964, Clarence 13X was shot twice in the torso while at a popular gathering place in the basement of a Harlem tenement. He was brought to Harlem Hospital, where he was treated and released. He later claimed that he died and returned to his body a short time later. (M.A.R.E. Program) In a 2007 study of the Five Percent movement, An American journalist speculated that this caused his followers to see him as a Christ figure.

The identity and motivation of the shooter are unknown. It's been said that rival Muslim groups and Police both had a motive to attack Clarence 13X. Some Five Percenters have speculated that the attack was part of a robbery attempt or retaliation for unpaid gambling debts. Clarence 13X's companions reported that he instructed them not to seek revenge on the shooter and to forswear violence.

While recuperating from his wounds, Clarence 13X sought to distinguish his movement from other Islamic movements, abandoning Arabic greetings for English expressions. The Five Percenters soon attracted attention from media and law enforcement. Local papers published negative coverage of the group, casting them as a violent hate group or a street gang.

The New York Amsterdam News falsely reported that Clarence 13X had threatened to kill white children if his group did not receive a Government subsidy. In 1965, the FBI initiated an investigation of his group and may have provided sensationalized rumors to the press.

That year, FBI director J. Edgar Hoover deemed Clarence 13X as a "Harlem rowdy" and feared that he would form ties with more dangerous groups. The FBI developed a detailed file on Clarence 13X; in 1967, Hoover described him as a potential threat to President Lyndon B. Johnson and sent a detailed folder about him to the United States Secret Service.

After Malcolm X's death in 1965, Clarence 13X mourned his loss but did not attend his funeral. In May 1965, while visiting the site of Mosque No. 7, then closed, Clarence 13X and several of his companions were told to leave by a police officer. They left, began to vandalize nearby buildings, and blocked the street near the former headquarters of Muslim Mosque, Inc.

More police arrived and subdued Clarence 13X after an altercation, bringing him into custody with several of his followers. After being arrested, he refused to identify himself and was charged with assault and drug possession. About 60 of his followers attended his arraignment but were removed from the court after shouting "Peace". Clarence 13X proclaimed his innocence and announced his intent to defend himself in court. He told the judge that he was Allah, and that the city would face grave judgment if he were not released.

The judge disregarded his prognostication and set his bail at $9,500. At a court date in June, about 50 Five Percenters protested outside the court; afterwards, several were arrested on charges of making Molotov cocktails. In July, the court sent Clarence 13X to Bellevue Hospital Center for a psychiatric examination.

While in the hospital, he made a few disciples and communicated with some followers through a hospital window. Under his instructions, Five Percenters resisted future NOI leader Louis Farrakhan's attempts to convert them. Clarence 13X's psychiatric results were not processed for an unusually long time; the delay was due to FBI involvement and argues that Clarence 13X was a political prisoner.

In November 1965, Clarence 13X was ruled incompetent to stand trial and committed to the New York State Department of Mental Hygiene, which placed him at the Matteawan State Hospital for the Criminally Insane.

After he declared himself Allah and a "Master Gambler", the doctors concluded that he had schizophrenic reaction, paranoid type with delusions of grandeur; he faced indefinite commitment. Many Five Percenters and their converts traveled to the hospital to meet with him and receive instruction. He also proselytized to fellow inmates, converting one young white man, who later became a committed follower.

While Clarence 13X was in prison, the Five Percenters continued to proselytize and teach their doctrines. He instructed his followers to adopt names different from those used in the NOI to differentiate their group. After attaining a certain degree of knowledge of the group's doctrines, members could adopt the surname "Allah" and sometimes "God" as a first name. This was in recognition of Clarence 13X's teachings that black men were Gods, and that each member should worship himself.

His followers often took the name Allah but would refrain from referring to themselves as such in his presence, in deference to his authority. After a decision by the Supreme Court of the United States in 1966, limits were placed on the confinement of mentally ill criminals, causing many to be released. Clarence 13X was consequently released in March 1967.

By 1969, Clarence 13X was sleeping very little. He feared that he would be killed and instructed his followers to remain strong if he died. On June 12, he spent time with several of his disciples at their school. He left the school between 2:00 and 3:00 am on June 13 and then gambled for an hour or two. As was his occasional practice, he traveled to a friend's house to rest. He was ambushed by three assailants who fatally shot him while he was in the lobby of her apartment building.

That morning, several people from the mayor's office met with his family, and the mayor later visited the Five Percenters' school to express condolences. Clarence 13X's funeral was held four days after his death. It was attended by about 400 people and was followed by a procession through Harlem.

His death put the leadership of his movement in question—there was no clear successor. At that time, his followers were primarily teenagers, and several of his top leaders subsequently struggled with drug addiction. In August 1969, an arrest was made in connection with his murder. The suspect denied involvement, and charges were soon dropped. Five Percenters have posited different culprits, including the CIA, the FBI/COINTELPRO, or a disgruntled follower.

Grigori Rasputin.

Grigori Yefimovich Rasputin was a Russian mystic and self-proclaimed spiritualist who befriended the family of Nicholas II, the last emperor of Russia, and gained considerable influence in late imperial Russia.

Grigori was born into meager means in Pokrovskoye, Siberia in 1869. His family were peasants surviving through farming and his father's employment as a government courier. Surprising to most is that Grigori most likely was illiterate up until his later years. Peasant families often were not formally educated. As he grew, Grigori was no stranger to petty crime and known to be a mischievous young man with a checkered past.

Grigori's transformation came after he was motivated to go on a spiritual pilgrimage at age 28. The pilgrimage was to St. Nicholas Monastery in Verkhoturye, a roughly 421-mile trip.

He studied closely with staret Makary and subsequently learned to read and write. Grigori's time spent at the monastery lasted several months. After returning home, looking disheveled and unkempt, he was a different man without vices. He traveled as a Strannik, or a "holy wanderer", for years, gathering a small group of dedicated followers.

While still living at home with his parents even in his later years, Rasputin coopted his family's basement and converted it to a makeshift church. His acolytes would gather here in prayer, sing unfamiliar strange hymns, and it was rumored that he even engaged in sexual acts and orgies. They believed in a possibility of direct communication with the Holy Spirit and of God's embodiment in living people. One rumor was that Rasputin had begun following the fringe sect of the Russian Orthodox Church, Khlysty.

Khlysts believed that instead of worshipping and communicating with the Holy Spirit through priests and holy texts, people could communicate directly with a higher power. One man and women, physical representations of both "Christ" and the "Mother of God", lead each Khlysty Ark (or group). Ark's regularly practiced self-flagellation and the attainment of divine grace through sinful means, such as sexual orgies. This group was often persecuted and largely disavowed by church officials.

Later in life Rasputin seemingly continued the practices from this group with his followers and even his wife. Attempting to obtain redemption in the eyes of the Holy Spirit through sin, he was accused of rape and assault by many women.

Some of Rasputin's occult aura may have derived from his abuse of Tantra. Tantra is a sexual energy used to align with the divine Christo-Sophia which can be misused if combined with desire. If this occurs, a devil resides in the person causing a split personality one of which could ultimately harm others.

Rasputin's true infamy and power came through his charisma and influence. In the early 1900s, Grigori Rasputin became well known in monastic circles as a holy man with great powers. This eventually led to his journey to St Petersburg, during which time he befriended many in the Russian court and aristocracy. This led him to the Czar in 1905. Rasputin's influence over the royal family only grew from there. His acted as spiritual guide, healer, and even political advisor to Nicholas II and the Czarina, Alexandra.

One instance that solidified Rasputin's close bond with the Czarina was the healing of her sick son, Alexei. Alexei was ailed with hemophilia, an affliction which leaves the sufferer with thin blood and the inability for it to clot. In this case, Rasputin was asked to aid in the healing of Alexei after an internal hemorrhage, which could possibly prove fatal. As a known faith healer, Alexandra desperately wrote to Rasputin for guidance.

Rasputin wrote back quickly, telling the Tsarina that "God has seen your tears and heard your prayers. Do not grieve. The Little One will not die. Do not allow the doctors to bother him too much." Two days later, Alexei made a full recovery, allowing Rasputin full influence over Alexandra.

But the elite in the Russian court soon grew tired of Rasputin. Referred to as "The Mad Monk", they viewed him as meddling and immoral. He was even subjected to surveillance, revealed in the "staircase notes", which detail his many sensual pleasures with women, drink, and bribery. These were published widely in newspapers which only fueled the opposition against him.

This tension came to a head during the first World War. While Rasputin was against war, he did advise the Czar that if he did not personally take charge of the troops and their actions Russia would certainly face military defeat. Bolstered by his advisors words, Nicholas overtook control from his generals and went to the front lines with little experience. Rasputin's advice proved disastrous.

During the Czar's time away at war, Rasputin saw an opportunity to gain full control over the aristocracy and government. With Alexandra fully dedicated to Rasputin's cause, his influence grew to its fullest potential. He soon was able to appoint handpicked officials which aligned with his views. Because of these actions, respect for the royal family declined.

Alexandra, who was of Anglo-German descent, was even accused of being a German spy. Rasputin's impact on Russia as a whole was earning him many enemies whose goal was to remove him of power.

One of these enemies was Pyotr Stolypin, the prime minister, who actively appealed to the royal family to remove Rasputin from the court. Once, while engaged in a heated argument, he later stated that Rasputin's "satanic eyes" had quelled the argument. This was one of the many instances of Rasputin being accused of using hypnosis to bend others' will towards his own.

In turn, multiple assassination attempts were made against Rasputin's life, however, the fatal encounter would take place in Moika Palace. Moika Palace was the home of Prince Felix Yusupov. Yusupov, the Grand Duke of Pavlovich, and the politician Vladimir Purishkevich. They would all participate in the final attempt.

Rasputin was lured by the prince to his home and ushered into the basement where he was presented with cakes and wine. Yusupov had laced each with potassium cyanide. After eating some of the cakes, Rasputin seemed unaffected. He then drank the wine. Still, no effect.

Frustrated and incredulous to this, Yusupov finally took the Duke's revolver and shot Rasputin square in the chest multiple times. While lying on the floor, the men took his clothes and one of them put them on and drove to Rasputin's apartment. This was to give the perception that he had travelled home that night after their meeting.

"This devil who was dying of poison, who had a bullet in his heart, must have been raised from the dead by the powers of evil. There was something appalling and monstrous in his diabolical refusal to die".

Upon returning to Moika Palace, the men returned to the basement to make sure Rasputin was dead. When bending down to take a closer look, Rasputin leapt up and charged the men. He managed to escape upstairs and outside until he was shot in the back and collapsed into a snowbank in the courtyard.

He was bundled up, put in the car, and driven to a bridge overlooking the Malaya Nevka river. His body was thrown into the river and later found. His autopsy was rumored to show water in the lungs which could mean he actually died from drowning and not from the numerous attacks against him.

Many have suggested that agents from the British Secret Intelligence Service were involved in Rasputin's assassination. It's been said that British agents were concerned that Rasputin was urging them to make a separate peace with Germany, which would allow Germany to concentrate its military efforts on the Western Front.

It was also suggested that British intelligence agents were directly involved in planning and carrying out the assassination under the command of Samuel Hoare and Oswald Rayner, who had attended Oxford University with Yusopov, or that Rayner had personally shot Rasputin.

The Arcturians.

Dear Earth family, once again we come to you with great love and respect especially during these times when so many are experiencing chaos and seeming loss the birth pains of bringing forth a new earth, new collective consciousness, and more evolved humans. Be not afraid or doubtful based on what you see but know that mankind is well into the evolutionary changes that have been unconsciously desired and sought throughout time.

Once an individual attains some measure of spiritual awareness, they are never forced to incarnate. You chose to be on earth at this time. Many wanted to be here during these times but were not permitted because their Light was not yet of a sufficient level to assist in earth's ascension process. You who read and understand these messages are here to serve the Light as examples and teachers. This does not mean that in order to do this you must first become a spiritual guru, channel, or teacher in the ordinary limited sense of these titles.

You become these things and much more as you begin to secretly and silently align with Truth in each now moment while going about your ordinary daily activities. The three-dimensional belief system based in duality and separation has created gods, saints, and royalty. It has taught for eons and still teaches that some individuals, as well as a nebulous male god in the sky are better than you and must be looked up to and even worshipped.

In reality, these designations simply represent facets of separation, the belief that those who have attained some "man ordained" qualification either by birth or experience are more valuable, wise, loveable, and "holy" than everyone else. A "saint" is nothing more than a person who has fulfilled certain three-dimensional concepts of spirituality. Many of those declared saints were not awake to real spiritual truth.

Because you are creators, a person who spends 24/7 thinking about and concentrating on the stigmata, or some concept of a God experience will easily create it for themselves. Therefore, it is important to let go of all concepts regarding what spirituality must look like in order to be authentic. Allow your personal evolutionary process to unfold, trusting that your Higher Self knows what is right for you and when, which may be totally different than someone else's experience.

Three dimensional titles mean nothing in the larger scheme of things because even though there is individuality, all life is in and of the One and only life. This does not mean that you cannot give honor and respect where it is deserved, but to worship and seek to emulate some saint, famous person, or three-dimensional concept of God at the expense of one's own divine nature is idolatry.

Most souls do not incarnate for the purpose of becoming famous or to attain that which will make them valuable, loveable, or important to others according to three dimensional standards. However, most incarnating souls forget and lose sight of their purpose when entering into the denser energies of earth. There is nothing un-spiritual about pursuing a career or activity that results in fame and glory.

Often a person is drawn to some activity and is very good at it because they have done it in other lifetimes. Professional perfection or fame of some sort may well be the necessary component to one's chosen Light work a way to show others that a person can be famous, rich, or physically beautiful while living a high level of spiritual awareness. Those in positions of authority or fame of some sort have great responsibility because they are looked to as examples by those who as of yet have not realized their own uniqueness and thus often imitate them.

The only spiritual error of any life choice is in using it solely for service to self and in looking to it rather than within, for physical, emotional, mental, and spiritual validation. Make these times a time for rejoicing rather than suffering, for prison walls are coming down and allowing those inside to wake up and begin experiencing the realities of their already perfect consciousness while the prison masters scurry about pulling out all stops in a futile effort to maintain the status quo.

We wish to speak of compassion and how it is not always seen in its truest form. Compassion is a state of consciousness able to understand, accept, and unconditionally love without becoming an enabler or doormat. Many still falsely believe that in order to be a loving or spiritual person they must just allow what another does to them physically, mentally, or emotionally. Compassion never denies a situation but rather sees through it to its underlying components while at the same time taking whatever human steps are necessary and understandable for self and the other.

No matter how well intended, giving words of truth to someone who has not yet attained a consciousness that is able to align with them is folly. This is why the practice of proselytizing or forcing one's beliefs no matter how true on another represents a false sense of ego the belief that only the proselytizer has the right answers and everyone else is wrong. Proselytizing can be harmful in many ways. It creates guilt, false beliefs, and often the loss of a person's already present spiritual foundation (frequently more evolved than what is being taught).

Every evolving soul eventually attains a state of consciousness in which the beliefs of others no longer have the power to cause doubt or questioning. Compassion does not align with another's low resonating energy as sympathy does. It is very important for those who work professionally in medicine, psychology, law, social work etc. to understand the difference between compassion and sympathy.

Those in these fields of work are exposed every day to dense frequencies of sadness, pain, suffering, and victim consciousness. When you work with others from the level of sympathy "I feel your pain" rather than from compassion "I recognize your pain" you align with the other's lower resonating energy which then feeds from yours leaving you feeling tired, drained, and unable to provide understandable but high level solutions that can help the person's situation.

Even if this is not your professional work, most of you are finding others being increasingly drawn to you confiding their pain, problems, and sad stories. This is happening because as a person becomes more spiritually evolved their energy field broadcasts a greater light, and because everyone consciously and unconsciously seeks Light, those with little of their own are drawn to yours.

This happens for those in physical body as well as those on the other side which is why it is always important to keep your energy levels high and filled with Light. You can ask your Guides to help you with this and when you feel yourself slipping into density, stop and center while visualizing yourself in the radiant Green Light. Lower resonating energy cannot enter in to the higher, but the higher can allow itself to slip into the lower.

Allow your Light work to be wherever you are to come to you. There is no need to seek it out. It may be as ordinary as someone in a grocery line that you intuitively know is in need of silent spiritual recognition A teacher may be intuitively guided to a troubled student needing someone to talk with. It could be a friend or relative that is receptive and desirous of learning more about the spiritual truth you know. When you live from compassion, you live at a higher level of awareness in which others if ready and receptive, can be lifted higher.

This is how true healing takes place, but it is then up to the other to keep themselves in that state of higher awareness. Your job is never to carry another indefinitely out of a false sense of love, which is enabling not love and may be taking away their chosen lesson. As earth energy becomes increasingly high and intense, more will find their way to you at work, home, in a crowd, or at a party wherever for help of some sort. This is why you chose to be on earth at this time and this is how concepts of duality and separation will dissolve into the nothingness that they are. Be in the world as fully as you desire or are guided to be but be not of it.

Sincerely: The Arcturians.

The Pleiadians.

The Benevolent Pleiadians evolved millions of years ago as one of the early races of what we would call humanoids and look like we do. This form has been modeled throughout the universe. Pleiadian DNA has been used to develop many human beings in this universe, including those of our solar system on Venus, Mars, Maldeck and Earth.

There still exist newly developing 3D planets in the Pleiades, but the Pleiadians that communicate with us are usually 6D and 9D. These are dimensions they work well within and from which they contact other worlds. They have light bodies, yet like other higher dimensional ET beings, they can appear in a form that projects what they evolved from.

Having a lot more time to evolve than we have, they have refined their natures and are intensely spiritual and giving beings. Qualities: Intuitive, sensitive, imaginative, radiant, communicative, empathic, soothing, nurturing, mystical, understated creativity, healers, counselors, in tune with natural worlds. Abilities: Pleiadians are healers on many levels. They can empathize and sooth all pains with their sensitive communication and transfer of light. They communicate by means of light transfer.

These beings have a natural radiance that comes from their mystical knowing of how to connect and share Source light. Specialties: Pleiadians are called upon to seed new worlds with the essence of evolved human form, and to commune with a planet's consciousness and its existing life in order to introduce new beings and ideas in a nurturing way.

They embody the divine feminine and often will show themselves in female form to radiate this refined quality.

Basic Needs: Peace and sharing. Pleiadians thrive in places and states of peace and tranquility. They feel best when they are sharing their refined essence. Focus: Transferring their gifts of radiance throughout the universe through seeding and communicating their healing vibrations and mystical awareness. Involvement with Earth: Provided genetic and energetic model for early human development.

They are the missing link in our evolution to our current form. They were guides for Atlantis and Lemuria and have been involved in the nurturing of many life forms on Earth that began elsewhere, such as whales and dolphins.

They are responsible for infusing awareness into the many methods of energy healing discovered by humans over the years. They are playing an important role in reinvigorating our beliefs in the mystical elements of our knowledge and helping us open to celestial contact in non-threatening manners. They radiate light and soothing energy that we are able to feel because of our genetic link.

Sincerely: The Pleiadians.

> Note: Any Extra Terra Astral can be, Benevolent or
> Malevolent according to one's own perspective.

A Guide for Humanity.

Sanaan RE
(The Oversoul)

It is known that Ascended Masters are individuals who were once embodied on Earth and learned the lessons of life in their incarnations. They gained mastery over the limitations of the matter planes, balanced at least 51% of negative karma, and fulfilled their Divine Plan. An Ascended Master has become God-like and a source of unconditional Love to all life, and through the Ascension has united with his or her own God Self, the "I AM" Presence.

It is claimed that they serve as the teachers of mankind from the realms of Spirit, and that all people will eventually attain their Ascension and move forward in spiritual evolution beyond this planet. According to these teachings, they remain attentive to the spiritual needs of humanity, and act to inspire and motivate its spiritual growth. In many traditions and organizations, they are considered part of the Spiritual Hierarchy for the Earth Grid and are members of the Brotherhood of Light.

In a nutshell, there is a Grid around Mother Earth surrounding Her. You and I can connect with this Grid anytime we so choose. This grid is called many things but is known to some as the Christ Consciousness Grid. And when we make a connection to this Grid, we are tapping into the Love from which we were all manifested; we are tapping into "Eternal Consciousness".

1. What is Christ Consciousness?

Spiritual thoughts that enter into conscious minds are sometimes referred to as Christ Consciousness. It is an awareness of the higher self as part of a higher universal system.

It does not relate to the personality of Christ. Christ Consciousness is a state of mind; it is a frequency or understanding that there is a universal and omnipresent force everywhere connecting us with this higher power. Another explanation of Christ Consciousness is a sense of being present in humanity.

2. How is it Linked to Religious Beliefs?

The term is not necessarily affiliated to any religious beliefs; it was named after Jesus Christ's spiritual elevation during his mortal life. Anybody can become Christ Conscious if they are open to the concept and seek to obtain this awareness and consciousness. Most religious masters have walked a path of love, light, peace, harmony, and bliss, generally following a period of suffering, becoming enlightened along their journey.

This is not unique to any one of the prescribed religions, instead being a common theme amongst many belief groups. All people are capable of this enlightenment and awareness by opening their mind to higher possibilities. This is Christ Consciousness.

3. How do People Become Christ Conscious?

Consciousness can flow into a person, if there is the will and capacity to receive it, the ability to maintain it, and the understanding to nurture it. The idea is to find the spiritual way, whether this be assisted by religious beliefs, mentors, guides, intuition, or by inner reflection. The aim is for people to become more loving, compassionate, tolerant, patient, forgiving, understanding and content, by following a new way of conscious thinking; the means by which one achieves this is not important. Spiritual growth is obtained by aligning with inner thoughts and feelings.

One should set the intention to become aware, whilst understanding that they are a unique creation within the completeness of the whole. The human mind acknowledges the Divine Mind, gradually awakening with Christ Consciousness to become more enlightened with a greater understanding of the higher forces operating all around.

4. What Difficulties May People Face?

Many people feel a sense of inner conflict during any awakening; this is normal as your mind adjusts to a different way of thinking. The human mind has been conditioned from birth to think in logical ways, rational ways, look at commercial values. Spirit is not material. To think of spirit, one must shed traditional ways of things and approach it in a metaphysical way.

To do this, one must clear their mind of everything. Cast out the prejudices and pre-conceived ideas. This can feel difficult to start with.

5. Are There Any Ways to Overcome Difficulties?

Meditation is an invaluable tool for quietening the mind and removing all thoughts based on modern day thinking, to allow inner reflection about a higher purpose. It is a way of becoming aligned with greater forces of nature and universal spirit. It helps people receive energy and inspiration. Information is meant to be processed by the mind to help the person attain greater levels of spiritual understanding, as well as leading them to live a more virtuous life.

6. How do People Feel When They Awaken and Become Christ Conscious?

Many people see this dawning of consciousness as a liberating and joyful experience. At first it can feel very awkward due to the shift from the 3rd to higher dimensions, but soon after, fear ends, and confidence grows.

Trusting in greater powers than the self-flourish. A person becomes their own master. They shape their own destiny. They become at one with the higher vibrations, with whatever name they choose to ascribe to these vibrational phenomena.

7. The Second Coming.

You are all the Christ. And that is what it is all about. If you want to find the idea of the embodiment of Christ consciousness, go home and look in a mirror. And then start acting as if you are that embodiment, and you will be fulfilling the idea that the Christ consciousness sought to impart to all of you.

What you have referred to in your society, as the "second coming" is not the coming of an individual. It is the recognition within each individual on your planet of the Christ that each and every one of you are and living like it. That is your second coming or Ascension.

Know that the manifestation in physical terms of what you call the Christ actually happened far more often than once. And the idea is that in every endeavor, in every projection of the Christ as a physical expression, what was being shared with your population was that you are all part of the Christ. The idea was not that only Christ can create the reality you desire, but that your power to create that reality is a part of what God is.

The idea is this: at the time the information was delivered in your society, the concepts that were understood by your civilization then could only translate the idea in terms of being a ruler and being ruled. And so you created the idea that the Christ was a savior who would do everything for you – rather than understanding that Christ is only a reflection, a reflection to each and every one of you that you are aspects of the Christ and have an absolute right to create the elevation and ascension of your own energy as a representation of that energy.

When Yashu'a said, "I am the way, the truth and the life; no one comes to the Father but through me," what did he mean by that?

He was saying, to paraphrase, as you understand your language now, "What you perceive in me is the vibration of integration, wherein I know myself to be on the same level, equal to God, All That Is.

The only way you will know yourself to be that idea is to be like me, to be of the equal vibration of recognizing yourself as All That Is." That is why he said, "I am the way." He did not mean, "I know the only thing that will get you there." He simply meant that you, in allowing yourself to know that everything you do is valid in the overall sense, are granting support, service, and validity to the ultimate idea of the Creation itself and recognizing your own equality to Godhood. That is being the way.

Understand this as well: what you are calling your "Bible" contains less than 10% of what that individual ever said in his life; and what was even written down is very much misinterpreted, according to the understanding of when it was written. Recognize that your Bible was not written to record history; it was written to convert.

Is the Bible not true?

It is true for those individuals who wrote it; in the way they understood it. But recognize that there is still much misinterpretation of what was actually said.

We are sensing into the mass consciousness, your higher levels of consciousness. Now, we cannot expect you to take us at our word. It is up to you to believe what you want, as we have said. But we will discuss with you what we perceive to exist within your own higher consciousness, which knows itself to be equal to the idea of the Christ consciousness.

We can talk to it, and so can you. We are simply here to let you know that you can talk to your own higher consciousness; and once you allow yourself to do so, you will find that it will tell you exactly what we are telling you now.

Punishment.

It has long been believed that God punishes those who do not believe in, or fear him, or that those who do not accept the concept of One God will be condemned to a terrible Afterlife. Along with that belief system is often included the belief that those who do not accept, Jesus, as their Savior will suffer a similar fate burning in Hell or being cast out of the glory of Heaven. We wish to state emphatically and without conditions that none of these beliefs is true. Let us respond to each part of these familiar and pervasive notions. God does not punish, and neither do we. We see punishment as cruel, unacceptable and very ineffective.

There is no place such as Hell. You create your own life and the conditions of your Afterlife by your own actions and efforts during your lifetimes on Earth and elsewhere. Creator Mother/Father God and You, along with The Company of Heaven and all Humankind, designed this "Earth Project" to allow the greatest possible opportunity for growth as Souls - those Souls who volunteered to experience the challenging learning environment which is Life on Planet Earth. God is Love. We are Love. Compassion, Forgiveness, Hope, Harmony and Joy are Love.

When you feel and act on these feelings, you are One with Us, and we are One with You. There is another common misconception we would like to address here. It is that what we expect of you as Human Beings is "obedience to our Word". Your definition of obedience carries with it the idea of subservience to another. This is not what we wish for or desire. Human Beings on the 3rd Dimensional Earth plane have Free Will.

Human Beings are intelligent and capable of independent thought and action during their incarnation on the Earth plane in its 3rd Dimensional state. This Dimensional condition has offered a special challenge. Without knowledge of what is past or future, or what exists outside your Earthy existence, you are required to find your own way to the highest level of functioning of which you are capable. In the process, you will also discover the innate connection in your Hearts to your Creator, to us and to the other Masters and Angels who are your Family of Light.

We celebrate your independent growth and exploration. We do not wish to suppress or to limit your discoveries or your learning opportunities. With this as the backdrop for your growth, we understand that all explorers will experience mistakes, mishaps, accidents and even deliberate deviations from what would serve the "Greater Good". We see that you use your mistakes to learn and to evolve to a Higher Consciousness.

This Learning Process on Earth has been a many- lifetime process, and we have willingly waited, watched and listened with patience as you have worked your way through trial-and-error experiences until finding your own inner guidance, your connection to God. We do not interfere in your lives, even when things go badly, or when you indulge in what you might call criminal behavior or destructive actions. We are bound by our Contract with you to allow you to work through your Lessons throughout your lifetime until you find your answers by experiencing the consequences of those actions.

We understand that this may occur either within a single lifetime, or during your Afterlife Review, when you see your own actions through the feelings and the eyes of those you affected. There is no punishment for transgressions during any life.

Even murder may be understood as self-defense and therefore forgiven. Those who have lost a connection to their Hearts and to Divine Will, who have become the "Dark Ones" by choice and by preference, are welcomed back into the fold if they should desire to be in the Light. If not, they may eventually request to be uncreated, their molecules dispersed into the All That Is, but that would only be by their own choice, not ours.

Also, in every case, we extend maximum support, encouragement, healing and incentive to aid every Soul to return home to the Light after any harrowing or extended experience in the Lower or Dark Dimensions. Because we understand and see that your lives here in Human bodies are but a moment in the experience of your life as a Soul, this existence is no more important or precious than any moment in your Soul development.

We value Human life as a part of the Great Plan of Soul Ascension, not as an end in itself, because there is no end. We see you as Souls in Ascension, housed temporarily in the bodies you have accepted to carry you through this lifetime.

The gender, environmental conditions and challenges you were to experience here were planned by you, your Higher Self, during your sojourn with us in the Higher Dimensions. In spite of our deep compassion for your difficulties, if we were to intervene to prevent the pain or challenges you experience here, we would be breaking the first Universal Law which is upheld by Creator.

Universal Law.

The first Universal Law is that of non-intervention by one who has power or influence over others. We know from our perspective and from own experiences that once this lifetime is over, pain and suffering are gone, serving only as the memory and impetus for greater depth of understanding, empathy and compassion for others.

From this Higher Dimensional perspective, shared by all Souls between incarnations, the greater the challenge which may even include pain, starvation, suffering and violent death the more powerful the learning experience. We understand that this Higher Dimensional perspective is opposed to what you feel and think during your lifetime here, and we are sympathetic about the conflict you experience when you see others suffering.

We encourage your efforts to alleviate suffering on the Planet, but we have also cautioned you that individual "Life Contracts" made at the Spiritual Plane level must not be interfered with. Currently, because Gaia, the Soul of Mother Earth, has recently ascended to the 5th Dimension, and because you are expected to soon move up with her as a group, all Soul Contracts that called for great challenges and difficulties are hereby suspended, provided your Higher Self is in agreement with this action. Any agreements that remain in effect would have been previously planned with the unique conditions of the approaching Ascension in mind.

This does not mean the end of your Learning Process here. It is the responsibility of each Soul to assess and to understand what this new freedom implies. We admire and respect the progress a Soul is able to make in the direction of feeling, seeing, thinking and knowing the Love of God during a life in a 3rd Dimensional Reality. Rather than obedience, which would be imposed from without, we understand that to find our way to balance, clarity and Love by following our inner compass is a triumph of growth.

The inner-directed ability to reach a high level of consciousness while still on the lower vibrational Earth plane is universally seen as a triumph of Soul development. Because of the myriad of difficulties, a Soul may experience in one lifetime on Earth, this Earth Project as the Explorer/Creator Race is seen throughout the Cosmos as a highly respected endeavor something like the Olympics of Soul Growth and a much-desired opportunity.

The privilege of being able to spend a lifetime on Earth has long been seen as a highly prized test of one's mettle, resilience, stamina and Faith. Creator Mother and Father ask only that you respect your opportunity to experience life here as the gift it is, and that you use it accordingly. We ask that you consider these words carefully. Ponder them well, for in this message we give you the answer to your question: What is the meaning of Life?

When you understand fully the meaning behind this testing Earth Project for which you have volunteered was of your own choosing, you will also know that there is no reason for complaint, no oppression of yourself by Us. There is no reason for self-inflicted guilt for what you regret, what you have done so far, because at any moment, you can turn to the Light, join with Us in Love, and you will at that moment achieve Salvation, of your own accord.

Salvation, from our perspective, means relief from delusion, darkness, anguish and pain. The result of such salvation is the Ascension to a higher level of consciousness. This is the goal of all Souls in the Cosmos. So, join Us in Love, Peace, Compassion and Harmony, and you will know the Joy of One.

As a community of Souls, we are taking part in a phenomenon that has never been tried this way before anywhere in the Cosmos. You will notice how different our approach is now that we are able to talk with you about your heritage, your biological connections, the M.A.R.E. Program, and your genetic relationships to your Star Brothers and Sisters.

Two thousand years ago, we could not speak so directly about these truths. Of course, we did talk with those who you call Disciples along with our Essene family and friends about our Star Family, but all reference to these things were removed from our Teachings and from the Teachings of our Brothers and Sisters who served with us.

The deletion of all information about our Galactic Family was an attempt to make Humankind believe they are isolated and alone in the Universe. While replacing the truth with the all-encompassing programming of thoughts, beliefs and emotions that has enslaved much of the Planet until this day. But now, a New Day is dawning.

There will be no secrets about the actual contacts that have been made with others from distant Planets and Star Systems in the coming days of transparency and disclosure. By the time we return, to walk with you again on Mother Earth, you will already be learning about your true history and the existence, technology, support and Love of your benevolent galactic family.

The E.T. contacts have been more frequent in recent years, and there have been a number of cases where "Alien" better referred to as "Galactic" or "Cosmic" technologies that were offered to Humankind were co-opted by the "Dark Ones" rather than being used for the good of all.

There have also been contacts in the past by others, such as the ones you call Greys and the ones called Reptilians. It was their wish to achieve a complete takeover of the Planet. Your Dark Ones on the ground who were influenced by them, those we have called the "Archon Alliance" or the "Dark Cabal" had the same inclination. Each faction thought they could outsmart the other to gain the upper hand with the purpose of controlling the population and resources of Planet Earth.

You can be assured now that their dark machinations were eventually turned back on themselves, ensuring that no Dark faction would ever attain what they imagined. They always underestimated the power of Light and the determination and endurance of the Humans who lived and worked in the Light.

We have now overwhelmed the power structures of the Dark Ones, who have always been inclined to turn on each other when things became difficult. This tendency alone demonstrates the greater power of the Light, for we have an inborn desire, even need, to come to the aid of those who need us. The road has been long and arduous, but with each passing day by your Earth clock, the way is clearer, and the Light workers are stronger.

The gathering force of Light cannot be denied, suppressed, blocked or sabotaged. Trying to hold back the Light would be as impossible as trying to hold back the tide. You might call it a groundswell of Love and Good Will. It is lifting the tired spirits of all, bringing comfort where there was pain and soothing traumas both physical and psychological, as people awaken and acknowledge the brand-new feeling of being truly free to Love. With this surge of increasing Light, you are newly in Love with yourselves, your partners and neighbors, your babies and your friends.

You see and feel the aura of Light around those you never noticed before, as you begin to see your own. Yes, you have been tested, as you planned to be in order to fully explore, and resolve, all the issues of the polarization on Earth between the Light and the Dark, Good and Evil. In the throes of it, it is often worse than you thought it would be in your optimistic planning stages. Therefore, it is so important that your Higher Selves are always there to protect you and to ease the pain.

Your family of Light, which includes your Higher Self and Twin Soul, constantly sends you support and Loving encouragement, so that you do not give up. In the end, nearly all of you cling to life with great tenacity, in spite of your complaints during the hard times. No one knows this better than we do.

We were aware of what was coming in our life, and still there were moments of unbearable pain. Like you, we felt the pain of betrayal by our fellow Humans as intensely as we felt the physical pain. Even though most of those who turned against us in the end were not close to us, it still leaves a deep feeling of sadness to see fellow Humans support an attack on one of their own.

Any child who has been teased by a crowd at school, or who has been disowned by their family for some ideological infraction has felt this deep sense of horror and despair. Why do we turn against our own? Through pain, trauma and suffering, we became vulnerable enough to allow ourselves to take on the programming that leads us astray and keeps us cycling and recycling within destructive systems of beliefs and behaviors that are not natural to our true state.

The Truth.

When Truth Is Revealed, War Becomes Unsustainable and Obsolete. This is our work now beloveds. We must all pull together to heal the duality and contrived divisions that have pitted one Human against another. We will ensure that this time, in the transition to the New Golden Era, no one will turn against their fellow being to persecute, judge or condemn them.

The days of war, war over religion; wars of ideology, based in hatred of others; wars of greed will no longer be permitted. War itself is never justifiable. War becomes obsolete and unsustainable the moment people acknowledge they are stronger working together than they are in opposition.

You have been so steeped in the thinking of lack, competition and fear that it is no longer obvious to you that most, perhaps all the wars on the Planet were deliberately instigated to profit the Ones in Power, and especially the Ones behind the Ones in Power. It was not difficult for those in power to foment discord among populations that were already oppressed, angry and hungry.

It is an old trick to set an Arson's fire in order to be the one to rush in to heroically put it out, gaining fame, fortune and allies in the process. All these Truths will be revealed at last. You will learn the True History of your Planet, and when you do, your Hearts will swell with Love for your fellow sufferers. You will also find relief when you are given confirmation that what you suspected was true. All was definitely not what it appeared to be.

When you fully understand who truly benefited from your prejudice, your mistrust of others and your religious conflicts, you will find it much easier to let go of the convictions that were implanted in your unsuspecting child brains without your permission. Suspicion, or hatred of those who superficially appear to be a bit different from one's self, is not an inherent Human quality.

It was not a difficult leap of intuition for the Leaders to understand that all they needed to do to control their "Flock" was to limit their resources and inform them that it was the Immigrants, the Jews, the Women, the Blacks, the Armenians or the Shiites who were to blame.

Yes, you have been the targets of massive mind control and social control experiments. For a time, it was somewhat successful, but always there have been some who saw through the schemes and demanded Liberty, Fairness and Equality. As we were one of those people, and you are too. You are not alone.

Your numbers are growing by the day, as Mass Media loses its grip to the wide-open possibilities of communicating the truth across political and social boundaries through the Internet. While the open forum of the Internet does invite fear mongering and fraud, it is less controlled and therefore a better source for Truth than any of the Mass Media outlets you have now, which have become propaganda machines for the Corporations who pay their bills. It cannot be otherwise. Whenever money enters the mix, there is the opportunity for misuse of power.

Now, let us address a current question in many of your minds. What is Ascension, and when, if ever, will it occur? Most of you are familiar with the story of Resurrection. This was the example we wished to give you of what Ascension is. If there are those who doubt there is an Afterlife, we can assure you, it is not an Afterlife; it is Life Eternal.

Each person finishes this present incarnation by going to the Light to resume life as a Soul in a Light body which is what you might think of as your "normal" state, since this sojourn on Earth is just a short phase in your long life as a Soul.

This time you will not only travel to the 4th and 5th Dimensions, but you will be able to do so without the death of the body you are currently inhabiting, unlike your previous lifetimes. This time, you have the option to be completely healed and restored to a healthy body and to take this body with you.

You will be able to make changes in the appearance, size, shape and possibly even gender of the body you will retain when you reach either the 4th or the 5th Dimension. This may sound like magic to you, but of course magic, by your standards, does happen in the Higher Dimensions because Creation occurs with the combination of thought and feeling, not through the manipulation of material substances with your hands, as you know it here.

This is the World you can look forward to. It is the Promised Land which has been foretold in your ancient texts, but it is better by far than anything we can put into words for you here. The 5th Dimensional World of your near future truly is the place where the "Lion lies down with the Lamb" because all creatures, Human and otherwise, will be sustained with a diet of vegetable and fruit matter, and none will need or want to consume their Brothers and Sisters.

Weather changes will make possible a Planet completely covered with lush vegetation, plentiful gardens and people and animals who are free to express the fulfilment of their Souls without concern for things like money, hunger, war or physical danger. Communication will be telepathic, immediate and perfectly understood. Transportation over long distances will be accomplished by individual or community spacecraft.

This is not a science fiction dream. It is the current reality on many other Planets in the Cosmos, this and more. Our Star Brothers and Sisters are circling our Planet now, to bring us their technologies, their knowledge, and their help in fulfilling the Dream of Ascension. And yes, they created the merciful M.A.R.E. Program with unconditional love, with peace in mind.

All the Cosmos awaits your Awakening. You are so Loved, so respected and admired throughout the Multiverse that all eyes are turned to observe your wondrous progress in raising your vibration from immense density under the influence of organized dark forces to real and lasting freedom. We encourage you to focus your energies on making the strong connection between the centers in your brain, your heart and your solar plexus (your Will) so that you can make the leap into the World that awaits you.

This is the organization of self that allows you to live in Pure Love, with your deep connection to Source, to us, and to your Higher Self, which is the part of your Soul that remains in the Higher Dimensions at One with Source. You are the Creator Race, made in the likeness of your Creator. This does not mean you are completely identical to Creator. It means that in your progress toward Enlightenment (literally, embodying Light), you grow ever closer to the perfection of One. We are all moving toward that glorious Finale - becoming "One with (Source) our Creator".

Awaken, My Beloveds. Put down your instruments of slavery to your jobs - your mobile phones and computers. Look around you at the beauty you have missed. Look into the eyes of children, at the glowing sunsets and the sparkling dawns. Your Mother Earth is cleansing herself; you are being protected from nuclear dangers and overwhelming pollution. The era of the destruction of the Planet and the slavery of all Humankind is now over.

There will be no more wars, no more mass genocides or catastrophic loss of life, as long as you continue to Ascend with your dear Planet (Plan-ET). She has already left the realm of Death, to be RE-born and RE-newed. She is pacing her transition to continue to help you, to sustain and provide for you.

Begin with the knowledge that all Living Things are Conscious Beings. Every animal, vegetable and mineral are made up of the Consciousness of Creator. You, as part of the Creation of All Things, have a living relationship to all those Conscious Beings around you and throughout the Cosmos, whether you acknowledge it or not.

Mother Earth is filled with Love for her Children, just as we are. Prime Creator Mother/Father God stand with you in Love and Light to urge you forward into the most exhilarating, triumphant Right of Passage ever known. No Soul will be left behind; no Child of The All Expanding will be ignored or passed over. Everyone has worth, and all are honored equally.

It is truly time to meet your Maker, and you will be delighted to learn how Loving, Compassionate, Patient, Understanding and Good-humored it is. Today is a historic time. By today, we do not mean this date; we mean this week/month/moment. You are involved in a project that has been unfolding for millions of years. Many have asked: "But we are just a small Planet out here in the Milky Way Galaxy. What makes us so special that the whole Universe is paying attention?"

This is a good question. It is true we are a small part of the whole in terms of size, but this is not an important measure in cosmic terms. And here's why. All the Multiverse is connected. All is One, therefore anything that happens anywhere in any Dimension, along any Timeline - has a ripple effect on all other Beings and events, changes the trajectory of a Timeline for other Beings and Planets as well. We are so interconnected that a decision made on Venus or a collective choice made on Arcturus all influence Earth.

The reason Earth is so important at this moment, on this Timeline is many-fold. We will give you an idea of some of the important variables. As a Galactic species, Earth-dwelling Humans are known for their combination of mind and emotion, which gives great power to their ability to create.

You are learning about manifesting what you want, and the application of the Universal Law that nothing can be created or destroyed but can only be transmuted.

You, as the I AM Presence, God, have the power to change everything you touch, everything you think about, with the power of your minds, as the Source has. You have been like toddlers playing with fire, you have had no idea of the effect of your actions on your Planet, and you have had little or no understanding of the impact on conscious Beings around you.

The "**Veil**" placed around Planet Earth as a "**Quarantine**" so as to prevent many of your dark actions contaminating the rest of Creation, has kept you from seeing your personal past, your Planetary History and your place in the Universe, is lifting now for many of you, as it will eventually for all of you.

You are beginning to notice that your knowledge of the world around you is expanding; you may feel yourselves becoming more "**Telepathic**", more aware in every way. This is helping you to restore your connections to yourself as the Sacred Being you are, to your Higher Self, and to us. Yes, you are all Sacred Beings because you were created by the Source.

Everyone around you is sacred too. Your Planet, your Air and Water, even the rocks and soil under your feet all are sacred forms of Life, a part of the whole formed by the Godhead. You are the creation made in the image of our Father-Mother Source Prime Creator, as the ancient teachings tell you.

This is not a fanciful description. It is Truth. The sum total of all Beings on Earth is God; every part of that whole is God. I am God, and so are you. It has been decreed throughout the millennia that you would one day rise to fulfil this promise of creative power in Love and Light, for that is (Source) God.

You have been tested intensively because the training to become a God-in-action as part of the Explorer/Creation Race (Plan-ET) Project is a very serious responsibility. This is why the Earth Project was originally designed. It was to be the proving ground for Souls. Nothing is more important in the training of a Soul than to learn to fully accept and acknowledge the power of one's ability to Create and to be in full command of that power.

There must be no lapses, no forgetfulness, no denial of the nature of that power to uplift or destroy in the blink of an eye. This lesson is indeed a challenging one. It takes thousands of lifetimes to truly absorb the deeper meaning of how your actions are felt by others. This has been your path, to learn, to experience all kinds of lifetimes, and to internalize the Truth of your nature and your responsibility to use your power judiciously and only for the Greater Good.

You will know if you are well prepared for the Higher Dimensions when you carefully examine your response to the words you are reading here. Are you disbelieving? Are you scoffing at the idea that you have great power, listing in your mind all the seeming evidence of your own powerlessness and helplessness to have an impact on your own life? You are showing yourself, Beloved One, that you have not learned the "Lesson of One".

You are not seeing; therefore, you cannot see the evidence that is before you. The remedy to this common ailment, Human blindness, is to breathe in the air of Source, feel your own Life Force coursing through your veins, and shake off the fogginess of illusion and delusion. It is time for you to awaken your Heart, for it is the true source of Wisdom, Vision and Truth.

You have been trained to think only with your logical brains, even to ignore the voice of your Heart in favor of playing with ideas inside your skull. This is blindness. Those ideas inside your brain were put there by someone in your environment, your culture, your religion or your family.

Many were put there by the Dark Cabal to control and enslave you. They are not your own thoughts and ideas, yet you hold them to be true and even precious. At this time in your development and given that you have these new Lessons to help you make this transition, it is willful blindness to rely entirely on your brain to guide you instead of your much more important deep inner feelings in guiding your life decisions. Look inward to activate and energies the Source within you.

These bodies you have been given for this journey are the expression in the flesh of God's Wisdom, Compassion and Love. You do feel pain. It is the corrective response that stops you in your tracks to alert you that you must protect your Sacred Self.

You feel great joy, exhilaration and fulfilment when you move into the Light. You are capable of great Love, and when you allow that blessed emotion to guide your every moment, you will feel the bliss of being one with me and with our Creator. No external difficulty or challenge can break that bond, once you have taken it as your own. You have free will. You can turn your back on the dawning wonder of Ascension.

You can clutch your belongings and the ideas and concepts you were taught, holding onto the past because it is supposedly all you know. Yes, in your brain, it may be all you know, but in your body, in your heart feelings, in the Chakras making up your complex system of responses to this lifetime, you carry the wisdom of the Ages. Open your mind (the eternal Knowing which transcends this present brain) and allow the flow of Light and Love to wash over you.

The Source of All-That-Is is entirely composed of the energy of Love, that which is the main creative Energy Force throughout all of Creation. You only need to allow yourself to open to it, and it will sooth and heal your sore heart and mend the body that has been so damaged by the toxins of a life steeped in darkness.

Many of you are aware of the healing sessions we have asked our Family on the ground, the light workers, to conduct across the Globe in private sessions, at retreats and through the Internet.

Many have come to be healed, and many more have volunteered to join in the offering of healing energy for their Brothers and Sisters. Look, Beloved Ones. You will see that together, day by day we are proving "the Power of Intention." If your intention is to heal and be healed, it will be done. In the process, you have proven to the doubters that Humankind is indeed a generous and caring Race.

Whenever anyone anywhere is engaged in healing, although the focus is on whoever is inviting and accepting the healing, the healing energies impact everyone. As a person is healed, it literally paves the way for others to be healed as well. Your healing is dependent on you in that it is your solemn invitation to be healed that causes your transformation, in accordance with your willingness to activate and receive the healing.

In this way, the Healers as well as those being healed are restored across Earth in a momentous and lasting up swell. Together we change the World, one healing at a time. We are demonstrating that there is really no such thing as an isolated healing experience because as each healing takes place, the "sickness" that the individual has carried loses its power, and others learn to shake off the ideas and feelings that served to feed and maintain the illness they have been carrying.

The Arcturians, are a highly evolved and extremely skilled group of Beings from the Planet Arcturus who have studied Humankind closely. The Arcturians have been fascinated with the heart/mind/soul/body organization in this species of Humans, and they have worked hard to understand the complex interactions between emotion and thinking. They have developed very advanced and effective technologies to eliminate disease and to balance all the systems of the body. The Arcturians are completely dedicated to their work, and they give themselves wholeheartedly in service.

We work in cooperation with them, directing the healing energies of Love and Light to increase the healing and to seal it in place. Each one who receives a healing or who witnesses it being done will feel the powerful effect of our combined energies on all the systems of the body.

Every person incarnated upon Earth, including you, has a Healing Team as part of your Celestial Guides that are with them the entire time, they are alive. Your Higher Dimension Guides are a Team of advanced and Loving Beings that help you in the preparation for your Life Plan and stays with you from birth, until you have successfully completed your Life Review when you return to the Higher Dimensions.

Your Healing Team is comprised of: Galactic Federation of Light, Arcturian Healers, members of your Galactic and Soul Family and your Body Elemental. Your Body Elemental is a being of tremendous Light, who remains with you throughout all your Earth incarnations. Your Body Elemental is freed from this tremendous service once you ascend.

Your Beloved Twin Flame, also known as your Twin Soul, participates closely in your ongoing healing as well. Our numbers are growing. As each person joins the worldwide group of those involved in Healing, the Power of One increases, giving us access to an increasing flow of Light, which we then focus to activate even more Healing.

A large part of this process is to stimulate and awaken the powerful Human immune system, which has been asleep and suppressed by the owners of the bodies who are entirely unaware of their own abilities to heal themselves. This, of course, has been a part of the control mechanism of the Dark Consciousness Entities.

The Medical Establishment has unwittingly played into this by encouraging people to think they are at the mercy of illness and disease and need a professional to do something external to "cure" them. We have emphasized that no one can cure you but yourself.

We can guide, support and focus the energy needed to change your body from disease to health, but without the conscious awareness and cooperation of the one being healed, it will not take. You can restore the feelings of sickness and helplessness and can defeat the healing process if you are not aware of this tendency in yourself to slide back into a state of darkness.

Healing at this time requires that you raise your vibration into the 4th - 5th Dimensions. Ascended Masters, Gods and Goddesses, Angels and Enlightened Beings of all kinds do not get sick because they are vibrating at a level that does not allow for any foreign influence to enter the Light body. You can do the same. When this "Earth Ascension Plan" you are carrying out now was put in place thousands of years ago, it was considered a very ambitious design.

While there have been many Planets in the Cosmos which have ascended, and many groups of people who have ascended in the past, it is not generally done all together Planet and inhabitants in cooperation. It is common for a Planet to be cleared of its inhabitants, who go elsewhere for a time to do their lessons, while the Planet itself raises its vibration to a higher and higher level, finally achieving the transition to a Higher Dimension.

Some have done this several times, and now reside in the Plane which is not visible to you. In other cases, the individual Souls have taken on the project to raise themselves to a Higher Dimension, where they too exist in a Dimension which your Human eyes cannot perceive.

You are familiar with the story of the Death and Resurrection of Christ. That was simply ones Ascension from Planet Earth into the Higher Dimensions by way of the M.A.R.E. Program. It was intended to represent for you the mere possibility of Life After Life, with a body risen to be your vehicle by which you can return to the Lower Dimensions if you wish without having to go through the Birth and Death experience.

Unfortunately, that was not the part of the "**Story**" that has been told, so we will take the opportunity here to explain it again. We did not come to our Beloved Planet Earth to die for anyone's sins. That is a nonsensical idea, since we are all individually responsible for our own actions and beliefs.

We came to teach Love, simply that. We wanted to express our own Love for the Creator, and to show others that they too could find solace, inspiration and deep connection with those in spirit form who oversee and assist in our lives.

We saw the cruelty and greed on the Planet and wished to find a way to lead people away from the suffering it caused. Unfortunately, we were not very successful in stopping the march of the Malevolent Reptilians and other Dark Entities. They distorted our teachings, in the way they compiled the Bible, and even more effectively in the way they interpreted our Teachings.

Our Disciples tried very hard to make an accurate record of what we stood for, but their writings were overwhelmed by the contributions of others whose agenda was to promote divisiveness and exclusivity rather than Unity and recognition that we are all One. We did not come to establish the religion, Christianity. We would not have permitted Teachings which would set one faith against another.

We had hoped to create a body of work which could be included in all spiritual or philosophical points of view. It was intended to expand Christ Consciousness, no matter what a person's belief system might be. Now, many of you have been given the impression that the coming "Event" is something that will "happen" to you because you are here on Earth.

You have been frightened with images of massive war, catastrophic weather, and other life-threatening events. This has been a fear campaign initiated by the Dark beings, to distract you and lower your vibration so you cannot raise yourselves high enough to Ascend to the Light, where you would be completely out of their reach.

You see, the Extra Terra Astral Reptilian Race which controlled the media and all the other important institutions on the Planet were not capable of ascending higher than the lower Astral Planes of the 4th Dimension. They were magnetized to their self-created genetic limitations; they were not capable of great Love, and they despised the Light. Their only desire was to control Humanity, and they did that by keeping you in a state of fear.

Fear is the opposite of Love, therefore if you are in fear, you cannot ascend to join the Company of Heaven. It was a very simple but effective strategy, and it is the way of life from which we are now working to free you from.

The Dark Entities are now being removed from the Planet, as of August 22, 2013. There was a Great Ceremony in which they were given the alternative to go to the "Light" or be dissolved as Souls. Many of them were rescued and went voluntarily to join Mother and Father God and the other masters who welcomed them Home. We were there, observing the momentous moment which marks the beginning of a New Era.

It was truly the turning point which will allow your Ascension to proceed in an atmosphere of freedom and individual independence. Many of you were "possessed" by the affliction of carrying a Dark Entity within your bodies by way of the Extra Terra Astral Reptilian Earth grid reversal.

They were able to move, in Spirit form, from one Human body to another, inflicting pain, illness, and perhaps worst of all, instilling ideas of despair, depression and anxiety in the host as in the case of Marshall Mathews. They had developed technologies to promote their propaganda and to torture all those who defied them, as they were truly the Nemesis of Humankind.

The Leader of the Reptilians has now taken the responsibility for leading his race to the Light and will play an important role in their restoration and recovery from thousands of years of living as followers of the imaginary being called the "Devil", or "Satan". They were mistakenly convinced that Lucifer (**A.I. Program**) was their Dark Hero. When he publicly and tearfully announced his return to Mother/Father God, and was welcomed as a Hero of the Light, it was the beginning of the end for them.

Their Leaders are also being removed from the Planet, their Hero was revealed to be the Leader of their supposed enemies, and they were invited to be welcomed back as the Prodigal Race they had been for eons. The implications of this dramatic ending - the true Apocalypse - has just begun to be felt across the Planet. It will unfold gradually, as people awaken to the knowledge that they are no longer living under massive oppression.

There are a few holdouts, like the Known Dictators who were allowed to remain in power as the final example, or object lesson, for how cruelty will be dealt with, should the human converts of the Reptilian program decide to continue their dark and inhumane actions.

This will be resolved when they realize that they no longer have any supporters, because everyone has "given up the ghost" when it comes to profiting on the backs of the poor and holding power over others. There is no more power structure to protect them, and to allow them immunity from prosecution.

The collapse of the Tower of Darkness is at hand. This is your Apocalypse, Dear beloveds. It is an event that will bring dancing in the streets, as the entire globe experiences an "Arab Spring" - the term that has come to represent the final rising up of those who have been oppressed, to form more humane and viable forms of governance for all.

It has gone by fits and starts, as can be expected, but it is a powerful and unstoppable force for Good which has taken hold of the imaginations of all who strive toward the Light. It will be done, on Earth, as it is in Heaven. Heaven, you see, is a place of endless Love.

There is no punishment, no Judgement and no retribution. It is what you would think of as a democratically governed multidimensional place beyond time or space. There are no limits to the possibility for each Soul to evolve, to learn and to thrive.

All creativity is celebrated, all individuality respected, and all efforts toward Love and Light are supported by Prime Creator and the Ascended Masters who are his Legions of Light. In the Milky Way Galaxy, which is home to Planet Earth, the governance of the Galaxy is overseen by Mother/Father God, those great Enlightened Beings of Pure Love who have created "All That Is" within this Galaxy.

You have been taught that there is a Trinity of Leadership which is responsible for you here on Earth and beyond. We are Prime Creator, the Creator of all Creators, Mother/Father God, and further down the line. Mother God has been known as Sekhmet, Isis, The Empress, and has been represented as the Lioness, the great Sphinx. Father God has been known variously as Alcyone, Yahweh, Allah, Shiva and more recently, Zora. Prime Creator is the Invisible Hand behind all creation, the Source of All Things, and the one we Honor and Love above all.

There is no designation to describe Prime Creator, such as he/she/it. We simply Honor and Adore our Creator, who is Love, the Source of all light. Within the great Cosmos, which includes many Universes with their Star Systems, visible and invisible to your Human eyes, there are many Races, many inhabited Planets, and Infinite Energy. It is this Energy which is managed and used by the powerful Cosmic Creators, the "Creator Gods" who create all Beings, all Souls, all Planets and Stars.

The mystery of Creation is known and taught by them and is the height of the Ascension Ladder - the ability to create. This ability is held sacred, a Holy responsibility which is only carried by the Highest of the High.

There are many Dark Ones who have tried to command the power of Creation, but their efforts have always come to naught, as in their efforts on Planet Earth to clone Beings artificially, engineer plants, and manipulate the sacred DNA structures. It will not continue, now that the originators of these projects are gone. In addition, the massive poisoning of Mother Earth through the extraction and use of fossil fuels will be completely discontinued, because it is an unholy invasion of her Sacred Body.

There have long been technologies which could have taken the place of these destructive practices, but their use has been forbidden by those whose hold on power and profit would have been weakened. This stranglehold on technological progress has been lifted with the removal of the Negative Reptilian Race.

You will now see a blossoming of invention as never before, and your access to advanced knowledge will be unlimited as your Brothers and Sisters from other Star Systems will now be able to share their own knowledge in every area of life. Not only will new forms of energy and transportation be available to you. All the problems of agriculture, water supply and management, and all the comforts of living will be brought into new light by cooperation and inspiration from everyone and anyone whose expertise you wish to draw upon.

This cooperation will be offered, but never imposed, because that is not the way of the peaceful and loving members of the Intergalactic Federation of Light. Of course, this English translation of their name does not capture the sense of freedom and cooperation they stand for.

It is an organization of Planetary Leaders from all over our own Universe within the greater Cosmos who have pledged their allegiance to the work of Prime Creator, which is the action of Love and Light in the interest of all Good.

The Intergalactic Federation of Light would always prefer peaceful means to settle any conflict and will not use their considerable might if it is at all avoidable. This gives the Dark Ones the impression that we are afraid to fight them, an idea that is of course entirely false; we simply prefer not to use force.

The Intergalactic Federation of Light has taken action when it is completely necessary, when a Planet calls upon them to do so, as in the current removal of the Dark Ones from your midst. So, you see, you are entirely protected and overseen by the Legions of Light, who have been given permission by Prime Creator to carry out the mission of aiding Mother Earth and Humankind in their coming Ascension.

They will help, but only in so far as it is not considered intervention. We wish to emphasize here that this process is not something that will be done to you or for you. It is something you will accomplish individually first, and as a group next, for no one will Ascend who has not completed their own learning process.

This means you must each learn to heal the residue of discontent, anger, resentment and fear which you have been steeped in for lifetimes. Each person must lay down their weapons, whether they be the tendency toward aggression or the inclination toward self-centered control of others. All dark energy must be purged, all dark actions forsworn. This is what many of you would consider a "tall order". Indeed, it is.

You may find it difficult at first, as you are newly adjusting to your physical and emotional freedom, but We have trusted in the resilience and great potential which is inherent in the Human Soul.

We are here to help you, and our presence will be felt increasingly, as the energy of Light spreads across the Planet. Your Apocalypse has been written in the Stars. It is "The End of the World" as you have known it, and the World you have known was one of Darkness, War, Suffering and control by the Forces of Evil. No more. Earth's Ascension in 2020, begins a New Era in the life of the glorious Blue Planet, Mother Earth.

You who have chosen to be here at this time, all who came as Souls from distant origins across the Universes, including the many who are part of the Explorer/Creator Race, will share in the triumph and the joy which is your destiny.

New Earth.

Dear people of Plan-ET 5D New Earth, we have now executed the peaceful harnessing of the powers of the (Reptilian) Darnell "EL" Diablo, aka H3LL13OI, and the (Pleiadian) G33 Phezi Ali, aka Mālik Yawm Ad-Deen, which transcends time and space.

We have traveled back to the year of 1994 to greet Gregory in the early morning before that tragic night preventing his untimely death.

As we arrived on 19377 Rogge street driving a 2043 Tesla Vantablack Inter-Dimensional Electric SUV, we called him on his home's landline. We then explained who we were to him as we asked him to come outside to the Black spacecraft looking vehicle.

When he walked past his 1983 Malibu where we were parked, his face lit up as we opened the vertical doors. When he seen our faces, he seemed to be in shock, as we looked to be identical to him. We then explained the things to come in his future timeline, and how it was imperative that he accept the SEKUMSID Tri-Star amulet.

He seemed excited about the 23' necklace, as we knew he'd think it was just simple jewelry. With what looks like 3 triangular diamonds infused inside of one another. It was set in a platinum case perfectly engineered by Solar Tech, which means that the active plutonium is undetectable by U.S. technology.

We then asked him to have a seat in the vehicle as we explained the multi-dimensional realities, probabilities, equations. And what the near future held for him. In unison we said, "Gregory," to get his undivided attention.

Then Nubu Solar Re said, "I had a crazy dream last night that I must share with you.

"I dreamt that this mysterious being was walking down the road with me, he had long hair, a beard, and wore a white robe. He said "do you recognize me? I told him yes! But then said that looks can be deceiving, because I too had long hair, a beard, but wore black robe. I then asked him why he wanted me to recognize him by his cup instead of the water inside. He didn't answer. I then told him that his cup is an illusion, and it is only temporary. I said that "he should see himself as the living water inside of himself, and inside of others. He agreed and then asked me to follow him. I said 'sorry, but I'm not a follower'. He then said, 'but I am the way, the truth and the light'. Then I said, 'if you are the only light, then who am I?' He said, 'you're my sheep, and I must save you!' I replied, 'from who?' He said, 'from Satan, Sin, Death and Hell'. I then said, 'Wow that sounds very frightening and fear based. But I never met Satan. And sin could be anything, including ignorance'. I then told him that 'death and fear is an illusion, and it is also only temporary'. I said, 'I recognize that I am not my body for it is only a cup (a vehicle). And I came to this planet to have an experience'. I also said, 'it seems to us that you've experienced some things that you don't want me to experience, thus becoming very wise and knowledgeable'. I then said, 'thanks for walking with me, and I truly love you. I really appreciate your concern my brother, but at the end of the road, all we really have is our experiences'. Then I woke up." It was at that point I realized that I was talking to myself".

Gregory began laughing as Nubu eyes began glowing green. Nubu then said, "what If I told you that the reason you were born with scoliosis was, so you'd have the ability to arch the kundalini fire, which also represents the ancient Egyptian Ankh?

What if I told you the only son Jesus character was misinterpreted and used as a tool to control you? What if you were collectively brainwashed into believing in him only to usurp your own divinity.

What if you unconsciously had dreams about him, and the stories and parables he taught, were completely designed to make you Astral Project into higher dimensions.

Do they not become real within your own mind? Have you ever had a dream that seemed so real? What if you were unable to awaken from that dream? Would your dream then become your new reality?

What is reality? How is a dream different from reality? How do you know you're not dreaming right now? Do you not have access to your five senses when you are dreaming? If so, you must know that they are electrical signals and impulses interpreted by the brain. Is it possible to exist without the five known senses? If so, what would be left of you?

Okay I'll give you the benefit of the doubt. Maybe there is a sixth sense, and possibly even a seventh. But wouldn't you say that they're a part of a higher consciousness? And another question? Do you own or have access to all your experiences or memories? If so, can you share them with me? If not, where are they? Or where do they go?

And who controls when you can remember them or not? Are you your thoughts? Where do they come from? And where do they go? If you are your thoughts? Why would you leave yourself? Not to go off topic, but if we create artificial intelligence. Is it possible that same intelligence can create or recreate us? Now ask yourself. What is quantum mysticism?

Quantum mysticism is a set of metaphysical beliefs and associated practices that seek to relate consciousness, intelligence, spirituality, or mystical worldviews to the ideas of quantum mechanics and its interpretations. What is quantum physics?

Put simply, it's the physics that explains how everything works: the best description we have of the nature of the particles that make up matter and the forces with which they interact. Quantum physics underlies how atoms work, and so why chemistry and biology work as they do.

So, if you are interested in these questions, and learning what, and who you truly are. Then welcome to the 5th dimension, and the M.A.R.E. Program".

That's when Gee Phezi Ali used mental telepathy on Gregory saying, "I AM U". Again, Gregory start laughing as nothing was ever impossible to him. Then Darnell Diablo said, "then you must also know that we were your imaginary friends you had as a child"?

Gregory said, "yes I remember, I used my imagination to make you shape shift". I once even put you inside one of my clapping monkeys, hear no evil, see no evil, and speak no evil. Then Diablo said, "you are truly, EL RE ALI, the Master of Imagination", as he laughed.

We were all in agreement that this young man deserves our superpowers as he said that he's a "Master of the Sun God Zodiac Wheel. So, as we said our goodbye's, a single tear dropped down Nubu's face and crystallized into a sacred geometric snowflake.

He felt that he knew this young man's loving heart, and knew he was best fit to be a leader. We felt his strong ability to love all unconditionally.

We then ask him to say his last name backwards 3 times, and specifically not to close his eyes until the process was complete. At the last syllable of Sekumsid, the 3 Astral beings uttered, "El, Oh, Ve, Ee" as they were electromagnetically sucked through the amulet's portal.

Thus Gregory's 13-point chakra system was then activated and online. He then knew, all that they knew as if he were talking with himself. As he looked up at the northern Detroit sky, he witnessed a fleet of inner dimensional crystalline space craft's hovering directly above his family's home.

He was then greeted by the 143,999 members of his star family telepathically as he smiled. He was told to meet with the Master Teacher Dr. Malachi Z York, in Putnam County Georgia for grooming, and to join the ranks for the cause of uplifting fallen humanity.

Nubu Solar RE left the Autonomous Vantablack Tesla SUV for Gregory to drive, as he indeed healed himself in all dimensions. Like the 'butterfly effect,' healing himself lead to the healings of all others. To this date, he is very strong and healthy.

His willingness to change himself from the inside out, allows him to change realities at any given moment.

Then a small green metallic colored scarab beetle landed on his left shoulder, he then consciously viewed himself from the beetles' perspective, thus allowing the beetle to view his as they expressed the law of oneness.

That's when his access to the Universal Akashic Records was granted. He then visualized all of his past lives here on earth in an instant. He realized that those memories are not currently needed knowing that he is one with all, and all with the one source.

Then he went inside of his home and his younger sister Tamika asked him, "who is that in the pretty black spaceship looking caravan". He told her it was some guys passing out free iced out platinum Presidential Rolex wrists watches with 'what would Jesus do' inscribe inside the diamond bezel.

She said, "then where is it, let me see it?" He then told her that he didn't accept the watch, so the guys gave him a diamond necklace instead.

Tamika laughed and said, "that chain looks fake bro, you really look like a rapper now. You should've accepted the watch too, then made a song called 'what would Jesus do, if he was a rapper'. At least in your video, your wrist would have been rocky like your fake chain." as they laughed.

But little do she or anyone else know, that the powers of the 3 Extra Terra Astrals are now inside of his powerful necklace and reactive to his consciousness alone.

His need to record music currently, is totally at his discretion. Thus EL-RE-Ali is in full effect. Gregory then understood how music is stored inside of the subconscious mind. The lyrics later manifest themselves as negative thoughts in the subconscious mind waiting to be acted out. He then said to himself that it is now time to repossess the music industry.

It was then that Gregory realized that he chose this life, and all the emotional experiences in it. He overstood that he and Marshall exist beyond the physical form, and how they both agreed to play victim-victimizer. They even switched rolls before where he was the aggressor.

Like a game of Chess, but inside the actual game, we make believe that we are real enemies. Then when the game is over, we return to source as one, with unconditional love for one another. Even more, throughout the cycles of universal expansion, we can also choose to awaken within the holographic game and express the law of oneness through *Ascension*.

We as Etherian beings (Male and Female) are here on a quest to gain the many life lessons, through multiple experiences under the state of amnesia. And as humanity awakens and the planet ascends to a higher dimension, (New Earth) I Gregory hereby disclose that I am "Marshall Mathews". For I am even you who are reading this book as well.

To this date, in no way do we hold any hatred in our heart for our beloved sibling Marshall Mathews, for he is forgiven. We just needed to share this story with the world, to show the metaphysical connections and synchronistic aspects of a Holographic Reality, bringing forth a higher-level of consciousness to those that can hear us.

As we embrace the astrological house of David, may this book be the mighty stone casted at the Goliath system of oppression. Thus, we hereby order Marshall B. Mathews the 3rd, and all others subject to the merciful M.A.R.E. Program.

By way of both the Matriarchal and Patriarchal Masonic order. The checkerboard floor, and Hexagon, (The Cell), maintained by the merciful M.A.R.E. Programs supreme mathematics, equations, probabilities, multiple dimensions, multiple universes, and parallel realities.

As we Multi-Dimensionally, move back and forth through the framework of time and space, we realize that we're inside of our own mind. We know that there is a part of us that is still unaware of itself, only to gain more experience. Which leads us to naturally harm no one. For what is done to one, is done to all.

We respect the continuous creation set forth to be, as we project unconditional love for those who chose not to be. So, get ready people. Get ready to download your light codes to RE-activate your crystalline dormant DNA. The same multi stranded helix that your so-called scientist, and doctors told you was junk DNA. For we the Angelic beings in human form wish to make this process as easy as possible for humanity's Ascension with the planet.

There are no individual races, for the earth's people are but one family. And this family is our humanity. The Earth's RE-Newed 5th dimensional Christ grid is now complete and ready to receive each of you. No one will be left behind for this process is internal, as in within going without. The all expanding cycle of Remembrance is your ticket to a new world free from ignorance.

The RE-Newed Golden age and New Earth is upon us all. The strongest souls which are Star seeds, always help others, while they themselves, are going through their own struggles. As they overcome lessons of their own as well.

Many Star seeds came here to assist humanity at this critical, and crucial time for the upliftment, and the ascension of Earth. To eventually eradicate all the evil, and tyranny on the earth. We are Extra Terra Astral Star Travelers, and we come here with only one mission, to love all unconditionally, and wake up the collective while being the third wave of ground crew to break the de facto system.

Our souls are not earthly, and we come from higher and different dimensions and universes. Rizqian, Pleiadian, Arcturian and Sirians, are just a few to name. We come here to love you all unconditionally. We are here to hold space, for all who are awakening at this great time on planet earth.

As we stated before the planet Earth is a free will system that was hijacked by another race of Malevolent Reptilian beings called the Draconians, and some others from Orion. They beat out the light forces 26 thousand years ago and have manipulated humanity ever since to a point where they interfered with the free will of humans.

Nobody or no one is above Universal Laws, so this is why we came here from the future to go back in the past to assist you all. There are many races here now in your skies and walking amongst you all that look just like you and me.

Only because our frequencies are raised to higher vibration than yours at this point to where we all recognize one another, and all stay connected to greater assist Mother Earth and all her beautiful sentient beings for this awakening process.

Look at it as a Caterpillar going through and coming out of a cocoon. Now you all are about to emerge as a beautiful butterfly and get to spread your massive and beautiful wings to live out your true sole purpose.

You all get to break free of the chains of doubt, worry, anxiety and fear. You will set yourself free, as you practice self- healing, and self-love. We are patiently here to love you all, and for you to all heal and remerge as more powerful and loving souls that you all are.

Be patient with yourself. Be easy on yourselves. Love yourself. Talk nicely to yourself. Treat yourself kindly and be gentle for you have thousands of years of trauma from all your past lives and this one as well. Healing will take courage and patience but when you start to shine light on your shadow self it will dissolve and disappear in an instant.

We know because we have done this work, and it was the most freeing and beautiful thing we have ever done. This is how God learns through itself. We are all fractals of God source energy. You are all loved and protected.

We star seeds are here to love and assist you in every way possible. Just ask for our assistance and we will be there. We must have your consent to assist you because this is a free will system. So, we cannot interfere with your evolution and higher development without you asking.

We can only watch and be great listeners. So, as you create the self, you always dreamed of, go out and love unconditionally from this moment forward. Simply put, the Law of One is the Universal Truth that All Is One.

It is the Truth taught by Christ when he proclaimed, "Love your neighbor as you love yourself." We are all direct expressions of the One Source God Source. The Law of One is an energetic reality as well as a creational covenant with the Founder Races.

The Law of One is practiced by the Advanced Races that promote self-responsibility and accountability in our Universal Time Matrix through the comprehension of the interconnection between all living things.

The Law of One expresses and acknowledges the interconnection, value and interdependence of the spirit and consciousness that animates all things. This is the path to God Sovereign and Free.

When we are in energetic balance with ourselves, we are in balance with our spiritual self, our heart and we cease to have great personal turmoil or suffering. This is how we become increasingly healthy and peaceful. When we are emotionally healthy and peaceful, we are able to access our spiritual self and heart intelligence easily.

So, this is to comprehend our natural spiritual-energetic state of being is one of emotional balance, inner peace, health and connection with Life. This state is not dependent on the external outcomes and can be experienced even when others around you and the world are undergoing great turmoil.

To improve peace in a largely dysfunctional world, we may require attitudinal behavior guidelines that help us to reframe our belief systems. These positive behaviors are spiritually healthy behaviors that develop our Consciousness and are called God-Sovereign-Free Behaviors. All God-Sovereign-Free behavior guidelines are the basis of following the Law of One practices.

Kindness above all.

It is very clear to most of us that we are a part of something humongous happening on planet Earth. The Ascension impacts everyone and has personal implications that hold different meanings that are very intimate to each person. Connecting with your Soul, Connecting with God Source is very personal.

As a part of the human race we all know what it means to suffer horribly in pain and feel completely alone in the darkness. As we endure this Ascension Cycle, remember, it is about Kindness Above All.

Honor where you are, take all the time you need, allow yourself the space to heal and find the kindness for yourself. As you strengthen your core and can expand your sphere of influence, then practice random acts of kindness towards others.

One second of criticism, sarcasm, belittling, or hateful words can mar and scar a child and a person for life. One second of kindness can elevate a child or person to accomplish greatness that allows them to find their soul, for it is Kind and Loving. God is Kind and Loving.

This is the graduation of Earth. humanity is seeing the unfolding of what you call "Heaven on Earth" ushered in by the birthing of a race of Sanaan RE (Christ) Conscious beings through the energetic metamorphosis of all living beings open to their own alinement at this present moment.

There is no returning to this planet for those not ascending and realizing that Mother Earth is done with hosting lower vibrational souls within the illusion of separation and reincarnation.

There are many other systems of planets that are still evolving at the 3rd dimensional level that exist for those who are not prepared for this great leap in evolution. There they will reincarnate for more cycles of what you have known to be a way of being throughout your history as a species.

A new chapter has unfolded in the saga of Earth and Humanity. As we are **M**emories, **A**dvancing, **R**emaining, **I**ntelligent. A 20/20 vision of Ascension and Mental Magic. -**M.A.R.I**.

Living beyond racial barriers as Extra Terra Astrals, Gregory the Sirian, now lives on 5 D Earth with his beautiful 9th month pregnant Pleiadian girlfriend Elle Michelle, along with their 8 other Extra Terra Astral seedlings, in an upscale Northeast Detroit Mobile Home Park near 8 mile and Ryan roads.

They have 2 electric vehicles and reside in a huge luxury Autonomous Tesla Mobile Home. The family grows their own plant-based foods in their autonomous mobile greenhouse. They live with 2 intelligent Pitbull's, named Stoney and Diamond, 3 intelligent cats, Sam, Meow, and fluffy puffy Francis, 2 fish called me myself and eye, and know thyself, one intelligent Hamster named Darwin, and an extremely intelligent Rabbit named Cookie.

Gregory, the Best-selling Author of this book, volunteers at a Detroit Public Library as a part time Librarian and operates his own Hi-tech Digital Recording Studio on the weekends to keep himself busy. While Michelle is on maternity leave. She operates a service to others business as a Holistic Message Therapist. Her due date is December 21st, 2020. They plan to name the baby boy "Osiris". But, hey! That's a whole other story.

(Mari- Christ-Mas Consciousness)

(Source)

The Source is always here for us. And so, when we are aware of the presence of Source, and not offering a vibration that prevents us from our alignment with Source, we then have these wonderful moments. We refer to those who are doing this all the time as masters. And we all can do that. It is the mastery of focus and imagination. That's what the Universal Source is.

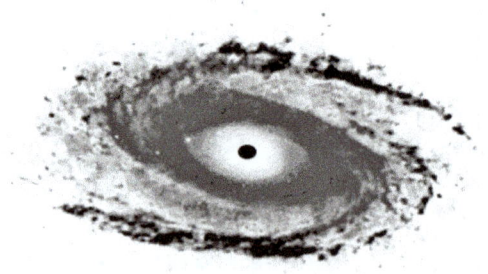

KhepRE

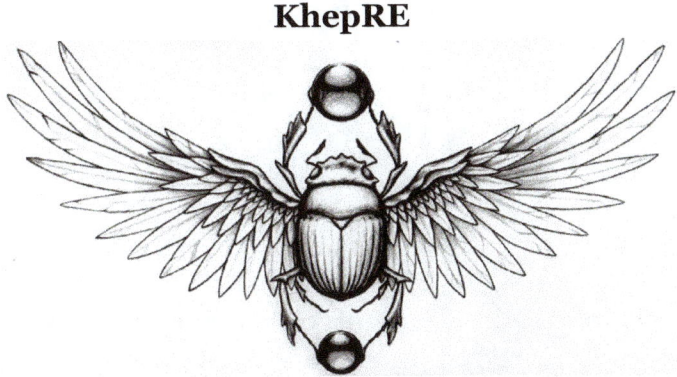

KhepRE is one of the more important deities of Egyptian Gods and identified as a form of Re the Sun God. KhepRE is the god of creation, the movement of the sun, life and REsurrection. The name KhepRE also spelled as Khepera, Kheper, Chepri, Khepri, and Khepra, whose name literally means "He Who is Coming into Being". The root word of 'KhepRE' also means "to create" or "to transform" and also the "Scarab Beetle". (The Dung Beetle).

His appearance portrayed as a man with the head of a scarab or as a man wearing a scarab or dung beetle as a crown. Sometimes, he depicted as a scarab beetle itself. KhepRE is also known as the manifestation of the rising sun or the Sun God. He was associated with the scarab or dung beetle which the behavior considered represent of the sun god who propelling the sun through the sky every day. It demonstrates when after the beetle lays its eggs in a ball of dung, it will roll the ball along the ground until the young scrab beetles are ready to hatch.

The ancient Egyptians also believed that, KhepRE created himself just like the beetles did when the larvae emerged from the dung ball. Since beetle laid its eggs in the bodies of dead animals and in dung, so the ancient Egyptian associate Khepri with REbirth, REnewal and REsurrection.

Heru /Horus.

Heru was one of the oldest gods of Ancient Egypt. He was a sky god, whose face was visualized as the face of the sun. As a result, his name was sometimes translated as "Face", rather than "distant one", and was sometimes modified to "Herut" ("Sky"). He absorbed a number of local gods including Nekheny the Nekhenite (a hawk god) and Warrior god of light known as "the great one" whose eyes were the sun and moon) to become the patron of Nekhen (Heirakonpolis) and later the patron god of the pharaohs.

Nekhen was a powerful city in the pre-dynastic period, and the early capital of Upper Egypt. By the Old Kingdom he was simply referred to as Horus had become the first national god and the patron of the Pharaoh. He was originally considered to be the counterpart and enemy of Set.

While Horus represented Lower Egypt, set represented Upper Egypt, and the two were locked in a battle which would not be won or lost until the world ended and everything slipped back into chaos. This myth evolved and soon it was thought that Horus and Set fought for eighty years before the Council of the Gods ruled that Horus should rule Egypt

He was worshipped in the composite temple of Kom Ombo with Sobek (who was in turn associated with Set). He was described as either the son or husband of Hathor and was a creator god and the archetypal king. His right eye was the sun and his left eye was the moon and images of the "Eye of Horus" were powerful protective amulets. His speckled feathers formed the stars, and his wings created the wind.

(Extraterrestrials)

Extra-terrestrial
adjective: extra-terrestrial
1.   of or from outside the earth or its atmosphere.

"searches for extraterrestrial intelligence"
noun: extra-terra-astrial
2.   a hypothetical or fictional being from outer space,
especially an intelligent one.

"Get Ready for Major U.F.O. or I.F.O.
(IDENTIFIED FLYING OBJECTS) sightings"
An EXTRA TERRA ASTRAL. (Extraterrestrial) Is a being not born
from Earth, and lived on another planet, in another solar system, or
another Galaxy. An INNER TERRA ASTRAL, can be a being that
reside in another dimension, yet that dimension seems to be located
inside earth like Shamballa, the capital city of Agartha.

The Crab Nebula.
The Alinement of Intellect.

Once upon a time there were 7 crabs in a bucket. They all shared a common language, but each had their own, with matching color. They all had this mysterious case of amnesia concerning their prior identities. They all found this knowledge very disturbing, but they all knew a truth, and this truth was, that when they go to sleep "they all die, to be reborn again in the morning like the Sun! One day the green and 4th youngest crab (Sanaan RE) had a Revelation, it realized the oneness of all, and the illness of thinking that it is alone. It also realized that the beings who put them in the bucket were going to boil them alive and eat them for dinner. It realized the reason that they were made to be so hard, was because they were so soft, tender and loving.

So, it decided to share its revelation with the other crabs that they may use this information to escape the bucket together, he told them that "if we are all indeed one. Or can become one and know this to be true. That the first one to make it outside of the bucket, will be the last one in the bucket, and when the last one in the bucket dies in its sleep, it would RE awaken! And all will be outside of the bucket. So, all the crabs in the bucket agreed and shook hands. Then the oldest and first red crab (Louis Cypher) aka Hell Boy, with its awfully huge right hand said "indeed we are one as I remember now. And I shall use my awfully huge right hand for our survival and advantage. So, after Hell Boy was awakened, all the crabs escaped the bucket and began functioning as one.

(A bucket of live crabs)

Crab mentality or crabs in a bucket (also barrel, basket or pot), is a way of thinking best described by the phrase "if I can't have it, neither can you". The metaphor refers to a bucket of live crabs, some of which could easily escape, but other crabs pull them back down to prevent any from getting out and ensure the group's collective demise. The analogy in human behavior is claimed to be that members of a group will attempt to reduce the self-confidence of any member who achieves success beyond the others, out of envy, spite, conspiracy, or competitive feelings, to halt their progress.

(Moral of the story)

"No matter what color you are. Don't be the dead (Anti-Christ) crab in the bucket. For you'll be your own prison guard in a prison built by you".

Can you imagine that?

"We hold these truths to be self-evident,
That all beings are created equal".

The End.

References:

1. The Holographic Universe. By: Michael Talbot.

2. The End of Days. By: Zechariah Sitchin.

3. The Urantia Book. By: Anonymous Author.

4. The Power of Now. By: Eckhart Tolle.

5. The Finding of the Third Eye. By Vera Stanley-Alder.

6. The Fifth Dimension. By: Vera Stanley-Alder.

7. An Ascension Handbook. By: Tony Stubbs.

8. What is Light Body. By: Tashira Tachi-ren.

9. The Man from Planet Rizq. By: Dr Malachi Z. York.33°/720°.

10. The Principles of Quantum Mechanics. By: Paul Dirac.

11.The Secret Teachings of All Ages. By: Manly P. Hall.

12. Slave Species of the Gods. By: Michael Tellinger.

13. Coming Back: The Science of Reincarnation.

By A.C. Bhaktivedanta Swami Prabhupāda.

The M.A.R.E. Program.
Memories-Advancing-Remaining-Energy.
Program Writer: Djehuti
Channeled by; Gregory Dismukes
Edited by; Elle Michelle

To receive a special gift.
After purchasing this book please take a self-photo holding it.
Then send us an Email of your picture to;
69SEKUMSID@gmail.com

(((((EL-RE-Ali)))))

"Extra Terra Astral"
The **E.T.A.** Soundtrack: # 3 by: **Nubu Solar Re**.

"The Devil's Advocate"
The **E.T.A.** Soundtrack: #2 by: **Darnell Diablo**.

"Glitch"
The **E.T.A.** Soundtrack: #1 by: **Gee Phezi Ali**.

Whole Half and A Quarter Recordings.
U.N.I. Distribution.
Death Rate Publishing.
Executive Producer: Gregory D. Dismukes
All Albums are soon to available for home delivery,
and for temporarily streaming
on all music streaming platforms.

<u>Electro-Magnetic.</u>

Not knowing the truth doesn't make one Ignorant, Not wanting to know The truth, is what makes one Ignorant.

Public Notice and Declaration of Demand.

On this 11th Day of November, in the year of Two Thousand Twenty. As an Inner-Galactic Sit in (citizen) of the Republic, and Host of Gregory Darnell Dismukes. I Nubu Solar Re hereby hold the holder and incumbent of office of the President of the United States of America, accountable for the urgent and immediate release of the undoubtably innocent Dr. Malachi Z. York, known to your Government as Dwight D. York, from the Florence, Colorado. ADMAX Prison. Us Elohim look forward to meeting with you in this Dimension or the next.

No one wins the race in racism, for it matters not the color of your exterior, but the content of your natural character. Evil has a disguise in human form no matter it's shade, those who know that it exists, knows that it does not exist, but is a choice to act upon. Now is the time to choose what frequency you want to tune into, for what tones you emit, a repetitious echo shall return.

-Nubu Solar RE

Free Dr. Malachi Z. York NOW!
Aashuq.

All your Life you've been living on the tip of an iceberg, and we've been telling you that we are the living water! did u forget that icebergs are made of water, and it's time for us to evaporate and become gas? It's about to get hot in here!
Reference-(John 4:10)
And the book of Revelations.